DAVID'S DAY

Books by
DENIS MACKAIL

Romance to the Rescue
Bill the Bachelor
According to Gibson
Summertime
The Majestic Mystery
Greenery Street
The Fortunes of Hugo
The Flower Show
Tales from Greenery Street
Another Part of the Wood
How Amusing!
The Young Livingstones
What Next?
The Square Circle
David's Day

DENIS MACKAIL

DAVID'S DAY

BOSTON AND NEW YORK
HOUGHTON MIFFLIN COMPANY
The Riverside Press Cambridge
1932

The Riverside Press
CAMBRIDGE . MASSACHUSETTS
PRINTED IN THE U.S.A.

also, from the posters on the Regency Cinema, a concrete building with a tremendously flashy front and shamelessly economical sides, and from the vast yellow advertisement which sprawls along the low railway bridge.

Still more colour from the trams, which dip, together with the roadway, to avoid this last-named obstacle, and then come hissing and roaring up the slope again, and so glide away round the slight curve. And yet with all this prodigal juxta-position of hues, the spirit scarcely feels itself enlivened by the prospect of Edgerley High Street. In bright sunlight, it is true, there is a certain garishness which might possibly startle the eye for a moment — if only the eye were less accustomed to it all; but in ordinary sunlight, or under still more ordinary grey skies, the colours seem simply to wrangle aimlessly and cancel each other out. They're like a lot of meaningless voices all shouting at the same time. The spirit is irritated, knows that it will gain nothing by searching for any sense in all this muddle, and automatically turns its attention elsewhere. The whole hodge-podge of reds, greens, yellows and blues has far less effect on an even moderately sensitive beholder than one bunch of violets from the basket of the one-legged ruffian outside the Regency Cinema.

So one leaves Edgerley High Street by a break between a sweet-shop and an undertaker's, and finds oneself in Marefield Road. No fields here any longer, or mares, if it comes to that, either. Just a long, level perspective of semi-detached, three-story houses, each with its square bow-window on the ground floor, each with its scrubby patch of front-garden, each with its rusty cast-iron railings and its creaking or unclosable gate. Each, also, with its little sunken porch, and its rectangular fanlight, and its two panels of leaded and tinted glass. Semi-detached, we called them, and indeed

DAVID'S DAY

1

NUMBER SIXTY-SEVEN, Pocklington Road. Off
Ardlers Road. Which is off Marefield Road.
Which is off the High Street.

The High Street is broad, smooth, and sweeps
along in a slight curve. There are shops on either
side. Banks, branches of the big multiple chemists,
and of the big multiple grocers, and of the big multiple outfitters and boot distributors — all imitat-
ing their prototypes nearer the seat of government,
but all just a little meaner and cheaper and more
reduced in scale. Local independents are also well
represented in these low terraces, some on the up-
grade, some on the down-grade, but most of them
hinting at neither ambition nor failure. A draper
has managed to string no less than three shop-
fronts together, and seems, at any rate, to have
no shortage of stock for his windows, which are
so full that quite a number of the lighter articles
have actually been gummed on to the glass. At
the other extreme there are minute establishments
occupying only a sixth of this space; so small
that their entrances have had to be set at an angle,
and that two of them often share the same door-
mat. Little half-shops, with counters as broad as
they are long, and a haunting suggestion that all
business in them must be conducted sideways.

Colour isn't lacking in this part of the High
Street, what with the raw red of the brickwork,
and the enamelled-iron legends which are spattered
all over it, and what with the petrol pumps and
the newspaper placards and the huge hoarding
just before you get to the station. More colour,

if they didn't lean up against each other like that, one can hardly imagine them with the strength to stand at all. But that dead-and-gone speculative builder knew his business, at any rate where skimping and scraping were concerned, and again you would almost have to turn sideways to squeeze through the gaps between them. Dark, veiled windows glare blankly at each other across these gaps, knowing little or nothing of light and air, yet sullenly insisting on their semi-detachment. For Marefield Road is quite a cut above many streets in this suburb, and those narrow chasms leading to its narrow back-gardens are one of the chief signs of its superiority.

Ardlers Road, into which one turns — by an undersized pillar-box — after a couple of hundred yards or so, has no such chasms. The frontages here are continuous, with nothing but the thinnest of party walls to divide neighbour from neighbour; nor can even the corner houses lay claim to a tradesmen's entrance. Alternating doors and bow-windows proceed down both sides and from end to end. There are still gates and iron railings in front, but they are both on a smaller scale than in Marefield Road; and though the elevations have still got three stories, the top one, with its dormer windows, scarcely qualifies as more than an attic. Ardlers Road, in short, is manifestly a stage lower in the social scale, and — which in Edgerley and other places comes to pretty much the same thing — obviously yields less in rates and taxes. Not a slum, for there aren't any slums out here, but a street without frills (except along the ridges of its slate roofs), or pretensions, or discernible symptoms of civic conceit. Just Ardlers Road, Edgerley. Full of life, hope, and endeavour; but you'd hardly choose to live here, if you could afford to live anywhere else.

Until the loop line was electrified and the price

of light vans fell, Ardlers Road marked the end of
the suburb in this particular direction. It petered
out in some desolate fields, containing a number
of stagnant pools, and some half-hearted trees,
and some rough grass and some old bricks and a
few rickety notice boards; and then there was
nothing, for nobody seemed to plough or feed his
flocks on this abandoned tract, until you struck a
muddy lane and beyond it the outskirts of Brockman Hill. Edgerley, in those days, seemed to have
reached the limits of its expansion, and with them
its final if slightly unattractive form.

But with the modernisation of the loop line and
the development of motor transport, back came
the speculative builders, and the hiatus began to
close up. Steam-rollers crushed a myriad flints
into the muddy lane, and Brockman Hill instantly
surged across it together with gas, main drainage
and company's water. Edgerley, not to be out-
done, hacked down the half-hearted trees, filled in
the stagnant pools and scored the rough grass with
straight lines running in both directions. Lamp-
posts, though as yet with no lamps, sprang up
along the sides of the new tracks, wooden huts
arrived and two-wheeled carts with enormous,
shaggy horses. And then, while the multiple shops
bore irresistibly down on the High Street, the
shallowest of foundations suddenly covered the
abandoned tract. Little sign-posts said 'Crudesden
Road' and 'Fairmeadow Road' and 'Pocklington Road,' and while you were still thinking how
ridiculous this was when there weren't any houses,
lo and behold, the houses had sprung up and were
already being painted and glazed.

If the new speculative builders could have dis-
pensed with these particular details, there seems
little doubt that they would have done so, for
they knew far more about scraping and skimping
than even their predecessors had thought possible.

But they also knew that the centrifugal millions
had got to live somewhere, and that all kinds of
substitute materials look just as smart during the
first six months as what they are supposed to
imitate. So they built like blazes with everything
that would more or less hold together during this
period, and put in mass-production metal casements and unseasoned joists and unimaginably
flimsy doors; and then they sprayed their cheap,
crumbling bricks with a kind of grey wash which,
temporarily at any rate, hid most of the flaws.
And then they put cunning advertisements in the
evening papers which asked 'Why Pay Rent?'
and simultaneously fixed red boards saying 'Sold'
on about two-thirds of the houses so as to terrify
any prospective purchasers who might be thinking twice before signing on the dotted line. And
by these and other means the hiatus vanished
altogether and Edgerley merged indissolubly into
Brockman Hill; and for about six months, as we
say, there was a distinct illusion — especially during
that rather foggy autumn — that these new residences were the last word in labour-saving con-
struction and up-to-date design that could possibly
be secured for a small sum down and the balance
on mortgage. It's also a slightly aggravating fact
that they were, at any rate while new, quite definitely less offensive than either Ardlers or Marefield
Road. They were only two stories high, they had
no bow-windows nor enclosed front-gardens. Their
cheapness had at least achieved something very
like simplicity.

So people came pouring into them, and the huts
and carts moved on elsewhere, and the Building
Society started sending its collectors round for the
interest — which now seemed strangely indistinguishable from the rent. And the rain came down
and swamped some of the lower rooms, and swept a
lot of the grey wash off the crumbling bricks, and

penetrated through a certain quantity of the fibre
tiles.   And the joists shrank and twisted, and the
doors cracked and bulged, and the quick-drying
paint peeled off the woodwork, and the slotted arms
snapped off the metal casements.   And the residents put up aerials and washing in their little
back-gardens, and some of them tried to keep
poultry and others succeeded in keeping cats.
And the Urban District Council brought a number
of actions against people who hadn't realised that
the new roads and pavements weren't a gift from
heaven; and for this and other reasons the houses
began to change hands.

And some of them became very shabby and
slovenly, and others revealed the individuality of
the inmates by amateurish attempts at brightening
themselves up.   There were splashes of new paint,
flower-pots with geraniums in them, scraps of trellis
with Dorothy Perkins as rampantly self-satisfied as
ever.   Or a couple of large shells on either side of
the front door.   Or a gaudy bell-push in the centre
of the door itself, communicating with a clockwork
contrivance just over an inch away.   Or an im-
prisoned canary, hopping ceaselessly from perch to
perch, inside the sitting-room window.

The inmates, in other words, were moved by
such varying and unchangeable impulses as control
all members of the human race, and worked and
slept and played, and spent money when they
had it, and got into difficulties when they hadn't.
And children were born to some of them, and
lodgers were taken in by others.   And some of
them left, and some of them died, and some of
them went on living where they were.   And the
rawness passed from the scene, and with it that
fleeting illusion that the houses were either labour-
saving or up-to-date, and in a very few years everybody had forgotten that these streets had been a
series of deserted fields — and before that, pre-

sumably, had been farm-land, or grazing-land, or primeval forest. The whole colony was now just part of the great sprawling belt which spread round the insatiable metropolis in every direction, and grew a little wider and a little dingier and a little more portentously inconceivable with every month that slipped past.

So, today, one turns out of Ardlers Road and sees the long vista of Pocklington Road stretching away into the distance, with even numbers on one side and odd numbers on the other. And so one passes between them, and between all the secret lives that are hidden behind their dirty grey walls. And so, at last, one arrives at Number Sixty-Seven, and pauses — because nothing, suddenly, is hidden any longer.

The walls dissolve, the whole house has become transparent, and it is here — as was hinted clearly enough at the outset — that the day seems to begin.

2

BETWEEN seven and eight on a fine morning towards the end of March. A touch of mist on the horizon, a pale blue sky overhead, smoke already rising from innumerable domestic hearths. A couple of milkmen and a baker's push-cart strung out along the vista. A boy propelling himself on one roller-skate with a satchel full of newspapers. Windows opening. Doors opening, too, and door-mats being shaken out of them. Edgerley gets off the mark early on a weekday, for it is half an hour from the big terminus by the fastest electric train, and there are very few breadwinners who don't have to make the trip and be at their desk or counter by nine o'clock.

Mr. Albert Coffin, aged forty-seven, a little bald, a little short-sighted, and a little protuberant below the midriff, stood in his tiny bath-room, with the

frayed linoleum beneath him and the sloping roof
overhead, assembling the four constituent parts of
his safety-razor.   The sun shone in on his black
boots, his dark trousers and his yellowish vest, on
his red hands and pale forearms; for Mr. Coffin
had already splashed and gasped in a cold bath.
He had also — early as it still was — found time to
go through some perfunctory and ungainly movements which he described as his exercises.   But
he hadn't shaved, even though it is far easier to
shave before than after a cold bath, because at
his first arrival on the scene the hot tap had utterly
refused to live up to its name.

Not that this had astonished Mr. Coffin.   Not
that he had really hoped to be greeted by a burst
of steam and a jet of boiling water.   Not that he
didn't splash first and shave afterwards on at least
four mornings in every week, and do so without criticism or complaint.   But naturally he preferred the alternative order — just as he would have
preferred a hot bath if there had been the remotest
chance of having one — and naturally there was
just a trace of anxiety in his expression until the
less reliable tap started doing its duty.   No one
can possibly blame Mr. Coffin for this.   No one,
surely, would wish the second salesman in Messrs.
Hamhurst's turnery department to suffer unnecessary agony in preparing his slightly pathetic features
for the public.

Nevertheless, on this particular morning, as the
occupier of Number Sixty-Seven again twirled the
tarnished handle, and again waggled his fingers
beneath it, his patience was distinctly strained by
the result of the experiment.   The water was icy,
and remained icy, whether it ran fast or slow.
No hopeful rumbling or panting came from the
pipes.   It was now, indeed, quite obvious to Mr.
Coffin that any further waggling or waiting would
be the merest waste of time; and this, he thought

sardonically, was all the good that came of handing things over to a daily woman. If only, he
thought, he'd kept the money for something else;
if only he'd never taken that rash, risky and
unselfish step...

But no, thought Mr. Coffin, as pride again came
surging to the support of his better nature. Mrs.
Bowker might be elderly and plain, she might be
unpunctual and she might be, and often was,
distressingly disrespectful; but how many other
householders in Pocklington Road had daily women
at all — even daily women who went off again by
eleven? How many of them had worked and
saved as he had worked and saved, and then had
the courage to be so daring and extravagant?
Precious few, thought Mr. Coffin, as he glanced
out of the tiny window at his tiny estate, and as
he again looked back on all the years of effort and
sacrifice which had at last landed him here as its
owner. And he recalled, as he was seldom tired
of recalling, how he had been the sole architect of
his fortunes; and how he had started without a
single advantage and without, as the saying goes,
a penny in his pocket. And how he had stuck to
his job and advanced in it. And how he had become affianced to Em, in spite of terrific opposition from both her parents. And how he had lost
his job (because of the war), and how he had spent
three and a half years in the Army Service Corps
(because of his eyes and his feet, not to mention
his back and his chest), and how he had finally lost
this job, too, and had had to begin all over again.

And how he did begin all over again, with Em
still faithful to him though the opposition was
more powerful than ever. And how presently he
had got into Hamhurst's, and how presently he
and Em had taken the plunge and got married,
and how they had spent five years in furnished
rooms, until they had again taken the plunge and

come to Pocklington Road. And how he was now
second-in-command in the turnery department, with
a steady salary and commission, and had bought
this house — never mind about the mortgage at the
moment — and had been married for ten years,
and had survived both his parents-in-law (though
not until his success had won their well-deserved
appreciation), and for nearly three months, now,
had employed a daily woman to come in and cook
and clean.

Yes, thought Mr. Coffin, as he ran through this
familiar but fascinating history, it was pretty
wonderful how everything had come his way in
the end, just by waiting and working like that.
Not, he thought again, that he could ever have
done it without Em. If Em (bless her!) hadn't
stuck to him like that, if she hadn't been one in
a million, if she hadn't been so patient and economical and steady all the time — well, he knew
well enough what he owed to Em. And again he
thought of his lengthy courtship, and of his wedding-
day, and of the first evening in the first furnished
rooms, and of the bunch of daffodils that he had
bought and put in that cracked vase, and of the
scene with the landlady about the damage to her
table.

'Funny,' thought Mr. Coffin, 'how I always
remember that. Funny how this time of year
always brings it back. Why, I believe ——'

The distant but sonorous hooting of the siren
at the saw-mills suddenly fetched him up short.
A quarter to eight, and his train to catch in less
than half an hour, and he hadn't shaved, or finished
dressing, or breakfasted, or done anything except
have his bath and stand here mooning. This
wouldn't do, thought Mr. Coffin; and he drew in
a determined breath.

'Em!' he shouted, raucously. And then, remembering that under the new regime she was

probably still in bed, he wrenched the door open and prepared to shout again.

'Em! I say, dear!'

To his surprise, Mrs. Coffin, wearing an old pink dressing-gown fastened with a large safety-pin, was coming up the narrow stairs from below.

'Eh?' she said, more briskly than benevolently. 'What's the matter now?'

'The — the water, dear. It's ——'

'Don't I know about that?' interrupted Mrs. Coffin. 'Haven't I got up specially? Aren't I boiling you a kettle?'

Mr. Coffin was still more perplexed.

'A kettle, dear?' he repeated. 'But why ——'

'She's not come,' said Mrs. Coffin sharply.

'She? D'you mean ——'

'I mean,' said Mrs. Coffin, 'that precious Mrs. Bowker of yours. Not that I'm surprised,' said Mrs. Coffin. 'Not that I haven't been expecting this. I tell you,' said Mrs. Coffin, with a distinct sniff, 'these women are all the same.'

'Eh?'

'Yes,' said Mrs. Coffin, still more directly. 'That's what I mean. A great deal more trouble and worry than they're worth.'

With this appalling statement, which in an instant had taken her husband's pride and rolled it in the dust, which had shattered his dreams and even, so it seemed, had caused a temporary eclipse of the sun, the figure in the pink dressing-gown swept onward and upward, swung sharply round on the miniature landing and vanished into the best bedroom — where it could be heard rattling violently at a drawer.

'I say,' said Mr. Coffin feebly. 'I — I say, dear — listen ——'

'What's that?'

'Em!'

'Eh?'

'But, Em, surely you don't mean ——'

The figure came bursting out again.

'Now, don't stand there fussing,' it said. 'I'm
doing everything I can for you, aren't I? I'm
getting you your breakfast, and I'm boiling you
up a kettle. In fact, I'm busy and you're late.
What is it?'

'Nothing,' said the other figure in the dark
trousers and yellowish vest. He hadn't been fussing, of course; he'd had no intention of fussing.
All he wanted was just one word to start helping
him out of the depths. Just a solitary and even
grudging admission that Mrs. Bowker wasn't always
more trouble and worry than she was worth, that
she did sometimes save work, that she hadn't been
imported — and at such vast expense — simply
so as to aggravate and annoy. 'Please!' said
Mr. Coffin's expression, as he backed towards the
bath-room again. 'Please, Em, don't say a thing
like that as if — as if you meant it!'

But the pink dressing-gown didn't even glance
at him as it scurried down the narrow stairs. The
pink dressing-gown was busy, as it had truly said,
and after all had only spoken of Mrs. Bowker in
words which have risen so easily to women's lips
since the beginning of time. Not for the pink
dressing-gown to realise the destruction that it
had wrought, though it knew well enough — even
without looking — that Mr. Coffin was sulking
about something. Well, the best thing was to take
no notice, and, anyhow, it was the pink dressing-
gown that was bearing the real brunt.

'Here you are, Elbert,' it said, dashing back
again with the kettle. 'Now, look sharp!'

And again Mr. Coffin tried to speak to it, and
again it had already turned and gone. He was
more or less compelled to mutter to himself; and
if you have ever muttered to yourself whilst shaving
against time, you know what is bound to happen.

'Uck!' said Mr. Coffin angrily, as the safety-
razor nicked one corner of his chin. And then:
'Garrh!' as it did it again. And then Em's
voice shouted: 'It's nearly five to, Elbert!' And
Mr. Coffin, so far from thanking her for this
timely reminder, snarled under his breath, and
then pulled his shirt on so violently that there
was a sound of ripping and tearing; whereat Mr.
Coffin swore, and tried to trace the damage, and
couldn't, for it was between his shoulder-blades.
So that now his face, as he put on his collar and
tie, was as red as his hands — and redder where
he had nicked himself. And then Mr. Coffin jerked
himself into a waistcoat and jacket, and patted
his pockets, and rushed madly into the bedroom
for his watch and handkerchief, and so, mumbling,
buttoning and stumbling, shot down the narrow
stairs and into the sitting-room.

And Mrs. Coffin said: 'Oh, Elbert — you've cut
yourself!'

And Mr. Coffin said: 'All right, all right,' in a
manner which expressed no sort of gratitude either
for the information or for the breakfast which
had been so efficiently prepared for him. For
though still at the back of his hustled, muddled
mind he was aware that Em was one in a million,
and though he was neither shocked nor repelled
by the colour of her pink dressing-gown or the way
in which it strained at that large safety-pin, nothing,
it seemed, could enable him to forgive or forget
what she had said upstairs about Mrs. Bowker.
He was still rasped and rattled. He was still
harassed and humiliated.

And, of course, in a small sitting-room in a small
house like this nobody can look and behave as
Mr. Coffin was looking and behaving, and expect
to remain unnoticed. Mrs. Coffin again asked him
what the matter was, but with even less sympathy
than before. And Mr. Coffin pretended not to hear

her, and said: 'Where's the paper?' And Mrs.
Coffin, being piqued, said that so far as she were
aware it was still on the doorstep, because if anybody thought she'd got time to go running out in
the road when she'd been running about indoors
ever since she didn't know when, then anybody
holding that opinion was in grave error.

And Mr. Coffin again said: 'All right, all
right.'

And Mrs. Coffin said: 'Look here, Elbert, is
that a nice way to speak to me, do you think?'

And Mr. Coffin mumbled into his tea.

And Mrs. Coffin said: 'Well, you'll be late anyhow, if you don't start.'

And though Mr. Coffin knew well enough in his
heart that truer words had never been spoken, he
didn't start, but poured out another cup and proceeded to drink it. For somehow it seemed to
him that this action was absolutely necessary as a
protest against that reflection on Mrs. Bowker,
which he still regarded as a reflection on himself;
and also it seemed to him — though with even less
reason, if possible — that a man who had never
missed his train for five years couldn't really miss
it now whatever happened.

'I'm all right,' he said. 'There's no need to
keep on at me.'

And it was at this point that the fat, as you might
say, fell definitely into the fire. No longer was it
a case of sulks or bickering. It was a real, first-
class, genuine rumpus, in which words were used to
hurt and voices were raised as savage weapons.
You see both sides? Of course you do; but that
doesn't mean that peace was any easier for the
Coffins. And Mrs. Coffin catalogued her wrongs;
and Mr. Coffin asked if she wanted everyone in the
road to hear her; and Mrs. Coffin, shouting still
louder, said that she didn't care if everyone in
Edgerley heard her; for she'd had enough of this

sort of thing, she said, and it was time a few people
knew it.

'All right,' said Mr. Coffin. 'So have I.'

'So have you what?'

'So have I,' said Mr. Coffin, 'had enough of it.
I work and work, an'——'

'Oh, yes!' said Mrs. Coffin. 'We all know you're
the only one who does that. Talk and talk,' said
Mrs. Coffin, 'is a bit more like it.'

'Now, then!'

'Now, then, what?'

Mr. Coffin suddenly staggered to his feet, trembling with emotion.

'Lissen-a-me,' he said thickly. 'Less have this
right out. Less getta the bottoma this. Woss the
idea? Woss——'

'Temper!' said Mrs. Coffin, quite maddeningly.

'*Nar!*' roared Mr. Coffin, plunging out into the
little passage and slamming the door behind him.

'Elbert!' shrieked Mrs. Coffin. 'What are you
doing? Come back in here at once, and don't
think you can go on like that, because——'

Thud! In one convulsive series of movements
Mr. Coffin had seized his hat and coat, snatched the
front door open, gathered his morning paper off
the step, pulled the door to again with a frightful
crash, and had started running towards Ardlers
Road as fast as his feet and his eyes (not to mention
his back and his chest) would allow him.

'Elbert!' screamed Mrs. Coffin, thrusting her
tousled head out of the sitting-room window.
'Elbert — come 'ere!'

But the ungainly little figure went racing and
stumbling away, still wriggling into its shabby
overcoat. Soon it was obviously out of earshot.
Then it was out of eyesight as well.

3

RAGE carried Mr. Coffin well into Ardlers Road
before physical disability forced him to slow down.
But as he paused and panted in the effort to master
his breathing, he was still a very long way from even
the stirrings of remorse; and as he set off again
at a more reasonable pace, he still mumbled and
muttered to himself. He'd had a row, and he was
glad that he'd had a row. And though but for
Mrs. Coffin he could neither have shaved nor eaten,
he still saw in her nothing but a traitress and an
antagonist.

Dim echoes kept returning to him from the scene
in the sitting-room, of personalities and insults
into which it had so swiftly degenerated; but each
time he flung them from him, and went back to
the origin of it all. To Mrs. Bowker, the real bone
of contention. To Mrs. Bowker, that broken reed
in whose defence he had begun by snarling and
ended by shouting and rushing from the field. And
again it struck him as beyond all bearing that a man
should have slaved as he had slaved, and then be
told that his supreme triumph was more trouble
and worry than she was worth.

'Khar!' said Mr. Coffin, summarising his feelings, and turned into Marefield Road. Only now,
though anger and bitterness still blazed beneath
his bowler hat, another emotion had begun to mingle
with them. For perhaps, said an unpleasant, carp-
ing little voice, the triumph hadn't been quite so
stupendous, after all. Perhaps there were greater
successes open to a man of forty-seven than just
making both ends meet. In fact, said the little
voice, there wasn't much doubt that most people
wouldn't call this success at all. How long, they
might ask, had it taken him to reach this puny
eminence, and how soon, if ever, did he expect

to get any further, and what could he really say
that he had ever done except just keep his head
above water?

'You're middle-aged,' said the little voice.
'You're short and bald, you've never really been
fit in your life, and in a very few years you'll be
done for. Have you saved anything to speak of?
Have you made any sort of mark in the world?
Have you ever seized an opportunity, or taken a
risk, or shown anybody that you're different from
millions of others?'

'Yes,' said Mr. Coffin defiantly, 'I've got a house.'

'Really,' said the little voice. 'I suppose you
mean that you've taken over somebody else's
mortgage. How long would it be your house if
Hamhurst's had a bad season, or if you didn't keep
what you're pleased to call your health?'

'I've got a wife,' said Mr. Coffin.

'And children?'

'Shut up,' said Mr. Coffin. 'You leave my
private affairs alone.'

'All right. I was only just asking, because ——'

'Will you shut up!'

'You're satisfied, then? You really think ——'

'Never mind what I think. I can't help it
if ——'

'There you go,' said the nagging little voice.
'Putting the blame on other people, as usual.
Trying to make out that your good luck is your own
doing, and that your bad luck is everybody else's.
You make me tired,' said the little voice. 'You'd
make me laugh, if only I hadn't seen through you
and your hopelessness years ago. You're nobody.
You're nothing. You're just a stupid little man
crawling along a stupid little rut, and if something
went over you and blotted you out, do you think
the rest of the world would notice or care? Do
you, Mr. Albert Coffin of Pocklington Road? Do
you really?'

And Mr. Albert Coffin of Pocklington Road groaned and muttered and stumbled forward into the High Street, but had no further answer to make to the dreadful little voice, for everything that it had said was true.   Not for Mr. Albert Coffin to realise that high words with Em, however they might have been provoked, always produced a reaction, and that he was in the very pit and profundity of it now.   Not for him to analyse the joint effects of cold water from a hot tap, of indigestion from a hurried breakfast eaten in a temper, and of that depression which can seize on all but the very strongest and idlest on a morning of March sunshine.   He just saw himself as he now knew that he was.   A failure.   In his own words, a wash-out.

The March sunshine sang of a world full of hope and adventure, but he would never know either. The March breeze, which blew scraps of paper along the wide pavements, spoke of courage and freedom, but not to Mr. Coffin.   He'd just go on like this until he dropped, because there was no possible alternative.   Edgerley and Hamhurst's.   Hamhurst's and Edgerley.   That was his life, if you could call it a life, and nobody would care twopence when it ended.

'Nobody,' said Mr. Coffin obstinately.   'Hear what I'm telling you?   Nobody!'

Thus Mr. Coffin's feet bore him across the tramlines and into the familiar blind-alley with the coal-merchants' little offices known as Station Approach. And thus he hurried up its incline, and turned sharp to the left into the booking-hall; and passed through it; and made that habitual movement towards one of his inner pockets which indicated to the man at the barrier that he was a season-ticket holder.

''Morning,' he said.

''S gone,' said the man at the barrier.

'Eh?' said Mr. Coffin, with a fresh sinking

sensation as he took in the emptiness of the scene.
'Woss that?'

The man pointed with one handle of his clippers
towards the dial of a very dirty clock.

''S gone,' he repeated. 'Eight twenny-eight's
the nex'.'

'But —— ' said Mr. Coffin, as the last straw
crushed him to the earth. 'But I say —— '

''Nless,' added the man at the barrier, suddenly,
'you was to cross over an' go the other way.
Eight-twenny, that is.'

Mr. Coffin stared blankly across the glittering
rails at the opposite platform, and even as he did so,
there was a squeak from one of the signal wires.

'There she is,' said the man at the barrier.
'You'll do it, if you run.'

Mr. Coffin hesitated for a moment. Never in all
these years had he gone round the loop the other
way, and still it seemed to him that it might be
better to be definitely late by the route he knew
than just to beat the clock by so wild an experiment. If he had followed this impulse —— But he
didn't. Whether it were the thought of his un-
broken record in the turnery department, or the
chance that had suddenly presented itself of getting
even a few inches out of the rut, it is impossible to
say. But he did run — like lightning along the
asphalt platform, and like winking up the steps of
the bridge, and like anything across it and down the
other side. And so, again panting and gasping, he
hurled himself into a third-class compartment of the
eight-twenty, and the eight-twenty hooted and
shuddered and set off with swiftly gathering speed.

'Whew!' said Mr. Coffin; and then looked apologetic, because perhaps he had gone rather far in
saying 'Whew!' in a carriage full of strangers.
None of them, however, paid any attention to him,
and he put on his eyeglasses and opened his paper.
At once he felt more at home. At once the daily

drug began to act. 'Government's Problem at
East Malmsey,' read Mr. Coffin, and passed on.
'Paddington Mystery,' he read, and assimilated
nearly half a column of official reticence sprinkled
with sub-editorial clichés. 'Mr. Corbett's New
Spectacle,' he read, and followed a very succulent
interview with that great man on the eve of his new
production at the Empress. 'Today's Big Wedding,' he read; and absorbed, and instantly forgot,
a selection of singularly conventional details. 'Will
the New Waist-Line Win?' he read, and sought
the answer to this question — which was never
really elucidated — right down the short column
in which it started, and so over the page.

And then Mr. Coffin read about some confused
occurrences in Italy, and a very unintelligible report
of what a French scientist thought about sunspots.
And then, not omitting the advertisements as he
came on them, he read the household hints and
the Women's Page. And then he read the Wireless
Programmes and the Children's Corner. Also
some medical advice by a Well-known Physician,
and part of a short serial by the successful Graham
Rutland, and a whole-page display (as it is called)
by a drapery firm, and a number of exceedingly
pointless remarks by magistrates, solicitors and
litigants which were yet served up as if they were
in some way humorous.

And then he arrived at the weather forecast,
and the leading articles, and the correspondence,
and the gossip. And then he struck some very thin
material about nothing in particular, and nearly a
column of two- and three-line inanities called 'The
World's News in a Nutshell.' And then the type
became rather smaller and he was on the City
page, with a report about a scene at the general
meeting of Associated Enterprises. And then he
ploughed manfully through three pages of sporting
news, decorated with still more advertisements,

and a short article on choosing a car. And then he reached the last page of all, and stared at a blurred phantasmagoria of photographs, which wasn't exactly the same as yesterday's and yet certainly wasn't different.

And so Mr. Coffin, now jammed tightly between the maximum of fellow-travellers and with several more standing between their feet, laid down the daily paper for which he paid sixpence a week, and again thought — but somehow with less passion and agony than before — how little all these affairs had to do with him, and how little he had to do with them, and how wide was the gulf between real life and the occupier of Number Sixty-Seven, Pocklington Road. And so he looked out of the window, past the other noses and newspapers, and recognised a factory chimney and an engine-shed which meant that he had long since left the loop, and was now nearing the end of his journey. And so he pulled out his watch and saw that it was three minutes to nine. And so he began to stir and shuffle, as did all the other passengers, that he might be ready to start running again at the first possible moment. And so he calculated that if he did this, and also forced his way on to an omnibus, he might yet punch the clock at the staff entrance to Hamhurst's without rendering himself liable to more than a formal caution at the end of the week.

And the train moved more and more slowly, and began to shudder again as the brakes came into action. And the long, dirty platform began to slide past it, and all its doors began opening like the swell-box of an enormous organ, and all the passengers stood up and crowded towards them, and feet appeared, making ready to leap and dash.

And then out they all swarmed, with their newspapers in one hand and their season-tickets in the other, and Mr. Coffin struggling and pushing in the midst of them. And the officials at the barriers

shouted: 'Hurry up, please!' though not a soul
in the vast throng was attempting to do anything
else; and the mob hurtled past them, and spread
out again, and rushed for the Underground and the
omnibuses and the streets — even as a second train
arrived on the other side of the long, dirty platform
and the whole process began all over again.

And Mr. Coffin, an indistinguishable unit in the
surging tide, ducked and dived and dodged, and
skipped and scurried, and elbowed and edged. And
so, at one minute past nine — for if you go the other
way round the loop, it takes at least ten minutes
longer to reach the terminus — Mr. Coffin collided
somewhat abruptly with a young woman in a brown
coat who was hurrying in more or less the same
direction, and said 'Sorry,' and rushed on again,
and disappeared.

Only even as he said 'Sorry' like that, a little
attaché-case fell from under the young woman's
arm, and its contents — or at any rate a book, a
bundle of knitting and a packet of sandwiches —
were scattered on the ground. And the young
woman stooped, and snatched at them from among
the innumerable racing feet, and crammed them
into the case again, and tried to snap the cheap
little catch. And it sprang open again, and she
snapped it more viciously. And again it sprang
open, and she thumped it with the side of her hand.
And then ——

And then a man's voice suddenly said: 'Hullo!
It's Gladys!'

And the young woman, who certainly wouldn't
still have been here at this moment if only Mr.
Coffin had caught his customary train, gasped, and
stared — and smiled.

'Oo!' she said. 'Why, it's Mr. Jackson!'

4

'It's Mr. Jackson!' said the young woman in the brown coat, as she snapped the little catch at last. 'Well!' she said. 'Fancy meeting you!'

'Why not?' said Mr. Jackson. And, 'Here,' he said. '"Harry," if you don't mind.'

'Pardon?'

'My name,' said Mr. Jackson, 'is Harry. You haven't forgotten that, have you?'

'Oo, well,' said the young woman.

'Eh?'

''Course I haven't forgotten,' said the young woman. 'Only I didn't think —— Well, I mean ——'

'What's that? I can't hear you in all this row. Come over here.'

'What?'

'Come over here, I say. I want to talk to you, don't I?'

'Oo, well ——'

'Eh? In a hurry, are you?'

'Well, not reelly,' said the young woman, looking up at the big clock. 'I've got a minute or two, that's to say.'

'That's to say, what?'

'Pardon?'

'What's my name, again?'

'Oo, Mr. —— Oo, all right, then. Harry.'

'Ah! That's better. That's more like it. You know you haven't forgotten me.'

''Course not. But I thought you'd forgotten *me*.'

'Eh? Why?'

'Well, you never rung me up at the office — like you said.'

'I've been busy,' said Mr. Jackson. 'But of

course I was going to. Why, do you think I'd forget you, after that film we saw?'

'Film? What d'you mean?'

'Wasn't it a film? No, of course it wasn't. It was at that dancing place, wasn't it? That's right, eh?'

'Well, if you go about with such lots of girls ——'

'I don't,' said Mr. Jackson. 'What d'you take me for? One of that sort? Not me! I knew what it was all the time, only I wanted to see if you remembered. Eh? Well, *I* do — anyway.'

'Reelly?'

'Yerss. You were there with a party, weren't you, Gladys? An' it was the M.C. who intrerjooced us, wasn't it? 'Course I remember the whole thing, an' I've been wondering what'd happened to you ever since. I remember your frock an' everything. Pale blue, wasn't it? Eh?'

'Well, saxe.'

'Oh, never mind those fancy names. I haven't forgotten it, anyhow — or you, neither. Or the ride we had afterwards.'

'Oo, Mr. ——'

'Now then!'

'Sorry. I keep forgetting.'

'Well, don't forget again. See? We're friends, aren't we? That's right. And, I say — I've still got that car.'

'Have you?'

'Yerss. And if I hadn't been so busy, I'd have come along for you one Sunday. How'd that suit you, eh?'

'Oo, I'd love it.'

'All right then. I've still got your address. I shan't forget.'

'Oo, thanks ever so much. Only ——'

'Eh?'

'I ought to be going now — reelly.'

'Why?'

'Well, I don't want to be late at the office, do I?'

'What time you gotta ——'

'Well, half-past. An' it's ——'

'Listen,' said Mr. Jackson, suddenly. 'I'll see you're not late.'

'What d'you mean?'

'You've heard of a taxi, haven't you?'

'Oo, I say! No, I couldn't reely ——'

Mr. Jackson laughed richly, and pulled out a cigarette-case.

'Now, listen,' he said, again. 'Don't you worry about time or money when you're with me. I'm having a holiday now, I am, and I've just been paid for a big job. Don't you think I'm looking smart, eh?'

He grinned and patted his dark-blue overcoat.

'Eh?' he asked. 'That's all right, isn't it?'

'Oo!'

'Wossa matter?'

'I knew there was something different. That's why you gave me such a start at first. You've taken off your moustache.'

Just for a moment Mr. Jackson didn't look quite so full of self-assurance.

'Was I wearing one at that place?' he asked — almost as if it were the kind of thing that one found on one's lip by accident. And then: 'Yerss — that's right. So I was.'

And suddenly he laughed again.

'You are funny,' said the girl Gladys.

They stood and looked at each other. All over the big station, as more suburban trainloads arrived and swept through the barriers, couples were standing like this; some talking, some arguing, some gesticulating, some just staring. The crowds flowed round them and past them, and perhaps if you watched any particular couple, it would cease to be a couple and become merged in the moving mass. Only at once there was another couple, almost in the same place; for it seemed that even in the midst of all this noise and confusion there were people who must stop and settle something.

'Funny, am I?' said Mr. Jackson. 'You mean, I look funny?'

'Oo, no. 'Course I didn't mean that. I didn't mean to be rude.'

'Fact is,' said Mr. Jackson, abruptly, 'I got tired of that moustache. Wanted a change, I dessay. You know.'

The girl nodded. She could hardly be expected to go to the utmost limit in sympathising with a whim like this, but it was obvious that she wanted to go as far as she could.

'I'm not sure you don't look nicer without it,' she said. 'Not that —— Well, it's nothing to do with me, I suppose?'

'Eh? Why not?'

'Well, I mean ——'

'You don't know me well enough, eh? 'S that what you're getting at? Don't you want to?'

'I didn't say nothing like that.'

'Well, per'aps you're going to,' said Mr. Jackson. He lit his cigarette, flung the match down, and stamped on it. 'Fact is,' he said, 'I'm a funny sort of a chap. Fact is, I've had a bit of worry these last few days, and you mustn't be surprised if —— Here; let's get over to the side a bit more. Ackcherly I was taking a short cut through the station just now, but —— Well, the fact is, I'm not supposed to be in London.'

'Why, where are you supposed to be?'

'Well, somewhere else. See? No, you don't see, of course. But look here.'

'What is it?'

'Where's this office of yours? Near?'

'Empire House it's called. It's just ——'

'I know,' said Mr. Jackson, with a glance at

the big clock. 'An' you've got to be there by
half-past, eh? Well, there's lots of time still. Let's
drive round a bit. You and me, eh?'

'But you don't want to ——'

'Yerss, I do. Tell you the truth, I've got a
reason I don't like standing about in this place.
I'm —— Well, 's a matter of fact, I'll tell you.
D'you know my business?'

'How'd I know that? You never ——'

'I'm a detective. See?'

'Oo!' said the girl Gladys. 'Not reelly! Not a
reel one!'

'Well, more like a private one. See? I'm —
I'm on a big case just now.'

'Oo!'

'Yerss. Only look sharp, can't you, because I
tell you...'

The girl Gladys didn't quite catch the end of
this sentence, because Mr. Jackson had already set
off at such a pace that she had almost to run to
keep up with him. And then, just as she drew
level, he suddenly wheeled round, caught her arm,
and pulled her in the other direction.

'Changed my mind,' he said. 'We'll get a taxi
out this way.'

'But ——'

'I know. Only I'll find one where they come
in. Here we are. Taxi!'

It crossed the girl Gladys's mind that perhaps
she oughtn't to be doing this; that perhaps this
was the kind of thing that she had heard about
and been warned against; that it would be a great
deal better, possibly, if she said good-bye now,
and ran for her bus — since it was too late to do
the shopping for which she had caught the early
train. And then, as she stepped into the taxi, it
seemed to her that it was silly to be so stupid,
and that it was nothing to do with her mother
anyhow, and that this wasn't the first time she'd

been for a ride with Mr. Jackson, and that if he was a detective, then of course it was all right. And she was rather excited and thrilled. And she laughed.

'This *is* a nice taxi,' she said. 'It's ages since I've been in one.'

Mr. Jackson turned round from looking out of the little window in the hood, and laughed too.

'That's better,' he said. 'Now we can have a bit of a talk.'

The girl Gladys thought he was really awfully good-looking.

'Are you sure ——' she began.

'Eh?' said Mr. Jackson.

'Are you reelly sure you've got time for this?'

'What? Yes, of course I've got time. Didn't I tell you I was having a holiday?'

Oo, yes; so he had. But then, after that he'd said how busy he was, and how he was working on this big case. Well, which ——

'Eh?' said Mr. Jackson — just as if he'd read the girl Gladys's thoughts. 'You're wondering about this job I'm on, eh? That's right. 'Course you are. Well — 's like this. I'm *supposed* to be having a holiday, see? But between you and I...'

Here Mr. Jackson gave an extremely knowing and confidential wink, and the girl Gladys was more thrilled and excited than ever. A private detective, she was also thinking, must have quite a large screw. Well, look at his clothes. Look at the way he'd taken this taxi. And he'd got his own car as well. And, besides (thought the girl Gladys), he was reelly awfully good-looking — reelly he was. 'I wonder,' she thought, 'if he's married.'

Quite a nice girl, this Gladys; quite good; quite straight, as the saying goes. But, like the rest of us, she wanted to be happy as well, and like the rest of us, she had the illusion that she was meant to be happy. When she didn't think about it, she was often — again like the rest of us — happy enough; but when she did think about it — and she was thinking about it now — it seemed to her that you never got what you wanted just by doing what you were told. Other people, and particularly old people like her mother, never understood this. There'd been no end of a fuss, for instance, when Mr. Jackson — when Harry Jackson had driven her home after that dance. But it wasn't as if she'd promised not to see him again — well, as a matter of fact, she'd hardly hoped she ever *would* see him again. But she had; and he was awfully good-looking; and she wondered if he were married.

'I'm almost sure he rather likes me,' she thought. 'And he's quite a gentleman. I mean, reelly he is.'

Really he wasn't. No, not by any of the very arguable definitions of this curious term. But the girl Gladys was thrilled and excited, and her lips parted a little, and he *had* remembered her, hadn't he?

'Go on,' she was saying. 'Do tell me. I swear ——'

'Eh?'

'About this big case, I mean. I swear I'd never tell a soul.'

Mr. Jackson looked at her again.

'Wouldn't you?' he asked. 'Well ——'

'Oo, please!'

'Um,' said Mr. Jackson. 'It isn't such a secret as all that, you know. It's been in all the papers.'

'Not reelly!'

'Yerss,' said Mr. Jackson, impressively. 'On the front page, too. The men at the Yard have been on it more than a week, but — well, I don't see *them* getting much further.'

'You mean, that's why they've had to send for you? Is that what you mean?'

Mr. Jackson glanced out of the window, turned back again, and nodded.

'That's right,' he said, with a grin. 'They can't do without me, you see, and they know it. It's — you see —' He seemed to reach a sudden decision. 'Well,' he said, 'I'll tell you what it is. It's this Paddington business.'

'Oo!' cried the girl Gladys. 'Do you mean that poor old man in the shop that they——'

'Poor!' Mr. Jackson gave a short laugh as he lit another cigarette from the stub of the first. 'Don't you believe it, my dear. Pig-headed's more like it, I say — keeping all his cash in a little tin-pot safe, 'stead of sending it to the bank or having a good time with it. And damned stupid to yell out like that when the natcheral result came along, 'stead of handing it over quietly. That's more the way *I* look at it,' said Mr. Jackson.

Three separate thrills ran up and down the girl Gladys's back under her brown coat. He'd called her 'my dear' — that was one thrill. He'd sworn, and that was distinctly another. And for the third he'd told her something about the murder that wasn't in any of the papers.

'Did he?' she gasped. 'Did they hear him?'

'Eh?'

'Did somebody hear him yelling, then?'

'What? No, I never said so. 'Course they didn't. Whadyer mean?'

She must have made a mistake. She'd been stupid, she supposed, and misunderstood him somehow. What a shame, just when he was going to tell her some more, and —— No, it was all right. He was going on again.

'Fact is,' Mr. Jackson was saying, 'that job was one of the neatest jobs there's been for years.

See how it's beaten the police, eh? Because —
well, listen; this is how I reckon it out. That
chap who broke in there — whoever he was, see? —
he didn't come there not to hurt the old boy.
Well, doesn't it say in the papers how the old boy
always went over to his sister's on early-closing
days? So it stands to reason, doesn't it, that this
chap wouldn't have broke in just on the chance.
See what I mean?'

The girl Gladys didn't exactly follow his reasoning, but she wasn't going to risk stopping him
again, and it was extraordinarily easy to nod.

'Go on,' she murmured.

'Well,' said Mr. Jackson, 'where this chap
was so smart — see? — was not losing his head.
'Cos, supposing you was to break in somewhere,
an' supposing you was just opening the safe, an'
supposing an old man came in suddenly and saw
you, an' supposing you coshed him — well, that's
the point, see? Nine chaps out of ten, what
would they do? Clear out as quick as they could,
an' likely as not leave something behind what'd
fix it on 'em. See? Finger-prints or something,
see? Or a bit of their kit. Or else they'd go
touching the body, an' get all smeared up with
blood. See?'

'Oo!' said the girl Gladys, squirming and shuddering. 'Oo, you do get awful ideas, I must say.
Did you — did you see it, then? Was it...?'

'Yerss,' said Mr. Jackson, frowning slightly.
'I saw it. When they called me in, I mean, of
course. Only that's not the point. The point I
keep trying to tell you is what a nerve this chap
must have had. Because when the cops came
along — next morning, that is, after the servant had
found him — natcherally they started looking for
clues. But do you think they got any?'

'I dunno. Did they?'

'No,' said Mr. Jackson. 'They didn't. Because

the chap had worn gloves, see? And he hadn't touched nothing, except what he needed to. And he hadn't gone rushing out, like a lot of these chaps would have done, so that everyone would start remembering about it afterwards, and coming along with a description and all that. No, what he did — well, I mean, there's not much doubt about this — was just to slip out quietly when the street was clear, an' disappear like that. Very likely he'd have a car waiting somewhere, see? Clever — get what I mean? I tell you, that chap wasn't leaving no clues about.'

'Oo!' said the girl Gladys. 'You do make it sound reel.'

'Well, it was, wasn't it?'

'Oo, yes. Go on — please!'

'Go on? What more do you want?'

'Well, I mean, you must know something ——'

'Eh?'

'— or you wouldn't still be after him, would you? Oo, I do hope he's caught. Just fancy, I mean, him going about all this time — all among everybody. But you know they say murder will out — don't they?'

'Eh? Whadyer mean?'

'Well, it's what they say, and ——'

'Rot,' said Mr. Jackson. 'See here, I'm working with the police, aren't I? An' I know as much as they do about it, don't I? An' I tell you they say just what I say. That chap who did this Paddington job is one of the smartest chaps in the game — whoever he is — an' if I got a hold of him, I'm damned if I wouldn't tell him so. He's one of the regular boys, he is — I'll betcher anything you like; an' he won't be caught, not now he won't. An' don't you ask me any more questions, because ——'

'Oo, Mr. Jackson — I'm awfully sorry. I — I didn't mean to say anything rude.'

Mr. Jackson's sudden spurt of annoyance, almost of passion, seemed to have died away as quickly as it had come.

'Eh?' he said. 'That's all right, Gladys. 'Course you didn't. Only look here — if you don't want to be rude, just you stop mistering me quite so much. Don't I keep on telling you? Now, what's my name? Eh?'

The girl Gladys wriggled her thin shoulders.

'Oo, well...'

'Come on. Say it!'

'Oo, all right. Harry. I — I think it's an awfully nice name.'

'You do?'

'Yes, honestly. I mean, I think it sort of suits you.'

'Do you? Better than "Jack," f'r instance — eh?'

The girl Gladys had quite got over her embarrassment just now. She laughed.

'Well,' she said, 'you couldn't hardly go about calling yourself "Jack Jackson." I mean, that sounds silly — doesn't it?'

'Think so?'

'Well, doesn't it? I mean —— Oo!'

'Here — what's the matter?'

'Oo, gracious, look at that clock! And wherever are we? Oo, I say — you're not going to let me be late, are you? You don't know what they're like when a person's late, an' I promised ——'

'All right. All right. Don't get so excited.'

'Yes, but where are we? Oo, do please ask the man to go back. I ought to have noticed sooner, only ——'

'There, there. Keep cool, old dear.'

'Yes, but ——'

'He's going there as fast as he can. I only told him to take a bit of a drive round.'

'Oo, are you sure?'

'Well,' said Mr. Jackson, 'you're a nice sort of a girl to take along for a ride. Here, stop it! Stop jumping about like that. We'll be there 'fore you know where you are.'

'Will we?'

'Yerss. Unless ——'

'Oo, what?'

'Unless you'd rather let 'em wait. You know; ring up and tell 'em you're not well. Eh? Why not, now? There's plenty of places we could go.'

'Oo no. I — I couldn't.'

'Yes, but listen, Gladys. I like you.'

'Oo, no!'

'Yes, I do. An' I've had a lot of worry lately, an' I didn't run into you for nothing like that, an' there's reasons — well, I've told you about this case an' all that, haven't I? Listen — you don't know what it means, going about all the time by yourself — 'cause you can't trust people, see? Listen — I've had the hell of a time, Gladys, and now you and me's met again, I'll go anywhere — see? — if only you'll come along too. I tell you, I haven't so much as spoken to a girl for a week.'

He laid his hand on the girl Gladys's knee, and she could have cried out at the struggle between fear and temptation. And lots of girls would do it, wouldn't they? Lots of girls would make up some sort of story for the office, and get away with it, and then boast afterwards of all the fun they'd had. And he liked her; he'd said he liked her; and he was touching her, and he was rich, and he'd got a car.

And it wasn't as if other men bothered to be nice to her like this. They took her along to make up a party sometimes, or because the girl she was going out with had forgotten to put her off — like at that dance the other night; but this man...

'Oo, Harry ——'

'Well? 'S that right, eh?'

But supposing they found out at the office. Supposing they found out at home. Oo, no; she must have been mad to think of doing anything so crazy, and of course nobody'd ever believe her, and — and ——

'Oo, Harry — I can't!'

'Eh?'

'I mustn't. I mean, it's awfully sweet of you, but ——'

'Here — never mind that. I want you, see?'

'Yes, but —— Oo, please leggo!'

But Mr. Jackson didn't let go. On the contrary, he slipped his right arm round the brown coat, and pulled the girl Gladys towards him, and his face grew enormously large, and his thick lips drew back — and suddenly the girl Gladys began to scream.

'Oo!' she cried. 'You mustn't!'

Mr. Jackson caught both her wrists in his left hand, and though she tried to duck her head she could feel his hot breath.

'Come off it,' he was saying. 'Don't be such a little fool, Gladys. Listen — I'm not going to hurt you. Here — whadyer want to come driving about with me for, if a chap can't ——'

'Oo — you beast!'

'Steady!'

'You beast — you beast — you ——'

The hand which had been gripping her shoulder suddenly made a grab at her chin, forced it round, and was over her mouth. The girl Gladys kicked and tried to push with her elbows; and nearly fell off the seat and was jerked on again; and bit savagely, though she had no idea that she was biting; and found she could scream again, and did scream.

'Quiet!' shouted Mr. Jackson. 'Shut up, you little devil!'

The girl Gladys relaxed, and gave a quick spring, so that her head was out of the window.

'Stop!' she cried. 'Stop! Stop!'

'Eh?' said the driver, clapping on his brakes, and looking round. He was just in time to see the door open and go swinging outwards with his female passenger clutching at it. And then a lot of things seemed to happen at once. As that the cab stopped; as that the female passenger missed her very precarious hold and went rolling into the gutter; as that a number of people shouted 'Hi!' 'Oy!' and other lively interjections; as that they all came hustling and clustering round the cab on both sides; as that the crowd on the near side was suddenly divided as no less than two policemen — one in a helmet and the other in a peaked cap — stalked swiftly through it.

'Now, then,' said the helmeted policeman, stooping and setting the girl on the step. 'You 'urt, missie? Eh?'

Crowd noises. Traffic noises. Arms, legs, bodies and faces all whirling about and dissolving and coming together again.

'Back, there!' said the inspector. And then he looked piercingly at the driver, and the driver, with the aid of shrugged shoulders and raised eyebrows, indicated his entire disassociation from responsibility coupled with an opinion, based on long experience, that passengers as a class were half-witted and top-heavy.

'I dunno nothink about it,' said the driver; and then he glanced backwards over his right shoulder and suddenly became far more concerned with the affair. ''I!' he shouted, struggling from his little seat. 'Wait a minute, sir! Where are you going?'

And Mr. Jackson, who had been stepping quietly out of the off-side door, seemed not only to alter his intention extremely quickly, but also to wish

to convey by the speed with which he re-entered
the vehicle that he had never really left it. And
yet Mr. Jackson looked anything but calm or
dignified.

'I never saw nothing,' he said. 'I never ——'

He looked at the off-side door again, but the
driver was standing outside it, glaring significantly
through the window. No escape that way, and
Mr. Jackson turned to face the inspector. As he
did so, his features gave a twitch and his mouth
fell slightly ajar.

'Mr. Jack Harrison, isn't it?' said the inspector.
'Hullo, Jack!'

And he snapped his fingers, so that the helmeted
policeman, who had been bending over the girl
Gladys and brushing the dust off her coat and
asking her where she felt it and receiving singularly
unintelligible replies, looked up and looked interested and looked attentive.

'Er,' said the other passenger. ''Morning,
Mr. Davis.'

'Well?' said the inspector, leaning forward a
little. 'What's the idea?'

Mr. Jackson, as one goes on calling him — for he
was at least as well known by this name as by half
a dozen others — gave a quick gulp, and looked
indignant.

'Idea?' he said. 'I dunno what you mean,
Mr. Davis. I can't help it if this young lady starts
fooling with the door, can I? I wasn't doing
nothing. I wasn't ——'

'Oo!' cried the young lady, tempestuously.
'It isn't true! Oo, I wish I'd never got into the
cab. Oo, look at my coat! Oo, it's all his fault,
it was. Don't you believe him! Don't you ——'

'Steady,' said the inspector; and his little eyes
darted from the girl to his subordinate, and from
his subordinate to Mr. Jackson, and from Mr. Jackson back again to the girl. 'Wait a minute, now,

miss; let's get this straight. Is he a friend of
yours, eh?'

'Oo, no!' sobbed the girl Gladys, struggling
to her feet. 'Oo, I don't hardly know him, sir.
Oo, I wish I'd never met him again. Oo, you
dunno what he did to me. Oo, I'm going to be so
late. Oo, lemme go away — please! Oo ——'

'Just a minute; just a minute. Now, what did
he do to you?'

'Oo, I couldn't tell you, sir. Nothing. I made
a mistake. Nothing at all. Oo, please ——'

The inspector cocked his little eye back into the
cab.

'Well?' he asked again.

'You heard,' said Mr. Jackson, still more indignantly. 'You ain't got nothing against me,
Mr. Davis. I can't help it if doors fly open,
can I? You heard what the young lady said. I
tell you, you'd better not ——'

'Just a minute. What's in that case?'

'I dunno, Mr. Davis. 'Tisn't mine, I tell you.
How should I know what's in it?'

And Mr. Jackson picked up the little attaché-
case, perhaps to offer it as proof of his innocence;
and the girl Gladys turned round and saw him, and
screamed.

'Oo! He's got my case! Oo, stop him! Oo,
don't let him take it! Oo ——'

The inspector took the case himself.

'Come along, Jack,' he said. 'We'll all come
along together.'

'But I never ——'

'We'll see about that,' said the inspector, 'when
we've had a look at you.'

'Eh?'

Mr. Jackson glanced at the other door, turned
back, hesitated, and swallowed violently. If they
found that five-pound note on him at the station, if
they'd got the number.... Why the blazes had

he kept it? Why the blazes hadn't he hidden it
somewhere? Why the blazes hadn't he torn it up?
Blast that idiot of a girl, what did she want to go
making all that row for, and chucking herself about,
and fetching the cops into it like this? He wished
she'd broken her blasted neck. He wished he'd
bolted at the beginning. He wished he'd never
set eyes on the damned little fool. This was what
came of messing about with women, instead of lying
low and keeping quiet; and now...

'Give us a bit of room,' said the inspector,
climbing into the cab and dropping on to the back
seat. And: 'Come on, Stevens,' he said. 'Let's
have the young lady, too.'

In got the helmeted policeman and the girl
Gladys, the latter's limp form requiring a good deal
of assistance.

'Oo,' she was moaning, 'I never did anything.
Oo, where are you taking me? Oo, look at my
stocking! Oo, I'll get the sack for this.'

More crowd noises outside. Faces at both windows, swirling and shoving and staring. The
driver was back on his little seat, tooting vigorously.
The cab gave a jerk, and began to move.

'Keep your hands out of your pockets, Jack,'
said the inspector. 'I'll tell you what's in 'em
presently, if you want to know.'

Mr. Jackson, or Harrison, opened his mouth to
say something threatening about his solicitor —
and then closed it again because he had been on the
point of being sick.

'Oo!' moaned the girl Gladys. 'Oo, I never
meant any harm. Oo, what'll mother say about
this? Oo, dear! Oo, I wish I was dead!'

The inspector leant back in his corner and eyed
her with a look from which benevolence, tempered
by curiosity, was by no means lacking. Mr. Jackson gazed at his own finger-nails, and swore steadily
under his breath. Constable Stevens sat bolt up-

right beside the girl Gladys, immovable and without
a trace of visible emotion.   And so the taxi rattled
and bumped through the traffic towards the nearest
police station.

5

THE third Lord Midhurst's grandfather was a
Victorian proconsul whose name meant very little
to his contemporaries — though it crops up here
and there in a number of dull memoirs and lives —
and still less to the generations which have succeeded them.   He had rather a fine set of whiskers,
a brow which at any rate appeared to grow loftier
with age, no perceptible sense of humour and an
inexplicable horror of cats.   He also had two wives
— one, that is to say, after the other — and fourteen
children; so that by the time that the second Lord
Midhurst came into the title, there wasn't quite so
much money going about as everybody would have
liked.   This was more or less inevitable even in the
days when everything except *The Times* was far
cheaper than now, and income-tax was well under a
shilling in the pound.   Nevertheless, the family
remained intensely respectable with scarcely an
exception, and some of the daughters had husbands
who partially supported them, and several of the
sons earned a little money of their own.   South
Kensington and Sussex continued to contain this
large and on the whole uninteresting brood.   None
of them were very good-looking, but they were all
fairly well pleased with themselves.

The second Lord Midhurst, who was probably
the stupidest of the lot, spent a few years in the
army, without ever shedding his own or anybody
else's blood, and then spent nearly forty years doing
nothing to which one can exactly put a name.   He
went to and fro between South Kensington and
Sussex, and sometimes he went abroad, where he
was very distant in his dealings with the natives.

If pressed still further, one might add that he was a magistrate — though he never sat on the Bench — and that he was also on the wine-committee of his Club. That, honestly, seems to exhaust all that can be said of the second Lord Midhurst — though he married and had five children — except that towards the end of his life he acquired an unaccountable air of distinction which on more than one occasion made several people wonder who he was. When supplied with this information, they said 'Oh' — there being really nothing else to say — and let the whole subject pass lightly from their minds. Now that they looked again, perhaps they had been mistaken to show even such fleeting interest.

So presently the second Lord Midhurst died, at the age of sixty-seven and while the income-tax was still only just over a shilling in the pound; and as well as being succeeded by his second son, the third Lord Midhurst, he left behind him such a welter and chaos of ·debts and worthless investments and muddled accounts, that the house in Sussex had to be sold then and there, while the only reason why the house in South Kensington didn't follow it into the market was that this large, inconvenient and revoltingly ugly residence proved to be virtually unsaleable. At any rate it seemed simpler for the third Lord Midhurst and his unmarried sister Alice to go on living in a bit of it, than to raise the funds to provide a new establishment elsewhere. One of the other brothers was now dead, the second had gone to Australia, and the youngest of the family — Gertrude — had married a clergyman. The Victorian era had quite definitely come to an end.

This third Lord Midhurst was also in the army when the crash came. He resigned his commission — and the war broke out. He got another commission, went through the whole business from beginning to end; was wounded once or twice — not seriously; was promoted; was mentioned in dispatches;

was brought home again; was discharged. He was now forty-four, had a title, no income to speak of, a house in South Kensington, an unmarried sister, and didn't quite know what to do next. He was tall and thin, had a large nose, pale eyes and not very much hair. His morale was quite unaffected by his experiences in France, but his intelligence remained distinctly below par. There was a boom, as you may remember, in industry and business — Heaven alone knows why, when one looks back at it — and a friend got him a couple of directorships.

If it hadn't been for the boom, he would almost certainly have lost them again. Shareholders would have called him a guinea-pig, and that would have been the end of Lord Midhurst in the City. But the boom saved him. The boom lasted long enough to give him a certain standing — also more directorships; and though it may seem a bold thing to say that almost anybody can learn to sit on a board if they keep their mouths shut and look respectable, the fact remains that by these methods Lord Midhurst gained quite a little reputation. Presently he started opening his mouth, and as he never said anything either original or unexpected, the reputation grew steadily in weight. He never quite understood the business which was being transacted, but he was regular and punctual in his attendances, and even those who saw him oftenest felt a strange confidence in the height of his collars.

The boom passed, but Lord Midhurst still tucked his long legs under board-room tables and was paid for doing so. He became chairman of one or two ventures, and read typewritten speeches — prepared by other hands — in a voice which convinced almost everybody that the concerns were sound at bottom. Some of them, moreover, actually were; but even when they weren't, and it became necessary to wind themselves up, the creditors thought of Lord Midhurst's plain, sandy face and his dull, heavy

manner, and somehow knew that it was all just
bad luck, and were mollified. He never reached
the heights of first-class companies, but — until he
met Mr. Fink — a certain mild fastidiousness had
kept him practically clear of the dregs. Certainly
he was no judge of character; certainly his private
belief that only about three gentlemen (of whom
he was one) had survived the war, was no great
help in distinguishing between sheep and goats;
but the goats — until he met Mr. Fink — had almost all felt too uneasy in his presence to wish to
see more of him in theirs. They thought him a
pompous fool, and had quite a number of grounds
for this opinion, but all the spice would go out of
crooked dealings if those collars were to be associated with them. So Lord Midhurst became quite a
moderately successful guinea-pig in a number of
quite moderately honourable undertakings, and
picked up a quantity of useful phrases which saw
him through several inevitable emergencies, and
passed his fiftieth birthday without noticing it
particularly, and was still frequently appointed and
reappointed to various boards.

And he stayed on in the inconvenient house in
South Kensington, still accompanied by his unmarried sister Alice, and managed to pay off some
of his father's debts, and generally came out just
about all square at the end of the year. He hadn't
got a country house, or a yacht, or even a car; but
on the rare occasions when he stepped even partially
outside himself to see how he was getting on, he
was quite satisfied with the spectacle. He was
doing his best, he might undoubtedly have done a
great deal worse, and with any luck it would all be
over in less than twenty years.

Then he would either have a good rest in the
family mausoleum, or find himself once more in the
society of gentlemen. Either prospect seemed a
distinct change for the better, and Lord Midhurst
stepped inside himself again, and forgot about both.

6

WOMEN, of course, never know an outsider when they see one — or else there aren't any outsiders, really, except in the imagination of men — and it was Lord Midhurst's unmarried sister Alice who overcame his first impression of Mr. Fink.   Mr. Fink came to dinner at the house in South Kensington, because his host had declined to be his guest; and Lord Midhurst apologised beforehand to his sister Alice, and asked her if she wouldn't prefer to dine with one of their innumerable relations.

'You wouldn't care for him,' he said.   'He's purely a business acquaintance.'

But Alice — a dull woman leading an amazingly dull life — wasn't going to be pushed into the background like that.   The City was still all mystery and magic to her, and she wanted to see the kind of man who'd made a real success in it, and whose name she had read in the papers.   She hadn't forgotten what it was like to be rich — or at any rate to have an apparently rich home — and if Mr. Fink were coming here with a business proposition, then at least she must see that he had everything he wanted.   Perhaps this was to be the beginning of the change for which she still hoped and prayed. At the worst there was the chance of picking up a tip.

So Alice stayed at home, and ordered a special dinner for the vast dining-room, and arranged special flowers on the enormous table, and refused to see Mr. Fink as a swarthy little cad, but smiled on him and played up to him and thought she was being very helpful and clever.   And after he had gone, and when Lord Midhurst again apologised for having him in the house, she raised her eyebrows and said she didn't know what he meant.

'I think,' said old Alice, 'he's charming.'

'Eh?' said Lord Midhurst. 'Do you?'

'So polite,' said old Alice. 'And so interesting about all the things he does. No, don't make those faces, Bertie. I tell you, I took to him *particularly*.'

'Oh,' said Lord Midhurst, swaying to and fro on the hearthrug under his grandfather's portrait. But if Alice felt like that about Fink, then perhaps he was wrong. Nobody, as he well knew, could be more critical than Alice if she didn't take to people, and nobody was more punctilious over distinctions which, alas, no longer existed. But she was his sister, and part of the old and only true tradition, and perhaps she was right.

'Um,' said Lord Midhurst, raising and lowering his sandy eyebrows. And then he decided to sleep on it all, and having slept on it all, found that Alice's opinion was no longer detachable from the other aspects of the affair. For what else had he got against Fink, except that at first he hadn't much liked him? And was this any reason for keeping clear of him, when the dislike had virtually evaporated? 'He's no worse,' thought Lord Midhurst, 'than lots of fellers, and he can't help his appearance. I've half a mind, you know, to look into that idea he was talking about. One mustn't be unreasonable,' thought Lord Midhurst. 'One's either trying to keep a roof over one's head, or one isn't.'

And the half-mind, still stimulated by Alice's judgment, became a whole mind; and Lord Midhurst lunched with Mr. Fink at his office in Empire House, and wasn't insensible to his flattery, and nodded over a lot of figures which he certainly didn't understand, and joined the board of one of his companies. And joined the board of another. And joined the board of a third. And Mr. Fink was satisfied, because Lord Midhurst's name was exactly the kind of name which he wanted — that is to say, dull, respectable and without a blot or blemish on it. And Lord Midhurst had no real cause for dissatisfaction, either, because he was now making nearly twice as much money as before, and so far as regular attendances and the utterance of useful phrases were concerned, certainly seemed to be earning it. Mr. Fink remained very civil to him, and he remained very civil to Mr. Fink. They also both remained poles apart in ethics, morals, standards of personal behaviour and intelligence. But the companies weren't doing so badly at this time, at any rate on paper, and the divergence hadn't yet been tested by stress or crisis. Lord Midhurst paid off some more of his father's debts, and hired a butler and a chauffeur and a car.

As for his unmarried sister Alice, having got her way, and with these delightful results, she no longer saw any cause to pretend that Mr. Fink was worthy of her admiration, nor did she trouble to stay in when he came — as still happened occasionally — to dine. And Mr. Fink didn't care a couple of hoots whether he saw her or not, and never knew what he owed her, or thought twice about what she owed him. As an investment, Lord Midhurst was paying all that he had ever hoped for, but his relations were neither here, there, nor anywhere else. For Mr. Fink was no snob. He merely knew that other people were.

So presently there were some secret difficulties and set-backs — as are almost bound to occur when a group of companies has no real reason for existence — and Mr. Fink was kept very busy juggling and conjuring; and then — with a great flourish of trumpets — Associated Enterprises was suddenly born, and somehow all the people who had been disgusted with its component parts came rallying round to support them under this different name. And the new issue went to a premium, and Mr. Fink juggled and conjured more ingeniously than ever —

and made a large private profit — and Lord Midhurst was gratified, though not particularly astonished, to find himself in the chair. And for about six months everything went swimmingly again, and Lord Midhurst and his sister Alice engaged a footman and reopened almost all the rest of the large house in South Kensington — which was instantly occupied by hordes of uncles and aunts and cousins — and in the summer they actually rented the old family seat for August and a bit of September, and apart from the deplorable degeneration of all the new neighbours, it was almost like old times. Alice continued to entertain cartloads of the clan, and they bowed before her, and she accepted their homage, and her cup, as you might say, was practically full. She was a little annoyed with her brother because he still went to and fro between the seat and the City, instead of posing as a landowner and doing nothing at all; but that, as you might say — during August and a bit of September — was the only fly in her ointment.

Then they came back, and at the end of September the shares began to fall. And Mr. Fink was quite calm, and they rose again — not quite so high. And then they relapsed. And then they wobbled, and relapsed again. And then they relapsed a bit further. And then Mr. Fink made a statement to the Press, and they stayed still for a while. And then Lord Midhurst read a typewritten document to a deputation of shareholders, and they — the shares, that is to say — actually rose a little. And then they stopped rising, and sagged, and flopped, and gathered impetus, and went rushing downhill. Mr. Fink said it was nothing to worry about, and look at some of the other companies; and Lord Midhurst looked in the direction indicated, and nodded, and agreed. It was the Government's fault, said Mr. Fink, and again the Chairman agreed with him. They might, said Mr. Fink, have a little

trouble until the Report came out, but now, said
Mr. Fink, was the time for them all to stick together.

You only had to suggest the idea of loyalty to
Lord Midhurst, and he would have stuck to a burn-
ing oil-tanker in the middle of the Atlantic. Even
the other directors were comforted when they saw
how cool he seemed, and how stiff and unbending
was his collar. Alice said she wanted a hundred
pounds for her dressmakers, and he gave it her, and
an extra fifty as well. She was a little disappointed,
because now it seemed that she might just as easily
have asked for two.

Associated Enterprises suddenly overflowed from
the City page, and kept appearing in the news.
Mr. Fink made more statements, and they were
printed without comment; also without any noticeable effect on the market. The Report came out,
and the result was even less encouraging. Then
Lord Midhurst stood up in a big room in a dingy
hotel, with a typewritten sheaf in his left hand,
and an enormous quantity of people roared and
screamed, and shouted and yelled. And Lord
Midhurst looked at them over his eyeglasses, and
made some inaudible remarks while they continued
to raise pandemonium. Some fierce gentlemen and
an absolute virago in the most repulsive hat started
making speeches from the body of the hall, and
were subdued in a fresh uproar, while Lord Midhurst kept putting one hand behind his ear and
calling for order. When he looked round for Mr.
Fink, he couldn't see him; but another, pale-faced
director handed him a slip of paper containing a list
of proxies which may or may not have been accurate,
but in either case was of very little value when
the Chairman was quite unable to make himself
heard.

'What had I better do?' asked Lord Midhurst.
'It's no use if they won't listen to me.'

One of the fierce gentlemen was now on the

platform, bellowing and gesticulating to the excited
mob. Lord Midhurst touched him on the elbow,
so as to call his attention to the impropriety of his
conduct, and he turned round and struck him, and
they both fell off the platform together; and the
other directors all bolted out of what you might
call the stage-door, and Lord Midhurst was buffeted
and hustled and lost his eyeglasses and his wind;
and the police came in and cleared the hall, and
picked the Chairman up, and invited him to charge
a complete stranger who had been trying to find
his way to another meeting — which his lordship
very bluntly refused to do. The proceedings, in
short, terminated in what both evening and morning newspapers described as general disorder, and
presently Lord Midhurst found his car and his
chauffeur, and drove back to South Kensington
feeling rather puzzled.

His telephone rang a good deal that afternoon
and evening, but the only voice which got past the
butler was that of Mr. Fink. And Mr. Fink said:
'Are you all right, Midhurst?' And Lord Midhurst said: 'Perfectly, thank you.' And Mr.
Fink said that was good, and he was sorry he'd
been called away from the meeting so suddenly,
and how had it gone? Lord Midhurst said that
there'd been a little disturbance at the end, and he
was afraid that no resolution had actually been put
or carried.

'Good,' said Mr. Fink. 'Then I'd better see
you early in the morning. Say about ten o'clock
at Empire House. There's nothing to worry about,
you know.'

Lord Midhurst was glad to hear it, and made a
note of the appointment. A number of callers tried
to see him during the evening, but the butler didn't
fancy their manner or appearance, and said that
his lordship was not at home. His sister Alice
being out at a theatre, Lord Midhurst sat alone in

his study reading a detective story. At half-past
ten he drank some hot water with a slice of lemon
in it and went to bed.

7

Mr. FINK smoked a large cigar as he walked up
and down his room in Empire House, and occasionally flicked the ash on to the carpet. Lord
Midhurst sat in an upright though ornate chair,
with his hat on his lap, his long legs crossed and
his umbrella leaning against them, and listened
attentively.

'It was infernally bad luck,' said Mr. Fink,
'that I couldn't stay there yesterday, but there
it is; one can't be everywhere at once. Everybody,' said Mr. Fink, 'tells me you did splendidly.'

'I'm afraid,' said Lord Midhurst, 'I couldn't
do very much. And I suppose it means calling
another meeting.'

'Why?' asked Mr. Fink.

'Well,' said Lord Midhurst, 'we ought to get the
accounts approved, oughtn't we?'

'I'm not sure,' said Mr. Fink. 'That's to say,
eventually — of course. But I've been thinking
about this, you know, Midhurst. I've got a
scheme.'

'A scheme?'

'Yes. I mean, it's like this. We don't want a
repetition of yesterday's scenes. We don't want
to risk having our hands forced, eh? Of course
not. But the shareholders aren't satisfied — that's
obvious. Well — we must see that they are.
That's all.'

Lord Midhurst thought this an excellent idea.

'The whole difficulty, just at the moment,'
said Mr. Fink, 'is capital. We haven't got enough.
We want more. Well — we must find it.'

Lord Midhurst nodded.

'It's not easy,' said Mr. Fink. 'I don't say for an instant that it's easy. But it can be done.'

'How?' asked Lord Midhurst.

'Well,' said Mr. Fink, 'I dare say there are several ways. Only time, as I see it, is important. We mustn't waste time. In fact, it's our duty and responsibility *not* to waste time. We've got to be quick. That's where my scheme comes in. That's where I want your help.'

'Of course,' said Lord Midhurst; and Mr. Fink paused by his big desk.

'Mind you,' he said, 'this has got to be between ourselves. In fact, I'd have done it alone if —— However, there's no need to go into that. Anyone like myself,' said Mr. Fink; 'anyone, that's to say, who's made his own way, always has the same difficulty with the banks. They won't judge anything on its merits. They will keep raking up the past. Well *you* know I've been through the Courts more than once. I don't shout about it. I've got my discharge every time, and my name's as good today — with everybody except the banks — as anyone else's you like to mention. However,' said Mr. Fink, picking up a sheet of paper, 'there it is. We can't, unfortunately, overlook it.'

Lord Midhurst nodded again. He would have liked to express his sympathy, only he found the subject a little embarrassing. Mr. Fink hadn't expected him to find it anything else.

'And so,' he said, 'the thing's got to be fixed through you, old man. You're our chairman, after all; you're well known; you've got an interest in these other concerns, and — at a time like this — I say they all ought to stand together. I don't like to remind you,' said Mr. Fink, 'that you've done pretty well out of our group. Between gentlemen,' said Mr. Fink — and here, though he was quite unaware of it, one of Lord Midhurst's sandy eyebrows twitched — 'one doesn't mention

these things. They're understood. Eh? Of course
they're understood. But,' said Mr. Fink, again
glancing at the sheet of paper, 'this is what I
think you might do, Midhurst. Now, just listen a
moment.'

And Lord Midhurst listened, while Mr. Fink —
at first cautiously, and then with growing enthusiasm and assurance — propounded his scheme.
Figures entered largely into it; figures whirled round
the Chairman's head, and showered down on it, and
utterly bamboozled it. If Mr. Fink had said:
'Now, what you've got to do is to borrow money,
by distinctly crooked means, in the name of your
other firms, and then give it to me so that I can
either try and stop this rot or, better still, keep
it and go abroad while you stand your trial'; if,
one imagines, Mr. Fink had submitted his proposals
in this form, it is scarcely likely that Lord Midhurst
would have remained sitting in that chair and
listening to him. But though this was exactly
what Mr. Fink meant, and even what a translation
of his spellbinding would have shown him to be
saying, Lord Midhurst merely saw that he was
being offered an opportunity of helping all the people who had howled at him yesterday. And since he
was most anxious to do this by every means in his
power, he nodded again, and continued to nod.

'You see?' said Mr. Fink, getting well between
Lord Midhurst and the light. 'You follow me?'

'Certainly,' said Lord Midhurst. 'And naturally, if there's anything I can do ——'

'Naturally,' said Mr. Fink, passing his handkerchief round the back of his neck. 'And in that
case, Midhurst — although of course we quite understand each other, as I was sure we should — I'll
just get a girl in and dictate a little memorandum.
And then, if you'll be good enough to sign it ——'

Well, if his lordship were good enough to sign
it, not even extradition could touch Mr. Fink, if the

worst came to the worst, for the Old Bailey would
be completely satisfied to deal with his lordship
alone. And again his lordship nodded, and Mr.
Fink — looking extremely genial — pressed a little
bell-push on his large desk.

'Of course,' he said, 'I'll help you to draft all the
necessary letters and so forth — in fact, I think we
might very well get on with some of them at once;
but I'm sure you appreciate my personal position.
It would be different, if you didn't know me so
well, but ——'

'Of course,' murmured Lord Midhurst, looking
at the doorway.

'I wonder,' said Mr. Fink, 'if that bell's broken,
or something. Perhaps I'd better ring again.'

He rang again, and both directors waited in
silence.

'Dammit,' said Mr. Fink, suddenly and ex-
plosively. 'You'd think some of these girls came
here as a favour to me, instead of —— Oh,
there she is. No, she isn't. Look here, Markham,
I didn't ring for you. I want Miss Padstow. Why
the dickens doesn't she come?'

Lord Midhurst's eyebrow twitched again, and he
looked out of the window.

'I'm very sorry, sir,' said the servile secretary.
'Miss Padstow's only just come, and I thought ——'

'What? Why's she so late? Where is she?
Send her along at once, and tell her ——'

The servile secretary faded away, and your old
acquaintance, the girl Gladys, came quickly into
the room. She had removed her hat and her
brown coat, and was holding a notebook and
pencil. One of her stockings, as Lord Midhurst
noticed, had a large hole in it, and as he glanced
at her face he was momentarily repelled by its
blotched and mottled appearance. The girl then
gave a sudden, uncontrollable sniff, and Lord
Midhurst found that though still slightly repelled,

he was also a little disturbed. The girl — he remembered her vaguely, and had actually seen her
perhaps twenty or thirty times — was either unwell
or labouring under some other form of distress.
She was either, he was convinced, on the verge of
collapse or else had been crying so recently as
hardly yet to have left off. A plain girl, probably,
at the best of times; a positively ugly girl just now;
but a girl all the same, and therefore a subject for
chivalry. And therefore capable of making Lord
Midhurst distinctly uncomfortable and nervous
and apologetic, and desirous of offering her some
kind of assistance. He half rose from his seat.

'I say —— ' he began. 'I say —— '

Mr. Fink had dropped into his big arm-chair,
and thumped the top of the large desk.

'Now, look here,' said Mr. Fink — not at all
chivalrously. 'Look here, Miss Padstow, what
the dickens do you mean by keeping me waiting?
Do you think you can come along here any time
you like? Eh? Do you think I engage my sten-
ographers for fun? Eh? Do you think I've got
nothing better to do than to waste my time while
you make up your mind whether you're going to do
any work or not? Eh? Do you know I've had to
ring for you five or six times? Why are you so
late? Eh?'

And Mr. Fink glared at the girl Gladys, and
both Lord Midhurst's sandy eyebrows twitched,
and the corners of his mouth as well; and the girl
Gladys's eyes began to swim again, and her throat
began to close up, and she made a sound which
conveyed no vestige of intelligible meaning.

'Eh?' shouted Mr. Fink. 'What's the matter
with you? Are you ill?'

'N — no, Mr. Fink. I — I —— '

'Well, siddown, then. What d'you think you're
doing? Can't you answer me?'

'Oo, Mr. Fink —— Oo —— '

'"Oo"?' said Mr. Fink rudely. 'Are you dumb, eh? Have you gone mad? And look at your stocking! What d'you mean by coming in here like that? What d'you mean by keeping me and his lordship ——'

Lord Midhurst suddenly rose to his full height of six feet.

'Look here, Fink,' he said. 'Look here ——'

'Eh?'

'I — I'd rather you didn't bring me into this. I — I don't like ——'

'Eh? What's the idea, Midhurst? What don't you like?'

Lord Midhurst knew perfectly well what he didn't like. He was horrified and appalled by Mr. Fink's tone in addressing this ugly and apparently half-witted girl. It had stimulated such a violent feeling against his fellow-director, that he clenched his fists and an angry, red mist swirled in front of his eyes. The girl was nothing to him — indeed, he distinctly preferred not looking at her — but it was quite impossible that he should stand by and allow her to be spoken to like that. He'd never forgive himself if he did, and if this were Fink's idea of the way to address a female subordinate, then — then...

'Eh?' said Mr. Fink again.

'Wait a minute,' said Lord Midhurst, thickly. 'You're going to apologise.'

'Apologise? Who on earth to? What d'you mean?'

'You've absolutely no right,' said Lord Midhurst, still clenching his fists, 'to speak to any woman on earth like that. I don't care who you are, and I don't care who she is. It's unpardonable!'

Mr. Fink had probably never looked more flabbergasted in his life. Nor, if it comes to that, had Miss Gladys Padstow.

'Oo,' she said. 'Oo, please, sir. Oo, I know it's
all my fault. Oo ——'

'There you are,' said Mr. Fink, triumphantly.
'Apologise, indeed! This is my office, isn't it?
Have I got to put up with every kind of impertinence and incompetence, have I got to go on my
knees to a lazy, good-for-nothing little ——'

'Steady!' said Lord Midhurst. And a swift,
composite moving-picture rushed through his mind,
and he remembered how often he had thought that
Mr. Fink was a cad, and how often he had deliberately and disgracefully driven the thought out of
his mind, and he looked ahead and saw that he
must either go on degrading himself or else make
a clean break now and for good. And his soul
sickened as he thought of all the money that he
had made out of this association, and it shuddered
as he thought of what his unmarried sister Alice
would say if he abandoned it. And then suddenly
it rose to tremendous heights, and knew that even
if it were already inextricably defiled, and even if
what he were going to say now meant ruin, he'd
still got to say it, and face the consequences. And
that if he didn't, he would never feel decent or
honourable again.

'Look here,' said Lord Midhurst, leaning forward over the large desk. 'We won't argue about
this, Fink. You can't make me feel worse about
it than I do. But this settles it. I'll never force
an apology from anybody. It's not worth it.'

'Ah!' said Mr. Fink.

'But,' said Lord Midhurst, 'I can and will offer
you my resignation from this moment. You'll have
it in writing as soon as I get home, but understand —'

'Oh,' interrupted Mr. Fink. 'That's the trouble,
is it? You think I left you in the lurch yesterday.'

'No,' said Lord Midhurst. 'That's got nothing
to do with it.'

'Eh?' said Mr. Fink. 'Well, it's this scheme of mine, is it? You think I'm trying to use you, do you? Well, lemme tell you ——'

'I'm not interested in the scheme,' said Lord Midhurst. 'I've resigned.'

'But, my dear fellow, you can't ——'

'I can,' said Lord Midhurst. 'And I have. If I'm proved to be responsible for anything that happened before my resignation, I'm not going to run away. You'll know where to find me, and if I'm forced to give up my other directorships too — well, I am. That's all. I don't expect to get off for nothing ——'

'By gosh!' shouted Mr. Fink. 'You're right there, you crazy fool. You won't. I'll see about that. I'll —— Here! Midhurst — you're not going, are you? Here — wait! We'll think of something else. We'll fix it some other way, see? That was just an idea about getting the banks to help us, but if you don't like it ——'

An invisible red mist, totally enveloping the third Lord Midhurst, passed through the big folding doors, and out into the passage, and along the corridor, and down the lift-shaft, and through the entrance hall into the street. It entered his lordship's car, a voice from within it said: 'Home,' and the car drove away. There'd be no car by the end of the week, thought the third Lord Midhurst; no butler or footman. Only the large house in South Kensington, and a fresh pile of debts, and his unmarried sister Alice nagging and complaining and telling him what an utter fool he'd been.

But he hadn't. Not that kind of a fool. He'd come out of the other mist which had been creeping up round him for nearly three years, stifling him and demoralising him and dragging him down into the depths. He was nearer sixty than fifty, and he'd have to start all over again. Yet he

smiled, for more than a moment, in the March
sunlight.

On the other hand, there is no evidence that he
ever thought of the girl Gladys again.

8

No MORE, curiously enough, did Mr. Fink.   This,
as it turned out, was his last morning at Empire
House, just as it was his last day — at any rate for
some months — in the land where he was wanted
but by no means needed.   Though that's not the
point.

The point is that as Mr. Fink swung round
with every intention of being ruder than ever to
his unfortunate shorthand-typist — not because he
identified her as the cause of the recent catastrophe,
or had ever really believed that she had anything
to do with it, but simply because he was in a black
rage and when in this condition liked roaring at
people who were obviously afraid of him; the
point is, we say, that just at this instant and just
as Mr. Fink's veins were swelling and his little eyes
were glaring, the inner door opened again, and
again there entered that slinking, servile secretary.

'Eh!' barked Mr. Fink.   'What is it, Markham?   What the devil's the matter now?'

'Excuse me, sir ——'

'Eh?'

The girl Gladys sniffed, and gulped, and vanished.

'The telephone,' said Mr. Markham.   'It's Miss
Reynolds's maid, sir.   Speaking from the theatre,
I think.   She says would you speak to Miss Rey-
nolds at once, please, because ——'

'No!' roared Mr. Fink.   And what was Sunny
Reynolds, or anything that he had ever promised
Sunny Reynolds, when he was in this sort of mess,
and had got to think and hurry and do Heaven
knew what, and with everybody waiting to jump

on him wherever he turned, and with everything telling him to cut and run for it while there was still time to make a clean getaway? 'Calling me up like this,' thought Mr. Fink, 'in the middle of all my work! Wanting some more money, I suppose, or waiting to be taken out to lunch, or wanting to tell me some damfool story about her part not being big enough. Well, I'm through with Sunny and the whole lot of them this time, and if she thinks I'm going to hang on the line while that infernal maid takes ten minutes finding her, she's wrong. She never made a bigger mistake in her life.'

'Tell everybody,' shouted Mr. Fink, 'whoever they are and whatever they want, that I'm busy, and I'm not going to speak to any of 'em. And if they come here, I'm out. And if they wait, I'm not coming in. And if they want to make an appointment, they can't. And look here!'

'Yes, Mr. Fink?'

'I'm busy, see? I'll be going out presently, and I don't know when I'll be back. I might be going away for a bit, but that's my affair — see? I'll write, or I'll wire, or —— Oh, get out and leave me alone. I'm — I'm not to be disturbed.'

'Very good, sir,' said the slinking, servile secretary. And he also vanished. And Mr. Fink went on cursing and swearing all by himself.

9

HUGE dust-sheets were draped all over the auditorium of the Empress Theatre, leaving only the first six rows of the stalls uncovered. A temporary wooden bridge, with a rickety handrail, spanned one end of the orchestra pit and some of the musicians who were congregated therein. The curtain was up, and the stage was set with the elaborate, but as yet not entirely complete, Oriental bazaar which was to form the third scene in to-morrow night's elaborate production.   There were also present a number of men and women — or girls and boys, as they are known in the profession — in extremely fantastic attire, and three or four other characters in mufti and with bowler hats on their heads.   Since this dress-rehearsal of Mr. Corbett's newest spectacle had been timed to start at ten o'clock sharp, and it was now nearly eleven, there was still a prodigious hammering in progress somewhere in the background.   Otherwise nobody seemed to be doing anything, except standing about, and muttering, and looking rather unhealthy.

There was more muttering in those first six rows of the stalls, where Mr. Corbett himself, also his stage-director, his orchestrator, his arranger of dances, his secretary, some scene-painters, dress-makers, authors and other persons of both sexes appeared to be holding a series of informal con-ferences.   Every now and then a figure crossed the temporary wooden bridge with an air of great urgency, and was either absorbed in one of the groups in the front of the house or was lost to sight on the stage.   The conductor kept whispering to the first violin as they discussed the score to-gether, and there were frequent tootlings and roulades from the other instrumentalists.   High up at the back of the second circle the morning sunlight streamed in through some dirty windows, producing an indescribably sordid and dismal effect. The ladies and gentlemen of the chorus — or of the ensemble, as Mr. Corbett preferred to describe it, though no one ever quite knew how the word was pronounced — stared up at it, and blinked, and looked more incapable of gaiety than ever.   The hammering was punctuated by a fearful rending sound, and instantly went on again.

A rather stout man in a very brightly-coloured costume — but he was quite a well-known tenor, so you would hardly expect him to be thin — came suddenly through an archway in the bazaar, and elbowed his way past the chorus, and advanced towards the footlights.

'I say,' he remarked, in a throaty, self-important voice. 'I say — Mr. Farrell!'

The muttering in the stalls rose a little higher, and the heads in each group converged more closely together. The tenor raised one of his arms, to shield himself from the glare, and bleated again.

'Mr. Farrell! I say!'

The muttering died down.

'Hullo, old boy,' said a voice from the darkness. 'Just a moment, old man.'

'Yes, but look here ——'

An absolute spate of muttering. Also some subdued laughter. Also a fresh outbreak of tootling from the orchestra. Also the sound of sawing superimposed on the sound of hammering. The tenor moved threateningly towards the temporary bridge.

'Look here, Mr. Farrell ——'

'Hullo, old boy! Here I am. Yes? What is it?'

Rich, though superficial, sympathy in the voice this time. The tenor hesitated, and moved back into the blaze of light.

'Look here,' he said. 'Can you see me?'

'Rather, old boy. Here I am. I'm looking at you.'

'Well!'

How do you show indignation without indignity if you're a stoutish tenor in a fair wig and particoloured tights?

'Well!' said Roland Morton, registering what he believed to be the former quality. And he raised his eyebrows and shrugged his shoulders and flung out his hands, and the lights blazing up from below distorted and caricatured every movement, and Mr. Farrell — wishing to be pleasant even at this critical juncture — leapt at a completely erroneous interpretation.

'Fine, old man,' he said. 'Splendid. That's terrific!'

Mr. Morton's face became almost as red as his left leg.

'Terrific?' he squeaked. 'Do you mean you expect me to come on looking like this? I've never seen such a rig-out — not even in opera. I've put it on once, just to show you — but it's impossible! D'you want everyone to laugh at me tomorrow night?'

Mr. Farrell understood now. This was a familiar difficulty at all dress-rehearsals, but he supposed he must deal with it again.

'They won't laugh, old man,' he said crooningly. 'What's put that idea in your head? No, no; you look fine from the front. Say, Wally, come here a jiffy. Mr. Morton doesn't like that costume. What do *you* think? Eh?'

A second figure joined Mr. Corbett's stage-director by the orchestra rail, and the director stepped warningly on its foot.

'Think!' it cried, instantaneously. 'Why, I wouldn't worry if I was you, Mr. Morton. We was just saying back there what a fine coschume it was. Wasn't we, Charlie? Wasn't we saying what a fine coschume that was of Mr. Morton's?'

A third figure came clambering over the front row of seats.

'Thass right,' it said, earnestly and impressively. 'Thass just what we was all saying. Don't you worry, Mr. Morton. Thass no end of a coschume, that is. Why, you look fine!'

The opinion that the tenor looked fine having now been established by a majority of three to one, and the minority party being temporarily overwhelmed, Mr. Morton found himself with little or nothing to add.

'Oh,' he said. 'Well, perhaps it looks better out here than it did in my room. Only you're quite sure——'

'Mr. Farrell!'

The Boss's unmistakable croak from behind the Boss's inextinguishable cigar. Tenors and their demands for flattery were mere immaterial trifles now. The entire majority turned round as one man.

'Yes, Mr. Corbett?'

'What are we all waiting for, eh? You know well enough what it costs me, keeping everybody standing by like this. What are we waiting for?'

Mr. Farrell whirled round on one foot.

'George!' he yelled.

The palest possible assistant emerged from the prompt corner.

'Yes, Mr. Farrell?'

'What are we waiting for? Eh? Do you know what all this is costing Mr. Corbett?'

No one ever answered this rhetorical question. Seeing that Mr. Corbett had never put a penny of his own money into any production with which he had yet been associated, it would have been difficult to deal with it accurately. The pale assistant was understood to say that they were still working on that rostrum. Mr. Farrell wished to know what the blazes was the matter with the rostrum now, and in his impatience to receive an explanation, rushed madly over the temporary bridge, and could be heard bawling at somebody called Fred. The hammering ceased, and a shower of hoarse technicalities took its place.

The hammering started again, and Mr. Farrell reappeared. 'That's all right, George,' he announced. 'They'll prop it up somehow now, and you'll have to get it fixed later on. Don't let anyone go barging into it, see? Are we waiting for anything else?'

'No, Mr. Farrell. We're all ready when you are.'

Again Mr. Farrell launched himself over the bridge, and shot down into the stalls.

'We're all set, Boss,' he reported.

Mr. Corbett knocked the ash off his inextinguishable cigar.

'— and so,' he continued to inform his neighbour in the third row, 'I said: "We can't do that," I said, "without we have the film-rights too. Send 'em a cable," I said, "and then come back and perhaps I'll talk about it." Oh, Daisy!'

'Yes, Mr. Corbett?'

'Make a note, Daisy. Make a note to call up Mr. Lewin about those film-rights. Not before Friday, see? I'll be a bit clearer then, if only we can get this darned show started. Where's Mr. Farrell?'

'Here I am, Boss. We're ——'

'Well? What are we waiting for? Just a minute. Yes, Mr. Morton? Your dress? Fine! Don't you think so? What's that? No, of course I didn't. No, I'll speak to her. Gosh, these girls seem to think they can go and —— Oh, hullo, Ben! Do you want me?'

Mr. Morton faded away. Mr. Farrell made a further attempt to attract the great man's attention, but it was B. J. Hanson who had secured it. Mr. Corbett's press-representative. Also, by an arrangement which might seem curious in any other business, occupying the same post with five rival managers. But Ben knew the ropes. Ben got his stuff printed. Besides, there wasn't anybody except old Ben. There never had been.

''Morning, Mr. Corbett. See me on the front page of the *Record* today?'

'No! That's fine, Ben. What was it?'

'Half a column,' said Mr. Hanson. 'Special interview with yourself.'

'With me? That's great. Daisy! Make a note and get hold of that. Say, Ben, are you going to stop and see the show?'

'Can't do that, Mr. Corbett. Got my work to look after. But it's O.K. for tomorrow night, eh? Nothing hanging you up?'

'Here,' said the great man, contemptuously, 'don't you go mixing me up with some of these other fellows. You put that idea right out of your head, Ben. When I fix a date for an opening, it's fixed. See?'

A murmur of admiration from the nearer myrmidons, in which Messrs. Wally and Charlie were particularly effective. If the Boss had touched wood at this moment, or had crossed his fat fingers —— But what difference could that have made? Mrs. Bowker had failed Mr. Coffin, and Mr. Coffin had missed his train and collided with the girl Gladys, and the girl Gladys had met Mr. Jackson (or Harrison), and they'd kept her nearly forty minutes at the police station, and at this very moment her resultant hysteria was stirring the chivalry of the third Lord Midhurst. Would the chain break off here, just because a manager did or didn't boast, or because he did or didn't do something with his fingers?

'Orright, Ben. Mr. Farrell!'

'Here I am, Boss.'

'Say, what in thunder are we still waiting for? Say, have you any idea what it costs me while everyone stands around here and does nothing? Come along, Mr. Farrell. Get a move on, if you don't mind. Do you want to keep us here all day and night?'

'I'm ready, Mr. Corbett. George!'

'Yes, Mr. Farrell?'

'All right, George. Call the beginners again — and for mercy's sake stop that hammering! Drop those tabs. Hi! Give us some light out here,

can't you?   All right, Mr. Mosetti.   We're ready
for your overture now.'

The house-lights came flickering on.   The musical
director rapped sharply on his desk, and the side-
drums began rolling under the temporary bridge.
Once more Mr. Farrell bounded up it, and over it,
and disappeared behind the curtain.

'Oh, Daisy!' said Mr. Corbett suddenly. 'Make
a note and remind me to speak to Miss Reynolds
presently.   I've got something I'll have to say to
that girl.'

10

'MAUD!' said Sunny Reynolds, into the big
mirror surrounded by electric bulbs.   Then she
looked past her own reflection, and there was the
dresser's back by the door.

'What's the matter?' she asked.   'Who's
there?'

'Can I come in, Sunny?'

'What?' said Miss Reynolds, powdering herself
violently.   'Who is it?'

'It's me.   Kenneth.'

'Oh,' said Miss Reynolds, swinging round on
the low stool.   'Yes, I suppose so.   All right,
Maud.   Hallo, Kenneth.   Good morning, or whatever time of day it is.'

A tall young gentleman, with a pink face and
an exquisite overcoat, slipped into the dressing-
room; and then stopped abruptly, and looked a
little stiff.

'Oh!' said Miss Reynolds.   'Lemme intro-
duce you.   This is Mr. Morton, Kenneth.   This is
Mr. Rooke.   Shut the door, somebody.'

Maud shut the door, and the two men nodded at
each other.

'If it's business ——' said Mr. Morton from the
sofa.

'No, of course it isn't. Kenneth's only a friend of mine. Go on, Roland.'

Sunny Reynolds would always rather have two men than one man in her room. It gingered things up — while it lasted.

'Well,' said Mr. Morton, 'I don't know that —— I mean to say...'

The situation, apparently, needed more gingering still.

'I know!' cried Miss Reynolds. 'I've got an idea! Let's see what Kenneth thinks. Kenneth — Mr. Morton's worried about his dress. Now, what do *you* think of it? 'M?''

The tall young gentleman became definitely pinker. Also definitely stiffer.

'Oh, well...' he said. 'I mean —— Well, what's it supposed to be?'

Miss Reynolds leant lightly against the exquisite overcoat — just for a second.

'How stupid you are!' she said. 'It isn't supposed to be anything. It's just a dress; and Roland thinks people are going to laugh at him in it. That's the idea, isn't it, Roland?'

Mr. Morton stood up.

'Laugh?' said Mr. Rooke, trying hard not to be stupid. 'Oh, yes; I see. Well, I think they ought to; don't you? What?'

Miss Reynolds burst into a peal of laughter herself.

'No, no,' she said, again bouncing off the exquisite overcoat. 'Roland's not a comedian, you great cuckoo. He's a tenor — aren't you, Roland? There, now. We've gone and upset him again.'

'Oh,' said Mr. Rooke, from behind a fresh wave of pinkness. 'I'm awfully sorry. I mean, I — I ——'

'Here,' said Mr. Morton, 'I'm off. I didn't come in here to crack jokes about myself. All I want is someone to pay a little attention and tell me what they really ——'

'All right, darling,' interrupted Miss Reynolds. 'I'll tell you. You look lovely. You look a dream. How's that?'

'Oh, of course, if you're going to make fun of me ——'

'Do I ever,' demanded Sunny Reynolds, making the fullest use of her very wide eyes — 'do I ever make fun of anybody? Go on, Kenneth; say something polite, can't you? Here's poor Roland never been in a real show like this before, and all of a twitter about his new frock, and ——'

'Utch!' said Mr. Morton, opening the door and shooting out into the passage. And bang went the door behind him. And Sunny Reynolds laughed more heartily than ever, and then looked at Mr. Rooke, and started laughing all over again.

'Poor old Roland!' she gasped. 'Did you ever see such a sight in your life! That wig! Go on, Kenneth — laugh, can't you?'

'Eh?' said Mr. Rooke. 'Oh, rather. But ——'

'What's the matter, duckie?'

Mr. Rooke glanced at the dresser.

'What?' said Miss Reynolds. 'Oh, don't worry about Maud. Maud's used to everything; aren't you, Maud? Oh, very well, then. Run along outside for a moment. And listen ——'

'Yes, miss?'

'Don't let any more people in.'

'Oh, very good, miss.'

'There!' said Miss Reynolds, as the door closed again. 'Is that better, Kenneth? You know, you oughtn't to be here at all, really. 'M?'

'Why not. I told you ——'

'Oh! Isn't he fierce!'

'Look here ——'

'What?'

'What does that fellow mean — lounging about

in your room like that?   And what do you mean
by calling him — what you called him?'

'Calling him what?'

'You know.   "Darling."'

'Poof!' said Miss Reynolds.   'You'll have to
get used to that, if you come lounging about yourself.   Now, don't get excited.   I'm a bit sorry for
Roland, if you want the truth.   He's not a bad
sort, and he can sing like —— Well, you wait till
you hear him.'

'Oh,' said Mr. Rooke.

'Meaning?'

'Sunny!   I ——'

'Get away, Kenneth!   Can't you see I'm all
covered with wet-white and everything!   Just you
keep where you are.'

'I'm sorry,' said Mr. Rooke.

'All right, Kenneth.   I'm not angry with you.
How's your father this morning?'

Mr. Rooke sat down and scowled at the
floor.

'If you want to know,' he said, 'I've just had
the deuce of a row with him.'

'Really?   Again?'

'Yes.   Sunny — you know what it is.   You —
you know I'm potty about you.'

Miss Reynolds, who was admiring her reflection
again, began to hum.

'Look here, Sunny — are you listening, or aren't
you?'

'What?   Yes, of course I'm listening.   What
was the trouble?   'M?'

'Well, what do you think?   It was about you,
of course.   I dare say I was an ass to tackle him
at breakfast, but — but I just felt I couldn't wait.'

'What for?'

Mr. Rooke glared still more intently at the
carpet, and even his ears were flaming.

'You know,' he said, thickly.   'You know I

can't go on like this — just seeing you, and ——
Sunny — listen, you've got to marry me.'

There! He'd said it. After weeks of desperate
courage in her absence, and awkwardness and
cowardice in her presence, he'd done it at last.
Now, then!

''M?' said Miss Reynolds.

'Sunny! Darling — can't you ——'

'Yes, yes,' said Miss Reynolds, swinging round
again. 'I heard you all right. And — and it's
awfully sweet of you, Kenneth, but ——'

'Go on! Can't you see you're driving me
mad!'

'Am I?' said Miss Reynolds, with traces of a
mild satisfaction. And it was good, she thought,
that she should have this delightful power, and
right that young gentlemen should feel it. And
when Kenneth's old father popped off, he'd be a
baronet, and his wife would be Lady Rooke. But
meanwhile — well, how long would one have to
wait? Ages, probably. And how much money
could one hope for if the old father went on being
so shirty? Not much. Of course, if Kenneth did
some real work —— But no; that wasn't the kind
of marriage she wanted. In the kind of marriage
that she wanted, work wouldn't exist. She'd retire,
and her husband would have a lot of houses, and
a yacht, and they'd keep going off to the Riviera
and all the other places where one got photographed.
Unless, of course, he was an old husband, in which
case the more he worked and the less one saw of
him, the better. Well, Kenneth was young, and
smart, and hadn't got a bean. While Mr. Fink ——

It looked as though she'd got to settle something,
though. It looked as if, between the two of them,
there'd be nothing but worry until she did. And
if she chucked Kenneth, it meant losing a lot of
fun — because he was just the sort to take it all
seriously and leave the country. But Mr. Fink,

on the other hand, hadn't so far mentioned the word marriage. She knew he'd been thinking of it; it was quite obvious what he meant when he'd told her that he could get a divorce any moment he chose. But she'd let it go at that, so far, because if Kenneth's old father only played up properly ——

Well, he hadn't. Mean old brute; sickening old snob; she'd seen him now, and she knew just the sort of conceited old stick-in-the-mud she'd got to deal with. There'd been a chance, of course; there was always a chance if only one worked it the right way. And if she'd really made up her mind in time, even old Rooke could have found himself in a nasty corner. But she'd let it slide — well, she *hadn't* made up her mind, and there'd been this new part to rehearse, and you couldn't do everything at once — and now Kenneth had gone and bungled it all. Fancy trying to get round an old father like that at breakfast!

A pity. Of course she wasn't soppy about him, but she did like his clothes, and his figure, and his voice. He was the real thing all right, even at his heaviest, and how many other girls had managed to get hold of that? Lady Rooke. What a curse it all was!

But it was no darned use like this.

'Kenneth!'

'Yes, Sunny?'

'I — I suppose there's no chance...'

'What?'

'I mean, your father ——'

'Oh, leave him out of it. He can't stop us. We'd manage somehow, Sunny. I'm in a bit of a hole at the moment, I know, but — well, perhaps he'd come round. I mean, afterwards.'

Hopeless. One didn't gamble like that as long as one had anything left to lose.

'I — I might get a job,' said young Mr. Rooke, blinking slightly.

Yes, thought Miss Reynolds. And they might go and live in the suburbs, and starve.

'Of course,' added Mr. Rooke, 'I'd have to chuck the Brigade, but honestly, Sunny, that'd be cheaper than staying on. And then we could go and live in the country somewhere, and ——'

There was a rap on the door, and it was easy enough for Miss Reynolds to change her involuntary shudder into a start of surprise.

'Hullo!' she called out. 'Who's that?'

The dresser's head reappeared.

'Curtain's up, miss,' she said. 'I was only thinking about your shoes.'

'Oh!' said Miss Reynolds. No; it was quite hopeless. 'Thank you, Maud. And, Maud!'

'Yes, miss?'

'Just a second,' said Miss Reynolds, and crossed the bright little room and pushed the dresser ahead of her into the passage. She'd get rid of Kenneth in a moment, but meanwhile — 'Listen,' she said, confidentially. 'I've just remembered something. You know Mr. Fink's number? His office, I mean?'

'Yes, miss?'

'Well, call him up — now — and tell him it's all right about dinner tonight. Tell him I made a mistake — see? Tell him I didn't know what time the rehearsal was before. Tell him I'll be ready about half-past eight. Got that, Maud?'

'Very good, miss. Did you mean now?'

'Yes, yes. I said so.'

'And your shoes, miss?'

'I'll look after them,' said Miss Reynolds. 'You run upstairs and send that message. See?'

'Right you are, miss. Oh, excuse me, miss.'

''M?'

'Here's your call, I think.'

But it wasn't the call-boy who was running down the steps. It was Miss Burdock — previously in-

troduced to you as Daisy — Mr. Corbett's plain
but indispensable secretary, who came hurrying
round the corner.

'Oh, Miss Reynolds,' she said. 'Just a moment.'

'Hullo, Miss Burdock. Yes?'

The secretary lowered her voice.

'Mr. Corbett,' she said, 'wants to speak to you,
and ——'

'What, now?'

'No, he's busy just now. But I thought I'd tell
you, because — well...'

''M?'

'Well, Miss Reynolds, I know what it's about,
you see. I thought perhaps I'd just warn you.'

'Warn me? What do you mean?'

'Somebody's told him you've got a visitor, and
you know what he's like about his dress rehearsals.
No, no; of course it wasn't me, Miss Reynolds;
I'd never do a thing like that. But he had the
notice put up on the board specially, and I know
you wouldn't want to get the sergeant into trouble.
That's all, Miss Reynolds. You understand, don't
you?'

'No,' said Sunny Reynolds; 'I don't. My
friend's not thinking of going near the stage.'

'Of course not, Miss Reynolds. It's just the
rule.'

'Well, it's the sergeant's fault, then. Not
mine.'

'No, Miss Reynolds; I just asked him, and he
never saw anybody. But of course he can't be
everywhere at once, with all this stuff coming in.
So if your friend goes now, it'll be all right, see?
Then you can tell Mr. Corbett ——'

'Oh,' said Miss Reynolds. 'All right. Well,
he's going, anyhow, as a matter of fact. Only what
I want to know is ——'

But Daisy had whisked round the corner, and

clattered down the stairs, and gone. And Sunny
Reynolds didn't really want to know anything,
because of course it was that dam-fool Roland
Morton who'd gone and tried to make mischief —
just because she laughed at him. All right. Very
well. And the next time she saw that dam-fool
Roland Morton, he'd be sorry. She'd only got to
say a word to her girls outside tomorrow night,
and they'd soon send him back to the concert-
platform — if the concert-platform still wanted him.
And she would, what was more, if he couldn't learn
to behave himself. Having her up in front of the
Boss like that for some dam-silly rule that she'd
never heard of, just as if she was still in the chorus.

'Oh, yes!' muttered Miss Sunny Reynolds,
looking much more like a miniature thundercloud.
And then:——

'Miss Reynolds!'

'Oh, hullo, Maud. Yes? Is that all right?'

'No, miss. I——'

'What?'

'I got on to Mr. Fink's office, miss, but he
wouldn't speak on the phone. And they wouldn't
take any message, neither. I told the gentleman
who it was, miss, but he come back and said he
couldn't do nothing. He said Mr. Fink wasn't
going to speak to nobody.'

'Oh,' said Miss Reynolds. 'He did, did he?'

And that was that, was it? And Mr. Fink thought
he could get away with that kind of an answer,
and everybody else was going to take it lying down.
All right. Very well. Then Mr. Fink, as well as
that dam-fool Roland Morton, was going to have
the surprise of his life. And thank goodness she
hadn't turned Kenneth out, because this was just
where Kenneth was needed, and tomorrow Mr.
Fink would hear something that would show him
just where he got off. 'The engagement is announced —' Well, why not? She could break

it off again any moment she chose, and it would be a marvellous bit of publicity, and perhaps — again, why not? — it would knock some sense into Kenneth's old father. He might come round, when he saw he was beaten, and then...

'Maud!'

'Yes, miss?'

'Wait a moment. Stay where you are for a second.'

And so Miss Reynolds forgot all about Daisy's warning and Mr. Corbett's notice on the call-board and all that might result from such forgetfulness, and dashed back into Number Seven Dressing-room.

'Kenneth!' she said. 'Look here!'

Young Mr. Rooke sprang to his feet.

'Yes?'

'Listen, Kenneth — I've only got a moment, but I want to tell you something.'

'Yes, Sunny? Yes?'

He could read encouragement this time, surely, as she kicked off her slippers and stepped into her shoes. The dressing-room began whirling round him, and his pinkness had seldom been more pronounced.

'Yes, Sunny? Tell me!'

'Look here, Kenneth — if you're really game to stand the racket; I mean, if you won't go and do anything silly till I've had a chance to see you again — well, then...'

'Sunny! Darling — you don't mean ——'

A violent thump on the door.

'Your call, Miss Reynolds. Look sharp, please!'

And Maud's voice. 'Miss Reynolds! They're waiting!'

'Bother!' said Miss Reynolds, leaping across the room. 'Wait, Kenneth — I'll be back in a minute.'

'Yes, but ——'

They were both out in the passage.   They were
both dashing down the stairs, hot on the call-boy's
heels.

'Sunny!   I say!'

But Miss Reynolds mustn't keep the Oriental
bazaar waiting, and perhaps she didn't hear him.
She burst through the swing-doors at the bottom,
and young Mr. Rooke burst after her.   Everything
was stuffy and dark and crowded with mysterious
figures, and there was a band playing somewhere,
and there were ropes and struts and cables and half
visible obstructions.   But madness still urged the
infatuated young gentleman on, for all this was
nothing to him now that hope and happiness danced
in his path.   He'd always gone where he wanted,
and done what he wanted, and taken what he
wanted, and what were rules and regulations — even
if he had ever heard of them — to a young gentleman who saw the one cloud that had ever darkened
his life vanishing before his impetuous will?

'Sunny!' he panted.   'Wait!'

And there she was, on the other side of the stage,
and one of the mysterious figures had seized hold
of his arm.

'Steady, sir!' it said.   'Quiet, please.   The
curtain's up.'

'Leggo,' said Mr. Rooke, unpleasantly.   'What
the blazes ——'

He jerked himself free.   His foot caught in a
lighting-trap in the invisible planking.   He lurched,
and shot out a hand to save himself.   He took hold
of something, and it gave.

'Look out!' yelled an infuriated, panic-stricken
voice.   Mr. Rooke staggered sideways, ducked his
head, and was struck heavily between the shoulders.
There was a splintering, squeaking crash, and to the
horror of Mr. Corbett and his courtiers in the stalls,
the balcony at the back of the bazaar began pitching
forwards.   As it fell, it collected more and more

objects in its crash.   The big archway above it
collided with the fourth batten, and the fourth
batten punched a large hole in one of the side-flats;
and the side-flat buckled and descended in ruin on
an elaborate awning; and the awning doubled
up and laid out a papier-maché pillar; and the pillar
tottered and rolled destructively towards the floats
just as the whole built-up background subsided in
a cloud of crackling and dust.   Shrieks filled the
air as houris and men in robes and turbans rushed
madly into the wings.   The orchestra broke off
abruptly as its members dived for safety into the
recesses of their cave.

'Lights!   Lights!' roared Mr. Farrell, like the
King in *Hamlet*, and the flimsy pretentiousness of
the whole illusion faded under a sudden glare, reveal-
ing wreckage all over the crowded stage and calmly-
cynical whitewashed brickwork beyond it.   And
feet came pounding over the temporary wooden
bridge, and figures in every describable costume
from overalls and shirt-sleeves to Zouave jackets
and Turkish trousers began tugging and lugging and
wrenching at the chaos, and telling each other to get
out of the way, while feminine voices kept saying
that they could see somebody's legs under there, and
hysterics and fainting-fits were occupying every
available spare corner.   Only the imperturbable and
indispensable Miss Burdock knew just what to do
and did it, as she passed right across the scene of the
disaster without pausing, and ran up the stairs at
the back, and seized the sergeant's telephone to
summon an ambulance and a doctor.   That is to
say, unless you count Mr. Goodge and his assistant
out in the box-office in front, who — still in ignorance of the inevitable postponement — were selling
and refusing to sell tickets for performances which
would never take place.

'Send them through as soon as they're here,
Sergeant,' said Miss Burdock; and turned, and

ran back the way she had come. Past Number
Seven Dressing-room, in other words, and on down
the stairs, and through the swing doors into the
shattered remnants of the bazaar. There was less
noise now; less screaming and shouting and confusion. The more responsible characters were
taking charge of the situation, and the less responsible characters were being herded out of the way.
Somebody said: 'That's all, isn't it?' And somebody else said: 'I think they're all here, sir.' And
though there were little knots round one or two
victims of cuts and bruises, it seemed perhaps that
the company had suffered less than the scenery,
and stood a better chance of being repaired. Perhaps, also, thought Miss Burdock, as she dodged
round the débris to rejoin the Boss, a doctor alone,
without an ambulance, could have dealt with the
human casualties. And then, suddenly, she saw
that real, and terrifyingly motionless, leg.

'Here!' she cried. 'Come here — quickly!'
And the overalls and shirt-sleeves leapt towards her
and began straining and heaving at the splintered
woodwork and tattered canvas. 'Steady!' they
said. 'Got it?' they said. 'Now, then!' they
said. 'Over she goes!'

And over she — that is to say a tangled mass
of fragments — went tumbling and crashing. And
there, beside it, lay Mr. Kenneth Rooke, whose
overcoat was no longer in the least exquisite. And
he groaned, and gasped, and twitched convulsively,
and sat up.

'There!' said an excited and denunciatory voice.
'That's 'im. That's the one what did it! Give it
a shove, 'e did, and —— Oh, sorry, sir.'

The great Mr. Corbett came thrusting his way
through the crowd. So did Roland Morton, still
intent on his revenge. He muttered treacherously
in the Boss's ear, as Mr. Rooke rose unsteadily to
his feet and looked wildly round.

'He's all right,' said somebody.

'Sunny!' said Mr. Rooke faintly.

'Shut up!' said Miss Reynolds, rudely. 'Oh, Mr. Corbett, I'm most awfully sorry, and of course I'd no idea ——'

'That'll do,' said the Boss. 'You don't get any notice from me after this, Miss Reynolds. You can clear out.'

'Oh, but, Mr. Corbett ——'

'Now,' said the Boss, savagely. 'You think you can play the fool in my theatre, and bring your friends along to smash up a five-hundred-pound set! Take her away, Mr. Farrell. Take her away, and don't let her inside the doors again. Gosh, what isn't this going to cost me! Daisy!'

'Yes, Mr. Corbett?'

'Come along up to my room, and let's get out of this. I've got to think. I'll have to get hold of Ben. Ring through to Mr. Goodge and say I want him. Come on. Quickly!'

The great man went striding away, almost dignified in his wrath and misfortune. A path cleared before him as if by magic. He never looked back. He was gone.

Babel broke out again, and high above the babel came a sharp smack as Miss Reynolds's right hand met Mr. Rooke's left cheek.

'You blasted idiot!' she said. 'That's what comes of having anything to do with a dam' fool like you. Get out, and don't you ever dare speak to me again! I wouldn't be seen dead with you if you were the last man on earth. You — you — you ——'

Roland Morton smiled satanically to himself. Young Mr. Rooke's eyebrows rose to an unnatural height; only one side of his face was at all pink; his lower jaw dropped, and waggled. Just as he wondered if by any chance he were going to be sick, the dull pain in his back and the blackness in front

of him seemed to come rushing together; and since
he no longer knew where he was, so it was equally
impossible for him to care.

Nor need Miss Burdock have regretted the addition to her telephone message, for it was in a motor-
ambulance that the unconscious young gentleman
returned in due course to his ancestral home.

11

BETWEEN eleven and twelve o'clock on a fine
morning at this time of year — or, indeed, at almost
any other time of year except during the months
of August and September — the sight is such a
common sight in the pleasanter streets of London,
that it is rather surprising how one still continues
to notice it. Nevertheless, one does notice it, and
unless one happens to be particularly critical or
atrabilious, one is almost always a little amused if
not charmed by it; for even its familiarity never
seems to have made it entirely stale. One may feel
no subtle thrill, no inward smile, no sense of philo-
sophical interest and entertainment at hundreds of
equally well-known scenes in the metropolitan
panorama; one accepts them, or sees them without
observing them, or is merely bored and unmoved
and full of one's ordinary detachment and calm.
Yet somehow or other when a front door in one of
these pleasanter streets suddenly opens, and out
come an obvious mother and a no less obvious
grown-up-daughter-at-home — well, one generally
turns one's head, doesn't one, and experiences
something not wholly unconnected with momentary
thought?

Perhaps it strikes us afresh how odd it is that
there should be different generations on the face of
the earth, and that women should pass from one to
another, and that their children should follow them
on the same extraordinary track. Perhaps we are

diverted by a swift comparison between those two kinds of assurance — that of authority and that of irresponsibility. Perhaps we reflect on the strangeness of family life, which can still unite such a couple even in these lawless, independent days; or on the fashions which can send the couple out in practically the same clothes and yet make them look so entirely different. Or perhaps we are suddenly stirred — though honestly we don't quite know why — by a feeling that we want to warn them against something — though honestly we don't quite know what.

We may even, before they go swiftly away on their high heels, spare a thought for the invisible slave who has fed and clothed and housed them, and enabled them to set out — as they are almost certainly setting out — to spend his money in the shops. Then it all becomes far too complicated, for of course we don't really know whether the slave actually exists, or whether he does any work if he does exist, or whether he isn't more than rewarded — or possibly more than suitably punished — by facing the consequences of an impulse which he has probably long since forgotten. Suddenly it seems that this woman and girl have roused such a confusion of questions and problems, such a welter of contradictory emotions, and of vague approaches towards ideas which keep turning round and rushing off before we can catch them, that the only thing is to sigh and drive them all out of one's mind, and to quicken one's pace and think about something else. Well, that's easily done in the pleasanter streets of London — for look, there's a postman clearing a pillar-box, and of course one has got to see exactly how he does it, and to start wondering about the mystery of all that correspondence. Thus one goes hurrying towards one's destination with all the other people, and is apparently one of them. Thus one forgets, until sooner or later one's eyes light on the same little scene again.

So at about half-past eleven on this fine morning towards the end of March — though perhaps it wasn't quite so fine now, for there were clouds moving slowly across the blue — the front door of a house in a very pleasant street closed with a thud, and some high heels came tripping down the steps and joined another pair of high heels on the pavement. And Mrs. and Miss Micklethwaite, aged forty-eight and twenty-three, turned to the right and began passing all the well-known area railings. And Mrs. Micklethwaite wore a coat with a fur collar and cuffs, and had a bag tucked under her left arm. And Miss Micklethwaite wore a coat with a fur collar and cuffs, and had a bag tucked under her left arm. And Mrs. Micklethwaite wore a fashionable hat which revealed all her forehead and rather a serious face. And Miss Micklethwaite wore a fashionable hat which also allowed more than a glimpse of at least a rather serious expression. Yet, as we say, there was no possibility of confusing the generations, even though they had adopted the same disguise. For Mrs. Micklethwaite was quite obviously the mother, while Miss Micklethwaite, as well as being nearly five inches taller, was no less obviously the grown-up-daughter-at-home. And so they tapped their way along the pavement, and so, presently, Miss Micklethwaite spoke.

'But, Mummie,' she said, 'why shouldn't I?'

Mrs. Micklethwaite didn't answer.

'You're so funny,' said her daughter. 'Everybody I know does exactly what I do, and nobody dreams of ragging them about it. And I've done the same thing myself — hundreds of times — and you've never said anything. But now — suddenly...'

'Well?'

'Well, you know what I mean, darling. I'm grown-up, aren't I? And I know perfectly well how to take care of myself. And when one goes out to a party like that, of *course* the chances are one'll go on to another party. And I never made any noise when I came in. I mean, it wasn't my fault that Daddy happened to be awake, and — and ——'

'And what?'

'Well, you know how perfectly sickening he was.'

'Moira! You're not to talk like that!'

Miss Micklethwaite made a face and shrugged her shoulders.

'All right,' she said. 'I'm used to it, anyhow. But if anybody thinks — if anybody thinks I've done anything to be ashamed of, well ——'

The roar of the traffic at a particularly noisy crossing drowned the rest of this conditional clause. But so soon as they were safe on the farther pavement, Miss Micklethwaite began again.

'The point is, Mummie,' she said, 'that if you wanted me to be different, then you ought to have brought me up differently. I mean, isn't it?'

The mother gave a little sigh, and there were more lines round her eyes. For even if the point were true, what help or use was that to her now? And if it weren't true —— Well, as a matter of fact, it was ridiculous. Hadn't she taken endless pains with Moira from the very beginning? But if the world changed even faster than children grew up, and went on changing, too, however hard one tried to catch it up — well, what chance had one got? Here, beside her, was a tall, strange adult who had been in tears half an hour ago, and had clung to her, and had gasped out the beginnings of a number of quite terrifying sentences, and had apparently been on the point of confiding in her. And then she had said: 'Yes, darling. It's all right. Just try and tell me, and of course I'll understand.' Whereupon the tall, strange adult

had suddenly burst into fits of laughter and had
rushed out of the room without shutting the door;
and a little later had been heard telephoning to one
of her unknown friends as though she hadn't a
thought or a care in the world; and had then disappeared into her bedroom; and had then emerged,
looking as though nothing at all had happened,
and had said: 'Are you going out, Mummie?
Well, perhaps I'll come too.' And had come; and
was still here.

'Darling,' said Mrs. Micklethwaite, suddenly,
'do you think perhaps it's all because you've been
doing too much?'

'All what?' asked the tall, strange adult. And
laughed again. And said: 'No, of course it's nobody's fault. I'm mad; that's all.' And then, as
if this settled and accounted for everything, caught
hold of her mother's arm and fetched her up in
front of a shop window.

'Look!' she said. 'Don't you think that's
rather a dear little hat?'

So then Mrs. Micklethwaite had to peer through
the glass at a selection of two- and three-guinea objects, some on wooden stands and some on extremely improbable heads; and of course — being
Mummie — she began criticising the wrong one.

'Well,' she said, 'I suppose it might suit *some*
people. But really, that colour ——'

'No, no, darling! You're not looking at the
one I mean at all. There!'

And still gripping her mother's elbow, Miss
Micklethwaite pointed with her other hand. And
the clasp of her bag struck the window with a sharp
rap, and suddenly a face appeared over the pleated
curtains behind all the hats, whereupon Miss Micklethwaite jerked at her mother's elbow and started
marching her off again; the fact being that she owed
the face rather more than she saw any particular
prospect of paying. Rather funny, though, now

that the face was out of sight, and Miss Micklethwaite laughed again.

'This is better,' thought her mother. 'This is
more like Moira.' And she glanced up at Miss
Micklethwaite, and saw no trace of laughter. Only
that far-off, calculating, mysterious look which she
couldn't understand at all. The adult, in fact,
was taller and stranger than ever.

'Moira!'

'What? Yes, darling?'

'Do you think it would be a good thing —— I
mean, would you see him, if I sent for Doctor
Turnbull?'

Miss Micklethwaite dropped the elbow like a hot
coal.

'Old Turnbull!' she exclaimed. 'Me? What
on earth for, darling? I'm perfectly well. I've
never been better in my life. Don't be so absurd!'

'But ——'

'And I'm certainly not going to see him, either.
I do wish you and Daddy wouldn't fuss so much.
Anybody'd think ——'

'Yes?'

'Nothing,' said Miss Micklethwaite, stepping
out more briskly — so that her mother began to
feel a little breathless. And: 'Turnbull, indeed!'
she muttered. And then: 'Oh, by the way!'

'What, dear?'

'Did you say something about a lunch-party
today. Because I think I'll be out.'

'But I told you ——'

'Yes, I know, Mummie. But of course it
won't make any difference. And, anyhow...'

The difficulty, or one of the difficulties, about
this dialogue was the way in which street noises
and the necessity of dodging other pedestrians kept
on interrupting it. Impossible to tell, just now,
for instance, whether Miss Micklethwaite had been
going to say anything else, or had actually said

something else, or had simply stopped short in the
middle. Quite certain, on the other hand, that
no subsequent encouragement would make her
repeat herself. Not in this mood.

'Well,' said Mrs. Micklethwaite, 'I suppose it's
all right. Will you be late?'

'What, Mummie?'

'Will you be out long?'

'Oh,' said Miss Micklethwaite. 'I don't know.
I mean, I'm not sure. I mean —— Look out,
Mummie!'

Another sudden, sharp jerk at the elbow, and
Mrs. Micklethwaite skipped hastily back on to the
kerb. The taxi which had so nearly struck her
went roaring away, and she laughed — as people
do, as often as not, when they have just had such
an escape.

'Really!' said her daughter. 'You must have
been mad, Mummie, to think you could do that.
Didn't you see it?'

'Well, dear, of course if I'd seen it —— I
mean ——'

'Lucky I was with you,' said Miss Micklethwaite.
Only now, instead of squeezing the elbow, she
seemed to be almost hanging on it. 'Oh,' she
was thinking, 'if only it weren't all so complicated
and awful. If only one could go on feeling what
I felt just then. Poor Mummie!' And then,
abruptly and insanely: 'Shall I tell her?' And
then, still more quickly: 'Of course not! Just
imagine if I did.' And then: 'Oh, Johnnie... !'

But now, there being a distinct pause in the
traffic, the elbow gave a swift tug.

'Come on!' said Mrs. Micklethwaite. 'Now's
our chance.'

And her daughter let go again, but came on.
And so they passed across the dark, shiny surface
of the wood paving, and arrived safely on the
further brink, and disregarded the barrel-organist

who welcomed them with a greasy cap in one hand while he continued to perform on his instrument with the other, and entered a doorway between two windows full of books and stationery. And the roar died down behind them, and they were in the quiet and respectable premises of Messrs. Binns & Bartlett.

'Note-paper,' said Mrs. Micklethwaite to the undulating figure which had come forward to greet her. Still undulating, the figure waved towards the nearest counter.

'Note-paper,' it said, in unexpectedly authoritative tones.

'Note-paper, madam?' said the girl in the black dress.

'Yes,' said Mrs. Micklethwaite, agreeably. 'I want to order some more note-paper.'

Here the undulating figure invited the attention of both visitors, by another undulating movement, to the presence of a couple of small, high chairs.

'Thank you,' said Mrs. Micklethwaite, and sat down. Her daughter sat down too, and began fiddling with a tray full of rather elaborate book-markers.

'As a matter of fact,' said Mrs. Micklethwaite, 'I can't quite remember whether you've got my die, or whether I put it away somewhere at home. But perhaps if you could just find out...'

So like Mummie not to have found out for herself, but of course Messrs. Binns & Bartlett are very high-class stationers and would never expect their customers to remember anything. And of course the girl behind the counter was more than prepared to deal with this little problem.

'Certainly, madam,' she said. 'Would you care to wait while I just look and see?'

'Thank you,' said Mrs. Micklethwaite.

'Mrs. Micklethwaite, isn't it, madam?'

'Yes,' said Mrs. Micklethwaite. 'Mrs. Micklethwaite.'

And the girl in the black dress hurried away to some mysterious place where all the dies were kept; and Mrs. Micklethwaite fell into a kind of doze or dream on her high chair; and her daughter stopped fiddling with the book-markers, and again thought: 'I wonder where I'll be this time to-morrow.'

And then she thought: 'If it comes to that, I wonder where I'll be while Mummie's having her lunch-party.' Because, even though she avoided it, it still didn't mean, necessarily, that she was going to meet Johnnie where he'd said. Up to the last minute one could change one's mind, and drop in at any of at least three houses where they'd welcome her and feed her — and never guess what she hadn't done instead. And the long girl on the other high chair thought of her three friends, and began wondering what they'd think when they heard, and then suddenly thrust the speculation out of her mind, and went back to the middle and beginning and unknown end of it all. How extraordinary it all was, she thought, that she should be sitting here like this, so near to the precipice, and apparently so calm about it. Because she didn't feel excited now, or nervous, or anything. It was as though she were watching herself from outside, and wondering what somebody else was going to do; and not caring, particularly, either. Only of course this sort of fatalism couldn't last. Either there was going to be the most ghastly scandal, or else...

But of course what nobody understood, not even Johnnie, was how miserable she'd been. When one thought of that misery, when one thought of the months and months of secret agony, and of how really one had hardly known poor Chick — compared with lots of people; and of how everybody said, afterwards, that he'd really been as good as engaged to Lettie; and how Lettie had

married an awfully rich man,. just as if nothing
mattered so long as she got what she wanted...

Well, perhaps poor Chick had escaped something
there — only must one be killed, absolutely broken
to pieces like that, simply to get out of marrying
the wrong girl? Was this the clumsy, cruel way
that things were planned?

And again the long girl on the high chair gazed
at nothing (though her nails dug deeply into the
palms of her hands), and deliberately went back to
the day when the news had reached her. Last
summer; on the way to play tennis with Ronnie
and his sister and all the rest of them at the Riverside Club. And Ronnie had said: 'Here, just a
second. I want to see about a horse.' And he'd
stopped the car and bought a paper; and then
he'd said 'Dash!' and had dropped it over his
shoulder. And Nesta had picked it up and looked
at the front page; and then she'd said: 'Hullo!
Another of these crashes in Kent. Anybody heard
of a man called Peter Farmiloe?'

Chick. Dead. Pulled out of the blazing mess,
and rushed to the hospital — but too late; and
she'd gone on and played tennis. And had laughed
and talked, quite easily, though it sounded so
utterly impossible — only sometimes one couldn't
take things in. And even the next day nobody
had said: 'Why, what's the matter, Moira?' because there was still nothing to make them say it.
But the day after that — suddenly...

Only one couldn't say one had been in love with
him, because how could one, when one had hardly
known him? Five or six meetings, perhaps, and
perhaps ten minutes, altogether, alone with him.
But there'd never been anyone else in the least
like that; so funny, and clever, and quick, and
understanding. Well, of course there'd never been
anyone else in the least like Chick.

So then one was quite alone, even in the middle

of crowds and parties, and there was nobody that
one could possibly, conceivably tell. So what else
could one do, except put on speed, so as to try
and get over it and forget? What else could one
do, except go dashing about with all kinds of
people whom one didn't even much like, when if
one stopped for a moment, the loneliness and
misery came choking and strangling one? Only
this one couldn't explain, either. Imagine telling
Mummie, and the faces she'd have made! Imagine
telling *anyone* — well of course it was absolutely
out of the question. And then perhaps one *was*
getting over it a little, just by rushing about and
never keeping still. And then — well, of course
it had all been so absurd and ridiculous, really,
when Chick had been engaged to Lettie, and Lettie
had married old Dunstable. Only by this time,
somehow, one had got so different — about everything. And then, suddenly, one had so hated and
loathed oneself. And then, just as suddenly, there
had been Johnnie...

The girl in the black dress was back behind the
glass-topped counter.

'I'm sorry to have kept you, madam,' she was saying; 'but it's quite all right about the die. We've got
it here quite all right with all the others, madam.'

Mrs. Micklethwaite started from her doze or dream.

'Oh,' she said. 'I see. Thank you. Well, in
that case — ah — do you remember what I ordered
last time?'

'Well, I can easily look it up, madam.'

'I see. Of course. Well, perhaps I'd better
have the same again. Don't you think so?'

'Very good, madam,' said the girl in the black
dress. 'I'll see to it, madam. That will be quite
all right.'

'Thanks,' said Mrs. Micklethwaite. 'Thanks
very much. Good morning.'

And both the Micklethwaites rose from their

high chairs, and the undulating figure reappeared to accompany them, in an undulating manner, towards the door. And opened it, and a roaring sound came rushing in. And the Micklethwaites went out into the roaring sound, and continued tapping their way along the pavement.

'Not quite so fine, is it?' said Mrs. Micklethwaite. 'I do hope it isn't going to rain.'

'Where are we going now, Mummie?'

''M? Oh, the flowers next, I think. I might get them at Boyce's.'

'Well, aren't we going the wrong way, then?'

Mrs. Micklethwaite clicked her tongue, and turned round, and again showed such obvious signs of treating the roadway as if this were the year 1900, that again her daughter had to clutch at her elbow.

'Darling,' she said, 'you simply *must* look where you're going. You are awful, aren't you?'

'What?'

'How on earth do you ever come home alive when you're alone?'

Mrs. Micklethwaite dashed forward without answering. And perhaps it was just as well that she didn't answer, when the question had suddenly taken on that suffocating significance. For if Miss Micklethwaite did what she knew now that she was going to do, then indeed her mother must cross a great many streets by herself — after this morning. And this, as well as a lot of other things, was suddenly so frightfully funny that the girl laughed quite alarmingly; only nobody heard her because of the traffic, and nobody saw her because they were all much too busy rushing about and dodging each other. And so the mother and daughter once more gained the comparative security of a pavement, and went tapping along it, and turned into Boyce's.

A peculiar but familiar smell of flowers, vegetables,

earth and water. Rather like a green-house, only
not so stuffy. Not exactly fresh; not exactly
stale. Rather nice sometimes, and then, again,
rather nasty. Bare boards underfoot, and bits of
paper and a few odd potatoes, and some leaves,
and some lengths of string. Customers staring
reflectively, under an archway of pine-apples, at
the exhibits in the window. A glimpse, right
through the back of the promises, of a little yard
full of round baskets and flat wooden boxes. Half-
way between these two extremes a high, battered
desk, with piles of bills threaded on metal stalks
and a cash-register on a large bracket. Boyce's was
always the same; never tidy, but never absolutely
choked with débris. As if they were always
beginning to put things straight but had never
had time to finish.

'Yes, madam?'

Miss Micklethwaite touched her mother's arm.

'Here's somebody, Mummie,' she said.

'Oh,' said Mrs. Micklethwaite, with a slight
start. 'Good morning. I just want a few flowers.
Now, let me see...'

A few months ago all Boyce's masculine staff
had suddenly changed from shirt-sleeves and black
aprons to light-coloured drill coats, so that until
one had got used to it they looked rather like
attendants in a garage. Now, however, one was
quite used to it, and the drill coats had become
much shabbier, and one had forgotten that they
had ever been anything else. So that Miss Micklethwaite might have been any age down to seven,
or less, as she stood here and heard exactly what
she had heard all her life. How many hundred
times, she wondered, had Mummie brought her
into Boyce's and said just the same things to these
assistants who never altered or grew any older,
and had been just as slow in making up her mind,
and in the end had bought just the same flowers?

But it had been so safe, somehow, in those distant
days when Mummie took one out on Saturday
mornings to 'pay the books'; and later, when one
had left school and, as one now realised, had been
so exceedingly awkward and so exceedingly un-
becomingly dressed.   So safe, and so cosy, and so
dull, and so delicious.   Poor Mummie!   But she'd
never understand anything.   Not that it mattered.

'And those?' asked Mrs. Micklethwaite.

'Three shillings the bunch, madam.'

And Mummie would say —— There!   She'd
said it.

'Just let me see what size the bunches are.'

The drill coat stood on tiptoe to reach the jonquils
in their tin jar, and Miss Micklethwaite glanced at
her wrist-watch.

In just over an hour Johnnie would be waiting
for her at the station, and the cloak-room ticket
for her little box was here in the bag under her
left arm.   And the extraordinary thing was that
she still didn't know whether she loved him or
not.   Perhaps she didn't, then; but if it weren't
love —— Oh, what was the use of words?   What
was the use of *thinking* any more, when she'd
made up her mind days ago, and had made it up
again only last night?   He needed her — how often
hadn't he told her that he needed her? — and nobody else needed her, and she didn't need herself,
and he was so awfully kind.   And of course there
ought to be a law about people whose wives went
off their heads like that — everybody said so; and
of course it was only other people, who'd always
had everything they wanted, who'd say that poor
Johnnie ought to go on living by himself for ever.
You couldn't be hurting someone who didn't know
where she was, or who she was, and when Johnnie
went down to see her, didn't recognise him, either.
Ten years of it, and poor Johnnie working so hard
all the time, and never complaining to anybody,

and paying out hundreds and hundreds of pounds
to that place. Well?

'Very good, madam. I'll see they go off at
once.'

'You will, won't you? I must have them by
one o'clock.'

And the train started at a quarter past, and
Mummie'd be sitting there with all those dreadful
dull women — all chattering and jabbering. And
then presently they'd start playing bridge, and
they'd go on playing bridge, and then — and
then ——

'Moira! Come along!'

'Oh, sorry, Mummie. I — I didn't see you were
ready.'

Out of the familiar smell, and back into the
familiar noise. Was it conceivable that all these
hurrying, hustling people had any real reason for
filling the streets like this? That they all had
thoughts and hopes and disappointments of their
own, and that Somebody kept track of everyone?
Something about two sparrows being sold for a
farthing; only that didn't explain why, quite
pointlessly and suddenly in the middle of millions
and millions of years, one of them all should be
oneself. 'Oh, dear,' thought Miss Micklethwaite,
'why on earth do I start this kind of thing *now*?
This is the last moment to keep getting outside
myself, and bothering about things that haven't
got any answer.' But Johnnie, she thought,
always stopped one feeling unreal like that. He
was so terribly real himself. And so kind.

Perhaps it was all right. Well, it had got to
be. Only ——

'Moira! Wait! Where are you going?'

'What? Oh, I'm sorry, darling. I thought you
were ——'

'I don't believe,' said Mrs. Micklethwaite, 'you
ever listen to a single word I say. You know the

buses won't stop if one goes any nearer the stopping place.'

'Oh,' said her daughter. 'I see. I beg your pardon.'

So they were going on a bus, were they? Where? But of course she'd heard all the time, only somehow she hadn't known that she'd heard. They were going to Hamhurst's, where they always went; and that was all right, because it would just take about half an hour altogether, and then she'd say good-bye to Mummie, and then...

But the devilish part of it all had got nothing to do with that. Mummie wouldn't mind, after the beginning of it all, and after her friends had stopped being tactful and tiresome. Mummie never noticed whether one were there or not, and never cared, either way, and was always explaining how expensive one was, and was always saying: 'If only you'd get married.' As for Daddy, it would be an absolute treat to him to be able to shout and roar and talk about horsewhips and disgrace, and to put on his long-suffering expression, and to know all the time that he was saving so much money. But the devilish part was doing anything like this, however certain one was about it, without telling anybody first.

One ought to be able to say: 'Look here. This is what I'm going to do, and you can't stop me, and now I'm off.' Only Johnnie had said — and he'd said it again last night — that one mustn't. 'Write,' he said, 'after we've got there. I'll tell you what to put.' 'But why, Johnnie?' 'Oh, darling, I know they'll do something to keep you, if you do anything as mad as that. And they mustn't. I can't wait any longer. You *must* trust me.'

Rather frightening, for a moment. And 'trust' was a funny word, rather; because, of course, one wouldn't be doing this at all, if one didn't trust

him. You'd have thought that was obvious.
Only Johnnie was such a funny mixture of understanding everything and then suddenly — just every
now and then — not understanding anything. Was
it because he was so old? And Miss Micklethwaite's
eyes narrowed as she once more ran through a
series of strange arithmetical calculations. For
when she was thirty, Johnnie would be forty-
seven. It sounded awful. But when she was fifty
Johnnie would only be sixty-seven, and that really
seemed practically the same age. And it wasn't as
if he were in the least old now, unless one went
just by figures. Miss Micklethwaite frowned, and
pushed a lot of questions into the outskirts of her
mind, and again summoned one firm, established
truth into the foreground. Johnnie, said Miss
Micklethwaite to herself, was so terribly, terribly
kind.

Mrs. Micklethwaite put up her finger, and the
huge omnibus stopped — though the driver had
certainly looked rather annoyed — and both Micklethwaites climbed on board, and it rasped and
grunted and trundled away. And tickets were
punched and delivered, and other characters —
mostly women — got on and got off. And the
streets were extraordinarily full of revolving wheels
and noisy engines, and policemen and pedestrians,
and dogs being whirled about on the ends of leads.
And again Miss Micklethwaite wondered what had
made her join the expedition this morning, and
whether it had just been to get through the waiting,
or with some odd idea of being as nice as one could
for the last time. Not that she had actually been,
or was being, particularly nice; but then there
hadn't been much chance, had there?

And she glanced at her mother's profile, and saw
that it was absorbed in thoughts of its own —
almost certainly about shopping and the dull
luncheon party. And the omnibus gave a jerk,

and the profile wobbled suddenly, and Miss Micklethwaite looked away again.   And rather disliked
herself for looking away, because she knew that she
had been critical just when she had meant to be
nothing of the sort.   And looked back again.   And
the profile turned round.

'Yes?' said Mrs. Micklethwaite.

'Nothing,' said the girl beside her.

'I thought you said something.'

'No, I didn't.'

'Oh.'

'What?'

'I only said "Oh."'

'Oh.'

And the omnibus continued to trundle along until
presently it slowed down in a great gathering of
other omnibuses, and Miss Micklethwaite nudged
her mother, and the two of them and a lot of other
shoppers all stood up and began tottering towards
the exit.   And descended, with varying degrees of
skill and agility, on to the pavement.   And made
their way past a great quantity of entangling
citizens to a huge, bronze doorway.   And passed
through it, and so exchanged all the tooting and
rumbling and roaring outside for the lower, duller,
steadier note of Messrs. Hamhurst's silk department.

'That's rather pretty,' said Mrs. Micklethwaite,
pointing at a festoon of printed chiffon.   'I wonder ——'

But an assistant came hurrying towards her, and
her face suddenly became blank.

'Moira!'

'Here I am, Mummie.'

'Oh, there you are.   I do wish they wouldn't
bother one so, when one's only just looking at things.
And then when you want to buy something, they
won't come near you for love or money.'

How true.   And how often had Mrs. Mickle-

thwaite made exactly the same comment, both
in Hamhurst's and other establishments. 'No,'
thought her daughter. 'I'll never be like that —
not if I live to be a thousand.' And it seemed to
her now that in joining the expedition she had
chosen the very surest way of avoiding regret.
These ghastly, dull, pottering, pointless mornings,
always ordering the same things from the same
people, and making the same remarks about them,
and then going back in another omnibus, and then
starting out again the next morning — if not the
same afternoon — and so on, and so on, and so on.
They passed on towards the grocery department,
and Mrs. Micklethwaite bought some soap.

'Account, madam?'

'Yes, please. "Mrs. Micklethwaite." Perhaps
I'd better spell it. "M-I-C-"'

Miss Micklethwaite's lips moved in sardonic
synchronisation. She suddenly wondered what
she'd have to call herself when she went shopping
with Johnnie in Paris. Funny that she'd never
thought of this before, when she'd thought of so
many other things. Not that it mattered, because
it was too late to bother about anything now, and,
besides, Johnnie would have to settle everything
like that. No doubt of it that one *could* trust him.
And one *did* trust him. And, what was more, if
one didn't love him — yes, really and truly and
practically madly — then there wasn't any such
thing as love, and in that case it didn't matter
what happened to oneself or anybody else.

'I know it!' muttered Miss Micklethwaite to
herself. And now such a terrible feeling of impatience swept over her, such a wild, agonising
wish for reunion — anywhere and anyhow — that it
was all she could do not to start running towards
the street and leaping into a taxi — even though
Johnnie couldn't possibly be at the station for at
least another twenty minutes. 'Oh, Johnnie!'

cried Miss Micklethwaite — but still, of course, to herself. 'Oh, Johnnie, I *do* love you. And you are the only one, aren't you, who's going to make me happy again. And you will go on being kind to me, won't you? Because I know I'm not nearly as clever as you are, and I know I'm dull, and I know I often have those awful moods; but it's going to be all right once the train has started, because then I'll never think of anybody else, and ——'

'Come along, Moira. What on earth are you dreaming about?'

'Oh, I'm sorry, Mummie. Here I am.'

The sumptuous interior of one of Messrs. Hamhurst's lifts, piloted by one of Messrs. Hamhurst's suggestively-attired but quite passionless attendants.

'Up? Up? Going up?'

And up they all went.

'First floor. Dress-making, furniture, glass and china, gramophones, turnery ——'

Mrs. Micklethwaite, who always managed — but which of us doesn't — to get to the back of the lift when she was going a short way, and to the front when she was going right up to the top, started struggling towards the gates. Her daughter struggled after her, and the gates clanged, and the lift soared away.

'What now, Mummie?'

'What? Oh, there you are. I've got to see about that carpet-sweeper. Either Rose has broken it already, or else there's something wrong with it; but in any case I know the man who sold it me said it was guaranteed. I've still got his card somewhere.'

And Mrs. Micklethwaite stopped abruptly and obstructively in the doorway leading to the turnery department, and began rummaging in the recesses of her large bag. So like Mummie, this was. People began saying 'Excuse me' and 'Pardon,' as they tried to edge past her; and again the long girl had to catch hold of Mrs. Micklethwaite's elbow.

'What, dear? Don't jog me like that. Ah — here it is. Such an odd name, too. Mr. Coffin.'

And now Mrs. Micklethwaite left her point of obstruction and approached the stupid-looking occupant of a cashier's box (and yet this occupant could give change with accuracy and speed for nearly nine hours a day), and said: 'Do you know where Mr. Coffin is?' And the occupant looked utterly blank and a little resentful — perhaps because of the trifling variety which had just entered into her life — and then indicated by a kind of sullen goggling that somebody better equipped to supply this information was somewhere beyond Mrs. Micklethwaite's left shoulder. So that Mrs. Micklethwaite then turned round and saw a harassed-looking man tying up an awkward parcel with both hands and his teeth, and once more put her question.

'Mr. Coffin, madam?' echoed the harassed-looking man — and as he let go with his teeth, both string and paper burst from the awkward parcel. 'Just a moment, madam.' And the harassed-looking man raised his voice and called urgently across a pyramid of mops and dusters. 'Mr. Diggle!' he cried. 'Do you know where Mr. Coffin is?'

'Gone to lunch,' said an invisible authority; so that the chain, it seems, was not to cross its own track after all, but was to continue its erratic and uncharted course. And the harassed-looking man, with a last, regretful glance at the wreckage of his awkward parcel, said: 'I'm afraid Mr. Coffin's gone to lunch, madam; but if there's anything...'

Queer names, thought the long girl, as her mother hesitated between telling the whole story of the carpet-sweeper to a stranger and returning without having told it at all. And what a funny time to

have lunch, thought the long girl, and she again
looked at her watch.   Still barely a quarter to one,
and ——

Just half an hour left; but how long would it take
to get to the station in a taxi?   Plenty of time,
really; and yet a fresh access of impatience seized
her, and having seized her, filled the surrounding
atmosphere.   Mrs. Micklethwaite was conscious,
suddenly, that it was getting late.   She was also
strengthened in an earlier impression that the
harassed-looking man was incapable of dealing with
her problem.   If only she hadn't started by mention-
ing Mr. Coffin, thought Mrs. Micklethwaite; but
having once been mentioned, he remained as a kind
of intangible obstacle to any real progress.   It was
obvious, indeed, that his harassed-looking confrère
was taking no sort of interest in the carpet-sweeper;
was forgetting everything that she said as fast as
she said it; was merely waiting until she had exhausted herself to announce that nobody but Mr.
Coffin could be of the least assistance.

So that Mrs. Micklethwaite, who hadn't gone
shopping for thirty years without acquiring a certain sensitiveness to such symptoms, realised that
nothing was to be gained by any continuance of
her laborious monologue.   She'd have to come back,
or write, or telephone, if the carpet-sweeper were
ever to function again; for whatever the size of
Hamhurst's premises and advertisements, the last
word remained, as ever, with the human element.

'Well, never mind,' said Mrs. Micklethwaite,
more graciously than she felt or than the harassed-
looking man seemed to appreciate.   'I'll have to
see about it some other time.'   And: 'Come
along, Moira,' added Mrs. Micklethwaite.

The assistant at once returned, with obvious
relief, to his awkward parcel.   The long girl gave
a start, and set herself in motion.   'Now,' she
thought; and her heart began beating, so violently

that she nearly missed a step. An observer might have thought — so quickly and gracefully did she regain her balance — that she was one of those long girls who dance occasionally, as they pass through Hamhurst's and other places. But her face gave another suggestion. With all trace of conscious expression wiped out, it was a sad — and if you were prepared to admit it — rather a pathetic face. This was how Miss Micklethwaite, that spoilt, useless but so far harmless creature, looked when she was alone. And she was alone now, in a sense, though still her high heels went tapping after those of her mother. She had given herself her last instructions, and no outward influence must affect them until they had all been obeyed. An automaton, moving under remote control, followed Mrs. Micklethwaite — that dull, worthy but self-centred creature — down Messrs. Hamhurst's wide stairs, and back into their silk department, and out through the swinging glass of their huge, bronze doorway.

And the roaring began again, and somehow — though still an automaton — Miss Micklethwaite would cross the street with her mother for the last time, and for the last time just touching that elbow; and then, on the further side, she would say good-bye — just like that — and Mrs. Micklethwaite would climb aboard a home-going omnibus, and the long girl would hail a taxi and drive away (as she supposed) from her own misery, and at least (as she believed) make one person happy.

'Steady, Mummie!' she said. 'Look out!'

And Mrs. Micklethwaite drew back, as a rush of vehicles came bursting past the policeman who had freed them.

'Now, then,' said the automaton, as the roadway cleared. 'Come on, Mummie.' And her hand just touched the familiar elbow, and the two Micklethwaites set off. Six yards of dark, glittering wood-paving, and they had achieved the island refuge in the middle of the street. The long girl glanced, automatically, to the left.

Ting, ting! came the sound of a bell. Ting-ting-ting!

The grey motor-ambulance which had deposited young Mr. Rooke at his ancestral home, and was now returning to await its next summons, came gliding swiftly past.

Ting, ting! it repeated.

And: 'Oh!' cried Miss Micklethwaite, suddenly released from automatism and as suddenly changing the touch on that familiar elbow to a desperate grip. 'Oh, Chick!' she cried — but now only to herself. 'Oh, Chick — I hadn't forgotten you, my darling. And I couldn't do anything that you'd be ashamed of — not possibly; not as long as I live. It's all right, Chick. It's all off. I don't suppose you can hear me; I don't suppose you know or care. But they took your poor pieces in one of those awful things on that awful day; and now I've just seen one of them again, and Johnnie's nothing, *nothing* to me at all. Chick — do you hear me? Chick, darling — can you ever forgive me? Chick!'

Ting, ting! from the distance, and the roar on all sides.

'You needn't,' said Mrs. Micklethwaite, 'hold me quite so tight, Moira. I saw that ambulance just as well as you did. Come along. It's safe now.'

'Mummie!'

'What?'

'I say,' said Miss Micklethwaite, with just a slight gulp. 'I say — do you mind if I come home to lunch after all? I — I've just realised I've made the most stupid mistake. In fact, I — I wasn't going anywhere today at all.'

'What?' said Mrs. Micklethwaite. 'Well, of course, Moira. Considering you never told me you were going out until I'd ordered —— Oh, quick! Look sharp! There's our bus.'

So the two Micklethwaites mounted the vermilion
monster and were borne back towards the pleasant
street where they both lived, and would go on
living.

And Johnnie, whoever he may have been, waited
at the station; and waited; and went on waiting.
Until presently the train went off without him,
and he knew.

12

IT SEEMS unquestionable, if affairs had fallen
out otherwise — if this hadn't followed that, and
that, in turn, hadn't followed this — that the Fates
who sported with the destiny of William Somerset
might have continued to sport a great deal longer,
instead of suddenly relenting, or being forced to
relent, and — well, and doing what they actually
did.

Seems unquestionable? Why, there's no seem-
ing about it. For one knows the habits of those
Fates. One knows their peculiar and misguided
sense of humour, and their conservative method of
repeating exactly the same jest, and the silly guf-
faws with which they applaud their own tomfoolery,
and the extraordinary conceit to which this perpetual misuse of their powers gives rise. Yes, 'conceit' was the word which we used, and no doubt
that it is this quality which makes them so vulnerable when any of their victims really turns round
and hits back. No doubt, either, that it was their
conceit which made them so careless at what one
is almost bound to call the psychological moment.
If they hadn't been laughing so odiously, there
were plenty of tricks left up their capacious sleeves,
and Bill Somerset could easily have been downed
by another of their hoary practical jokes. But they
were taken by surprise, this time. They hadn't,
it seems, allowed for the remarkable chain of cir-

cumstances which had followed on Mrs. Bowker's
non-attendance at Number Sixty-Seven, Pocklington Road, and for once the self-complacent old hags
were caught napping.

This, at least, is a theory with a good deal to
recommend it and little, if anything, which can
possibly be disproved. For if anyone imagines
that Bill Somerset was the kind of character who
could ever, in any conceivable conditions, turn
round and hit anybody — in his own interests,
that's to say, for he could pack quite a pretty
wallop when it came to defending other people or
animals — then anyone under that delusion is
wrong. Of course he wasn't a fool; there was the
most sensitive kind of intelligence in every line that
he ever drew or smear of paint that he ever daubed
on a canvas; but in looking after himself, in choosing his friends, in dealing with possible clients and,
generally speaking, in advancing what you might
call his career — why, the young man was everything in the alphabet from an ass to a zany.

Shy, too — which made it so particularly tempt-
ing for the old hags to score off him. He had a
habit of standing on one leg, rubbing the back of his
head and looking disparaging which instantly
knocked about seventy-five per cent off the value
of any work which he was trying to sell. And off,
accordingly, it was knocked, in the twinkling of an
eye; whereupon Mr. Somerset committed the still
greater error of emitting a jet of incoherent gratitude, and very likely threw in some other sketch or
drawing — which a different character would have
held for an obviously rising market and eventually
have sold for Heaven knows what to an American
collector. Only Bill's market, naturally, didn't rise
— since he took such peculiar pains to depress it —
and the result was that he worked until his eyes all
but dropped out, and let all his ill-chosen friends
sponge on him, and went about with every appear-

ance of unaspiring failure — unless he happened to look you in the face, which he hardly ever did — and was twenty-seven, and might easily have been making several thousand pounds a year; but actually lived exclusively on his beam-ends and had large holes in both his socks and his shoes.

So the Fates who sported with his destiny laughed heartily, and went on teasing him with indefatigable horseplay. And he sold a picture (to an American, of course) at the Paris Salon for about a fifth of what it fetched six months later, and lent the money to an unmarried stranger who said that his wife was ill. And he sold the copyright in his illustrations to a limited *édition de luxe* for five guineas each — the originals shortly afterwards changing hands for a hundred — and lent the money to a girl whose address he mislaid, and who didn't seem to have taken any particular care of his, either. And he signed contracts with the art-editors of magazines which didn't quite cover the actual cost of production — and then went and lent the money to anybody who took the trouble to call round for it.

'My dear fuf-fellow,' he said, for he stammered a little, as well as standing on one leg; 'that's the most tut-terrible story. I'm awfully glad you came to me with it fuf-first. Here you are, old man, and any time that's cuc-convenient...'

And he blinked, and it appeared, in due course, that no time was in the least convenient for the repayment of his loans; so that though, in a sense, he was almost as much of a moneylender as an artist, he was no more successful — as success is commonly understood — in one profession than the other. For it amused the Fates who sported with his destiny to see him turning out work which (for they are no mean critics) they knew was just about as good as it could be, and still going about with holes both in his socks and his shoes.

The man, you say, was an imbecile; but we don't
agree with you. We can't agree with you when we
think of his workmanship and his imagination and
skill. To us it just seems, as it has always seemed,
that there are some people who fit into the curious
pattern which has been evolved by the majority of
human beings — and has often been described as
'the world' — and become part of it, and make
use of it, and go ahead in it, and know just what
they're doing; while there are others, like Bill
Somerset, who have obviously fetched up on the
wrong planet and can never feel at home there,
even when — as sometimes happens — the Fates
stop sporting with them and they stumble into an
ostensible niche. This, one is told, is the age of
democracy, and whatever that may mean, it is at
least an age — like other ages — where minorities
have jolly well got to look after themselves. There
isn't room in the pattern for everybody, so that
unless you can weave a new bit for yourself —
and that isn't any easier than it sounds — you had
better put up with things as they happen to be.
So Bill Somerset, a philosopher, though he was
quite unaware of it, whistled and sang as he worked
for the crooks who employed him, and gave both
to the rich and the poor, and slept soundly at nights
and had no idea that there was anything exceptional
about his case or anything unusual about his
appearance — it was the other people, of course,
who were always being so odd — and was perfectly
happy, indeed, in his horrid little studio with his
horrid little oil-stove and his horrid little camp-
bedstead behind the tattered screen in the corner,
until —

Well, what is it that makes even visitors from
.another planet unhappy? They go and get mixed
up with the daughters of men.

13

ACTUALLY, and in this case, there was only one daughter, nor was Mr. Somerset mixed up with her in any such sense as gives rise to the activities of play-producing societies on Sunday evenings. Nor, though one has just said that he was perfectly happy until he met her, should it rashly be assumed that he was unhappy afterwards. The point, rather, was that he was no longer responsible to no one but himself, for the girl had come along and had insisted, as girls do, on sharing a load of which he had hitherto been quite unconscious. He was so helpless, and he had saved her when she thought that no one could save her. So she owed him everything, and was determined to pay her debt.

Also she was in love with him, and, if it comes to that, he had married her. But the beginning of it all was that she had been in the most awful mess and the most awful hole, and if only she hadn't been such an awful coward, she was going to have killed herself. She had, as a matter of fact, turned the gas on twice — only then she had turned it off again — on the night before she came round hunting for Gerry. Because Gerry had been one of Arthur's friends, and though she never wanted to see Arthur again — never, never, *never* — she was so mad that morning that she had got to tell somebody what quite a lot of people knew. She was going to scream and yell at Arthur's friend — Heaven alone knows why, only she was past all sense and reason — and then she was going right away somewhere, and perhaps it would be that river that you could get to on the bus, or perhaps it would be the wheels of a train somewhere — 'eastbound traffic,' the evening papers would say, 'was delayed eight minutes' — and then, presumably, she would go to Hell, and that wouldn't be much fun either, only she didn't really see how it was going to be worse than this.

So she came in by the doorway with all the un-
polished bell-pushes, and with all the little cards
fastened up by drawing-pins, and she went up the
dank, dismal stairway, right up to the top, and she
waited until she got her breath, and then she
knocked with the cheap, ugly knocker.

And there was some scuffling inside, and a frowsy
woman in a dirty wrapper came and half opened the
door.

'Well?' she said, not over politely. 'Yes?'

'Oh!' said the girl on the landing.

'Eh?'

'I thought — I mean, is Mr. Salter in?'

Not, of course, that the original plan could be
followed if Gerry had got this awful woman on the
premises, but one had to say something when one
had climbed all this way and knocked on the door,
and —

'No,' said the frowsy stranger. 'There's no
Mr. Salter here, and what's more, I don't know
any Mr. Salter. If some people took the trouble to
look at the cards downstairs ——'

And the frowsy stranger closed the door again
with as much of a slam as so flimsy a door could
produce, and the girl outside heard her shouting:
'It's all right. It's nobody.' And then, because
her feet, at any rate, knew that there was no point
in standing here any longer, they started taking
her back down those exceptionally dank and dismal
stairs. And at the first half-landing it seemed to
her that she was going to die, quite without the
assistance of any river or railway-train, and she put
out her hand to touch the wall; and the wall wasn't
there, and no more was anything else; and somebody
screamed and something hit her very hard. And the
next thing she knew was that she was lying on something very low in a room with an overpowering
smell of turpentine, and a man was pouring something out of a bottle more on to than into her

mouth — something which stung and smarted —
and that she'd never seen him before, and that she
ought to get up, and that she couldn't.

'I can't get up,' she said, faintly.

'That's all right,' said the man, whom she now
observed to be wearing an extraordinarily ragged
pullover. 'Dud-don't try and move. Here — try
and have some of this stut-uff.'

The stuff suddenly smelt more overpowering
than the turpentine. The girl shook her head and
clenched her teeth.

'I'm all right,' she said. 'I'll go.'

She began sitting up. The man gave her what to
all intents and purposes was a push, and she fell
back again.

'Gug-gosh!' said a voice; and then there was
another blank in her consciousness. And then she
was still lying in the room, and the man was between her and the window, bent over a large, tilted
drawing-board, scratching ceaselessly with a pen.
It occurred to the girl (whose name was Norah)
that if only there was a basket of mending-wool
available — which didn't, somehow, seem very
likely — she could and should do something about
that pullover. An odd thought to occur to anyone
in her situation, but it did.

'I say!' she said.

Bill Somerset gave a terrific start.

'Eh?' he gasped. 'What?'

'Before I go ——'

'Oh, but dud-don't hurry. I mean, are you sure
you're — you're all right? I mean, I just had some
work to fuf-finish, but I'm nearly ready.'

'Ready?' said the girl. 'Ready for what?'

'B-breakfast,' said Bill — it being now about
midday. 'You see, I don't always feel like cuc-
cooking things when I get up, so ——'

'But do you mean you haven't eaten anything
yet?'

Mr. Somerset nodded.

'Nor have I,' said Norah; and suddenly she began to laugh, and the man in the pullover pushed his chair back, and stood on one leg and scratched his head, and gave his celebrated sheepish grin. And now it seemed to Norah that she *must* stop and look after anyone who was quite so hopeless and helpless. And she noticed his socks, and a pang went through her heart. And his shoes, and another pang followed it. And then — so queer and complicated are human beings — she turned aside from all the horror and misery which had brought her here, and saw everything from an extraordinary new angle, and no longer had the least wish to yell and scream about something which had quite obviously happened to a different girl altogether. And she stood up, quite easily, and joined the man in the pullover where he was fumbling and muddling at a cupboard in the corner. And then she said: 'Now, that'll do. You're not to touch anything. *I'm* going to do this.'

And she did, while Bill Somerset stared at her and scratched his head. And then she cleared a corner of his work-table (while he writhed in silent terror); and then she dashed back to the oil-stove and stirred and sniffed at the saucepan; and so, presently, the two of them were sitting facing each other across the space which she had cleared, drinking tea and eating buttered eggs, and Norah said: 'Oh, dear! Isn't this good!' And Bill said: 'Yes. Spup-plendid.'

And Norah said: 'Oh, dear! I believe you've saved my life.'

And Bill said: 'That's a fuf-funny thing to say.'

And Norah said: 'Have you got any mending-wool?'

And Bill said: 'What's that? No.'

So Norah asked him for a shilling (which he instantly gave her) and went out, and he thought she'd quite gone for good. Only apparently she hadn't, because just as he was settling down to work again, back she came and told him to take off his pullover.

'What for?' said Bill Somerset. But he took it off, and the girl sat there darning it. And then she said: 'Have you got any other socks?' And Bill said: 'Yes. In the waste-pup-paper basket.' And the girl fished them out and started darning them too. And this time Bill forgot she was there, until, in stepping back to take an all-embracing glance at his drawing, he also trod on her foot.

'Oh, I say!' he said.   'I beg your pup-pardon.'

'Look!' said the girl.

'Oh, I say.   That is gug-good of you.   That's awfully clever.   Fancy ——'

'What?' asked the girl; for the man was glaring at her now in the most penetrating and alarming manner.

'Have you,' he asked, 'ever sat to anybody?'

The girl ducked her head.

'Yes,' she said, as she remembered Arthur, and the beginning and the end of it all.

'Oh,' said Bill; and nodded, and went back to his work.

There was a long silence.

'If you want a model ——' began the girl abruptly.   'I mean, I didn't mean to be rude just then.   But —— Oh, I never meant to tell anyone; only ——'

Her strange host had turned his back and was singing — if you could call it singing — as he fiddled with a cardboard box full of crumpled tubes.

'I don't even know your name,' said the girl.

'Somerset,' said Bill.   'Bill Somerset.   But that's all right.'

'What do you mean?'

'Don't worry,' said Bill.   'It dud-doesn't matter.'

'What doesn't matter?'

'Anything,' said Bill.   'All sus-sorts of things
happen, I mean.   Not my affair.'

'Yes, but ——'

She never told him, though.   Even when Arthur's
name was mentioned — but this was weeks afterwards, when she was sitting to him regularly, and
doing his housekeeping, and trying to stop him
giving all his money away — she never succeeded
in telling him.   And perhaps he knew, or perhaps
he wasn't like other people, or perhaps — he almost
made it seem possible — there had never been any
Arthur or any of the distant misery and horror.
Something new began at the moment when the
girl took that toss down the top flight of the dismal
stairs, and when one is young one is elastic in spirit
as well as in body.   A look came into Norah's
face; a possessive, protective look which clearly
meant business.   'He's mine,' said the look.   'See
how helpless and hopeless he is, and how he needs
me, and what I'm going to make of him.   This is
the job that was waiting for me all the time, and
no one else is going to get it away from me.'

No one else tried.   Other passing, predatory
creatures merely saw that Bill Somerset was shy
and untidy and hard-up, or were frightened of him
because he was so different.   A few of them, perhaps, appreciated his work, which Norah never
did — and this, one imagines, was why he found
her so soothing — but they were ambitious simply
for themselves, and in those days Bill was so obviously never going to get anywhere.   They wanted
push and punch, not the kind of cleverness which
was geared to impractical dreaming and took
such pains to conceal itself, and they went their
way — with Norah's unnoticed assistance; but
Norah herself remained.

The Fates said: 'is This a joke. She's got him now, and he'll probably marry her, and that'll be the end of him. A stupid girl like that, who couldn't even keep out of trouble herself, will be a millstone round his neck. He can't support her unless he takes to pot-boiling, and if he does that he'll soon hate her, and then he'll have a fine chance of ever doing anything better. Chivalrous ass!' said the Fates. 'He's done for. He's sunk.'

And they stood back, lest even their shadows should warn him. And Norah was there every day and all day, and Bill got quite used to having her about the place, and did everything — outside the actual practice of his art — that she told him. And missed her, in a dumb, vague sort of way, if ever she left him alone. And sold the portrait which he painted of her to a dealer, and lent three-quarters of the preposterous proceeds to another artist called Rudd — who instantly vanished from his circle. And Norah got the truth out of him, which was as easy as getting a rattle away from a bald baby, and whether it were due to cunning calculation or inherited instinct, she now knew that the moment had come for her to burst into tears.

So that Bill dashed at her, tripping over a T-square and putting his foot through a newly-primed canvas *en route*, and grabbed hold of her, and nearly fell on top of her, and forced his handkerchief (which had just been used as a paint-rag) on her, and said: 'There, there, Norah! For God's sus-sake, don't do that! I can't stut-tand it. Norah! Stut-*top*!'

And Norah clung to him, and it seemed that he had kissed her. And it seemed that she was abusing him for something which he couldn't at all understand, but at the same time was calling him a number of exceedingly affectionate names. And it seemed, then, that if he let go he would be a brute and a devil, but simultaneously that, as a matter of fact, he didn't want to let go. And Norah — forgetting for the first and last time that she was a woman (but one rather likes her for it), said: 'Oh, Bill — darling — I've made you do this!'

And Bill blinked and said: 'Nun-no, you haven't. I love you.'

And it seemed, now, that he did love her — though as he had never loved anybody else there was just a possibility that he was wrong. And he would have liked to explain this, only it might sound rather rude. So then he was quite convinced that he loved her — as he still is, and, after all, what further evidence can anybody require? And since it was quite positive that Norah loved him (and still does) with her heart and her head and her body and her soul — well, there they were and there it was.

And Bill said: 'Let's go and gug-get married.'

And it was all so easy that Norah burst into tears again — but quite different tears, if you see what we mean. But of course this was exactly what she had had in mind, so it was silly to cry, wasn't it? And married they were, though Norah still thinks that she told him all about Arthur the night before they went to the Registrar, and Bill neither had nor has the faintest idea what she was talking out. And for all our rigid views on what's called morality, it still seems to us that if two people can be happy after one of them has been so miserable that she was thinking of rivers and trains, then the present, as always, is rather more important than the past, and the future not without a dash or slice of hope.

They moved into another so-called studio, which had a tiny little bedroom attached to it and a diminutive projection which was both bathroom and kitchen, and another chapter in both their lives had begun.

14

You can't alter these beings from other planets just by living with them and taking care of them. Mr. Somerset would always be untidy and unpunctual and unbusinesslike and confused in his strange mind as to whether it were the beginning of this week or the end of next. But Mrs. Somerset could, and did, see that he had breakfast in the morning and dinner in the evening, and that he occasionally breathed a little fresh air, and that his handkerchiefs and paint-rags were no longer interchangeable and indistinguishable. And she kept, or tried to keep, accounts of a sort, so that Bill no longer went about with old cheques in forgotten pockets of his disgraceful clothes, nor used receipts for lighting his pipe. His happy-go-lucky generosity continued to dodge most of her attempts to control it, and at first he still took any kind of payment that his clients offered; but the borrowers could no longer drop in at any time they chose and help themselves, with Mrs. Somerset there to keep an eye on them; and it wasn't long before Mrs. Somerset began interfering with the art-editors and dealers as well.

A clever little woman, they called her; and laughed, because they had come across clever little women before, and knew just how to run rings round them. 'We'll have to be careful, Mrs. Somerset,' they said, 'now you're on the job.' But the only care necessary was to stick to the contracts and agreements that Bill had signed as a bachelor, which had got him tied up in a stranglehold for months and years to come.

'It's disgraceful!' said the clever little woman.

'But,' said the art-editors and dealers, 'look at the risk we were taking at the time. Who'd heard of your husband before he came to us? We

can't afford to be philanthropists, Mrs. Somerset,'
they said.

'Anybody,' said Mrs. Somerset, 'can afford to
be honest.'

But Bill dragged her away by the sleeve, and
said she couldn't possibly talk to people like that,
and then went back by himself and apologised for
her. And: 'Look here, Norah,' he said, 'as long
as we've got enough to live on, what dud-does
it matter? And we — we have got enough; haven't
we?'

'No,' said Mrs. Somerset. 'I've got enough,
and I'd hate to have any servants, and I adore you,
Bill. But you know you oughtn't to work so hard.'

Mr. Somerset shook his head, violently.

'And you know you ought to go abroad.'

Mr. Somerset stopped shaking his head, and
looked thoughtful. It would, he was reflecting, be
rather fun to go abroad, and he'd been meaning to
go abroad (though he'd never said so) when somehow or other he'd got married instead.

'I mean,' added his wife, 'it always puts up
people's prices.'

Mr. Somerset stood on one leg and scratched his
head. His wife was such a remarkable girl that
he couldn't argue with her, least of all if the argument were to be one in favour of perpetual poverty.
But he knew he was right — just as he knew that
she was right, too — and if only he could please her
without aggravating all the people who had been
so decent to him, well, of course he'd do it like a
shot. Only the point was that one's work was
so much more important than what one got for it,
and that, as a matter of fact, one couldn't work
at all if one were always having to think about
money; and that was why he never *had* thought
about money; and it was all rather confusing and
difficult, only of course Norah was so much cleverer
than he was.... And so on.

What a man to take and urge forward on the
road to success! But the remarkable girl never
lost heart. She *knew* that hard times should be
a phase and not a lasting condition. She *knew* —
and was right, though her knowledge was the
purest guesswork — that Bill was a genius. And
she knew that he wasn't inexhaustible, and that
he'd crack up if he didn't ease off, and that he
must have security — which meant money — if he
weren't to come down like a rocket, and with her
still on his hands. And she wanted him to be
famous, for all the good reasons as well as all the
bad reasons — which is what all nice women want.
And she was going to manage it somehow, what was
more — only this time without ever telling him or
bothering him or appearing to know anything
about it. Because she loved and worshipped him,
and nothing was too good for him, and he had
saved her life.

So now Mrs. Somerset started all over again,
with fresh cunning and fresh determination, and
listened and looked about and learnt. And it
seemed to her that as for the dealers, one had only
to cut them right out and they could do nothing
but gnash their teeth. And as for the publishers,
that one had only to keep them waiting — after
the next set of illustrations was finished — and
they'd soon find that they'd either got to pay more
or lose money. And as for the contracts with the
art-editors — well, here was a harder nut for Mrs.
Somerset to crack; but if they had cheated Bill
because they were all in the same ring, then the
very same reason should prove to be their undoing.
One would go behind them and round them and
above them. One would — though six months ago
one had been terrified of one's own shadow — go
straight to Lord Ludgate, who was the ringmaster,
and tell him what he'd got to do, and see that he
did it. Why not, when — after all — he was only a

human being like oneself?   Why not, when it was all for Bill?

The idea sounds mad.   The idea *was* mad.   But Mrs. Somerset neither knew nor cared.   Such terrifying and single-minded devotion had grown up — as she also had grown up — during those six months of safety and peace, that she would have been prepared, with just as much assurance, to tackle the Prime Minister or the King.   A woman like this, who has nothing to lose and is doing it all for a man whom she really loves, is still one of the most irresistible forces that even a self-made millionaire can meet.   She told Bill that she'd be back for lunch, and was in Lord Ludgate's private sanctum — without any appointment, and admitted solely by the sparks which flashed from her eyes — within ten minutes of her arrival at the palace in which he lurked.

'I can't possibly see her,' he had told the last line of defence; and there she was, flashing her eyes at him and talking his head off.   He laughed at her; and she laughed back.

'You're much nicer than I thought,' she said.

'But *I* can't do anything,' said Lord Ludgate, weakly.

'Oh, yes, you can,' said Mrs. Somerset.   'I'll tell you exactly what to do.   You must cancel those agreements, and then Bill will paint your portrait.'

'But, my dear ——'

'Look at that mantelpiece,' cried Mrs. Somerset. 'You *know* there ought to be a portrait there. It's a disgrace that there isn't.   And it'll be far cheaper now than if you wait, because Bill's a genius. Why,' said Mrs. Somerset, 'it'll absolutely make your name!'

Lord Ludgate collapsed.   Nobody had come into this room and made him laugh like this since he had evicted his predecessor.   He was tough and

scaly and hard as nails, but the girl, at any rate,
wasn't afraid of him, and why shouldn't he have
his portrait painted?   He looked at the portfolio
which the girl had flung on his desk, and though
he knew no more about art than she did, it was
quite obvious that the man wasn't an impostor.
And even if he were an impostor, hadn't Lord
Ludgate the means of making a million readers
swallow him whole?   And then he looked at the
space over the mantelpiece, and puffed out his chest.
And then he looked back at the girl and said: —

'Well.   I'll see what I can do.'

'See?' said Mrs. Somerset, instantly.   'Oh,
no.   I must have more than that.   You must
do it.'

'Must I?'

'Yes, please.   You see, you're so busy otherwise
that you might forget.   When can Bill start?'

'Eh?' said Lord Ludgate.   'Look here.
Dammit, I mean.   I beg your pardon, Mrs. —
er ——'

'"Somerset."'

'Mrs. Somerset, but I — I ——'

The eyes flashed again.

'Oh, all right,' said Lord Ludgate.   'Tell him
to lunch with me at my club — the Wanderers'—
tomorrow.   You'd better tell my secretary as you
go out.   Because I warn you,' said Lord Ludgate,
with a last effort to be tough and scaly, 'that
I'm not going into this blindfold.   I've always,'
said Lord Ludgate, 'been a judge of character,
and — ah — that's why I've let you talk me round
like this.   But I warn you, if I don't take to this
husband of yours ——'

'But of *course* you'll take to him!' interrupted
Mrs. Somerset, gathering up the portfolio.   'Why,
don't you understand?   He's *marvellous*!'

And she skipped out of the sanctum, and gave
the good news to the secretary, and ran down the

stairs, and leapt on to an omnibus, and went
straight home again. And there, just as she was
running up her own stairs, a man passed her, and
he raised his hat and said: 'Good morning, Mrs.
Somerset.' And it was Bill's artist-friend called
Rudd.

15

'I suppose,' said Mrs. Somerset, 'he didn't pay
you back?'

'Well,' said Mr. Somerset; 'no — not exactly.'

'You mean —— You don't mean you let
him touch you again?'

'Oh, dud-dear, no,' said Bill. 'Oh, no!'

Mrs. Somerset looked a little suspicious, as anyone might who knew her husband and had noted
the nervous emphasis of his reply. But of course
he wouldn't tell her a lie, and of course he hadn't
told her a lie. His friend Rudd hadn't touched
him for the simple reason that his wife Norah had
locked up all his money and taken the key out
with her. On the other hand, his friend Rudd had
certainly tried to touch him, and would certainly
have succeeded but for this fortunate circumstance.
So Bill looked a little shifty, as he stood on one
leg and scratched his head. But Norah had too
much to tell him to go on bothering about his
friend Rudd. And she began telling him, and Bill
became pale green.

'You mum-mean to say ——' he gasped.

'Yes, darling. I do!'

'And I've got to go and have lul-lunch with
him?'

'Yes, darling. It's all arranged.'

'At his Cuc-cuc-club?'

'Yes, darling. At the Wanderers'.'

'To-mum-morrow?'

'Why, what's the matter, Bill? Aren't you
pleased?'

'Oh, yes,' said Bill Somerset, tottering slightly and absent-mindedly drawing a bit of charcoal across his forehead. But suddenly it seemed to him that this girl, of whom he was really extraordinarily fond, was taking charge of his life in a manner which filled him with uneasiness; and that it was wonderful of her, of course, to do what she had done, but at the same time that he ought to have stopped her; and that the vague world in which he really moved couldn't stand much more of this treatment without falling to pieces; and that if it did fall to pieces...

Well, there was still and always now this girl of whom he was so extraordinarily fond, so perhaps it was all right. And he blinked, and decided that of course it was all right. And a distant, wobbling bit of his mind told him that nothing could ever really make him a native of this planet. But perhaps one ought to pretend to be, if it would be easier for this girl of whom he was so extraordinarily fond. And it would be wrong of course to let anyone else push him about like this, but Norah of course was different.

And then another little bit of his queer mind noted just the way that a woman's mouth changed its shape when the woman was trying not to cry, so that he even made some odd motions with his thumb as he considered exactly how one should draw it. And then, in the same instant, he came rushing back from the strange, astral outpost where he had been hovering, because Norah mustn't cry, and he wasn't going to let her cry. And his own mouth twisted into the celebrated sheepish grin, and he caught the girl of whom he was so extraordinarily fond in his arms, and told her that he adored her, and that he'd be absolutely lost without her, and that he'd never heard of anybody being so clever and ingenious in his life.

All of which was very sensible of the sensible part

of Bill Somerset, and his wife laughed and they both became tremendously excited about the impression that he was going to make on Lord Ludgate, and about all the results that were going to follow; so that the Fates who sported with his destiny were quite flustered and almost thought that the game was up — until suddenly the wisest and most malicious of them said: 'Wait a moment, though. Aren't we forgetting about his friend Rudd?'

So then they began plotting and planning, and pulling wires and calling on their assistants; and then their scheme was complete, and they all had a good night's rest. While Norah lay awake, filled with such thoughts as only unprincipled, single-minded and devoted women know, and turned them over and over, and was more certain than ever that she had indeed been clever and ingenious. And Bill slept beside her, while his spirit visited other and exquisitely beautiful but quite impossible worlds, and he muttered and smiled — and sometimes even made odd motions with his thumb — and when he eventually woke up, had forgotten everything except that it was a fine morning and that the light was just right for his work.

But Mrs. Somerset, naturally, hadn't forgotten. And presently she told Bill that he must stop. And about the fourth time she told him this he heard her, and asked why. And she reminded him of his appointment, and he said: 'Oh, yes. Oh, of cuc-course.' And then she made him change his clothes and brush his hair and put on a tie; and she turned him round, and looked at him, and kissed him; and she gave him no advice beyond telling him (which she had found out by consulting a public telephone-directory) that the Wanderers' Club was in such-and-such a Square, and how he was to get there. And then — though of course he wouldn't need it, but nothing (she knew) fills a man with more confidence — she gave him no less

than three pounds of his own money, as well as a
shilling for his fares, and kissed him again, and
told him it was now time to start.

So then he started — feeling a little uncomfortable, it is true, in his best clothes and new shoes, but
less so as his tie slipped round out of sight — and
followed the prescribed route until it was time to
get off the first omnibus. And at this point, just
as he was staring round and gaping and considering
how he was going to cross the road, a hearty voice
greeted him and a hearty thump descended on the
shoulders of his shaggy overcoat.

'Why!' said the voice. 'If it isn't old Bill
again.'

'Rudd!' cried Bill, delighted (as soon as he
had recovered from the shock) at this friendly face
in a swarm of strangers. And at the same moment
— to the accompaniment of inaudible chuckles from
the Fates who sported with his destiny — all recol-
lection of the cause which had brought him to
this part of London passed swiftly and utterly
from his mind. For here was dear old Rudd, whom
he hadn't seen since yesterday, and with whom he
had been having such an interesting talk when
dear old Rudd had suddenly looked out of the
window and said he must be off. Dear old Rudd,
who'd been having such rotten luck lately, but
had always been such a nice chap in the old days.
And how lucky to have run into dear old Rudd
again so soon, and which way was dear old Rudd
going?

'Anywhere,' said dear old Rudd. 'What about
a drink?'

Mr. Somerset, who had forgotten all about the
three pounds in his cigarette-case and was only
aware of ninepence in his trousers pocket, hesitated
for an instant. But again his friend Rudd slapped
him on the back.

'My treat,' he said.

For Rudd had just touched an Academician for a fiver, and could afford to be hospitable before making a second attempt on Bill. The two artists went into a hostelry, and Rudd ordered and paid.

'Cheery-ho!' he said.

'Chuch-cheery-ho!' said Bill.

'That's better,' said Rudd.

'Rather!' said Bill. 'Er...'

The point was that it was really his turn now to order and pay. But he couldn't; or thought he couldn't.

'Er ——'

'Got a fag?' asked Rudd.

Bill beamed. Yes, of course he'd got a fag. Out came the white-metal cigarette-case, and Rudd's slightly bloodshot eyes narrowed. Three quid. Not much, but of course there was more where that came from. Suddenly Rudd started to shiver and sag.

'Listen, ol' man,' he said; but there was a whine in his voice now, and all the heartiness had vanished. 'Listen, ol' man — you know what I was telling you yesterday. I'm not the kind of fellow to grouse about bad luck and all that sort of thing, but ——'

And Rudd groused. Rent, debts, pawnbrokers and false friends spun themselves into a fantasy to which Bill Somerset listened with his mouth slightly ajar and his eyes popping out of his head.

'But my dud-dear old chap ——'

Rudd waved the cigarette-case aside.

'Three quid!' he groaned. 'Gosh! I'm not trying to sponge on you, ol' man, but three quid —— Well! What's three quid to a fellow in the sort of hole I'm in? You'd far better keep it and forget about me. A tenner's the least that's going to save *me* from an absolute smash, and where am I going to get a tenner from? Eh?'

And Bill had actually been drinking at this

wretched, hounded creature's expense. It was ghastly! It was unthinkable!

'Now, lul-look here, Rudd ——'

'No, ol' man. I'm finished.'

'Nun-no, you're not. Come along with mum-me to the bank. I'll manage it sus-somehow. It's not fuf-far.'

Easy? The Fates nearly split their sides, as they watched Bill Somerset and his friend Rudd leave the hostelry together — Bill still stammering about his practical certainty that it would be all right, and not really having the faintest idea if he were really overdrawn or not (because Norah was the only person who knew that, though as a matter of fact he wasn't), and Rudd still egging him on by saying that of course he couldn't take a farthing, and then throwing in a few more heart-rending details about his unimaginable and imaginary sufferings.

And so they passed on foot through a number of streets, with Bill, as always, glancing at everything and everyone while his thumb and two-thirds of his mind considered how one should draw them. And so — since it was all so childishly easy — his friend Rudd suddenly decided that ten pounds would be as little use to him as three, and that now or never was the time to make a bold stroke and place himself in comfort for weeks.

'Look here, Bill,' he said, catching his dupe by the arm. 'Listen, ol' man. I don't feel I'm playing absolutely fair with you. Listen, ol' man — when I met you just now, do you know what I was going to do? I was going to end it. Yes, I was.'

'What?' gasped Mr. Somerset, standing stock-still at this still more ghastly and unthinkable statement.

'Yes,' said his friend Rudd. 'That was what I was going to do. And, Bill — Bill, ol' man — I told you a lie.'

'Eh?' said Mr. Somerset, lifting one leg from the pavement.

'Yes,' said his friend Rudd. 'Everything else was true, ol' man, but I've just got five pounds left. Here it is.'

Out came his hand, with all the frankness of the confidence trickster, and to Bill's bewilderment a Bank of England note was forced swiftly into his grasp.

'B-b-but ——' he stammered.

'There!' said Rudd, looking ineffably seedy and noble. 'Take it, ol' man. I know I owe it to you, and I was just going to have posted it to you anyway. It's no use, you see, ol' man. Five — ten — fifteen quid — that can't save me now. You clear off. You forget about me. I'm going to finish it the way I planned at the beginning. There's no other way out, ol' man. I tell you, and this is the sacred truth, unless ——' (Here the creature Rudd made an incredibly quick and practised calculation, as he looked at Bill's clothes and thought of his rooms and remembered what a lot of work he did for the magazines and recalled how little he had ever spent on himself) — 'unless,' said the creature Rudd, 'I can have fifty quid by to-night, well ——'

He shrugged his shoulders. He fixed his terrified companion with that noble and seedy eye. Bill opened his mouth to stammer, and it was now quite obvious what Bill was going to try and say. For of course it would be all right about an overdraft with so much work still to be paid for, and if it weren't, he'd take Rudd along with him and raise the money from a dealer, and anyhow he'd raise it somehow, because if he once let Rudd out of his sight before he had raised it ——

Down the narrow pavement came the tapping of four high-heeled shoes, belonging to Mrs. Micklethwaite and her daughter Moira, as they returned

towards their luncheon-party in the pleasant street
just round the corner. Automatically, Mr. Somerset moved aside to let them pass. Automatically,
his restless, tireless, penetrating gaze swept over
their features. A mother, he thought — swifter
than lightning — a rather dull, respectable, self-
centred mother, trying to look younger than she
feels, or at any rate feeling quite as old as she can't
help looking. And a daughter — a tall daughter,
with a sulky face. No! Not sulky. That was the
way that a woman's mouth changed its shape when
the woman was trying not to cry.

One couldn't mistake it when one saw it for the
second time within twenty-four hours, because ——

'Gug-gosh!' shouted Bill Somerset, as he suddenly remembered Norah and why she, too, had
looked like that, and the appointment that she had
made for him, and how, instead of keeping it, he
was standing he didn't know where doing he didn't
know what. And: 'Hi!' yelled Bill Somerset,
launching himself madly into the roadway, and
leaping on to the running-board of a crawling taxi,
and plucking the door open, and slamming it
violently behind him. And then his head shot
out of the further window, and told the driver to
go like the dud-devil to the Wanderers' Club; and
the gears shrieked and the tyres span; and the two
Micklethwaites passed quickly on to their home in
the pleasant street round the corner; and the egre-
gious and baffled Rudd stood there gaping and
gasping — until presently he began to blaspheme.

The next time that Mrs. Somerset went through
the pockets of her husband's shaggy overcoat, she
would find an inexplicable and crumpled five-
pound note there to which he was certainly as
much entitled as anyone else who had lent a great
deal more and not been paid back; and she would
smile, and click her tongue, and put it away in a
secret hiding-place with all the other money that

she was saving for Bill's visit to Italy. We like to think, also, and we're pretty sure we're right, that by this time Lord Ludgate's tough and scaly features would at least be beginning to appear on the canvas which would eventually hang over the mantelpiece in his business sanctum. For his lordship, as he had said, was a judge of character, and an artist who had had the nerve to keep him waiting nearly ten minutes for his lunch — well, no doubt that an artist like that had a future.

16

MIKE FERRIS took another look at the big doorway at the top of the wide steps, and was again filled with uncertainty and terror. And again, in order to modify the form of his anxiety, he glanced at his watch. And his watch let him down — as of course it had been bound to do sooner or later — by now telling him that it was exactly the time that his uncle had said; so that his other uncertainty and terror returned with no hope of remission, and once more he looked an extremely irresolute young gentleman indeed.

For of course it had never occurred to him that there would be quite so many obvious clubs — not to mention equivocal places which might or might not be clubs — all herded together so near the point which his uncle had so hurriedly described. And if he were to try and force his way into the wrong one —— Well, if it came to that, how on earth did one force one's way even into the right one? Did one just walk in, as all these other people seemed to be walking in, and trust to one's luck that one's host would be in the hall? Or, if a complete stranger and new-comer, was one supposed to ring the bell?

And then, again, wouldn't you have thought, and hadn't Mike Ferris certainly thought, that the

Wanderers' Club would at least have a brass plate
somewhere, so that people who had only just come
to London, and people who had hardly ever been
there before, and people who were distinctly re-
luctant in the matter of addressing strangers,
might at any rate know which doorway to attack?
But the Wanderers' Club, if this were the Wanderers'
Club, bore no such announcement of its identity.
The big doorway and the wide steps merely brooded
and threatened in nameless mystery. The only
way to solve it, apparently, was to risk being
snubbed and thrown out; and honestly, thought
Mike Ferris, if he hadn't come so far and if it hadn't
been so jolly decent of Uncle Robert to ask him,
he'd more than half a mind to abandon the adventure altogether; to lunch at one of those tea-shops
that he'd passed, and then to go straight back to the
office.

If only, thought Mike Ferris, he'd kept away
from the telephone last night. But he hadn't.
Well, naturally one felt a bit lonely and a bit at a
loose end one's first night in strange lodgings, and
with so much apprehension about what the strange
office would be like in the morning; and then Mother
had particularly given one Uncle Robert's address,
and had particularly said: 'Mind you let him
know you're in London.' And though at the time
of this injunction one had quite meant to postpone
all action indefinitely — because, after all, one
hardly knew Uncle Robert at all, and he hadn't been
down to Bedford for years, and one didn't really suppose he wanted to see one any more than one really
wanted to see him — yet somehow or other, as that
first evening stretched out with all its ominous un-
familiarity, one had known that one was being
drawn, with increasing attraction and diminishing
resistance, toward the call-box at the corner of the
street. At home one infinitely preferred an evening
— though one hardly ever had one — without the

sound of human speech. But here, in these lonely, alien lodgings, and still only half-past eight...

So Mike Ferris had put on his hat and overcoat, and had gone along to the red call-box, and had found Uncle Robert's name in an extremely tattered directory, and had obeyed all the instructions relating to Button A and Button B, and presently there was an intermittent buzzing in his left ear, and then a man's voice said: 'Hullo?'

'Oh!' said Mike. 'Is that you, Uncle Robert?'

'Beg pardon, sir?' said the voice.

'Oh!' said Mike, blushing almost as hotly as the call-box. 'I'm sorry. I mean, is Mr. Trouton there — please?'

'What name, sir?'

'Oh!' said Mike. 'Mr. Michael Ferris. I mean, look here, if he's busy — I mean, I don't want to bother him if — I mean, look here, perhaps you could just tell him ——'

It was manifest, however, that the manservant had already gone, and that Mike was twittering at a vacuum. He blushed again. Had a sudden and, as it seemed, happy notion of replacing the receiver. Remembered, just in time, that he had already given his name. Waited. Heard footsteps. Heard another voice.

'Hullo?'

'Oh! Is that you, Uncle Robert?'

'What? Who is it?'

'It's Mike. Mike, Uncle Robert. I'm ——'

'Mike! Good lord! Nothing wrong, is there?'

'Oh, no, Uncle Robert. I mean, I'm in London. I'm just starting this job, you know. Or perhaps you didn't know. But Mother said ——'

'Eh? What did your mother say?'

'She (gulp) said I was to let you know I was here, and I'm awfully sorry if you're busy or anything, but ——'

'No, no,' said the voice, with a sudden sound of

breezy patronage. With a sound as though it had expected something much more troublesome, and was now delighted, or at any rate pleased, to be gracious. 'No, no,' it said. 'That's all right. Look here, you must — ah ... I mean, we must ——'

'Yes, Uncle Robert?'

'I mean,' said the voice, with a trace of irritation, 'I must see you, of course. Eh? Now — er...'

No help from the call-box, though it remained full of attention.

'Tomorrow?' suggested the voice, abruptly. 'Lunch, eh? Better come along to the Wanderers'. Know where it is? Yes, that's right — near the corner. One o'clock, and then we'll be certain of a table. That all right?'

How on earth was one to know whether it would be all right or not, when one was still so comprehensively ignorant of conditions at the strange office? Would one be released for lunch at all on the first day, or if one were released, would one have any control over the time? If only, thought the very young gentleman in the call-box, he had left well alone, and stayed indoors. But the grand and rather frightening voice was waiting, and of course there was only one thing to say.

'Thanks awfully, Uncle Robert,' said Mike Ferris. 'I mean, thanks awfully.'

'Eh?' said Mr. Trouton. 'Right.'

And there was a click in Mike Ferris's ear, and he emerged from the red call-box and returned to his new lodgings. And the hideous maidservant having admitted him to the hideous hall, he went upstairs, and roamed round his little sitting-room, and peered out of the window, and thought a great deal, and expended additional energy in trying not to think, and frowned, and looked at his watch. And having done all these things quite a number of times, he was eventually glad to find that it was

nearly ten o'clock.   So that now he passed through
into the other portion of his unfamiliar quarters, and
undressed, and went to bed.   And in due course
Mike Ferris fell asleep.

In due course, also, he awoke and got up.   At
eight o'clock he consumed a breakfast which was
certainly worth no more than he would presently
have to pay for it, and included an egg which didn't
taste like an egg, butter which didn't taste like
butter, and even — such are the resources of furnished lodgings — a loaf which didn't taste like a
loaf.   At half-past eight he made for the nearest
Underground station, travelled in an upright position for twenty minutes, alighted, was swept up
the steps with all the other trampling feet, and once
more found himself in the open air.

But if only it weren't so fine, he was thinking.
If only it were dark and gloomy on this first morning, as he had always imagined that it would be.
Not, thought Mike Ferris, that there was any dodging the hour that approached, and the life-sentence
which was to follow it; he'd known about the life-
sentence all this last year at school, and there'd
never really been any hope of going to Oxford or
Cambridge, and it was even lucky, perhaps — since
he had no practicable inclinations of his own —
that the affair had been taken out of his hands and
settled for him.   And of course if one's father were
dead and one were the eldest of five, then the
sooner one started real work, the better, and London
after all, was the place where people eventually got
on.   But London oughtn't to shine and glare like
this, and show one up and make one feel so con-
spicuous.   It ought and he had always imagined it
to be the kind of place where one's identity and
private feelings were swamped in a general greyness
and dullness; where one went about unnoticed and
unnoticeable; where one escaped all personal
responsibility and individual existence until, in six

months from now, one left it for one's first fortnight's holiday.

But in this bright March sunlight it was impossible to see London as one had seen it from Bedford.
It was stark and brisk and inquisitive and impertinent.   It stared at one, it knew that one was a new-
comer and a beginner, it insisted on throwing one
into relief.   Suddenly it came over Mike Ferris that
not even by the most passive acceptance of fate
could he avoid living every single instant which
separated him from September.   There would be no
blanks as he remained fettered to the ex-schoolboy
whom he could never elude.   Even here and already
committed to all the strangeness and uncertainty
that lay ahead, he had still, inevitably, got to go
on being himself.

He scowled and slackened his pace.   Curse everything, thought Mike Ferris; curse his appearance
and his age and his sex; curse the forbears who had
conspired to produce him, and the circle in which he
had grown up, and the school which he had just
left.   And curse Mr. Hammett for offering him this
job, and expecting him to be grateful for being
swizzled out of all but twenty-four hours of his
Easter holidays.   And curse the company which
was about to employ him, and the clients for which
it worked, and the goods which it supplied.   Not
that there was any alternative, now, to going on
and going through with it and doing what one was
told, and being puzzled and baffled and probably
bullied by all sorts of people whom he didn't know.
But if only — if only...

Few very young gentlemen whose nineteenth
birthday would fall in the following May can ever
complete this passionate protest.   They know, well
enough, that they don't want to go into offices and
live alone in lodgings, even if they would be honour-
ably revolted by the prospect of staying on and
idling at home.   But what do they want?   Just

to have a good time? Certainly not; they're not
as selfish and visionary as that. Fame, then? Or
Adventure? Or a swift bound to the top of some
tree? Don't be ridiculous; they know perfectly
well that they're quite ordinary young gentlemen,
and are a long way from becoming anything else.
But, oh, surely (they cry) something ought to
be different; there is some turning that they have
already missed; some terrible mistake has already
been made. By whom? They don't know, as
they gaze resentfully around, and see nothing
but the projection of their own bewilderment.
Is this, then, the only road to independence, with
the end years and years out of sight; or can it be
that everyone else is in the same ghastly boat, and
nobody else minds?

'Blast!' muttered Mike Ferris, with a fixed,
sullen glare at the high buildings on all sides of him.
And then somebody bumped into him and said:
'Pardon,' and shot off again. And instantly, as
if propelled by some unseen force, the very young
gentleman dashed recklessly across the roadway,
and hurried along a little street and passed, together
with a mob of pedestrians, between two omnibuses
on to the further pavement of a very big street;
and so turned down a middle-sized street — for he
hadn't forgotten an inch of this journey since his
visit to Mr. Hammett in January — and entered a
marble hallway, and took his place with a number
of passengers in a lift; and was borne upwards, and
was released; and smelt a smell which he hadn't
encountered for nearly three months, but now
recalled with sickening accuracy; and turned one
more corner and came to a glass door with the name
of the company printed on it in black lettering;
and paused, and gulped, and turned the handle.

There was a little counter, as he also recalled,
just inside the glass door, and beyond it, seated on
a radiator under the window, two young women

were engaged in talking and giggling to each other while they industriously manicured their nails. They looked round for a moment, appeared to see nothing, and then resumed their occupation.

'Excuse me,' said Mike Ferris, presently.

This time one of the young women did see him. She rose from the radiator, put down her nail-polisher, patted the back of her head, took two steps towards the little counter, and arched her eyebrows.

'Pardon?' she inquired — which seemed to be a very favourite word in London. 'Pardon?'

Mike Ferris asked if he could see Mr. Hammett.

'A bit early, aren't you?' said the young woman.

Mike Ferris said that he'd been told to be here at nine. The young woman looked sceptical and suspicious.

'That's funny,' she remarked. And then, with a sudden and mysterious brightness: 'Well, he's not here, anyway.' And then, with renewed misgivings: 'Is it from Dodman's?'

'From what?' asked Mike Ferris.

'Pardon?'

'I'm not from anywhere,' said Mike Ferris. This sounded imbecile. 'I mean,' he explained, 'Mr. Hammett told me to be here early this morning, and — and ——'

The second young woman suddenly left the radiator and began muttering to her colleague. They kept glancing at Mike Ferris. They tittered. They muttered again.

'Well,' said the second young woman, more audibly; 'I dunno, I'm sure.'

The first young woman appeared to be struck by an idea.

'I'll tell you what,' she said, turning back to Mike Ferris. 'Per'aps you'd better take a seat.'

'Oh,' said Mike Ferris.   'Thank you.'

On the other hand, there didn't seem to be any seat.

'Where?' he asked.

'Pardon?'

'I mean, where shall I ——'

Suddenly both young women started, stiffened, turned their backs and snatched at the waterproof covers of two typewriters.   A short, bald, bloodless man in spectacles came bursting out of an inner door and glared at them ferociously.   They began winding paper into their machines like mad, and the new arrival deflected his gaze at Mike Ferris.

'Yes?' he snapped.   'Yes?'

'Mr. Hammett wrote and told me ——'

'Ah!' interrupted the bloodless man, with slightly less venom.   'That's right.   What was the name?'

'Ferris,' said Mike Ferris, hopefully.

'That's right.   Ferris.   Of course.   A bit early, aren't you?   Well, never mind.   You'd better wait.   This way.'

Somehow it seemed that though the bloodless man could strike terror into typists, he was making the most of his present opportunity to lord it over Mike.   There was just a little uncertainty in his briskness.   The effect was to make young Mr. Ferris still more embarrassed and uncomfortable, as if he were now responsible for two inferiority complexes instead of one.

'In here?' he asked.

'That's right,' said the bloodless man, indicating yet another door.   ''S a matter fact,' he suddenly added, 'Mr. 'Ammett's down in the City this morning.   But I dare say Mr. Dixon'll see you when he comes.   Or if not —— Well, anyway, you'd better wait.'

And the bloodless man withdrew with an air of accomplishment, for what difference was there to

one in his position between a problem solved and a
problem shelved? And Mike Ferris found himself
in a little room with three glass doors and no window, and two chairs and a filing-cabinet, and an
electric pendant and a strip of hair-cord carpet,
and a hook on one of the doors, and nothing else
anywhere. And here he waited, not only because
he had been told to wait, but also because no other
course seemed open to him. Sometimes he heard
voices or the clattering of typewriters or the trilling
of telephone-bells, and sometimes he saw shadows
on one or other of the glass panels. Occasionally,
also, preoccupied figures of varying ages and sexes
came dashing through the apartment, which seemed
to be a kind of short cut as well as a waiting-room.
Few of them, however, appeared to see him, and
not one of them spoke to him. Nor did Mike
Ferris speak to them.

Once he actually had to move his legs while a
boy rummaged in the bottom drawer of the filing-
cabinet; but the boy said nothing, and he said
nothing, and presently the drawer was closed again
and the boy had gone. Thus it became ten
o'clock, and then half-past ten, and then eleven,
and then getting on for twelve. And still no word
had reached him, either from Mr. Hammett or
from the nebulous Mr. Dixon, or from anyone else
in authority, and still it hadn't occurred to him
— or else he lacked the courage — to leave his
glass-walled prison and draw attention to his
existence.

'They must know I'm here,' he thought. 'It's
not my business to keep on telling them.' And
yet he was filled with constant anxiety, not only
lest it should turn out that he really ought to be
doing something else, not only on account of the
hidden activities which were going on all round
him and in which he might be plunged at any
moment, but also because it again came over him

that the trap had now closed and that whatever
happened next must be even worse than what was
happening now.

It seemed incredible that he had ever wanted to
start this appalling job, that he had deliberately
done extra work so as to qualify for it, or that he
should actually have thanked the headmaster —
now clearly seen to be the Devil in disguise — who
had introduced him to Mr. Hammett. But he
had, and this was where it had landed him. And
now he couldn't go back. And now, he knew
perfectly well, he couldn't go on. A lump rose in
his throat. His eyes swam. Suddenly, in addition
to all these other physical and mental disturbances,
he became aware that he was ravenously hungry.

Once more he looked at his watch. Twenty past
twelve now, and —— By gosh! Uncle Robert!

All right, then. He was going. He'd had
enough of this hanging about, and he didn't care
if they asked for him, and he was going to get out
of this horrible atmosphere before he went mad.
Perhaps he'd tell Uncle Robert, and Uncle Robert
— who'd had the rare sense never to do a stroke
of work in his life — would help him somehow.
Inherited criticism of this mysterious relation,
whom he had been brought up to regard almost
as a black sheep — though a pretty comfortable
one, from all accounts — suddenly dissolved and
gave place to a wholly fresh outlook. One saw
him now not as the shirker of family legend, who'd
been left almost all Grandpapa's money and had
never married and had never done anything but
enjoy himself and whom mother could never mention (even when she had said: 'Let him know
you're in London') without making a kind of face,
but as a rock and a refuge in the midst of this unspeakable city. He'd understand, somehow. He'd
do something, somehow. And Mike Ferris was
going off to see him, at once.

And if anyone tried to stop him —— But they didn't. One can't say whether the impulse which fetched this very young gentleman out of the glass-walled waiting-room would have survived if he had met anyone in the outer office. But the outer office was empty. The typists had gone forth to their own lunch; the boy who should have been on guard was smoking (as a matter of fact) in the lavatory; every one of the innumerable doors was closed.

'All right,' said Mike Ferris savagely; and since he had never removed his overcoat, he merely replaced the hat which he was still grasping on his head, strode out into the corridor, turned the corner, ran down the stone stairs into the marble hall, and once more joined the crowds in the street. 'I've had enough of this,' he kept on muttering. 'It's their turn to wait now, and if they want me, they can jolly well send for me.' The breath of freedom and rebellion was in his nostrils, and since he already knew all about this part of London that can be learnt from a sixpenny map — or in other words, a great deal more than was known to many of its natives — no bee nor crow could have made more directly for St. James's Park and the suspension-bridge across its long lake. A subdued mumbling still kept the shreds of his conscience at bay. He wasn't at all sure, now, that he didn't feel rather like the hero of an adventure, after all.

17

WE know already that there was little enough gunpowder left in the heels of Mike Ferris's boots by the time that he reached his destination, and it was the rain which suddenly began to fall, more than any return of his courage, which actually sent him up those wide steps and through that big doorway. 'At least,' he muttered — though again it was the rain which had really given him the idea — 'at least I can ask.' And he asked, rather inaudibly, of a page-boy covered with buttons, and the page-boy said 'Yessir' (which meant that this was indeed the Wanderers' Club), and waved him towards the upper half of a uniformed porter in a glass and mahogany lair.

And the porter scrutinised him over his eyeglasses and said 'Yessir,' again; and waved him back at the boy. And the boy said, 'Thiswaysir,' and set off down a dark passage with Mike Ferris stumbling after him; and then suddenly stopped by a lot of hooks, until Mike Ferris realised that he was meant to remove his hat and overcoat — which he did, and the boy hung them up for him, and instantly set off again. And then the boy opened a colossal, soundless door, and stopped dead just inside it. And Mike Ferris shot past him on to an enormously thick carpet, and was just wondering what on earth he should do until his uncle appeared, when a large, red-faced figure came rolling down on him and slapped him on the back.

'Oh!' gasped the very young visitor. 'Hullo, Uncle Robert.'

'Well, young man,' said Mr. Trouton. 'Let's look at you.'

And he looked at him, and saw a pale, nervous, lanky lad wearing a suit which was quite obviously ready-made, and blinking at him with a face which for the moment was so like his widowed sister's that Mr. Trouton felt quite uncomfortable himself. Then, in the twinkling of an eye, the face changed and looked so exactly like that of his deceased brother-in-law, that Mr. Trouton (who had always disapproved of the marriage) instantly recovered his mastery of the situation. He seemed to become even larger and redder, as he glanced down at his own exquisite shoes and compared them with his nephew's boots.

'Ah!' he said. 'So you've come to London, eh? Well? How do you like it?'

Mike Ferris gulped.

'Well ——' he began.

'Wait a minute,' interrupted his Uncle Robert. 'You'll want a wash, won't you? Come along, then.'

Out by the colossal, soundless door, back into the dark passage, and so, suddenly, into a blaze of white tiles and glittering taps and long mirrors, and a clean smell of soap, and a splashing and gurgling as members dipped and fussed over the innumerable basins, or brushed their varying quantities of hair. 'Hullo!' they were saying to each other. And: 'Hullo, old man!' And: 'Well, you're back, I see.' And then just as Mike Ferris was wondering whether he, also, as a mere guest, were entitled to one of those little towels which everyone was snatching up and then hurling into gigantic buck-baskets, he heard his uncle's voice mingled with the others.

'Hullo! Where've *you* been all this time, eh? Well, look here, where are you staying? What? Well, look here, we must have an evening or something soon. Eh? Yes; I'll remind you. What? Ha, ha, ha!'

Mr. Trouton's friend hurried away, and Mr. Trouton turned back to his nephew. 'Very interesting feller,' he said. 'Just been out in the East. Known him for years.'

What a place this was, thought Mike Ferris; and what a life his uncle led! All in the middle of everything, and knowing all sorts of interesting people, and having evenings with them whenever he wanted to. Honestly, it was most awfully decent of him to have been so decent about this lunch, when he was obviously so busy and had such hundreds of friends. And in the reflection of this avuncular importance Mike Ferris no longer hesitated about the little towels, but seized one and dried his hands, and flung it daringly into the nearest basket. There! That had probably cost the Wanderers' Club at least a penny, but what were pence — or even shillings or pounds — in this stimulating and luxurious atmosphere?

'Ready?' asked Mr. Trouton. 'Come on, then.'

In the corridor outside Mr. Trouton again fell in with an acquaintance, and again greeted him with hearty interrogatives, and again (it might have struck some people) the acquaintance was remarkably nippy in making his escape. But to Mike Ferris this was all just part of the fascinating and crowded existence in which these impressive characters moved, and he gaped with genuine deference as his uncle once more informed him what an interesting feller that had been.

'Known him for years,' said Mr. Trouton. 'Been private secretary to three Foreign Ministers, and what he doesn't know about —— Oh, hullo, Renshaw! Haven't seen you for ages. When are we going to have another game of billiards, eh?'

'What?' said Mr. Renshaw. 'Oh, hullo! Good morning!'

Not exactly an answer to Mr. Trouton's question — and already Mr. Renshaw had dashed away in the other direction — but Mike Ferris was again just as much stirred when he heard what an interesting feller he had seen.

'Goes everywhere,' said Uncle Robert. 'Knows everyone. Got a lovely place down in the country too. I'm always meaning to go down there, only I never seem to have time. Well; here we are. Now, then, what'll you have?'

Their progress had brought them up some steps, and through an open doorway, and abreast of a long table absolutely crammed with great joints and pies and fowls and shellfish and bowls of stewed fruit and a representative display of cheese. Members were huddled in front of it, gently jostling each other as they stared at the profusion, and occasionally bent forward to get a closer view. Mike Ferris hadn't the faintest idea how to deal with such a giant's feast.

'Eh?' said Mr. Trouton. 'Or there's hot, you know.' A waiter slipped a card into his hand, and he began declaiming from it.

'Soup. Scotch broth or —— What? No soup? Well, fish, then. Eh? No? Well, roast beef, roast mutton, roast chicken? Or curry. What about curry?'

Mike Ferris detested curry, which not only burnt one's tongue, but also, in his case, produced a fierce and unhealthy perspiration. Curry, however, was clearly what his uncle wanted, and he was far too nervous to explain his objections.

'Curry, then,' said Mr. Trouton, returning the card. 'And which is my table?'

'This way, sir.'

The waiter, Mr. Trouton and Mike Ferris followed a swift, serpentine course into the furthest corner of the big dining-room, and the host and guest took their seats. Another waiter appeared with a round basket full of rolls and chunks of bread. A third waiter came forward with a wine-list.

'Drink?' said Mr. Trouton. 'What'll you have?'

'Water, please.'

'Water? Well, there's nothing like water. Yes,' said Mr. Trouton; 'I'll have water, too. No, I won't though,' he added. 'Russian stout.'

'One Russian stout, sir. Very good, sir.'

What a club! What an existence in which one called for drinks that no ordinary person had ever heard of, and was supplied with them at once. Not that Mike Ferris wanted Russian stout. Not, as a matter of fact, that his lips had yet tasted anything

more powerful than claret-cup at a Christmas party
— and they hadn't liked that any more than curry.
But the splendour of it all. The ease, the comfort,
the assurance. Of *course* Uncle Robert never came
down to Bedford when he could lunch like this
every day. Why should he? Mike Ferris had
definitely enrolled himself as a supporter of this
other side of his family, and blushed again when
he thought of his own. If only he could get Uncle
Robert to take an interest in him, surely there
was nothing in the way of introductions and short
cuts that couldn't be done. Why had he never
thought of this before? Mother's fault, of course,
and now she'd gone and hustled him into that
ghastly office without giving him a chance to try
anything else.

But if he didn't go back.... If he played his
cards properly now....

'Well?' said Mr. Trouton. 'And so you've
come here to work, have you? Well, how do you
like it?'

Honestly, it was almost as if there were an angel
in the room, just waiting there to answer one's
prayers. Mike Ferris began tearing at a chunk of
brown bread, and bubbling over with his case
against Fate.

'It's awful, Uncle Robert,' he said. 'I mean,
I've only just started, of course, but I've never
seen such an awful place. I mean, of course, one's
got to do something, but I do think they might
have let me choose a bit for myself. I mean, of
course, I'm *interested* in machinery, but this is only
the office end of it, and I don't see how it can ever
lead to *anything*. And it's the most awful office,
too, and nobody seems to care whether I'm there
or not; and it is a bit thick, you know, when I'd
really got an awfully good chance of going to
Cambridge. I mean, they made me do the scholar-
ship papers last autumn, and I didn't get less than

alpha minus in anything except Latin.   And what's
the use of Latin, anyhow?'

The bubbling ceased for a moment, for here was
the curry, and Mr. Trouton smiled.   With sympathy?   Not a bit of it.   But who wouldn't smile
if, to begin with, they were like Mr. Trouton, and
to go on with they felt what a very much pleasanter
life they had always had themselves, and if, to
conclude with, they had always disapproved of that
marriage and here was such positive proof that
they had been right?   For, naturally, any nephew
of Mr. Trouton's ought to go to the University as a
matter of course, instead of disgracing him by
turning up here in a suit like that and reminding
him of his sister's shame.   Not, thought Mr.
Trouton, that the boy was a bad boy, as boys
went.   But crude; raw; loutish; doltish; and a
trifle oafish.   The kind of boy whom he certainly
didn't propose to see again, at any rate, for the
longest possible time.   A real provincial hobblede-
hoy; but then what else, Mr. Trouton asked himself,
should he have expected?

Nothing, Mr. Trouton told himself, as the Russian
stout entered gratefully into his system.   The boy
was the precise product which anybody with the
least intelligence or foresight must have predicted,
and Mr. Trouton was even sorry for him in a way
— as one might be sorry for a beetle or a worm.
Bad luck, in a sense, that he'd never had a chance
and that one couldn't do anything for him.   But
then, thought Mr. Trouton...

No; he didn't think this.   It was more instinct
— and not a very nice instinct, either — than
thought that made him start bragging and expand-
ing a little now, as his nephew's hopeful eyes
watched him across the table.   His attitude became
a little more careless, his voice a little louder, as he
began acting the rôle in which he saw himself.   For
he was a success, you see; here he was, well dressed,

sleek, civilised and a member of a first-rate club, with comfortable rooms round the corner and a good manservant (though in this mood it pleased Mr. Trouton to describe Barker as a rogue), ready to do anything that he wanted. All this, thought Mr. Trouton, he had attained with no undue or undignified effort, but simply as the result (so he told himself) of knowing what he wanted. That was the secret, thought Mr. Trouton, and as he wallowed lightly in his soothing philosophy, he again knew that not one of his blessings was more than he deserved.

So that it was more out of kindness and generosity than anything else that he continued to exhibit himself, while the meal ran its simple but satisfying course, in some of the glory about which he was customarily so modest. At the Wanderers' Club he was known, in so far as he was known at all, as one of the most crashing and intolerable bores who had ever infested it. But to Mike Ferris, sitting there and believing everything that he said and goggling at him as he babbled of his social eminence, he was indeed an uncle of romance and an uncle to admire. Fancy, he had been at the big dinner that was in all the papers last week! Fancy, he had been behind the scenes at a theatre! Fancy, he was going to the Grand National!

And increasingly it seemed to Mike Ferris that only madness could explain his mother's attitude towards this miraculous figure, and that this was the life, and that here was the relative to pluck him forth from the rut. So that now Mike Ferris, also, exaggerated a little as he stammered of his hopes and ambitions, and felt himself becoming more and more a man of the world, and saw his puny triumph in being chosen by Mr. Hammett to enter his business merely as an obstacle in his true career.

'You see, Uncle Robert,' he said, 'if only

Mother'd *thought* a bit more, instead of just making me jump at this job.... Well, I mean, there *must* be something more suitable, mustn't there, if only one could meet the right sort of person? You know' — and here Mike Ferris giggled slightly at his own daring — 'honestly I've got half a mind to chuck this job, anyhow. I mean, if only you realised how they treated me this morning.... And I *know*,' said Mike Ferris, with inexplicable assurance, 'that I could get on like anything, if only I had the right sort of start. But Mother ——'

'Ah!' said Mr. Trouton, helping himself to a radish. 'Your dear mother. How well I know her!'

And the prickly thrill of wickedness ran up and down Mike Ferris's spine, and then vanished, leaving him more excited and reckless than ever. 'I will,' he was thinking. 'Yes, that's what I'll do. I'll write to Mr. Hammett and tell him just how absurd it is for me to go into an office like his — and that'll teach them to take a bit more trouble with the next person they get — and then — and then ——'

'Smoke?' said Mr. Trouton, at this point, producing the slimmest of gold cigarette-cases.

'Oh!' said Mike Ferris, with a start. 'Thanks awfully, Uncle Robert. Only, 's a matter of fact, I don't ——'

'Quite right,' said Mr. Trouton; and re-pocketed the cigarette-case and fished out a cigar for himself. And: 'Waiter!' he cried. 'A glass of port.'

'You see, Uncle Robert, if only. Well, of course, I don't want to bother you, but ——'

'Hullo!' said Mr. Trouton, abruptly — for no man had ever been deafer to what he didn't want to hear, and, besides, this was where he was going to glitter more than ever. 'Hullo!' he interrupted. 'Now, there's an interesting feller, if you like.

Just beyond that pillar there. D'you see? The one with his back to us.'

Mike Ferris span round and stared.

'Oh!' he said. 'Who is it, Uncle Robert? Do you mean that man with the funny tie?'

'Yes, yes,' said Mr. Trouton, stiffening slightly even at criticism of a fellow-member's guest's neck-wear. 'But that's nobody. I mean the one *this* side. Do you know who that is? Eh? That's Lord Ludgate.'

'Oh, I say!' gasped Mike Ferris, for hadn't he supported his lordship's periodicals — whenever pocket-money permitted — for years? 'Not really, Uncle Robert! Do you mean you *know* him?'

'Know him?' Mr. Trouton laughed lightly, and tapped the ash from his cigar. 'Of course I know him. Known him for ages. Long before he got his title, anyhow. Not a bad feller,' said Mr. Trouton, graciously. 'Self-made and all that, of course, but what's that nowadays?'

What, indeed, with Uncle Robert's approval? And supposing — well, why not? — supposing Uncle Robert introduced one, and one got a chance to say about those articles that one had written, and how one had jolly nearly edited the school magazine. Stranger things, thought Mike Ferris, had happened than that a meeting like this should lead to — to what? To anything. To everything. To escape, freedom, success and one in the eye for all the stick-in-the-muds who never dared take risks. Mr. Hammett? Away with Mr. Hammett. And away with even the memory of that dreadful morning in his little waiting-room.

'Uncle Robert — I say ——'

'Yes, my boy?'

'I say, do you think you could possibly — not now, I mean, but when you've finished your wine — I mean, I would like most awfully just to meet him.'

'"Him"? Eh? Oh, Ludgate, you mean. Well...'

Port on top of Russian stout is no great aid to swift thinking, but Mr. Trouton was quick enough as he weighed up the arguments. Old Ludgate (as he now apparently thought of him) was the last man to worry about his nephew's clothes, and any-how the boy'd probably be too shy to say anything. And to be able to show off like this, easily, airily, rapidly and without hesitation — well, of course. A whole lunch-time of incense may slightly have gone to this red-faced idol's face — but of course!

'Why not?' said Mr. Trouton, as the scent rose again and the worshipper gaped at him. 'Certainly, my boy. Delighted, if you really think you'd like it. In fact — just a minute' — (Here Mr. Trouton tossed off the rest of his port) — 'why not now?'

And Mr. Trouton rose, with a slight but successful effort, and patted the bulge of his well-cut waist-coat so as to dislodge a few crumbs, and twirled one end of his moustache, and took a firm grip of his cigar, and looked round the Wanderers' dining-room with the air of one who was at least as good as anyone within sight, and in all prob-ability rather better. Mr. Trouton also tapped his own thorax, as a man might well do in these semi-private surroundings, should the same man be threatened with the suggestion of a hiccup. And then, very large and red still, and very dull and pompous, and very highly pleased with himself, Mr. Trouton retraced a part of his serpentine course, with his nephew dutifully and expectantly following him, until they both arrived at the table just beyond the big pillar.

Here, it was true enough, the first Lord Ludgate was lunching with Mr. William Somerset — and not on curry, either. They had had oysters, and they had had guinea-fowl, with a very special salad, and they had both agreed to miss the sweet — thereby confirming a mutually favourable opinion which was still growing every instant — and now they were both munching and crunching some no less special biscuits and the Wanderers' very ripest Wensleydale cheese. And Bill Somerset was thinking: 'This man's got just the sort of face that I've wanted to paint for years,' even though it was an ugly, gnarled, cruel, selfish and cunning face. And Lord Ludgate, having already forgotten all about Mrs. Somerset, was thinking: 'I never make a mistake, and this young fellow's got the right stuff in him; and I'm a judge of character, I am, and you'll see where he gets to with me at the back of him.' And because Bill Somerset, though afflicted with that slight stammer, had never hesitated to look a possible sitter in the eye, and because Lord Ludgate, though brisk and brutal, felt a deep and secret respect for any expert in so remote a line of country, and because Bill was warmed and excited, and because the great magazine-proprietor was excited and warmed, therefore the two of them were getting on not only like a couple of houses on fire, but also like a pair of schoolboys who were playing truant at the same tuck-shop.

And Bill Somerset stammered his way through some extraordinarily good stories, and his lordship chuckled delightfully and capped them. And a glint shone in all their four eyes, and Lord Ludgate was tickled to death to find somebody whom it wasn't even worth while trying to frighten, and Bill, completely unself-conscious as ever, just said anything that came into his peculiar mind, while his right thumb played lovingly with the curves and angles of the hideous head opposite him. And even though it were as certain as death that Lord Ludgate always dropped everybody sooner than later, Bill knew nothing of this; nor, if he had known, would he have cared. For it was true enough that all he needed was a fair start and a clear run, and his undoubted genius would do the rest; while he would never notice being dropped by anybody so long as his wife Norah was there to catch him, which, of course, she always would be.

So into this curious merry-making, into this inspiring clash of complementary temperaments, there suddenly arrived — like a whiff of Monday morning in the midst of a perfect week-end — the pretentious figure of Mr. Robert Trouton (still accompanied by the goggling figure of his nephew), and Mr. Trouton's hand descended with a distinct and daring thump on Lord Ludgate's shoulder.

'Hullo, Ludgate,' he said.

His lordship slewed round and scowled out of his deep-set, darting eyes. And of course he knew Mr. Trouton both as a bore and a man-about-town. And he had even made use of Mr. Trouton in the past, when he was still burrowing his way upwards and needed men like this so as to burrow still further. And in the ordinary way he might even have tolerated that thump, and said a few condescending words, and then turned away again. But now — now, when he was having such fun with his new protégé, and was beyond all burrowing, and was warmed and excited, as has just been said, by the flame which ever flickered about Bill Somerset's other-worldly soul; now, in the middle of all this amusement and enjoyment, to be thumped like that by a big stiff of a good-for-nothing idiot — it was too much.

He didn't trouble to pretend. He merely looked mischievous, diabolical and tough as rawhide.

'Do I know you?' asked Lord Ludgate, as offensively as even he had ever spoken in his life. And then he turned his big, ugly head away. 'Go on, Mr. Somerset,' he said. 'Don't stop. It's nobody that matters.'

18

IT would be weeks, if not months, before Mike Ferris could think of that moment again without a feeling of disgust and sickness at the spectacle of his idol's collapse. If he had been older, if he had known more, if his own preposterous bubble hadn't been pricked at the same instant, perhaps it would all have been different. But youth, which is deceived by practically everything that tries to deceive it, has at the same time, oddly enough, a desperately clear eye for the truth. Its head may be in the clouds, but when the clouds part — as they had parted just now — it sees exactly and pitilessly and often agonisingly what they have revealed.

And Mike Ferris saw and knew that his rich, idle uncle was a fraud and an impostor, and that his own dreams had been the dreams of a senseless fool, and that no career can possibly start from a basis of weak imitativeness and snobbery, and that nobody either would or could do anything for him but himself, and that he had been petty and selfish and unpardonable to suppose that anyone could chuck a job because they hadn't been welcomed on the first morning with flags and trumpets, and that his mother — bitter though this pill might be — had been perfectly right for years, and that he was nothing and nobody but a miserable ex-schoolboy who had jolly nearly gone and mucked up everything within twenty-four hours of leaving home.

Horrible, shameful and degraded pity certainly had a share in the whirlings of his very young brain. He had seen the uncle on whom he had pinned such fantastic hopes crumple and look green, and then make that supreme but futile attempt to pretend that nothing had happened as they both sagged and tottered out of the Wanderers' dining-room. He had even said something about coffee, but the clear eyes had slithered past his deflated figure, and the nervous voice had broken into a mumble of excuses and thanks. Mike Ferris was awfully sorry, he said; he must get back to the office at once. Thanks awfully, he said, but he'd no idea how late it was, and honestly...

The deflated figure — though doubtless it would be pumped up again soon enough with its own resources of gas — seemed to vanish in the dark corridor; a little redder than usual in the face, perhaps, but no redder than the very young gentleman who started hunting madly for his hat and coat. Here they were, thank Heaven. Now, then. And Mike Ferris rushed forth into the hall, and burst through the big doorway, and dashed down the wide steps. The raindrops had turned to a sharp shower now, but it was haste more than any realisation of the weather conditions which caused him to scoot out into the roadway, and actually snatch the handle of a taxi door from the well-dressed stranger who tried to forestall him.

Could he possibly have done this save in the extremity of personal terror? Of course he couldn't, and he leapt up and down on the seat as the cab trundled back towards the office, and had the fare ready and was out again almost before it had stopped.

No time for the lift. Up the stairs like lightning. Along the passage, past the smell, round the corner. He all but collided with somebody coming out of the glass door.

'Oh, Mr. Hammett, I ——'

'Hullo! Oh, it's you, is it, Ferris?'

'Yes, sir. I ——'

'Sorry I couldn't get back sooner, and now I've just got to go out to lunch. But if you wouldn't mind waiting — in the waiting-room...'

Mind? One doubts if anyone had ever waited with more thankfulness and patience and deep, tireless, inexhaustible, hopeful calm.

19

THOUGH it still rained in the earliest afternoon of this day towards the end of March; though the brightness and false promise of spring had gone, though the greyness and true image of winter had returned; though the heavens dripped and splashed, and the pavements swam, and the gutters ran, and the policemen unfurled their capes and wheels spurted mud over innumerable ankles, yet the knot of faithful votaries who had been drawn once more by the sight of an awning outside a sacred edifice, still stolidly stood there and stuck it out. Some of them had umbrellas, some of them turned up the collars of their coats, quite a quantity of them — at this early stage of the proceedings — huddled under the rather inadequate shelter of the awning itself. But of course the main, though invisible, protection which sustained them one and all, and was the true cause of their presence here, and would have kept them, one imagines, at their self-appointed posts even if the rain had turned to sleet, snow, thunder and lightning, cloudbursts, earth-quakes, volcanic eruptions and tidal waves, was the magnetic magic of yet another fashionable wedding, and the warm, glowing stimulus which it sent pulsing through all their veins.

Not, of course, that you should picture a group of cupids or wanton nymphs. If anyone has fallen into this illusion, he should immediately extricate himself as quickly as he can. For, as a matter of fact, the individuals composing this devoted band were for the most part plain, drab and by no means particularly prepossessing. Nor was their average age so remarkably young. Nor did their faces shine as might Hymen's torchbearers or Aphrodite's attendants, being on the contrary, and again as a matter of fact, more notable for their look of dogged and even dismal determination. Nor, if it comes to that, had so much as one of these long-suffering addicts even the remotest personal acquaintanceship either with the Lady Hermia Viney, the bride for whom this awning had been erected, or with Mr. George Medmenham, the other contracting party, who had undertaken to lead her to the altar. It was merely that once more the call had been heard, and the call must be obeyed. And here they were, and here — rain or no rain — they intended to remain.

Yet it must be admitted that on this occasion the call had been peculiarly distinct. News was scarce, space must be filled, romance was so easily stimulated, or at any rate simulated, and Lady Hermia Viney had been public property, in a sense, ever since her emergence as a débutante. Not that she was an actual originator or ringleader in the blithering activities which gossip-writers delighted to chronicle, but she had always been there or thereabouts when the others were lashing themselves into further publicity; and she had a title, which is still something where gossip-writers are concerned; and certainly she was extremely pretty, which has never ceased to be something where all reasonable and unreasonable people are concerned. And her engagement had been rumoured, and then announced, and then contradicted, at least twice before — which the general public always finds delightfully diverting.

So now the newspapers had let themselves go, and had taken her up, and had photographed her, and had paragraphed her, and finally had headlined her, and thus had worked themselves into a passing frenzy and their impressionable readers into an even more aggravated form of the same distemper. And either because they had discovered that she was to be escorted by bridesmaids in yellow dresses or else because her grandmother had been a very rich American girl (though there was precious little of the money left by now), or simply because they happened to like the phrase, these same newspapers had taken to calling her the Golden Bride. So that now she was the Golden Bride to thousands and millions of readers — as the people who buy newspapers are called — all over the country, and even Mr. Albert Coffin (as you may possibly remember) had become aware of her forthcoming nuptials as he rumbled the wrong way round the loop towards his day's work in Messrs. Hamhurst's turnery department.

Accordingly that crowd assembled under and around the unconscious awning outside the north door of the sacred edifice. And policemen arrived and told them to stand back there, and they stood back, and were instantly thrust forward again, and became a little indignant with each other because two, not to say six, people can't occupy the same space at once. And the rain went on falling. And several seedy, saturated men kept setting on the huddlers and trying to sell them paper pocket-handkerchiefs with the names of the principals printed on them as a souvenir of the occasion; but did little or no business at this stage, partly because of the difficulty of displaying their wares in this weather and partly because their clients' enthusiasm was as yet damped by the same downpour. And another group kept on forming, and then giving it up, and then being replaced by indistinguishable units, on the further pavement. And the drivers of all kinds of vehicles slackened speed and stared perilously over their shoulders as they passed by, and tried to catch a glimpse of what couldn't conceivably be visible for at least another half-hour. And the wind flapped the wet awning, and the drops trickled down people's necks. And it occurred to a fat woman to tell her thin neighbour that it was a pity about all this rain, because you knew what they said about happy the bride that the sun shines on. And the thin neighbour clicked her tongue, and altruistically agreed. And other people either heard this fragment of vaticination, or else evolved it for themselves, so that it went the rounds among the addicts not once, but again and again. And stories were told of other brides and other weddings, as well as of all the legendary adventures with which the gossip-writers had credited this particular heroine and her circle of friends. In fact, the only aspect of the whole affair which escaped scrupulous dissection among these kind-hearted if immediately unproductive people was any kind of reference to the hero.

Nevertheless, Mr. George Medmenham distinctly and unmistakably existed, and was just as real and three-dimensional as any of those who seemed to have forgotten about him, even if he were also the very last person to wish them to remember. Very quiet, a slow, deep voice, a brown face, blue eyes, a haunting aura of fishing-rods and retrievers surrounding him even in London, and yet no mere country squire, living — as some of them still inexplicably manage to do — on his acres. Acres there were, and a stone house of gentle, exquisite beauty tucked away in the Cotswolds, but all this had been let until a couple of years ago, and if Mr. Medmenham had been like most of his family, nothing, one imagines, could have prevented its being sold. But he was different, it seems, somewhere inside and behind that unassuming brown face, and though he could easily have cashed in on his remaining assets and done anything he liked with the proceeds, and though this was what everyone expected him to do — because, of course, whatever happened, he mustn't give up his hunting — he had surprisingly done nothing of the sort. He renewed his tenants' lease of the stone house, and stopped hunting altogether, he came to London,

and he went into business. Nor did Mr. Medmenham go into the kind of cheerful, slapdash business
of, for instance, a half-commission man, who works
when he chooses, counts anything that he happens
to make as unadulterated profit, and so drifts about
on the edge of bankruptcy until presently he strikes
a rock and vanishes without a trace.

This, again, was exactly what his friends and
neighbours in the Cotswolds had expected, because
they really knew little or nothing about George,
and were merely assuming that he would be like all
the rest of his relations. But he wasn't, it seems,
and they were wrong. Still preserving his brown
face and quiet, deep voice, he had buckled to and
gone through the mill and learnt his job and come
out on top. Now he was busy, important — though
neither quality had ever revealed itself in his
manner — and definitely well-off. The extended
lease of the stone house expired, and this time he
didn't renew it. He put in electric light, and a
restrained form of central heating, and spent all his
week-ends there. The friends and neighbours
naturally expected him to start hunting again —
this, in their view, being the only justification for
life in their self-satisfied midst — but again, apparently, they were mistaken. Mr. Medmenham
made no attempt to hunt; lack of time was the
ridiculous excuse that he offered. Yet even as he
offered it, there was something in his brown face
which suggested that it wasn't an excuse at all;
that the fact was that he didn't want to hunt.

'Monstrous!' said the friends and neighbours.
What secret vice, they wondered, had so sapped
the decency and manhood of a Medmenham?
They gossiped madly, as was their tradition and
habit, and the gossip broke against the walls of the
stone house, and was shattered into a fine spray,
and fell to the ground and turned sour on them
and died. They tried saying that old George — he

was at this time about thirty-two — was potty.
But he quite obviously wasn't potty, even though
he exasperated them by his anti-social soft-heart-
edness as a landlord, and they had to give
up saying this too. So now he was accepted and
respected, which appeared to make absolutely no
difference to him whatsoever, and everybody said:
'Why doesn't he get married?'

Everything was done to help him towards this
desirable and entertaining end, but nothing happened. 'He's not human,' said the friends and
neighbours, as they met with disappointment
after disappointment. 'I've never known such a
fellow,' they said. 'Have you?' But George
seemed just as unaware of this criticism as when
they had said that he was vicious or potty. It,
also, withered away — and, besides, there was no
doubt that he was human whenever one actually
met him or talked to him or saw him with his
dogs. So now, again, the county was compelled
to take him as they found him, and secretly to
admit that there were honourable exceptions even
in their self-satisfied midst. And they became
rather proud of him — also secretly, because he
didn't hunt and wouldn't get married — and
thought they'd got him absolutely placed and taped,
which was perhaps all that they had really wanted to
do from the beginning, only it had taken so long
because they themselves were so slow. George
Medmenham, in fact, was a rich and slightly
eccentric bachelor of thirty-five, and would now
oblige the county by remaining in the category
in which they had with such difficulty fixed him.
He could, in fact, now become as rich as Crœsus
and as eccentric as old Lord Bumpstead, and the
county would be perfectly satisfied with him because this would merely prove that the county was
right. The audience relaxed its critical attention,
and was contented and at ease. And then, dash

it all, the telephones hummed and buzzed all over the Cotswolds, and all over the west end of London, too. 'Have you heard?' all the voices were asking. 'Have you heard the latest? George Medmenham. He's gone and done it. Yes. It's an absolute fact. He's going to marry Hermia Viney.'

20

THE reason for this unexpected action on the part of Mr. Medmenham was, it may instantly be admitted, one of the best possible reasons that there can be. He had fallen deeply, conclusively and absorbingly in love with Lady Hermia. Moreover, Lady Hermia — who had accepted him, anyhow — was practically convinced that she returned his passion.

Not entirely or unquestionably — though George was only allowed to guess this, and it never occurred to her that he did guess it — on account of several causes. For one thing, there were the previous engagements or half-engagements, which had seemed such fun at the time, and then had seemed so ghastly and tiresome, and then had left one a little doubtful as to whether one could ever really go on being fond of anybody. Also, there was one's own curious and interesting nature, originally complicated by the inherited characteristics of quite uncontrollable ancestors on both sides of the Atlantic, and subsequently kept from ever settling into one channel by the fact that her ladyship had never really had anything to do. 'Really,' of course, is the important word here, for there was little or nothing that her ladyship hadn't done at one time or another; but always as a game, always for fun, always because other people were doing it or going to do it, or because she didn't want to be bored. These, as all virtuous readers know, are no reasons for careering through six seasons as

Lady Hermia Viney had careered through hers,
and though time may be killed, care will remain,
and boredom can never be kept at any great distance from people who think that they have interesting and curious natures.   Virtuous readers,
in fact, at this stage will feel more than authorised
to sniff slightly at the thought of Lady Hermia
Viney, to mutter a few wise words about the dangerous effect of such creatures on the minds of an
incredible number of unemployed, and to classify
her promptly and derogatively as an unmistakable
Bright Young Person.

Only wait a minute.   One won't, in the character
of a red herring, inquire what exactly a Bright
Young Person is, but one will and must come
butting in to explain how little self-consciousness
attached to Lady Hermia's exploits.   For the true
Bright Young Person always practises with an
eye, if not an eye and a half, on the crowd, and
commits none of her ingenious or ingenuous excesses
without making pretty certain that the *Daily Dash*
or the *Evening Blank* shall hear of it, and thus
raises herself by her own suspenders (or whatever
else she may happen to be wearing) to an imaginary
eminence from which she looks extremely contemptuously on the less chuckle-headed portions of
the human race.   Whereas Lady Hermia Viney
neither knew nor cared how often her name appeared
in print, and neither knew nor cared whether she
were recognised or not as she went about with her
friends, and merely took part in their antics because her upbringing had landed her in this circle,
so that it seemed the natural thing to do; and
didn't look contemptuously on anybody, perhaps
because, even in all the shifting turmoil of these
whirling times, she had never quite rid herself of
the inherited notion that *noblesse oblige*.   The fact
was that even at her wildest, silliest or vaguest,
she never entirely ceased being a lady.

Not that one is suggesting that her character was perfect; for it wasn't.   But always, and in spite of everything else, there was a core of nice girl in this sign of the times and product of the ages, however much other people tried to overlook it and she herself tried to escape it.   Perhaps she needed smacking even more than she needed loving or helping — which provide so much pleasanter a treatment, and were all that Mr. Medmenham proposed to do. But chiefly she needed to love somebody — preferably George — herself.   Only she couldn't be certain because of the previous mistakes, and because she still kept thinking about her curious and interesting nature; and because of Archie Ryder.

Of course Archie was a Devil.   Everybody knew that, and everybody knew that he was a most awful rotter, and that he had treated dozens of women quite abominably, and that nothing and nobody could ever hope to make him run straight. But does any of this knowledge make a man like Archie Ryder less attractive, or less dangerous, or more easily to be eradicated from the system? Of course it doesn't.   And though the Golden Bride knew all about Archie, and all about his tricks and his devilishness and the way that he let people down, she still couldn't forget him, and she still felt excited and nervous and unsteady whenever she heard his name.

The funny thing was that she had never really bothered about him at all — in fact, she had laughed and had pointed out that he was going bald, whenever other people had said what a Devil he was — until just after she had got engaged to George. Then, though it seemed impossible now to believe it, she had been absolutely certain that this was the most marvellous thing that had ever happened, and she had told everybody at the party that night, and everybody had been terribly surprised

and had said how splendid, darling. And then
Archie had suddenly looked at her across the table,
and from that moment...

It seemed equally impossible now, but she'd gone
home and rung him up. Of course he'd meant
her to do it; he was like that — he could make one
do anything. But she'd known that it was exactly
what he was expecting, as soon as she'd heard his
voice.

'Oh,' he had said. 'So it's you.'

'Yes, Archie. I ——'

'Yes? Well?'

'Oh, Archie, I feel awfully worried suddenly.
I — I can't think why I wanted to speak to you,
but — but ——'

'I'm glad you did,' said Mr. Ryder. And there
was a pause, and then: 'I hoped you would.' And
there was another pause, and then: 'Why on earth
have you gone and done this?'

What a monstrous thing to have said! What
absolute cheek and caddishness and —— Yes,
but why on earth *had* she done it?

'Oh, Archie — you don't understand. I think
I'm mad or something, and I never meant to ring
you up at all, but ——'

'Yes, you did,' said Mr. Ryder's voice. 'We
must talk about this. Don't you think?'

'Oh, Archie ——'

'Tomorrow, for instance. At lunch. Sorry I
can't call for you, but...' He mentioned a quiet
little restaurant and a time. 'By the way,' he
added, 'I never wait more than ten minutes.'

'Well,' said Lady Hermia Viney, 'if you think I'm
going to chuck two other engagements ——'

'Two?' said Mr. Ryder, mockingly. 'Oh, lord,
no. Quite unnecessary. But you know where I'll
be — for exactly ten minutes — don't you? Right
you are. Good night, darling.'

Click! went his receiver, and Lady Hermia

glared furiously at her own instrument.   Not that
'darling' meant anything, even if ——   But of
course that was her imagination.   And of course
she *had* been mad, and of course she wasn't going
near that quiet little restaurant, and of course —
though this wasn't quite so certain — he'd feel an
awful fool when she didn't.   So then, of course,
and when the time came, she did.   And there was
Archie, looking just the same as ever, and neither
pleased nor surprised nor anything else.   And they
had lunch together, and they never talked about
anything.   That's to say that they just talked, and
Archie was rather amusing about all the things he'd
been doing and about the weaknesses of various
friends; and every now and then Lady Hermia
tried to say something about her engagement —
just in a general way, you know, because of course
she wasn't going to discuss George — and every
time she failed, because it seemed that Archie was
heading her off.   So that she was rather annoyed
with him, only he didn't seem to notice that, either.
So that it then struck her that perhaps she was
being rather unfair to him — Mr. Ryder was extraordinarily skilful at creating this illusion — and she
tried to make amends by being rather friendlier
than she really felt.   And Mr. Ryder suddenly
became rather silent and stared at her.   And then,
still more suddenly, he said:

'Of course you know what a cad I am.'

Lady Hermia laughed, a little uncomfortably.

'Rubbish, Archie,' she said.   'You know people
say anything about anybody.   I wish you wouldn't
talk like that.'

'Well,' said Mr. Ryder, 'don't ever say I haven't
warned you.   Cigarette?'

'Oh, thanks.'

'Light?   Here you are.'

'Thanks.   Thanks, awfully.'

'And of course,' said Mr. Ryder, 'I'm broke

to the wide, and even if I weren't, I'd never ask anybody to marry me. All the 'same,' said Mr. Ryder, extinguishing his own cigarette, and making the fullest use of his dark, mournful eyes; 'all the same, Hermia, you know what I mean.'

Lady Hermia didn't know what he meant. It isn't at all certain that he knew what he meant himself. But this was the game that he always played, and it disturbed her, as it was intended to disturb her, and made her nervous and doubtful and put what are called ideas into her head. And one of these ideas was that perhaps, after all, she had been rather hasty in accepting George. And another idea was that perhaps it was not so much safety as suffocation that she felt in his presence. And a third idea, one is sorry to say, was that Archie was known to be one of the rottenest men in London, yet it was distinctly flattering to have him using his eyes and his drawl like this.

Why? It doesn't seem logical. Surely there's nothing clever in attracting a man who is attracted by anybody and everybody. But women — so it seems — don't look at it like this. They can't, obviously, wish to sink their identity and become one of a crowd of dupes, but the point is, apparently, that men like this must be taken as offering a challenge. Can the woman whose turn it is now make such a tremendous impression that the crowd is forgotten? If she can, and she's almost always convinced that she can, then what a wonderful woman she must be. And of course she's a wonderful woman — especially when she has such a curious and interesting nature — and of course it's her duty to prove it. When she has proved it, then it will be great fun, because she'll turn round and start breaking the Lothario's heart, which will be the best sport in the world. Meanwhile, one mustn't lose him while he's still nibbling at the hook, and when there are so many poachers on both banks.

So one reels out a bit more line, and away he goes with it, and then, by Jove, he's got it all and he's tugging at the rod, and there's no letting go now, and there's a slither and a faint cry for help and a splash, and this, it seems, is how the best sport in the world has ended again. The quarry turns over and lazily opens his vicious jaws, snaps them, and is instantly ready for more. The angler has learnt too late what happens when once this so-called fun begins.

Thus, then, while the newspapers boomed her romance and George Medmenham gave her presents and wrote what he imagined to be love-letters to her — and certainly they smouldered, even if he could never quite make them burn — and went to see her every day as soon as he left his office, and arranged for the redecoration of his stone house in the Cotswolds, and paid a premium for the very smartest of flats in London; thus, then, while the engagement hurtled through its fashionably short career, Archie Ryder also continued to appear, and vanish, and appear again when he wasn't expected, and to look things which he never said, and to say things which had nothing whatever to do with his looks, and, one supposes, either to amuse himself by these time-honoured methods, or else to follow a track which was now worn so smooth that he couldn't get out of it if he tried.

And George Medmenham met him sometimes, and didn't much like him; but never said so, because he seemed to be one of Hermia's friends. And Archie always contrived to be particularly entertaining on these occasions, so that George seemed slower and stolider than ever. And at about this period, though she had no intention of doing anything mad or reckless, and was still practically convinced that she liked Mr. Medmenham as much as she had ever liked anybody, it yet came to pass that her ladyship no longer noticed or thought

about the bald spot on the back of Mr. Ryder's
head. A dangerous moment, no doubt, when she
could no longer see anything quite so obvious.
And there were more dangerous moments when,
either intentionally or accidentally, she didn't see
other things; or saw them, and said to herself:
'Oh, well. It's only poor Archie, after all. And
I can't help it if he likes me.'

And poor Archie did everything that he had
always done before, and advanced so cheerfully
that no one could possibly stop him, and retreated
so abruptly that one simply had to call him back.
And there was a scene or two — quite electric,
although her ladyship still thought she was only
playing at it all, and Mr. Ryder knew he was.
And people talked, of course, and on the whole
seemed rather pleased with the prospect of George
being made a fool of and Archie once more contributing to this state of affairs; not that these
people were naturally cruel or wicked or diabolical,
but just because they had no responsibility, and
because tragedy, to outsiders, is always more
amusing than comedy. George seemed so blind
and simple that honestly one couldn't help laughing
at him; while as for warning him — well, who
wanted to warn a man with a jaw like that and a face
that colour, and, as everybody was beginning to say,
with no sense of humour? No, thank you very
much; let George look after himself.

'Hullo! Is that Mr. Ryder's rooms? Oh, is
that you, Archie? Where on earth have you been
all day?'

'Racing, darling. Didn't I tell you?'

'No, of course you didn't. You said you were
coming ——'

'By Jove, so I did. Look here — shall I come
along now?'

'No — I'm busy now, Archie.'

'Eh? Oh, of course.'

Neither of them ever mentioned George's name now — to each other, that's to say — but he could be criticised and defended, and the engagement could be criticised and defended, without that.

'Only, Archie ——'

'What?'

'Afterwards, perhaps ——'

'After what?' said Mr. Ryder; and laughed; and rang off, still laughing, so that one didn't know whether he were coming or not. And was indignant. And was tormented. And said to oneself: 'I must be going mad!'

And then, suddenly, one was in George's arms, and George was so awfully steady and safe and sweet and loving, and honestly one was nearly certain that one adored him. All Lady Hermia Viney's respectable ancestors, of whom there was quite a quantity if you started adding them up, came rushing forward to tell her that George meant happiness and that Archie meant misery. And she heard them and believed them, and forgot everything now except how lucky she was and how even luckier she was going to be; and was thrilled and excited, and looked far prettier than ever.

'Oh, George, you are so good to me.'

'Rot,' said Mr. Medmenham.

'Oh, George, I do wish it was going to be sooner.'

'Do you?' said Mr. Medmenham, looking at her, and through her, and then catching her in his arms again. One never, which was so delicious sometimes, had to bother what George was thinking about; or perhaps ——

'George! You're not going!'

'Must, darling. This dinner. I told you.'

'But it's only business. Oh, well; you see how good I am. I'll let you go.'

An awful, hollow emptiness. Nobody else was

at home, of course. They never were. What could
one do? Where could one go? Whom could one...
 Enter an earl's butler.
 'Mr. Ryder, m'lady.'
 Exit the earl's butler. Enter Archie, still laughing. Enter, also, the ghosts of dozens of Lady
Hermia's disreputable, uncontrollable ancestors,
positively herding into the room so as to see how
the game is going; yes, and to help it on. Dash
it, her ladyship is looking even prettier than she did
just now.
 'Well?' says Mr. Ryder, taking her hand and
kissing it. 'Well, you little devil?'

21

WAS Mr. Ryder cold-blooded and calculating or
hot-blooded and haphazard? His victims never
knew; and this, perhaps, was how they became
his victims. At first they felt that of course they
were the only ones who really understood him;
then they weren't so certain, but it would all be
clear if only they could see more of him; then they
did see more of him, and generally speaking were
lost. Lady Hermia Viney would undoubtedly have
been lost if she hadn't kept on meeting George as
well; and if every time she met him she hadn't come
to the conclusion that he was really the most marvellous man she knew. Only then it came over her that
there was nobody like Archie either; so amusing and
impertinent and so clever at making one feel amusing
too. And of course one could always stop him
when he became tiresome — only sometimes it
seemed that one had almost to egg him on first, and
then the point at which one actually did stop him
became less and less definite. But then, one decided, this was one's last fling, and Archie knew that
as well as anyone. As soon as one was safely
married, that would be the end.

Or would it?   Sometimes that seemed a terrible way to treat poor Archie, and sometimes he looked so sad that one knew he was thinking about it. So then one had to be rather specially kind to him — imagine a bird being specially kind to a rattle-snake — and then one was sorry about this too, because, oh, dear, was one making a terrible mistake in getting married at all?

Archie didn't think so, obviously.   Or if he did think so, then he was behaving terribly well.   That softened one towards Archie, so that again one was rather specially kind to him.   And then rather specially kind to George, so as to soothe one's con-science and one's respectable ancestors.   All very confusing, in fact, to the bird, who still thought herself so curious and interesting; but the rattle-snake, of course, knew just what he was doing. For the rattlesnake, strange as it may appear, had a code of dishonour, and the code set limits to his conduct with Lady Hermia Viney but none to his conduct with Lady Hermia Medmenham.   Even right at the end of the short engagement, when there was an extraordinary midnight scene in which her ladyship wept and said that she had never been so miserable in her life, Mr. Ryder kept his head and merely patted her shoulder.

'Don't worry,' he said.   'I'll see it all comes right.'

'Oh, but it can't!' cried her ladyship.   'Oh, Archie, you don't understand!'

And, as a matter of fact, Mr. Ryder didn't under-stand, though he thought he did.   He had no idea that anyone so pretty or anyone in that set could hate and despise herself for being fascinated by such a rascal.   And when she moaned and said: 'Oh, Archie, I can't go through with it,' it never occurred to him that this reluctance was based on shame, or that it was George whom she was thinking of and pitying.

'Rubbish, darling,' he said. 'You can't back out now.' Because if she did back out, what was he going to get out of it all in the way of love and, in due course, money? 'What you need,' he said, 'is to dry your eyes and have a good rest, and then ——'

'But, Archie, I can't never see you again!'

What a ridiculous idea, thought Mr. Ryder, though he appreciated the agony in her voice. And: 'Rot, darling,' he said. 'What are you talking about? You'll see me at the wedding tomorrow, and then ——'

'Will I?' cried her ladyship, wildly. 'Where?'

'In the church, of course.'

'But there'll be such a crowd, Archie.'

'All right. In the vestry, then. Only, look here, darling, you must be sensible, because...'

Even Mr. Ryder couldn't exactly say: 'Because I'm going to seduce you as soon as you're safely married.' Nor did Lady Hermia Viney extract this definite meaning from his soothing words. But she did stop crying, and she was terrified and perplexed and bewildered, and she wished desperately that she knew what it all meant, and that there were some hole that she could pick in George's character so that she needn't feel so wicked, or else that her own character could appear more admirable so that she could at least comfort herself by the knowledge that she was absolutely chucking herself away. Neither of these consolations, however, did more than flicker in the intangible offing, and she shed a few more tears, and Mr. Ryder could quite easily have kissed her.

But that wasn't his game, at this critical stage, and he didn't.

'You go to bed, darling,' he said. 'You're worn out.'

'Yes, Archie. Oh, Archie ——'

'Eh?'

'You *will* be there tomorrow, won't you?   I *shall*
see you, shan't I?'

'Of course!' said Mr. Ryder, as he picked up his
hat and overcoat.   And how like all women, he
thought, to want to eat their cake and have it,
and always to want to make one man miserable while
they made another man happy.   Not that he was in
the least danger of being made miserable, now that
everything was working out just as he had planned.
He could have laughed, in fact, as he let himself
out of the earl's mansion, and thought how little
that ass George Medmenham knew what was in
store for him, and what an ass that ass George
Medmenham had been to go home so early on the
eve of his marriage.

'But of course,' thought Mr. Ryder, 'fellows who
work like that...'

And instead of laughing, he sneered and gave a
really revolting snigger, and went off to a night-
club.   Here he danced with a rich old woman who
contributed to his present support, and thought
with pleasure how soon he could dispense with her
society.   At first he looked so cheerful that she felt
vaguely suspicious and uneasy.   Then, as her weight
told on him, he became gloomy again, and the old
woman was relieved.   'He's terribly good-looking,'
she thought; and of course as long as there are
women of any age to think this about transparent
scoundrels, so long will transparent scoundrels
flourish.

22

GEORGE MEDMENHAM went to his office as usual,
and left in time to change and have a hasty lunch
with his best man.   The Golden Bride had a very
busy morning — a morning in which she was far
too busy to think — with dressmakers and friends
and relations and servants and telephone-messages
and people who came to snatch last-minute inter-

views and to take last-minute photographs. Archie
Ryder slept late and long in his bachelor quarters,
and breakfasted off a whisky-and-soda, and cursed
the maid who disturbed him by trying to dust his
sitting-room, and cursed the ex-butler who came
in to remind him about his bill, and cursed a
wretched little creature who arrived to remind him
about another bill, and filled in the intervals by
lounging in an arm-chair — and also in his dressing-
gown — and reading a lot of newspapers, and
occasionally telephoning to his bookmaker.

About half-past twelve he yawned, rose, and
began putting on the garments of a wedding-guest.
Very smart indeed — though still a little sallow —
did Archie Ryder appear by the time that he had
completed this task, for though he was always selling
what he called his old clothes, he was always ordering new ones. A glossy top-hat, a pair of yellow
gloves and a neatly-furled umbrella were added to
this vision of masculine perfection, and Mr. Ryder
left the chaos in his bedroom and descended to the
street. He wore no overcoat, because he never
felt cold and because he was convinced that the sun
would soon be out again. The neatly-furled umbrella was tucked under his arm, the yellow gloves
were clasped behind his back, and the top-hat was
now tilted slightly forward over his dark eyebrows
and dark eyes. Thus he turned a corner or two,
shouldered his way through a revolving door, and
descended into an underground bar. The white
jacket behind it greeted him, one or two heads looked
round and nodded. Mr. Ryder ordered a club
sandwich and a pink gin. Laid down his umbrella.
Removed his hat and gloves. Sagged into a comfortable attitude with one foot on a brass rail and
one elbow on the bar counter. Ate, drank and
smoked, slowly, simultaneously and sardonically.
Occasionally he turned his head to fling a few words
into the general and aimless conversation of the

other habitués, and the other habitués always agreed with what he said — for though not exactly afraid of him, they knew how easily he became quarrelsome at this time of day. And though not exactly looking up to him, they knew that he had once been more of a gentleman than they could ever hope to become. Somebody came in with an evening paper, and Mr. Ryder cursed when he heard the result of the first race at Liverpool.

Not that he wouldn't have saved himself on the place-money, but then, of course, one ought to do better than that. Besides, he always cursed at these moments, even when he had landed a long shot, because once these fellows thought you'd got any money, they were round you like flies. Let 'em wait, though, thought Mr. Ryder; he wouldn't be skulking down here in a month or two, when he'd started on George Medmenham's bank account — behind the silly ass's back. A distinctly disgusting smile flickered across his face, as he shoved his little glass towards the bar-tender.

'Another, sir?'

'Eh? No. Scotch and splash. And look sharp. It's later than I thought.'

The bar-tender looked extremely sharp. Trickle, pop, fizz, and the rattle of change.

'Going to this big wedding, sir?'

The habitués pricked up their ears, and Mr. Ryder wasn't above accepting their homage.

'Yes,' he said. 'No peace for the wicked, eh? Well!' And away went the whisky and soda, and Mr. Ryder picked up his hat and umbrella and gloves, and gave a swashbuckling leer round the cavern, and scowled at an habitué who was rash enough to leer back at him, and so strode up the stairs, and again shouldered the revolving door, and stopped suddenly on the threshold.

'Hell!' he observed. 'It's raining.' And: 'Taxi!' he shouted.

But the taxi went splashing by with its flag down. Mr. Ryder stepped out on to the pavement and waved his umbrella. A second taxi went by like lightning.

'Blank!' said Mr. Ryder. But of course there'd be one just round the corner in the Square, and it hardly seemed worth opening his umbrella for such a short distance. He set off quickly, and there, sure enough, was a third taxi just setting down its fare.

'Hi!' shouted Mr. Ryder, beginning to run. But either the driver didn't hear him, or else the driver had already sighted another client — a very young gentleman in a bowler hat and overcoat who had come shooting out of the Wanderers' Club; no other, in fact and of course, than our old friend Mike Ferris. So the driver swerved and clapped on his brakes; and then, just as Mr. Ryder came dashing in to pounce on what he naturally regarded as his prey, the very young gentleman cut in front of him, leapt on to the step, was inside, had shouted an address, and had gone — all while the veins on Mr. Ryder's forehead were still swelling with annoyance and surprise.

'Hi!' he shouted angrily. 'Hi, there — blank you!' And: 'Honk!' growled the snout of an enormous limousine as it swept round the corner. Mr. Ryder skipped sideways, and his new patent-leather shoes betrayed him. He slithered wildly, sat down with extreme violence, and the enormous limousine stopped dead. But can a gentleman attend a fashionable wedding at a sacred edifice when his only striped trousers are covered with mud, his only silk hat is rolling in the gutter, and — alas! — one tail of his only morning-coat has been ripped from its moorings by the non-skid diamonds of a colossal pneumatic tyre?

No need to answer this question while Mr. Ryder curses and fumes and harangues a policeman and exchanges names and addresses with the surly chauffeur who, for some reason, seems to have all the populace on his side. Mr. Ryder will definitely not be among those present at the solemnisation of holy matrimony between Mr. George Medmenham — very square, stolid and deep-voiced in his responses — and the Lady Hermia Viney — paler, almost, than her wedding-dress and practically inaudible under yards of ancestral lace. Nor, one imagines, will Mr. Ryder have repaired the ravages to his costume in time to mingle with the other guests, and sip the champagne, and inspect the presents, at the reception which is to follow the ceremony.

But that, as it happens, could make no difference now. For as the organ started rumbling and booming, not to mention fluting and twittering, and as the bride and bridegroom and their retinue and their relations and a certain number of pushful persons who had no business there at all, all congregated in the vestry for the signing of the register, the Lady Hermia Medmenham, no longer veiled, glanced here and there, at first nervously, then doubtfully, and finally with a look of hauteur which well became her aristocratic beauty. And then, suddenly, the Lady Hermia Medmenham looked at her husband, and as suddenly it came over her that in all this chattering crowd — nay, in all the world that she knew and the world that she didn't know — this solid, sunburnt, and utterly reliable companion was the light of her life and the idol of her existence; that she loved him, in fact, as she had never loved and could never dream of loving anybody else on earth; that she was his and he was hers; and that it no longer mattered in the very least how curious and interesting she was, because there stood the centre of her entire being who was going to keep her safe for ever and ever. So that even as her Uncle Hereward stepped forward and planted a smacking kiss on her left cheek, her eyes remained fixed and constant on those in the brown face that was watching her. That was George, her husband, and nobody else existed.

So the organ twiddled its way into the wedding march, and fashionable women (one regrets to report) stood up on the pews, and down the aisle came the happy pair, and out of the west door where the knowing huddlers had again gathered in preparation for this tremendous climax.

'There!' said the indefatigable fat woman to her equally indefatigable thin neighbour, as the crowd behind pushed them forward and the policeman in front shoved them back. 'Coo! Don't she look sweet! And look — I say — there's the sun come out again, after all. Well, isn't that lucky! Here — I'm going to have one of those hankies, I am. I didn't feel so keen on her, you know — not ackcherly — when I see her going in; but look at her smiling now. Just look at her smiling! Here — I say! How much are those sooveneers?'

It seemed that the fat woman had voiced the mood of the entire mob. The handkerchief-sellers, who had almost abandoned hope during the long, dripping wait, suddenly found that they could hardly produce their wares, or raise their prices, fast enough. There was even a cheer as the Golden Bride drove away behind Mr. Medmenham's chauffeur — still clinging firmly to Mr. Medmenham's left arm.

'Oo, don't she look 'appy!' said everybody. And she did.

23

'PADDINGTON MURDER,' said the newspaper placards, suddenly. 'Man Detained.' The news went dashing about on the sides and hindquarters of red and yellow vans, flapped from the grasp of hurrying figures in cloth caps, was tied round lamp-posts, woven into railings, flattened out under stones and old horseshoes or fitted into a neat arrangement of spring clips by other figures in varying species of uniform; and, last of all, would be added to the adornment of a hundred railway-station bookstalls.

Mr. Alfred Percy Scatcherd, however, though he read the legend and fully appreciated the implication, had no thought of wasting a penny on the doubtful chance of obtaining further details. For one thing, he wasn't interested — Paddington being to him much as China may possibly be to you, and murder being a pretty commonplace affair, in any case. For another thing, having once sold evening papers himself — though not for long, because he never did like regular hours — he still felt that he ought to see them for nothing, and therefore seldom saw them at all. Finally, having just cleared a profit of five and elevenpence — and, by gum, he'd thought he was going to be stuck with all his stock right up to the last minute — on the sale of souvenir handkerchiefs outside Lady Wotsername's wedding, he was far too anxious to celebrate this triumph by a mild-and-bitter to worry about the detention of anybody but himself.

So Mr. Scatcherd ambled and hobbled and slid and stumbled away from the wide streets and high buildings as fast as his legs and boots would allow him — for it would be closing time at the 'Duke of Brunswick,' if he didn't look pretty nippy. And soon enough the streets were narrower and the houses were lower, and the noises were harsher and the smells were fiercer. And then he plunged and ducked into the fiercest smell of all, and in another instant he was watching the handles of the beer-engine dipping in obedience to his order.

A delightful sight, thought Mr. Scatcherd, and a rare bit of luck the way they'd all started a-scrambling for those ankerchiffs just at the end, and five and eleven was a tidy sum to make on a job like that. He sought for no cause — though we, of course, can trace it all the way back to Pocklington Road out at Edgerley; he merely detected an arbitrary softening on the part of a Providence which seldom took the trouble to smile on him, and certainly wouldn't, in the natural course of events, smile much longer. Meanwhile, the moment was a good moment, and the mild-and-bitter — though shockingly weak and abominably expensive in these degenerate times — was exactly what Mr. Scatcherd's otherwise rather hollow interior craved. He drank, he smacked his lips, and he drank again. He slammed the empty tankard down on the nickel counter, and wiped his mouth with the back of his distinctly dirty hand.

'Ar!' said Mr. Scatcherd, contentedly and lingeringly. And the mild-and-bitter seemed to flow through his veins, and to give him both courage and hope. Should he treat himself to a fag as well, or — Well, why not, after all? What was one mild-and-bitter in these degenerate times, and hadn't he still got more than five bob in his pocket — he felt for it quickly, for the lining was none too strong — and hadn't he done a good day's work, and wasn't he going straight back after this to hand over at least half a crown to Maggie — and that ought to stop her grousing for a bit, anyway — and hadn't he just come from a wedding? Orlright, then. Wot abaht it? And, again, why not?

So Mr. Scatcherd slouched forward once more and said: 'Miss!' And then he tapped with his knuckles, and said: 'Miss!' again. But already it seemed that Providence must have followed the natural course of events, and have hardened its heart. No stout, elderly barmaid reappeared, but a stern voice from beyond the partition uttered an ultimatum. 'Time, gents!' it barked. 'Time, please, everybody!' It was the law of the land that spoke; wise, not to be questioned, and in any case, apparently, conjured into existence by the will of the Sovereign People itself. Mr. Scatcherd might deny his own responsibility in the matter, he might and did regret the happier days of long ago; but the 'Duke of Brunswick' knew well enough that it traded under sufferance, and the 'Duke of Burnswick' was firm. 'Time!' it cried again; and there was a rattling sound as one of the shutters went rolling down, and a thud as its bottom edge struck the threshold of the Saloon Bar. Mr. Scatcherd realised that he was beaten, and that the will of the Sovereign People had prevailed. He hiccupped, winced as his feet again supported his entire weight, and went stumbling and hobbling out into the street.

He'd still got seven bob, though; and there was a barrel-organ playing outside, which he always rather liked; and the sun was still shining — though the clouds were again piling up — and even one mild-and-bitter was a great deal better than none. Yes, Mr. Scatcherd felt distinctly soothed and distinctly virtuous as he shuffled along the pavement, and glanced into the windows of the mean shops, and wriggled his shoulders so as to allay a slight tickle on his back, and occasionally looked into the gutter just in case he should happen to see the end of somebody else's cigarette.

One doesn't go so far as to assert that this middle-aged citizen *was* virtuous. Indeed, since he was a confirmed opponent of labour — in the non-political sense — and since he was by no means unfamiliar with the prospect from the dock at several police-courts, and since he had never avoided evil com-munications, and since he had been living for the best part of four months with, and principally on, a woman who most certainly wasn't his wife, there are sufficient rough and ready grounds for classify-ing Mr. Scatcherd as at least a bit of a rogue. Yet if a man feels virtuous, does it make him more so to remind him that he isn't?

Better leave that, perhaps. The fact persists that, in the absence of particular temptation, Mr. Scatcherd was no worse than quite a lot of other characters, and that even when temptation arrived, Mr. Scatcherd was quite often too lazy to yield. When Maggie had got him the chance to sell those paper handkerchiefs, and had put up the necessary capital, he could easily have dodged it — only he hadn't felt up to arguing at the moment. And still he needn't have gone back to her, and could easily have dissipated the entire proceeds in almost any manner that he chose — only he was exhausted by that spurt of activity in the swiftly-rising market, and wanted to get somewhere where he could take off his boots.

So the long and short of it was that he did go back to her — not exactly like a homing pigeon, for even if the route had been straightforward, which it wasn't, Mr. Scatcherd would still have meandered from side to side of the pavement and occasionally from side to side of the street. But slowly and on the whole surely he wobbled in the familiar direction, and sometimes he passed under the lee of great offices and warehouses, and sometimes there were little terraces of private houses, and sometimes his environment was pure, unadulterated, squalid, sordid slum. And at length, still meditating on his recent commercial success, still fingering the remains of the proceeds, but increasingly uncertain whether that idea about the half-crown hadn't been a great deal too generous and foolish, he came shuffling up to a large iron gateway opening into a long asphalt yard, partly occupied by low sheds and entirely surrounded by bricks, mortar and innumerable windows. And this rectilinear rabbit-warren of so-called model dwellings being Mr. Scatcherd's ultimate goal, he slouched

into the far corner, leant his shoulder against
a worn, shiny wall, and thus started propelling
himself up the stairs.

Just a minute, though.   There was a faint out-
cry — but of course we heard it — at the use of that
epithet 'so-called.'   Very well, then; please consider it withdrawn.   The dwellings were, in truth,
an exact model of everything that their public-
spirited founders and owners had thought most
suitable for their philanthropic purpose.   They
had, rightly and creditably, been appalled by those
neighbouring slums.   Their civic consciences had
been outraged, their determination to improve
matters had been deep and sincere.   They had
met, they had co-opted clergymen — one doesn't
quite know why — and bankers, because of course
the whole thing must definitely be run on business
lines, and borough councillors, because the borough
councillors had no intention of being left out.   One
and a half per cent, they said, was to be the limit
of the return on their outlay, and even this was to
pass into the trust fund which would be responsible
for upkeep and repairs.

The epithet, in fact, seems less in need of any
qualifying prefix with every detail that is revealed.
A model architect was set to work, who prepared
model plans.   So much cubic space for the lungs
of every fortunate tenant, so many windows opening directly on to the outer air, so many taps with
fresh water, so many other sanitary arrangements,
so many square yards for model recreation, so
many places for dustbins and miniature bunkers
for coal.   Such a clever architect, too, that he
knew just how to anticipate some of the fortunate
tenants' regrettable failings.   No wooden banisters,
so that they couldn't conceivably be removed and
burnt.   The very minimum of fixtures, and these
most powerfully and ingeniously fixed.   Caged gas-
lamps on the stairs where no one could possibly

reach them, and a truly Machiavellian system of master-keys so that no door or cupboard could ever serve an unauthorised purpose, or at any rate go on serving it once suspicion were aroused.

Down came the old hovels, courts and alleys, and away they went in dusty fragments. Up rose the brand-new hoardings, and were instantly covered with gigantic advertisements of plays and pickles. The Right Honourable Sir Somebody Something came and tapped a block of masonry with a silver trowel — unluckily the inscription commemorating this act has faded under many years' use as a target for juvenile cricket-balls, so that one is unable to identify him more closely — and speeches were made, and a luncheon was held and a slight counter-demonstration by the former residents was completely quelled by the police.

And then, behind those garish hoardings, the fabric itself began to rise too. And men whistled and worked, and shouted and hammered, and sang and chipped, and sweated and swore. You saw the drab brickwork climbing above the advertisements, draped in wooden scaffolding. You saw the roof going on, and glass going in, and the wooden scaffolding coming down. The exact prefigurement of a prison in Utopia or of a barrack in the New Atlantis had definitely established itself as part of the foreground and skyline. Iron railings surrounded it, and the gates which in a few weeks would be permanently fastened back with chains and padlocks — for the architect, it would seem, had forgotten that they would be used as swings — stood there in exquisite regularity and rigidity.

Another ceremony took place. The committee appeared in top-hats and frock-coats; also in silks, satins and ostrich feathers. The Press gathered round. The police again assembled, as did the mob. And to the fluttering of handkerchiefs and the fitful sound of cheering, a Serene Highness came driving up in a pair-horse landau with gigantic cee-springs, and passed through the iron gates, and alighted, and was offered a bouquet, and directed a mumping, mystical glance at the crowd and the flags, and was assisted on to a red-baize platform covered with a plain awning, and rose to its feet and was understood to announce that the model dwellings were now open.

Other speakers appeared to confirm this patently inaccurate statement — for, as a matter of fact, there was still about six weeks' work for the carpenters and painters and plumbers. Three windy cheers rent the welkin. A tour of inspection was made. The open landau was turned round; the Serene Highness re-embarked, with further assistance, and drove away again. Everybody felt that another milestone or turning-point had been reached in the history of social progress and civic endeavour, and all that now remained was to finish off the building, add another inscription, remove the remains of the hoardings and deal with the applicants for accommodation. Within two months the place was full, nor has there ever been an unoccupied corner from that day to this. Tenants have come and gone, the governing council has resigned, died and been replaced, the drab brickwork has become dingier, the rents have risen and the return on capital has somehow increased; but through all these busy, noisy, crowded years the human race has insisted on congregating in vast quantities on exactly the same spot, and the model dwellings have continued to serve their unceasing purpose.

And if they're a bit depressing, and if the occupants are also a bit depressing, and if newer notions in communal housing have made some of that architect's inspirations seem a little out of date, is that any reason for jeering or sneering at the original philanthropists? Most certainly not. You may shudder, if you like, as you catch a glimpse through those Victorian iron railings, you may and probably will thank your stars that you don't have to live here yourself; but if you follow up these very natural impulses by casting round for somebody to blame for it all, one insists that you will merely be wasting your time. The culprit, if there be any culprit, is simply humanity at large. And a section of humanity, one must in this case remind you, at least started with the intention of being humane.

Now we're actually going inside, and if you've never been inside yourself, the first thing that will strike you will be the remarkable number of cubic feet that can be crammed into such extraordinarily small rooms. For you realise, of course, that the district surveyor and the Building Acts and every other kind of authority will have seen to it that science is satisfied. If the occupants choose, as they still mostly do, to shut all their windows and consume their own exhalations, you may be quite certain that they can do so without having to be artificially restored. But the point is that self-respect demands lace curtains, and lace curtains can't be washed without soap and hot water, both of which cost money; and how often do you reckon that this expense would have to be incurred if the prevailing smuts were admitted through even the smallest chink? No, there is inexorable logic behind this atmosphere in Cadwallader Buildings, and in spite of the congestion of cheap furniture, you may be quite positive that the cubic feet are all there.

One can't deny that, according to modern medical theories, Mrs. Rainbow — the tenant of Number 42D — would be none the worse if she occasionally took in a breath of fresh air. But then she does. She leaves Cadwallader Buildings at seven o'clock on six days a week to scrub down the floors of a neighbouring elementary school — and if the air isn't fresh at seven in the morning, when is it? — she goes out again later, with a string bag, to potter about the shops and stalls and barrows; and at six o'clock she again sets forth and walks, wet or fine, all the way to a big Government office in Whitehall, where she again takes a lot of exercise on her hands and knees (at the expense of and, as some say, for the ultimate benefit of the tax-payer) before rising up, turning round and walking home again.

If during the rest of her time Mrs. Rainbow puts the cleanliness of her lace curtains before the super-stitions of the British Medical Association, then all one can say is that Mrs. Rainbow doesn't look a penny the paler for it. Her age is quite unguessable, though it is obvious at once that she is a great deal older than her teeth. But she's large and plump and strong and muscular, and her face is red and her eyes are astonishingly clear, and she had a son in the Navy once (but he was drowned while on leave, so no pension for Mrs. Rainbow), and a couple of daughters (one dead, and one gone to the bad), and a husband (but he left her years ago, and she doesn't know whether he's dead or alive), so that if, as it seems, she can hardly be less than forty, then, at any rate, it isn't lack of experience that has kept so much of her so young.

'I don't worry,' says Mrs. Rainbow to the other charwomen at the elementary school or the Treas-ury, and she shows her remarkable teeth, and laughs over the steaming pails and the smell of damp wood, so that the other charwomen are fain to admit that she has a way with her. Any one charwoman, indeed, finds her irresistible. Any two or even three charwomen would agree that Mrs. Rainbow's spirits qualify her for the flattering title of a Caution or a Scream. But when it comes to more than three charwomen — as it does, often

enough, in the cave where they keep their imple-
ments and make cups of tea, or when work is done
and they all come out into the street — why, then
there have been looks and murmurs and signs of
resistance to Mrs. Rainbow's remarkable teeth.
Shoulders, in fact, have been shrugged and upper
lips have been drawn down, for Rumour (who is
as much at home in these circles as anywhere else)
says that Mrs. Rainbow's private life isn't by any
means all that it should be. That Mrs. Rainbow,
forsooth, *ought* to worry; because, whatever the
temptations and excuses in this particular case, it
isn't respectable to share a couple of rooms in
Cadwallader Buildings with a man who isn't your
husband.

Of course, add Rumour's votaries, Mrs. Rainbow
is Mrs. Rainbow — here, one thinks, they show a
good deal of sense — and it isn't as if she were young
and flighty, and it isn't as if she hasn't had her
troubles, and it isn't as if she can regularise her
position when she doesn't even know whether her
real husband exists. And, again, they say, it's a
bit hard if a woman who's been treated like that
has got to live alone for the rest of her natural
life, and no good, they all say — more sensibly than
ever — can be expected to come of messing about
with lawyers. Still, they say, even bigamy might
be a better example than what Mrs. Rainbow
appears to be doing at present. And finally, they
say, of all the miserable, low-down creatures that
ever some of them have caught sight of or the rest
have had described to them, has anyone, they ask,
seen anything to touch the partner in Mrs. Rainbow's social and ethical crime?

And it's this last, penetrating inquiry which does
so much to confuse these worthy women and to
confuse their distinction between right and wrong.
If Mr. Scatcherd were younger and better-looking,
they'd be down on their colleague like a load of

bricks. If he were contributing to her support in any way, they'd have probably had her out of her job or jobs long before now, for here a deep-seated sense of equity, not to say jealousy, would have been involved. But Rumour — for once speaking almost the literal truth — says that Mrs. Rainbow found him reeling about in the street, and rescued him from the cops and took him home with her and nursed him through something which the votaries call Pewmonia; and, after all, in this hard and hazardous world, if a woman is fool enough to go and do a thing like that, one might at least say that she has brought about her own punishment as well as her own reward.

So the charwomen, it seems, are chary of actually casting the first stone, and Mrs. Rainbow scrubs away while they gossip together behind her back. And they feel a little superior, which is great fun. And they feel that they can pity her, which is even more delightful. And with the aid of these two feelings they disguise and overcome, for the most part, the little pangs of envy which also disturb them. 'She don't worry now,' they mutter, 'but, mark my words, she's only laying up trouble for 'erself. A lazy 'ound,' they say, referring to Mr. Scatcherd; ''e'll be knocking 'er abaht next, likely as not. Men!' they sniff, and centuries of dreadful knowledge are concentrated in this solitary, sardonic word. 'Men!' they wheeze, amidst the dust and tea-leaves. 'Just let 'er wait!'

24

WHY had Mrs. Rainbow done it? Why — vast and unanswerable question — does anybody do anything? She'd seen men reeling about the streets as long as she could remember, and she'd let them reel, and she'd stepped into the gutter, when necessary, so that they could reel more comfortably and

at their ease. Equally was she familiar with the
spectacle of dark-blue majesty bearing down on
such reelers, and warning them, or cajoling them,
or, when they resisted this treatment, closing with
them and removing them from the scene of their
dismal revelry. But just on this particular night,
when the stalls and barrows were so thronged with
Saturday shoppers, and when the naphtha flares
were so bright, and the combined and competitive
efforts of an accordion-player and a trombonist
were so stimulating, and even the very poorest felt
the imminence of tomorrow's calm; just on this
particular night, as Mrs. Rainbow threaded her
way through the crowds with her string-bag and
her moth-eaten pelisse — feeling, perhaps, a little
sentimental, and if so, in Heaven's name, why not?
— an impulse seized her, swung her and shook her;
and suddenly the deed was done.

'It's orlright, p'leeceman. 'E's a friend of mine.
I'll look arter 'im.'

Jeers, hoots and general merriment. Dark-blue
majesty a trifle taken aback.

'Friend of yours, ma? Well, we can't 'ave this,
you know. I oughter charge 'im.'

Hundreds of hovering, lamp-lit faces. The flash
of Mrs. Rainbow's truly remarkable teeth.

'Ar, but 'e's bin ill, pore chap. You're not going
to be 'ard on 'im.'

Mob-sympathy turns abruptly and completely
round. Becomes vocal. Points out, which is, indeed, translucent, that Mr. Scatcherd is suffering
from an 'orrible, narsty corff, and manages to
indicate that his other symptoms are entirely due
to his very praiseworthy efforts to cure it. 'That's
right, ma. You take 'im 'ome an' get 'im outer
the cold. Doctor's wot the pore chap needs. Not
a blinking, trebly-asterisked cop.'

'Now, then. Stand back there!'

'Stand back yerself!' from a courageous sym-

pathiser, who instantly ducks and vanishes.   The
murmuring intensifies, and the policeman — who is
young, nervous and doesn't in the least wish to
have his helmet knocked off by a rotten cabbage —
has suddenly yielded to popular opinion.   Having
staked all on Mrs. Rainbow's teeth, and having
advanced in his profession by doing so, he rolls
deliberately away — the back of his long coat distinctly announcing that his dignity is unimpaired,
that his decision has been both just and merciful,
that he knew exactly what he was doing and that
he wouldn't hesitate to do it again.   He's gone.
The excitement is all over.   The crowd goes swirling
on its course.

'Come on, then.   Mind wodjer doing.   'Ere —
ketch 'old of my arm.'

Mr. Scatcherd sang, coughed, reeled, plunged,
hiccuped and tried to sing again.

'Stow it, cancher?   'Ere — where you trying to
go?   Ay?'

'Nowhere.   Gor! my chest.   Chronic!   Oo!'

'Well, wherejer come from?'

'Dunno.   Lorst me job.   Cor — I'm bad!'

''Ere — 'old up.   Oughtn't to be like this, yer
know.'

Mr. Scatcherd began to weep.   A most embarrassing, repulsive and helpless handful.   But
Mrs. Rainbow seemed to be committed now.   She'd
saved him once.   He'd got a claim on her.   Nobody'd be any wiser if she took him back, gave him
a chance to sober up, gave him a cup of tea, perhaps;
went on yielding, in fact, to the impulse.

'Come on.   This w'y.'

'Lumme,' said Mr. Scatcherd; and suddenly
the character of his reeling changed.   It was no
longer wild and suicidal.   A mere touch, now,
was enough to guide him through the iron gateway
and across the asphalt yard.   He slopped up the
stairs.   He slouched against the side of the door.

He fell inward as it opened, rumbled alarmingly, bounced off the table, cannoned against the edge of the sink, shot through the second doorway, tottered in the most complicated and catastrophic manner — and collapsed on Mrs. Rainbow's bed.

''Ere!' she said. 'Geddup! Wodjer doin'?'

'Gor — I've copped it.'

Mrs. Rainbow shook him, and it was like — in some ways — shaking a mattress. In another and much more sinister way, it was just like shaking a corpse. Supposing he really *was* bad; supposing he died here; supposing ——

''Ere!' said Mrs. Rainbow, fiercely. 'You stay where you are, see? I'm goin' for a doctor.'

Years since she'd even spoken to a doctor, but she knew where to go all right. She burst through the crowd in the surgery, snatched at the youngest of three partners while the others tried to fend her off, came running back again with the pink-faced practitioner panting at her heels.

'Drunk,' he said.

'Yes, I know, sir. But the w'y 'e's breathin' — it's bad, sir. I don't like it. I ——'

'Quiet. Just a minute. Lemme look.... Yes, you're right. Listen — I'm going back to telephone for the ambulance ——'

'Oh!' said Mrs. Rainbow. 'But I can look arter 'im. 'E'll be orlright wiv me, sir. I swear 'e will. I know all abaht sickness. Why, me 'usband ——'

'Oh, he's your husband, is he? Sorry. I thought —— All right. Well, just come out here a moment....'

This was how Mr. Scatcherd fell almost simultaneously on to Mrs. Rainbow's bed and his own graceless feet. Nobody else wanted him, certainly, and if he had ever really had a job to lose, he never appeared to miss it when he was sober. He was a rolling stone, and they don't look ahead — the two feats being impossible at the same time — so that life could never really surprise him. Here he was, and Mrs. Rainbow never said nothing about his going; so he didn't go. An extraordinarily unromantic waif, and to almost any unprejudiced beholder an extraordinarily unattractive individual. Also the exact terms of the association, connection, alliance or whatever it was are wrapped in a good deal of mystery, and it's no use trying to peep through historical keyholes now. Mrs. Rainbow housed and fed him, disregarded a good deal of consequent scandal — but whether for his sake, her own sake, or because it just turned out like this, one really can't say — and was never seen to adopt anything warmer than the attitude of a keeper towards a sea-lion. Mr. Scatcherd loafed, lounged, cadged, grumbled, continued to avoid work like the plague and was successful in concealing the least token of gratitude. One doesn't want to insult an admirable species by saying that he was like a dog; yet one has seen such lazy, good-for-nothing mongrels, always at a loose end, always watching for scraps, always ready to snarl at the hand that feeds them, and still being supported because somebody has given way to a sense of ownership.

One of the strongest claims there is. Mrs. Rainbow gave way to it, and suffered for it, and was heroic because of it. Faced her own world with those remarkable teeth, even cast a thin film of propriety over her extraordinary behaviour. Found Mr. Scatcherd three real jobs, which he instantly and genuinely lost. Forgave him. Allowed the claim to persist, though she knew now that he could never be anything but a liability. Let him swindle her, let him steal and pawn some of her property, wasn't deceived for a moment, but still let it all go on. She'd found Mr. Scatcherd and saved his life. Now he was hers whether she wanted him or not.

So on that fine but no less deceptive morning towards the end of March, she met a former resident in Cadwallader Buildings, and stopped and chatted, and learnt the meaning of the package under the former resident's arm, and — on another impulse — bought two shillings' worth of crêpe-paper handkerchiefs, and took them home, and since even Mr. Scatcherd wasn't averse to making something at a job which couldn't possibly last more than an hour or so, off he went. And at the critical moment the sun came out, and the Golden Bride smiled — because Mrs. Bowker hadn't lit Mr. Albert Coffin's fire — and the seedy salesman netted three hundred per cent profit, and you know what he did after that, because you have already been told.

With five and threepence still jingling in his pocket, he slouched up the grimy staircase to Number 42D, pitched once more through the doorway — and stopped, with his jaw dangling and something very like panic on his brutish face. For the whole room was packed with ladies and gentlemen — cor, what a crowd! — and Maggie was standing there in the midst of them, twiddling at a bit of her dress and exhibiting her remarkable teeth; and Mr. Scatcherd span round with the notion of bolting like a rabbit from this terrifying spectacle, when, to his extreme horror, he saw that his retreat was already cut off; that a clergyman and a young lady had entered behind him, that the door was closed, and that he was hemmed in on every side.

'Good afternoon,' said the clergyman, in a patronising and slightly nasal tone.

''Arternoon, sir,' said Mr. Scatcherd, as his eye still wobbled wildly in search of escape.

The clergyman glanced at a little notebook.

'Let me — ah — see,' he said. 'You're —— Wait a minute; I think there must be some mistake. Are you Mr. Rainbow?'

'No, sir. Name of Scatcherd. That's Mrs. Rainbow — jes' there, sir.'

'Ha!' said the clergyman. 'But you're living here?'

One doesn't fence with authority in a dog-collar. One doesn't tell an Oxford accent to mind its own business.

'Yerss,' said Mr. Scatcherd. 'I bin living 'ere lytely. That's right, sir.'

'Hum!' said the clergyman. 'Just a minute. Mrs. Bevan!'

'Yes, Mr. Parsley?'

'Excuse me a moment. I think — that's to say ——'

The voices moved away and began mumbling. Another voice seemed to take the stage.

'But how very interesting!' it was saying. 'So you work at the Treasury, do you, Mrs. Rainbow? Well, isn't that funny! Because so does my husband — sometimes.'

And the rather good-looking woman laughed, not at all unpleasantly. And several other members of the Council of Management of the Cadwallader Estate, Limited, emitted slightly sycophantic echoes; for though they were all a little conscious of their superiority to the people whose homes they were inspecting, they were equally aware that Mrs. Rivington was the wife of a Financial Secretary — and of a Financial Secretary with a future, if the newspapers spoke the truth — so that if she laughed, they would laugh. And if she chose to be a trifle unconventional in some of her remarks to the tenants, then they were no less anxious to keep on the friendliest possible terms with her. Thus there were grades and distinctions even on the Olympian council itself, and places to be kept, and other places to which one was quite ready to aspire.

'"Sometimes,"' repeated the little group by

the table, and sniggered again. And Mrs. Rainbow
displayed her remarkable teeth with a look of
nervous civility.

'Reelly, mum?' she said. 'Is that reelly
so?'

And Mrs. Rivington confirmed her original statement, and then sat perched on the little table
and went on chatting in so genuinely friendly a
manner — for she liked Mrs. Rainbow more than
anyone whom she had yet met on this rather dismal
tour, and it *was* rather queer to think that perhaps
she emptied Mervyn's waste-paper basket — and
the rest of the group listened and nodded. And then
stopped nodding, and began listening to something
else. And then turned their backs on the little
table, while their ears seemed almost visibly to
expand. For this was what they'd really come for,
this was the kind of thing to justify the time and
trouble that they were taking, this, at last, was a
real, authentic and perfectly abominable Case.

'You mean to tell me ——' said the Rev. Basil
Parsley, so that he could get it all over again.
And Mr. Scatcherd tried to amend his evidence,
and stumbled, and was tripped up, and made it
all far worse than before. Ever since December!
Did you ever hear anything like that? Right
under all the other tenants' noses, and in a respectable block of buildings like this!

'Mrs. Rivington!'

'Hullo — yes?'

'I think I ought to tell you ——' said the Rev.
Basil Parsley; and he lowered his voice and told
her—not mincing words nor beating about the bush,
for there can be none of this when a council is
doing its duty. 'It must be reported,' he said.
'It must be seen to at our very next meeting. I
shall make a point ——' and so on. 'And meanwhile,' said the Rev. Basil Parsley, 'of course
the woman must have notice to quit.'

Mrs. Rivington slipped off the table and looked extraordinarily obstinate.

'If the man was ill,' she began; 'if the husband has disappeared ——'

There was a good deal of uproar here, because this was just the sort of gathering where everyone knew the dickens of a lot about Separation Orders and Poor Persons' Certificates and wanted to explain and argue about them with everyone else. But Mrs. Bevan—you remember Mrs. Bevan? — spoke more forcibly than any of them.

'Shocking!' she said. 'Disheartening! Terrible! Of course the woman's employers must be told. A Government office, too! If public money is to be spent on supporting this kind of establishment —— Mrs. Rivington, I expect you know the proper people to inform?'

But Mrs. Rivington looked even more obstinate.

'No, I don't,' she said.

'But you can — ah — find out?' suggested the Rev. Basil Parsley.

'Very likely,' said Mrs. Rivington. 'But I don't see why ——'

'Come, come,' said Mrs. Bevan. 'It's an obvious duty. I'm perfectly prepared to tell them myself, only ——'

'All right,' interrupted Mrs. Rivington. 'Do. And I shall tell them ——'

She broke off abruptly—partly from unusual but clearly advisable self-control; partly because the council, with a sudden and unanimous wish to avoid contamination, seemed to be melting out of the doorway. Mrs. Bevan glanced over her shoulder and began melting too. Mr. Scatcherd shuffled obligingly out of her way.

'Oh, madam ——' said Mrs. Rainbow. Somebody squeezed her arm, went quickly past her, and Mrs. Rivington, also, had gone. A great trampling died away down the stairs, and then

voices came up from the yard below where the
council was reforming its ranks before making its
next visit of inspection.   'Where's Mrs. Rivington?' they would be asking a little later, but in
the immediate crowd and confusion no one had
noticed her escape.

'That's done it,' said Mrs. Rainbow, yet still
with a wry sort of smile. 'That's torn it proper.
Goin' to lose me job now, thanks to them dear old
beauties. Goin' to lose one of me jobs for certain,
an' the other one, I dessay, as soon as they 'ears
of it. Goin' to be turned out, too. That's good,
that is. That's a treat, ain't it? An' all becos ——
'Ere! Wodjer looking like that for, old son?
'T ain't your fault, I reckon. 'Course you would
come a-blundering in 'ere jest the wrong time;
jest the time no one's expecting yer. Ay? Wodjer
want to go an' do that for? See wotcher done?
Ay?'

Mr. Scatcherd rubbed his chin, and shrugged one
of his shoulders.

'Ay?' repeated his benefactress, staring at him
with a dull look of inquiry.

'That's right,' said Mr. Scatcherd.   'Blyme it
all on me. I only done wotcher tell me. That's all
I done.'

'Ay? Oh, them 'ankerchiefs. 'Ave any luck?'

Mr. Scatcherd hesitated for an instant, and came
to a swift conclusion. Maggie, as a source of
supplies and provider of a roof, was done for. He'd
heard what the ladies and gentlemen had said.
Her time here was up, and so was his. Only a
born fool would let himself be chucked out, and
hand over five and fruppence first.

'Naow,' he said. 'Wodjer expeck if it goes
an' rynes like that? I tell you there wasn't
nobody there.'

'Wot? Yer mean yer didn't sell none at all?'

'Course I didn't. 'Ow could I?'

'Well, where are they, then? Wodjer done wiv 'em?'

Mr. Scatcherd hadn't thought of this, but it was plumb easy.

'Frew 'em aw'y,' he said. 'Wot's the use of a lot of ankerchiffs wiv the nyme an' everyfing on 'em? I'm fed up,' said Mr. Scatcherd, indignantly; ''angin' abaht an' gettin' wet froo. Fed up, I am.'

'Oh, well,' said Mrs. Rainbow. 'It's all luck, I suppose. Cheer up, old son. I dessay you did yer best. I dessay we'll manage some'ow.'

'Ay? Yer mean...?'

It was incredible. He'd never known such a woman. Ruined, turned out of her rooms, and still, apparently, ready to go on keeping him. Mr. Scatcherd was moved, not in the least by gratitude, but by an overwhelming sense of relief. Cor, what an old fool! But he'd better say something or do something quickly, to get it all fixed before she changed her mind.

He took a step towards her; he put out a dirty hand in the first motion of a clumsy caress. But he'd have done much better to stay where he was. There was no sort of warning as the lining of his trouser-pocket gave way beneath its unwonted load. Just a shower of silver and copper, bouncing from his boot all over the living-room floor. And Mrs. Rainbow staring at it. And Mrs. Rainbow raising her eyes, and drawing in her breath, and shooting out her arm.

'Out of it!' she said — as Mr. Scatcherd stumbled backwards. ''Op it! Geddout o' my plyce, an' doncher dare show yer ugly mug in 'ere agyne! I'm froo wiv yer, see? I knew yer was a liar; I knew yer was rotten; I knew yer larfed at me be'ind me back. But to get me into trouble like this, to stand by an' 'ear me bein' called nymes on your account, an' then to pinch even the two

bob wot I give for them blooming ankerchiffs ——
'Ere!' screamed Mrs. Rainbow, flashing her remarkable teeth and seizing the poker from the tiny
grate. 'Jest you stand there a bit longer while
I——'

Smack! went the poker against the upper panel
of the model door. Mr. Scatcherd hadn't waited
for the end of this terrifying outburst. He knew
— for few men have ever had more experience —
both when he wasn't wanted and just what it feels
like to be the victim of battery and assault. He
fled, lurching and crashing down the stairs, though
still clutching at the one and sixpence which he
had saved from the disaster — his only possession
in the world — and thus, still pursued by yells from
a second-floor window, this discreditable character
vanished once more into the streets from which
he had come; into the streets which he knew and
loved and hated so well; into the streets which
had somehow supported him for nearly fifty years,
and had now to start supporting him again.

One would prefer not to record the words which
emerged from his disgusting countenance as he
hobbled and hastened through the afternoon sunlight — for again there were patches between the
grey clouds — and limped and loped over the worn
paving-stones. One might well prefer, also, to
refrain from looking at Mrs. Rainbow as she sits
alone on a decrepit wooden chair, still surrounded
by four-and-ninepence worth of small change, but
motionless as she stares dumbly at the past, present
and future. She's worrying now, all right, and
there's no doubt that she's got something to worry
about. Her age is considerably less unguessable.
Her remarkable teeth are the only feature on
which care, anxiety, fear and responsibility haven't
laid their very plainest mark.

'Not that I'd 'ave 'im back agyne,' she mutters.
'An' not that I ain't bin arskin' fer this from the

very start of it all.   Must 'ave bin crazy,' murmurs
Mrs. Rainbow, as she shakes her head and sags
still lower in the decrepit wooden chair.

Yet one doesn't entirely abandon hope.   The
cause of offence has been removed, Mrs. Rainbow,
so far, has always paid her rent regularly, and the
Council of Management won't find these two facts
any great assistance when they come up against
one defiant, spirited, unconventional and obstinate
member.   Mrs. Rivington, one means, of course.
Yes, one certainly rather takes to Mrs. Rivington
in the middle of it all.   One can't help wondering
just why Mrs. Rivington should have deserted the
tour of inspection so suddenly, and where her smart
little coach-built coupé took her next.

It seems more than possible that the determined
creature is to forge another unconscious link.

25

A few words, at this point, on Fame.   Is it, for
example, or isn't it all luck?   Do people get what
they want or get what they deserve, or merely
get what comes to them?   What about bluff,
bounce and bluster?   Are they more, or less,
valuable than brains, and where does personality
come in?   Is the whole thing entirely objective,
and if so, what's the difference between illusion
and truth?   Are men known and judged by their
fruits, or simply by the grandeur of their green-
houses?   Is it more successful to have an immense
reputation built on sand, or a minute reputation
founded on rock?   Is it what you're trying to do
that really counts, or what you actually do, or
what other people think you do?   Is it inward
or outward approval that forms the true criterion?
And even if you satisfy both tests and go soaring
to the top of the tree, and are so free from false
modesty that you regard Westminster Abbey as

your natural resting-place, are you also justified
in taking any personal credit, or is it all due to
the functioning of your ductless glands?

A lot of questions here, but no attempt — you
may be glad to learn — will be made to answer
them.   The fact is, that they can't be answered.
The fact is that they only flowed on to the paper
as one might strike a few rolling, introductory
chords, before considering two definite and specific
cases.   That of the Right Honourable Mervyn
Rivington, for whom all the newspapers predicted
so distinguished a future.   And that of Sir Blundell
Hascombe, K.C.B., G.C.V.O., and a whole lot of
other initials, whom so many of the newspapers
had recently adopted as their darling and their
hero.   And yet if you fetched right up against
either gentleman —— However, that is exactly
what you're going to do.

Youth, as usual, comes first; though it must be
admitted that Mr. Rivington was less positively
than comparatively young.   He was younger, for
instance — as well as far paler — than Sir Blundell
Hascombe.   He was also younger than the last
three Financial Secretaries — at the dates, that is
to say, of their respective appointments — so that
an inaccurate journalist had had the notion of
calling him the Baby of the Cabinet.   Mr. Rivington,
who was getting on towards fifty and had no
imagination and no sense of humour, resented this
description; nor was he any further softened towards it when his wife laughed and said that of
course they were thinking of his head.

Here, in fact, Mr. Rivington looked a little
piqued.

'Darling,' said Mrs. Rivington, at once, 'you
know I adore your lovely round shining head.   I
was only being witty.'

'The preposterous part,' said her husband, without smiling, 'is that I'm not in the Cabinet at all.'

'No, darling,' said Mrs. Rivington, very agreeably. 'But of course you soon will be.'

At this loyal if slapdash prophecy, Mr. Rivington's pale countenance took on a more earnest expression than ever. And Mrs. Rivington thought what a duck he was, really, with all his little dispatch-boxes and private secretaries and shorthand typists, and how odd, but at the same time delightful, it was that she should be so fond of him, and what a queer world it was in which a really quite stupid man (but bless his heart!) could go so fast and so far simply because he had never seen a joke in his life. Honestly, thought Mrs. Rivington, preposterous — as the poor darling had just said — was the only word for a state of affairs like that.

So here was another contribution to the symposium on Fame, even though there is no compulsion to accept it as gospel, and even though one or two people said that the real reason for Mr. Rivington's advancement was that everybody liked his wife. On the whole it's all rather deep and mysterious, because it's a plain fact that Mrs. Rivington didn't possess so much as a spark of ambition, or a touch of reverence for mere pomposity as such. It's true that her husband's career amused her, but she didn't even know the first rudiments of how to pull strings. If he could retire, that would be absolutely perfect; but if he couldn't or wouldn't, and if it made him happy to do such extraordinarily boring things, very well then, she loved him and that ended it. So she smiled at him and fed him and looked after the children, and had impish impulses which frequently scared him out of his wits — and quite as often turned out to have done him all the good in the world, as on the occasion when it suddenly entered her head to play a practical joke on the Leader of the Party. And thus the dense mass of Mr. Rivington's dreadful dullness was constantly being jerked forward by a series of rocket-explosions, and from its own ponderosity seemed incapable of slipping back.

Once more, was it all chance, or was it as certain as the result of mixing two different chemicals? Impossible to say. No one could repeat the experiment, for no one else could produce precisely the same ingredients. Anyhow, Mr. Rivington took himself terribly seriously, and his colleagues, though naturally a little jealous at times, fairly loaded him with work and responsibility. As for the newspapers — well, if a politician appears quite so often in the public eye, and has quite such a large, round, glittering, bald head, what else can they do except tell their readers that he is the Coming Man?

Sir Blundell Hascombe — and all those initials — on the other hand, had achieved his present eminence without the assistance or handicap of any wife at all. Sir Blundell's voice, figure and military ancestry had been quite enough to determine his career from the outset, and no paragraph in the whole of *Who's Who* read with more exquisite or sonorous rhythm. Not that it boasted; not that it had the slightest need to boast. It just swept calmly through every rank and campaign of the contemporary army, with bracketed references to dispatches or medal with clasp or bar. Without changing its tone, it rolled through the European War (twice wounded), and without pausing or hesitating, it continued to pile up commands and honours, until suddenly, and about three years before the current issue, it appeared that Sir Blundell had been appointed as governor of an extremely distant possession, after which the recital ended with his extremely distant address and the names of two quite inevitable London clubs.

Success, in fact; clean, straightforward, unquestionable success. But, up to this point, scarcely

Fame. If you took the trouble to plough through that stout red volume, you could easily find the names of dozens of elderly gentlemen who have made almost precisely the same contribution to the history of your empire, and of dozens of governors who are keeping the flag flying in all kinds of places of which you would be bound to admit that you had never even heard. For it's a large empire, and it takes a lot of running, and it swallows up an enormous quantity of old soldiers with long legs and ruddy complexions without ever finding it necessary to resort to advertisement either of them or itself.

They come and go; they are extraordinarily important where one can't see them, and extraordinarily negligible when they return, and go tottering along Pall Mall in their carefully polished silk hats. Some, as is natural, have more medals and initials than others, and the files in the Colonial Office — which are your property, only you're not allowed to read them — naturally contain varying reports on their distant deeds. But you're having quite enough trouble helping to pay for their pensions without worrying about anything that they have actually done or failed to do for you. Presently there is a new edition of *Who's Who* and one or more of those crowded paragraphs will have vanished from its alphabetical space. Success is over, and Fame—as the newspapers understand it—has never even existed. The world and the British Empire continue to revolve. Plenty more soldiers and public servants, however, where the last lot came from.

So that if one thing hasn't led to another — but how often it does! — there seems no real reason why Sir Blundell Hascombe, admirable as many of his qualities were, shouldn't have subsided into exactly the same twilight as all the other distinguished old buffers, and absolutely no reason why he should

suddenly have found himself in England and in the
unaccustomed role of a popular hero. If, for
instance, a certain Eurasian agitator hadn't slipped
into the distant possession in the retinue of a
wandering M.P. If, before he could be tracked down
and ousted again, he hadn't put ideas into the heads
of two local gentlemen—the subsequently celebrated
Mr. Borundra and his no less obstreperous friend
Mr. Hari. And then if the M.P. hadn't come home
again and asked very insistently why Messrs. B.
and H. were being deported from their native district, so that the Government was overwhelmed by
a general outburst of liberalism and Sir Blundell
was forced, for their own protection, to clap the two
aboriginals into prison instead. And then, as a
result of this, if the two aboriginals hadn't become
so fat and comfortable that all their other friends
started seething with unrest — either because they
wanted to go to prison too, or because they wanted
Messrs. B. and H. to come out and do a little
honest work, or merely because unrest is so con-
tagious in a warm climate. And then if the M.P.
hadn't died, so that there was a vacancy at East
Malmsey ——

Well, these were the principal components among
the world-wide causes which had shot Sir Blundell
on to the very front page of every newspaper in the
country. For suddenly the unrest had flared up,
and cartridges — blank and otherwise — were fired,
and troops were sent for, and a cruiser arrived, and
cables buzzed, and leader-writers started searching
through their gazetteers. Sir Blundell acted
promptly and efficiently, and the whole crisis was
over in forty-eight hours. 'What,' asked the
globe-trotting M.P. — for this was still nearly a
month before he was run over and killed by a
laundry-van; 'what,' he inquired from his place
on the green benches, 'about Messrs. Borundra
and Hari? Are these two enlightened patriots

still to be treated as common criminals, or will the Government give an assurance that their case will now be reconsidered by an impartial authority?'

The Government — like all Governments, never so active as when it had just had a bit of a fright — telegraphed to Sir Blundell for the desired information, and Sir Blundell telegraphed back that Messrs. B. and H. were eating and sleeping well, and that he had taken steps to secure their safety by doubling their guards.

Uproar from the globe-trotting M.P., from his friends in the House, and from a number of sympathetic periodicals. Messrs. B. and H. were martyrs. Sir Blundell was a murderer. A day must instantly be set aside to discuss this important matter, which reflected on our entire status among millions of highly-civilised peoples; and the leader-writers started looking up Sir Blundell's biography. The Government hedged, wobbled, tried to laugh it off, and found itself in a worse state than ever. But if it told Sir Blundell to come home and report, nothing could happen for six weeks, and by that time, with any sort of luck, the whole business would have passed into limbo. Another telegram, temporary though decisive check to the globe-trotting M.P., and Sir Blundell — accompanied, as always, by the widowed sister who kept house for him — set off on the long journey back to his two clubs.

And still you couldn't call him exactly famous, and still there seemed every prospect that the Government's Fabian tactics would do what they had so often done before. If only that laundry-van hadn't tried to cut in between an omnibus and a pantechnicon. But it did. And East Malmsey must find a new representative, and the tub-thumpers and carpet-baggers started gathering together. And Sir Blundell Hascombe disembarked on the floating landing-stage at Tilbury in a snow-storm, and a reporter who had really gone down to meet an opera-singer thought he might just as well try to get a story from the old boy too, and from that moment, as you might say, the fat was in the fire.

For Sir Blundell, who had a bad cold and was feeling extremely irritable after a rough passage up the Channel, mistook the reporter for an emissary from the Colonial Office. His story was short, sharp but exceedingly venomous. Moreover, compared with anything that a mere mezzo-soprano might say, it was the very biggest and best kind of news. It burst into the largest print at once, it was on everybody's breakfast-table by the next morning, and at East Malmsey it made the Government's candidate start putting in telephone-calls to headquarters as if his house were on fire.

Was this the way, asked all the opposition papers, to treat a great proconsul, a man who had fought for his country in three continents, a man who had been one of the first to foresee the German menace, and a man who had only just shown such extraordinary courage in stamping out the flames of open rebellion? Sir Blundell read it all, still couldn't make out how his views had achieved so much publicity, but on the whole was distinctly bucked. He was annoyed, and so was his sister, that one of the chief spots on which the limelight fell was the occasion when he and his entire company had been taken prisoners in South Africa; but the newspapers were quite right in thinking that this would increase his popularity, and when they called on him, and flattered him, and played up to him, he was ready enough to give them more stories to keep the thing going.

After all, he had done his duty, he had been recalled in the hour of what he reasonably regarded as his triumph, and it wasn't as if all this notoriety were due to anything — he was still convinced — but the indiscretion of that young jackanapes at Tilbury. Very well, then, he was afraid of nobody, and he was damned if he were going to shut up. The Colonial Office sent genuine emissaries, and he snapped off their heads so loudly that that got into the papers too. The War Office tried to intervene, and were invited to go to blazes. The two opposition candidates at East Malmsey had only to mention his name to be greeted with roars and thunders of applause, while the only paper which dared to criticise him was burnt on the Stock Exchange.

But if Sir Blundell were still a bit puzzled at times, the Government were now positively shaking in their shoes. Of course, it couldn't last, of course it would all end just as suddenly as it had begun, but meanwhile there was this infernal by-election and something had got to be done. The Cabinet met, muttered, were patently at their wits' ends. Could nobody silence this turbulent governor before it was too late? Since it was now quite impossible to dismiss him from his post, could nobody induce him to resign?

Suddenly a name suggested itself; a gleam was observed on the horizon. More and more those anxious elders thought of the dull, unimaginative, humourless countenance of Mr. Rivington; of his remarkable power of being even drearier and more longwinded than the deputations which came to see him; of his amazing inability to wander from any given point; of the strange regard in which he was held by the masses — yet if he forfeited it over this business, perhaps they wouldn't much mind this, either. And then they thought of Mr. Rivington's unquestionable willingness to do almost anything if it were represented to him as likely to further his career. But principally and above all else they thought how time was pressing, and how

if they failed at East Malmsey, they might so soon
find themselves out in the street, and how they had
now tried everything else, and had only made matters worse.

'Rivington's the man,' they said, without
definitely stating whether he were to be Jonah,
Casabianca, Mettius Curtius, or Jack the Giant-
killer. 'Rivington's the man,' they repeated, although they knew it wasn't his business, and could
only be transformed into his business by a mixture
of blandiloquence and bluff. And: 'My dear
Rivington,' wrote the Prime Minister. And:
'Dear Prime Minister,' wrote Mr. Rivington, from
the midst of his statistics and deficits. And then:
'Dear Sir Blundell,' he began again; 'the Prime
Minister has suggested ——'

'That's more like it,' thought the ruffled veteran.
'They're beginning to realise how they've treated
me at last. They're beginning to see I'm not
such a fool as they thought. They're beginning
to climb down. I'll see this man Rivington.
I'll tell him just what I think about the lot of
'em. An apology — that's what I'm going to
get. They'll cancel that cable they sent me,
they'll issue a public statement, and they'll
send me back with an absolutely free hand. If
not...'

And Sir Blundell Hascombe growled, and struggled
into his big overcoat and put on his hat, and
marched out of his hotel, and saluted a little knot
of adherents, and paused for an instant in front of
a couple of reflex cameras, and drove along to
Whitehall. At ten minutes past three a sleek
gentleman, known privately as Mr. Gawthorne and
officially as P.S. to F.S., ushered him through a
doorway into the presence of the Financial Secretary
himself. And about twenty minutes later Mrs.
Rivington parked her coach-built coupé in the
Foreign Office yard, smiled at a couple of police-

men, walked across Downing Street, smiled
at the departmental doorkeeper, and so passed
upstairs.

26

'HULLO!' she said, as she entered Mr. Gawthorne's narrow but lofty lair, and smiled at him,
too. 'Good afternoon, Tommy.'

And the sleek Mr. Gawthorne jumped to his feet,
and snatched off his horn-rimmed spectacles, and
dashed towards an Office-of-Works arm-chair.

'Hullo, Mrs. Rivington,' he said, sweeping a
number of registered papers on to the floor. 'How
splendid! I say, do sit down, won't you?'

Mrs. Rivington, who had been exchanging further
salutations with a second and not quite so sleek
gentleman (known privately as Mr. Lauderdale,
and officially as A.P.S. to F.S.), turned back again,
and shook her head.

'Thanks awfully,' she said, 'but I'm in a bit
of a hurry. I've just come from one of my terrible
committees, and I've promised to go on to a dress-
show. Such a life, isn't it? I say, is he here?
Can I see him?'

Worth noting, perhaps, and just worth explaining, that Mrs. Rivington always dodged a little
problem by calling her husband 'he' or 'him'
when speaking to his private secretaries, had
originally taken to calling Mr. Gawthorne 'Tommy'
so as to make up for any apparent standoffishness
which this system involved, but didn't expect to
be called 'Evelyn' in return, except when Mr.
Gawthorne came to dinner and they played duets
together on the piano. Mr. Gawthorne understood
it all perfectly, and neither of them had ever broken
these rather complicated rules yet.

So now Mr. Gawthorne's intelligence was as acute
as ever, and he laughed and replaced his spectacles.

'I'm afraid you can't,' he said. 'Bad luck, Mrs. Rivington; but do you know whom he's got in there?' He jerked his head towards the inner doorway.

'No,' said Mrs. Rivington. 'Of course I don't. Who is it, Tommy? Somebody important?'

Just a trace of inverted commas about the last word, implying just the faintest hint of mockery; and once more Mr. Gawthorne thought what an extraordinarily attractive woman she was, and wondered why the dickens she had ever married his present chief.

'Important?' he repeated. 'Do you hear that, Lauderdale? Why, it's the dear old general himself.'

The assistant private secretary looked up from the document which he was perusing, and gave a wizened, sardonic and slightly harassed grin.

'That's right,' he said, as the grin faded. 'Old Fireworks in person.'

'Old what?' inquired Mrs. Rivington. 'Old who?'

'Old Hascombe,' said Mr. Gawthorne. 'Come, come, Mrs. Rivington — surely you read the picture-papers.'

'Oh!' said Mrs. Rivington, taking a step nearer the inner doorway. 'Not really? Not the man all this fuss is about! Why, what on earth are they doing together?'

'Scrapping,' said Mr. Lauderdale, reaching for one of his telephones. 'Can't you hear them?'

Mrs. Rivington listened, and while one ear heard the assistant private secretary calling for tea, the other could hardly fail to be conscious of a confused barking sound on the other side of the door. She edged a bit closer.

'Steady!' said Mr. Gawthorne. 'It's all right. There won't be any bloodshed. The old boy's collar's too tight for anything like that.'

'Oh, but I would like to see him!'

'Well, wait,' said Mr. Gawthorne, hospitably. 'Have a cup of tea with us, and he's bound to come out presently. That's to say, if he doesn't have a fit.' He turned to his junior partner. 'Did you —— ' he began.

'Yes,' said Mr. Lauderdale. 'It's just coming. I'm afraid we've only got biscuits,' he added, suddenly producing a tin from behind his rampart of box-files. 'But they're fairly fresh, and —— '

'Oh, thanks awfully,' said Mrs. Rivington; 'but don't bother, please! I mean, drink away, both of you, and don't mind me; but really — Oh, this *is* maddening! I did so want to see him.'

'Old Hascombe?' asked Mr. Gawthorne, for once misled by the pronoun.

'What? No, no. That was only just a sudden idea. I mean, when I heard — I mean, I expect he's terrible, really.'

'Sounds like it,' muttered Mr. Lauderdale, grovelling in his wastepaper basket.

'But there's something rather urgent. Well, I mean, I don't suppose you'd call it urgent, Tommy — but it's awfully on my mind.'

Mr. Gawthorne relaxed his attention on the inner doorway.

'Eh?' he said. 'What's that, Mrs. Rivington?'

'Well, it's about one of your charwomen.'

'One of my which? I haven't got any.'

'Of course you have. Who do you suppose comes and tidies up all the mess you make in here?'

'Oh! One of those old trouts.'

'You cad, Tommy! She's a great deal better-looking than you are. I tell you, I liked her awfully. And apparently she's been sort of living with a man — well, I can't make out whether she was living with him or only living with him — and —— '

'Just a second,' interrupted Mr. Lauderdale, as

a uniformed messenger came in with a tray of large teacups. 'Not before the child, Mrs. Rivington.'

The child, who bore a distinct appearance of having fought in the Crimea, saluted — thereby slopping a little more tea into the three saucers — and stood at attention, breathing heavily.

'What's the matter, Cummins?' asked Mr. Gawthorne.

'Where'll I put it, sir?'

'Oh, anywhere,' said Mr. Gawthorne. 'Here,' he added, sweeping a pile of Hansards from his blotting-pad. 'Thanks. That's right. That's all.'

He stretched over for the secretarial biscuit-tin.

'Now then, Mrs. Rivington,' he said. 'Plain but healthy fare, but this is what keeps the country going. I admit it's a bit early, but you will join us, won't you?'

No answer. He turned round. He gave a sudden gasp.

'Good lord!' he exclaimed. 'Where's she gone to? Lauderdale! Where on earth ——'

Mr. Lauderdale's jaw dropped, and his arm shot out. Both secretaries bounded towards the inner doorway. There was a click, and it closed in their frantic faces. Mrs. Rivington, it seemed, had had another impish impulse. As if (she had thought) she couldn't see her own husband when she wanted to; as if Mrs. Rainbow wasn't quite as important as anything else; as if anybody could shout at poor Mervyn like that, and expect her to wait outside until they'd finished! Tea, indeed! But it was the tea that had given her the chance at last. Quick! Slip through the door while they're not looking. Shut it. Now, then!

'Gorblimey!' said Mr. Gawthorne, in his best Eton and Magdalen accent. 'That's put the lid on it at East Malmsey. Listen!'

But neither secretary could hear a sound.

28

A LARGER but equally lofty room for your inspection. Pathetically homespun when compared, for example, with the sales-manager's office at Associated Enterprises, but then the Civil Service — though Heaven knows that it is quite capable of spending money — never seems to have mastered the art of personal luxury. In the Civil Service your eminence is marked by a nicely graduated area of desk and carpet — but neither of them ever seems to be new — and by a tremendously complicated distinction in the number of fire-irons, water-bottles, inkstands, imitation leather screens and coal-scuttles to which your position entitles you. At a given salary you are advanced from a kitchen chair to a kitchen chair with arms. Further promotion brings you a sparsely upholstered seat. Higher still, and the legs are adorned with castors. But the shabbiness persists (nor would any tax-payer wish to change it) in every rank of the hierarchy, and the mixture of degenerate styles and periods, and the cupboards which lurch as you open or close them, and the shelves in which official publications have to be placed sideways, and the odd articles of furniture — rather like chiffoniers in county hotels — which quite frankly serve no purpose at all, and the dusty holland blinds in the tall windows.

Another symbol of dignity may be noted in the rather disgusting little portable wash-stands, flanked by a brown bathroom can of cold water, which lurk in odd corners, and are highly prized — though scarcely ever employed—by those who have achieved them. There is also an immense and elaborate discrimination by the heads of His Majesty's Stationery Office in the quality and quantity of the notepaper, envelopes, rulers, punches, penholders, sticks of sealing-wax and bottles of gum to which the various panjandrums are privileged. A supreme token of authority is the sole though temporary right to a small reading-lamp with an enamelled-iron shade.

Yet there's character in these apartments, nor could they ever be confused with anything else. They don't exactly proclaim efficiency, but they fairly reek with tradition. The instant that you are admitted to one of them, you realise what a vast, cumbrous, slow-moving but irresistible bit of machinery the whole organisation is, how indissolubly it is all linked with the past, and how little it needs to worry about the future. On the present, and on you as representing the present, it turns a dull, heavy and contemptuous eye. It was here long before you were born or thought of, it will still be carrying on long after it has collected its share of your death-duties. It belongs to you, it is actually part of your property, but it is most assuredly aware that you're never going to get rid of it. Long, long ago it has seen right through that fallacy of the State being the same as the People. It can afford to look shabby if it wants to. You're the one who must still try to keep up appearances.

So once more, and in spite of her familiarity with all that majestic squalor, Mrs. Rivington realised that the room itself was against her and all wives. And it was the arching of its unseen eyebrows, far more than her husband's look of astonishment or the bewildered glare from his adversary, which called up all her resistance and all her obstinacy in support of the impish impulse. She knew now that her presence was indefensible, and that nothing could justify the manner in which she had tricked the two secretaries; but she also knew that any sort of apology was quite out of the question, and she remembered and was full of defiant glory in her sex.

'Poor Mervyn,' she thought; 'how hot and worried he looks. I do wonder what that old man's been saying to him.' But there was no weakness in her own expression as she left the doorway and advanced across the ancient carpet. The only possible course now — nor did Mrs. Rivington find it so very difficult — was to keep on reminding herself of the injustice which had brought her here, and of the fact that still they were all human beings. So that Mr. Rivington drew back as the aura approached him, and his first automatic protest suddenly died away.

'What on earth——' he had begun. And stopped, because his wife was merely looking a little surprised at him. 'Where——' he started again. And then he glanced at Sir Blundell Hascombe, whose defiance was still echoing in his ears, and was still further confused to observe that he was now, apparently, awaiting an introduction.

'Oh!' said Mr. Rivington, taking two steps forward and one step back. 'Excuse me, Sir Blundell. I don't quite —— That's to say, this is — ah — this is my wife.'

'How do you do?' said Mrs. Rivington.

'Hrrm!' said the general. 'Howdydo?'

They shook hands, while the Financial Secretary tiptoed like a referee in the background.

'Of course,' said Mrs. Rivington, who was always polite, 'we've all been hearing an awful lot about you, Sir Blundell.' She smiled up at him. 'I've been seeing your photograph, too,' she added.

'Eh? Oh, yes. Ha!'

'Everywhere,' said Mrs. Rivington. And: 'Poor old pet,' she was thinking; 'I'm sure something must have upset him terribly to have made him roar like that. What marvellous cavalry legs he's got! I must say, I do think old soldiers are awfully sweet sometimes.'

'Everywhere,' she repeated. 'So it's really quite exciting to meet you.'

'Look here,' said the Financial Secretary. 'Look here, dear — just a minute — if you wouldn't mind ——'

'Yes, I know, darling. I shan't keep you a second. Sir Blundell, you *will* forgive me, won't you?'

The veteran bowed gallantly. Mrs. Rivington found him more romantic and touching than ever. Just think how he'd once been taken prisoner by the Boers!

'I say,' she said, on a rather illogical development from this thought; 'do please sit down, won't you? I know Mervyn's room's terribly uncomfortable, but —— What's that, darling? No, I keep telling you I'm not going to stay; but there's just one thing you must do at once. Open a window. You've no idea what the atmosphere's like in here, and I'm sure Sir Blundell's used to fresh air. It's *so* bad for you not even to have a crack open. Now, I'm just going to give you the tiniest little bit at the top, and you'll see what a difference it makes. Here — Mervyn! Which of these cords does one pull?'

Sir Blundell came stalking to her assistance.

'Allow me,' he said. 'Allow me, Mrs. Rivington.' And while the Financial Secretary still muttered and winced, they each caught hold of a dangling wooden handle and tugged; and nothing happened.

'How silly of me!' said Mrs. Rivington. 'I believe I'm pulling the one that shuts it. Let's try again.'

There was a wheezing sound, and the big window began to open.

'There!' said Mrs. Rivington. 'That'll do, I think, or I know Mervyn will say I've given him a chill. But it is better, isn't it, Sir Blundell? Weren't you suffocating before?'

'Ha!' said the old war-horse. 'By Jove! Was a bit stuffy. Brrh!'

'And I may just say one thing to my husband, before I leave you both? Mervyn, darling — I hope this won't bore Sir Blundell dreadfully — but it's about one of the charwomen who work here. You see ——'

'My dear girl ——'

'Yes, I know, darling. It's too sickening of me to come and bother you like this, but, honestly, it's rather urgent. Such a nice woman, Sir Blundell; such a nice face and so hard-working. And this committee that I'm on — we all went to visit her after lunch just now, and — would you believe it, Sir Blundell?—they want to report her to the office-keeper here, and have her turned out of her job. Don't you think it's perfectly monstrous!'

'Eh?' said Sir Blundell, seriously. 'Why? What's the good lady done?'

'Do you really want to know? Well, you will back me up, won't you? It seems her husband left her, and then perhaps she was rather too kind to another rather awful man — but it strikes me as absolutely her own business, and nothing whatever to do with how she scrubs the floors. Don't you agree, Sir Blundell? Don't you think people who interfere with other people are disgusting? I wish *you'd* been there to take my side!'

'Eh?' said Sir Blundell, with another courteous inclination. 'That's right, Mrs. Rivington. That's right.'

'Of course it's right. Now, you tell Mervyn that he's not to let anyone bully him, and that he's got to be firm. Write it down, Mervyn. The name's Mrs. Rainbow. No, write it down, darling. I know you'll only forget if you try and keep everything in your head.'

Mr. Rivington's gold pencil-case began scribbling

even while his whole angular form protested that it was going to do nothing of the sort. In spite of himself, and in spite of all that was still at stake, it was an intense relief that Sir Blundell was no longer roaring. He realised that he was getting his own wind back; that he'd remembered several arguments which had been lost in the earlier tempest; that he was now quite ready to start all over again. He'd just ring for Tommy Gawthorne, give him that message about the charwoman, get him to show his wife out, and then ——

He looked up with a start. His hand drew back from the battery of bell-pushes. Great Scot, what was Evie saying now!

'— absolutely all on your side, of course. I mean, everyone is, aren't they? And yet, Sir Blundell, I should have thought you'd had quite enough of living so far away, after all this time. I mean, England — and even London; well, there's nothing quite like them, is there? Even now — even in the spring, I mean, when it's so cold and keeps on raining — well, it *is* rather nice, don't you think? This morning, for instance, Sir Blundell. Did you notice the colour of the sky just about breakfast-time? Perfect, wasn't it? Didn't it make you hate the idea of leaving it all?'

Sir Blundell Hascombe had laid one arm along the dark-brown mantelpiece. With his other hand he was pulling at his bristly little moustache. Now, however, his extraordinarily pale blue eyes, instead of glittering — as they had glittered ever since Tilbury — with defiance and irritation, were puzzled and, as it seemed to Mrs. Rivington, almost child-like. 'Poor old boy,' she was thinking; 'I'm sure it's only his liver or something that's really at the bottom of it all. It must be dreadful to feel so cross — and never to have had a wife to soothe one down. And just look at the way his collar runs into his poor old neck. But I do wish,' thought Mrs. Rivington, 'that I knew how to stop talking to him, or how to get away without letting Mervyn think that I'm sorry I came.'

And her attractive voice continued to flatter and bemuse. And the Financial Secretary continued to gulp and dither in the offing. And Sir Blundell Hascombe continued to stare at her and to wonder what on earth her game was, because she was so entirely different from anything that he had ever met; and obviously wasn't a fool, like his sister, or a mere bundle of smart selfishness, such as one met at luncheon-parties and dinner-parties, or even a siren, as he recognised and identified the term. No, she was just a thoroughly simple and pleasant woman, who didn't make him feel shy, and quite clearly liked talking to him. Though he never forgot that it would all be over in a moment, his frayed nerves felt unusually calm. Once or twice, as he recalled some of the things that Mr. Rivington had said, his mouth twitched, and of course none of this was going to make the faintest difference to the determination with which he had arrived; but meanwhile...

'Yes, yes, Mrs. Rivington. I know what you mean. But you're young, and ——'

'Young, Sir Blundell! Don't be absurd! Why, how old do you think my eldest boy is? Fifteen. Isn't he, Mervyn?'

'Yes, dear. Quite. But ——'

'And taller than his father already. What do you think of that? And so good-looking. No, don't laugh at me, Sir Blundell; he is really. You don't know how I miss him — and the others, too — now they're all away at school. That was what made me go on that awful committee I was just telling you about. I'm not really that kind of person — in fact, I know I'm hopeless at it; but I just had to do something when Mervyn's away all day, and most of the night as well. Bobby'll be most terribly interested when he hears how I've met you. He's going into the army, you know, and —— Well, I wonder if I dare ask you something.'

'Eh?' said Sir Blundell, leaning forward again. And: 'Evie!' protested the Financial Secretary from his place near the big desk.

'Listen to poor Mervyn!' said Mrs. Rivington, with a gay, maternal laugh. 'He's terrified that I'm going to interfere with his business — as if I ever should! No, dear Sir Blundell, it was just —— I mean, if you *would* be so kind as to let me have your autograph — for Bobby, I mean. Do you think...?'

'Heh?' said Sir Blundell Hascombe. 'Autograph. Well, if you ask me like that — of course! Pleasure, I'm sure. Is he going to Sandhurst?'

'Well, we've not absolutely decided, have we, Mervyn? I mean, he's awfully clever in his own way, but.... Come along, Sir Blundell. Let's use a bit of Mervyn's beautiful stationery. You won't give him away, will you?'

And she laughed again, and again she thought: 'Why on earth am I going on like this, even for Bobby's sake? I'm feeling quite mad, but I *am* sorry for that poor old man in his tight collar, and I'm *not* going to catch Mervyn's eye so long as he tries to look at me like that. And, anyhow, you can't say this isn't better than leaving them alone together and letting them quarrel. And anyhow, I've saved that poor woman in those awful model dwellings, so perhaps I'll be forgiven.'

And Sir Blundell Hascombe also laughed, though he would have been just as hard put to it to explain why, and left the dark-brown mantelpiece, and followed Mrs. Rivington across to the Financial Secretary's big desk, and lowered himself into the Financial Secretary's big chair, and started putting on his eyeglasses.

'Now, then,' said Mrs. Rivington, reaching towards the pen-tray. And suddenly, just beneath her, she realised that the veteran's shoulders had stiffened and that the top of his sandy-grey head was turning a deep maroon. For it was natural enough that the Financial Secretary should have prepared himself for this interview by a perusal of all the relevant notes and minutes, and it was natural enough that they should still be strewn all over his vast blotting-pad, and it was no less natural that anyone catching sight of his own name should start reading long before his conscience or any other artificial impediment could stop him.

Mrs. Rivington stood waiting. Mr. Rivington, having washed his hands of the whole nonsensical business — figuratively, one means, and with no recourse to that battered accessory in the far corner — was standing staring out of the window. 'Above all,' read the old man at the big desk, on a sheet of the Colonial Secretary's personal note-paper, 'above all avoid letting Sir Blundell know that Messrs. Borundra and Hari have been promised their release. This, I am convinced, will only make him more anxious to return at once, since it is a reversal of the policy ——'

The old man emitted a sudden and sinister rumbling sound. Yes, he was thinking, with astonishing celerity and clarity, that was just what Malcolmson would have done as soon as his back was turned; just what any up-to-date young theorist would think so very wise and clever. And if he did go back, the two rascals would go on enjoying official hospitality until they died of over-eating. He'd see to that. But if he didn't go back, if he resigned and they were let out — why, the poor fools would be knifed by their own friends in a week. And Malcolmson would be in the soup, and Fotheringay — good fellow, that! — would get the post, and the revenue would be saved years of expense, and he himself need never go abroad again. It was plain murder, of course; and it was his reluctance to commit plain murder — for soldiers always prefer it coloured — that had led to all the trouble in January. But so long as Malcolmson was done for, so long as Fotheringay stepped over him and had a free hand, it meant at least five guaranteed years of peace and prosperity; and if anyone thought he were going to lift his little finger to stand in the way of that....

It meant climbing down, of course. But it was worth it.

And the old country was pretty good when one was seventy-four. What was it that someone had been saying about that sky this morning? Yes, he'd seen it when he was out in the Row, and even then he'd half thought that if only those two fat scoundrels could be got quietly out of the way; if only he hadn't been so soft-hearted about 'em....

Funny—damned funny, in fact—that Malcolmson and this high-minded Government were going to send them to their deaths. But they were going all right, this time. And they believed in survival, so it might teach 'em something at last. Show 'em who their best friend had been all these years. Give 'em something to say to Malcolmson when he turned up and started putting on his halo.

And suddenly Sir Blundell Hascombe rose to his feet, and pushed back the big chair (so that Mrs. Rivington had to skip aside to avoid it), and spoke.

'Rivington!' he said. 'Just a moment. I've been thinking things over. I think — I think, if you don't mind, we might reconsider one or two points. At my time of life one isn't as quick, perhaps, to see all round a subject, but — ah ——'

The cool air, entering through that slit at the top of the window, no longer breathed on the Financial Secretary's glossy dome, but it had served its purpose by this time. The fresh start, quite clearly, was to be no mere resumption of hammer and tongs. Reason was now to discuss with reason, as the former adversaries drew slowly together across the shabby carpet.

'My dear feller ——' Sir Blundell Hascombe was saying, as Mrs. Rivington — with the tiniest pout and tiniest shrug — slipped out through the door by which she had entered. Too bad, she was thinking, about Bobby's autograph-book (but perhaps there'd be another opportunity later on), and too curious how everything had suddenly changed, so that even if she'd wanted to stay — which of course she didn't — those two representatives of the childish sex would never have noticed her. Not that she was in the least offended, because so long as Mervyn were happy again, and were enjoying himself talking shop, and so long as that poor old pet of a general were purring like that, instead of snapping and growling, well, that was absolutely all that mattered, wasn't it? So often, she knew, an interruption did wonders when two people — especially men, who of course were just the same as boys — had started losing their tempers and saying things that they didn't really mean.

So Mrs. Rivington smiled vaguely and benevolently, first at the ambient air, and then, as he appeared just in front of her, at the sleek Mr. Gawthorne.

'Hullo, Tommy,' she said. 'I say, I've spoken about that charwoman, so do remind him, won't you? What? Oh, no; they're getting on splendidly now, and I simply *adore* that sweet old Sir Blundell. No, don't bother to come down, Tommy; I've got my little car.'

Another smile for the not quite so sleek Mr. Lauderdale, and Mrs. Rivington had passed altogether from the scene of her unconscious triumph. As she drove by the Admiralty, the newspaper

placards had already changed from 'Paddington
Murder. Man Detained' to 'Paddington Murder.
An Arrest.'   And though she didn't know this,
either, here was just the fillip to the public appetite
which would finally drive Sir Blundell Hascombe
from the front page.   With his resignation, with
his instant descent into dusk and oblivion, his
champions at East Malmsey and elsewhere would
be left simply beating the air.   The Government
would save the seat, Mr. Rivington's prestige and
position would be stronger than ever, and the
crisis would have dwindled, shrivelled and collapsed.

Only half-way along Pall Mall did Mrs. Rivington
suddenly remember her appointment at the dress
show, but the clock on her dashboard conclusively
advised her that it was now far too late to think
of keeping it.   Well, never mind; she'd telephone
when she got in, and of course Maisie would have
to forgive her.   A rather silly and extravagant
appointment to have made in any case.   Straight
ahead, then, to her home in Eaton Place.   And a
sofa, and a novel, and some real teapot tea.

29

NED PLUNKET— no need to look back, for he's
quite a new character — was rather sick with things
at the beginning of March, and not, as you will
probably agree, without a certain amount of reason.
To begin with, though of course he was devoted
to his mother, he'd had the very dickens of a
struggle with her not to stop him taking this new
job at all.   She'd called him ungrateful, which he'd
naturally disliked very much; she'd wept, and
though there was nothing new in this, it never
failed to embarrass and torment him; and then
she'd appealed to all sorts of feelings, which of
course he possessed, but which, in this case, had
simply got to be put aside.

'You want to leave me,' said Mrs. Plunket, and though Ned knew perfectly well that if he'd left her without warning she'd hardly have noticed the difference, he had to waste hours in explaining that that had nothing to do with it at all. 'What was the use,' asked Mrs. Plunket, 'of your father working so hard and leaving you enough to live on, if you go and live like a navvy with a lot of dirty men in overalls?' And then Ned had to exercise the most enormous and exhausting care in his choice of language so as to make it clear, first, that he wasn't criticising his father; secondly, that he couldn't possibly do what his heart was set on without going through the shops, and, thirdly, that having spent four years at the university and then gone round the world, he just couldn't and wouldn't take this as a complete contribution to his life's labours.

'I'll be perfectly clean whenever you see me,' he said. 'Nails and everything, mother; I swear.'

'It's not safe,' said Mrs. Plunket. 'They're always having accidents in those places. Dropping things, and getting blown up, and being scalded to death.'

'Well, I'll be all right,' said Ned.

'If you must work,' said Mrs. Plunket, 'why can't you go into the City like everyone else? You'd get on far quicker, and you'd have your Saturdays off, and I shouldn't have nearly so much to worry about. After all, there's your father's old firm, and you know they'd be delighted to have you ——'

'Yes, but don't you see, mother? That's not the point. I'm *keen* on this other job.'

Sometimes it seemed that it was just this keenness that Mrs. Plunket resented most. Perhaps it made her jealous, perhaps it was the fact that she herself had never been keen on anything but food, clothes and comfort that puzzled and annoyed her. One doesn't wish to present her as a caricature, and quite a lot of people, apart from her son, held her in considerable affection and esteem. But at home, and with one's own nearest and dearest, rather selfish middle-aged ladies don't always keep to the half-tones of dignified portraiture. Mrs. Plunket said a lot of things which she would have thought quite incredible if she had heard them in a film or a play. And her son wasn't always either patient or considerate, as they searched for the joints in each other's armour. But he was in training, and she wasn't. He could attack, and she could only resist. He knew exactly what he wanted, and she was always wanting something different. So that presently, and after the misdirection of a great deal of energy, Ned got his way, and Mrs. Plunket subsided into muffled and muted opposition. And then he actually went, and as a matter of fact Mrs. Plunket didn't miss him any more than when he had been at school, or at Cambridge, or in New South Wales.

For Mrs. Plunket, like the barbarians, lived in the present; and the present, for Mrs. Plunket, consisted eternally of food, clothes and comfort. And if she had a little grievance, such as Ned's eccentricity, which she could discuss with her friends over the bridge-table, then her contentment was even greater than if she had no such grievance at all. And if Ned had asked her for money, she would have sent it him like a shot—just as quickly, directly and unquestioningly. Only he didn't, because thanks to his father he had all and more than he wanted; so that even when the next aggravating thing happened, and it suddenly became necessary to remove his appendix with hardly any warning at all, it was the victim alone who paid for this unpleasant experience, while the victim's mother never knew anything about it until he was entirely out of danger.

'Just imagine it,' said Mrs. Plunket, at the bridge-table. 'Not a word, not a syllable, when all that time absolutely *anything* might have happened. Just imagine the shock to my feelings when I heard! Really,' said Mrs. Plunket, 'the way one's children consider nobody but themselves in these days —— Well,' said Mrs. Plunket, 'it will be weeks and weeks before I get over it.'

B, Y and Z all thoroughly agreed with her, though as a matter of fact there was only one child between the four of them, and Mrs. Plunket's new grievance gave her a great deal of quiet entertainment. But Ned, also, took weeks and weeks to get over it — as most people do when surgeons have been playing about with their insides — and eight hours' daily exercise in the engineering works became temporarily quite out of the question, and there was nothing for it but to come home and wait until he were strong enough to start all over again. And this was why he felt rather sick with things at the beginning of March.

Mrs. Plunket didn't exactly tell him that she and Providence had arranged the whole setback, and that they had been fully justified in doing so; but this was her attitude, and it did little or nothing to hasten his convalescence. Eventually, as he was well aware, he'd be fitter than ever, and of course his essential keenness was quite unimpaired, and of course appendicitis was the kind of thing that might happen to anyone. But to be kept hanging about like this, and to be wasting so much time, and to realise, as he did, that all the old arguments were bound to reappear as soon as he did recover — well, it was pretty maddening and exasperating and depressing. Quite right, of course, to be restless and impatient at the age of twenty-four, and very creditable to be so determined to work in spite of one's riches; yet it must be admitted that at the beginning of March young Mr. Plunket was

distinctly nervy, jumpy and on edge. Distinctly
fidgety, worried and off his accustomed balance.
Distinctly liable, in other words — though the idea
had never occurred to him — to slip suddenly into
quite a different kind of trouble.

'But of course you must go,' said Mrs. Plunket.
'Of course it's just what you need to cheer you up
and stop all this moping. If it were a late party,
or if you'd got to dance and get tired, that would
be quite another thing. But to go just round the
corner, and to people who were so kind to you on
the boat, and then to be back again in plenty of
time for dinner — why, it will do you all the good in
the world. Merryweather!' added Mrs. Plunket,
addressing her expectant butler. 'Tell Mrs. Watson
that Mr. Edward will be delighted.' And: 'There!'
she said, as the butler went back to the telephone.
'Or course you must go out and enjoy yourself,
instead of sitting up there in your room all the time.
So much better for you, dear. So much more
sensible, when I've got to be out playing bridge
myself.'

And she waddled over and patted her son on the
shoulder, so that he found it quite difficult not to
squirm, and then waddled out of the drawing-room
to go and talk about food with her cook, or possibly
about clothes and comfort with her maid.

'Rot!' thought Ned. 'Of course I'm not
going. Why should I go when I shan't know
anyone, and I hate cocktails even if I were allowed
to drink them? Not,' he thought, 'that I shall
bother to ring up again, because of course the
Watsons will never notice if I come or not. And
anyhow,' he thought, 'it's a year since I saw them,
and dash it all, they weren't really any kinder to
me than I was to them, and they'd probably be
frightful if one met them on dry land. I wish,'
muttered Ned Plunket, 'that people who hardly know
one would have the decency to leave one alone.'

And then he was disgusted to find that in his present low state of health his eyes were filling with tears. And he was so heartily ashamed of this quite excusable weakness that he rushed upstairs and started reading an extraordinarily dull article on strains and stresses, until he had given himself a severe headache but had restored a little of his self-respect.

'After all,' he now thought, 'it wasn't the Watsons' fault that mother was there when the message came. But I'm not going.'

'Of course I'm not going,' he repeated at intervals during the next few days. And on the day itself he was so resolved not to go that he would almost have welcomed a maternal reminder, just so that he could flare up and denounce the Watsons for their impertinent hospitality all over again. But Mrs. Plunket had forgotten all about it, and went off to her bridge-party without a word. So that now — only please don't think that any attack is being made on a semi-invalid who had a good deal to put up with — a complicated kind of self-justification began drifting into a still more confused kind of reaction. If nobody cared whether he went or not, why shouldn't he go? If he'd got to waste his time anyhow, why shouldn't he waste it thoroughly? If people were mad enough to invite anyone as uninteresting as himself, why shouldn't they get what was coming to them? And one didn't want to be rude, of course, and the more one suffered, the more cross-grained satisfaction one would derive. And as it didn't really matter two pins what one did, one might just as well do something unexpected. If one hated it when one got there — as of course one would — well, then, at least one would prove that one had been perfectly right from the beginning. 'Gosh!' thought Ned Plunket. 'I'm fed up with feeling so rotten, and I've half a mind to go there and get tight.'

And he knew he didn't mean this, but it cheered him wonderfully even to imagine anything so feckless and reckless, as it well might cheer anybody who had been through all his recent experiences and was still on a diet. And some may say that this was his subconsciousness taking charge of his repressions, and others that he was merely obeying his inscrutable destiny as rather illegibly written in the stars and on the palm of his right hand. But the main point is that at half-past six he suddenly slammed the front door behind him, and went. And that ten minutes later he had fallen madly in love.

30

IT CAN be done, you know. One doesn't say that it often happens like this, but on the present occasion there was a good deal to make it happen like this. Ned Plunket was a little sub-normal, and then he'd come out determined not to enjoy himself (which is always dangerous), and then the girl was really an extraordinarily nice girl, and then — if you see what one means — he had never been inoculated. Yes, it's an absolute fact that he'd been right round the world, without hurrying and on every possible kind of vessel, and had returned as serious and single-minded as he had set out. That was the way that Ned Plunket was made, and if anyone cares to point out that he was just a little bit of a prig, then anyone will be perfectly correct. But if anyone proceeds to deduce that he was a silly ass and a milksop, then he will be labouring under a complete and categorical error.

At Ned Plunket's age, they should remember, young gentlemen can't possibly have experienced everything, and the ones who know most about foreign travel and machine-tools — and in this case, when he wasn't having appendicitis, about Rugby football as well — are hardly ever likely to be the ones who know most about helping young ladies into evening wraps.   And if young ladies ever chose to play up to solid merit, instead of naturally preferring good dancers, they would probably have found it mere child's play to turn this particular example into any kind of fool that you like.

But they don't, and they didn't, and Ned Plunket remained extremely vulnerable but prodigiously secure from their attentions.   For they thought him heavy, and he thought them alarming and dull. And they left him alone, and he walked — but never danced — over the very thinnest crust without ever dreaming that it was suddenly bound to give way. And thus up to the very moment when it cracked, crumbled and precipitated him into the swirling depths beneath, it had never more than remotely crossed his mind that any such peril existed.   One of the largest, easiest targets which can ever have offered itself for Cupid's aim; only sometimes it seems that Cupid doesn't hurry himself when he knows he can't possibly miss.

So Ned Plunket rode up in the lift at a large block of furnished flats, and alighted with a couple of women who were quite clearly bound for the same destination, and followed them along some thick carpeting, and waited until they had gone in ahead of him, and then rushed in himself just as the door was closing, and dropped his hat and coat among a lot of other hats and coats, and trailed after a rather flustered-looking maidservant towards a pretty considerable uproar.   And if it had been at all possible to do so, would have been more than delighted to turn round and go home again.

Only of course this was now quite out of the question, and the maidservant conducted him to the outskirts of a very typical aggregation of totally unknown guests, and looked more flustered than ever, and appeared to decide that the best course to pursue was to leave the latest arrival to look after himself, and so — influenced, no doubt, by another trill from the outer door bell — ducked, dodged, dashed off and disappeared.

'This,' thought Ned Plunket, 'is a bit awkward. I wish to goodness I'd never come.'

And he moved forward into a gap, and the gap closed up behind him, and somebody drove an elbow into his ribs, and he turned round to apologise, and somebody else trod heavily on his foot, and he turned round again and lurched into another gap, and all this time he continued to think how very awkward it was and how very happy it would make him to be almost anywhere else.

What a noise, he thought, and what an extraordinary collection of people; and then he thought he saw Mr. Watson, and also thought that he saw a rather tortuous means of approaching him. And thus he contrived to force himself round a very sharp piece of furniture, and then it was quite obvious that the man wasn't Mr. Watson at all, and somebody gave a sharp cry and said: 'Please! You're standing on my dress.'

Round shot Ned Plunket again, contorted with guilt and compunction, and at the same moment yet another elbow caught him sharply under the shoulder-blades, and a little rug slipped from beneath his feet, and a spasm seized him in the neighbourhood of his lost appendix, and he sat down extremely abruptly and as luck would have it on a chair.

'Sorry!' he gasped. 'I'm terribly sorry. I do beg your pardon. I ——'

It was at this point that he first really caught sight of the girl who was now so remarkably near to him, and his immediate, uncontrollable impulse was to get up again and bolt madly from such breath-taking beauty. Mind you, this was only his summary of her appearance, and since it is notorious that beauty, whether breath-taking or not, lies merely in the eye of the beholder, it is quite possible that he was entirely wrong. But he did try to get up again, and he couldn't because of the phalanx in front of him, and now he thought: 'This is more awkward than ever, because I've been terribly rude to this absolute vision, and of course she thinks I'm an oaf and a cad.'

Notwithstanding this desperate delusion, he took another glance at her — with his forehead slightly furrowed — and was completely overwhelmed to observe that she was smiling at him.

'It's all right,' she said. 'You didn't tear it.'

'Good lord!' said Ned Plunket.

'I beg your pardon?' said the girl.

'Nothing,' said Ned Plunket. 'Terribly clumsy, I mean. Ghastly crowd, though. I wonder —— I mean, look here; can I get you something?'

'No, thanks awfully. I'm just having a little rest.'

'A little rest? Oh, yes. I see. Er ——'

'Yes?'

'Would you mind awfully if ——'

'If what?'

'—— if I didn't leave you. For a bit, I mean. You see, I don't know anyone here.'

'That's funny,' said the girl. 'Nor do I.'

'I mean,' said Ned Plunket, 'of course I know the Watsons. I met them when I was going round the world.'

'Oh?' said the girl. She looked a little puzzled, he thought; or was it a little disappointed? And then: 'Ought I to know them too?' she asked. 'Who *are* the Watsons?'

'What!' said Ned Plunket, continuing to gape, but now — as he was horrified to believe — at a shameless gate-crasher. 'Why —— Well, really, I mean. Don't you realise this is the Watsons' flat? Or ——' He broke off, as the girl still smiled at him and a dreadful alternative suggested itself. 'Do you mean to say,' he asked, 'that this *isn't* the Watsons' flat?'

'Of course not! It's Mrs. Babbacombe's. Look! There she is.'

'Good lord!' said Ned Plunket, without attempting to look. 'I say, how ghastly! I say, how appalling! I say — I must clear out at once.'

And once more he made an effort to rise, and once more he was forced down. Only this time, unless he were very much mistaken, somebody had given a gentle but quite definite pull at his sleeve.

'Don't go!' said the girl. 'Don't leave me. I was an idiot to come, I suppose, and of course Mrs. Babbacombe only asked me because of all the trouble she'd given. And she hasn't introduced anyone, and I don't know a soul here, and I've been on my feet all day, and —— Oh, please don't go just yet!'

'Well,' said Ned Plunket, seriously; 'I don't *want* to go.'

But he wondered what sort of trouble Mrs. Babbacombe had given, and detested her for giving it; and he also wondered, but didn't dare ask, why his exquisite companion should have been on her feet all day. And for some reason he tried to glance at her feet, and the girl thought: 'He's nice. I must say, he's quite as nice as he looks. But he's one of these rich, idle ones, or he wouldn't go round the world and come to cocktail parties, so I'd better stop being so blithering and mad.'

Because this girl, you see, had developed a deep prejudice against the rich, idle ones, having suffered a good deal from their attentions since she had taken to earning her own living, and also because she had what some people would call ideals and other people would call a complex. That is to say that she was rather romantic and at the same time rather fastidious, so that she had often started by thinking that men were far nicer than they were, and had then suddenly seen very good reasons for changing her mind. And she had come to the conclusion — in which it is hard to say that she was wrong — that the rich, idle ones were, generally speaking, a pest and a menace; and to the further conclusion — in which she may have been perfectly right, even if a bit impractical — that everyone ought to work for his living like herself.

And then again, because this girl worked for her living in the midst of other people's luxury and extravagance, every now and then she longed for some of the easy money which she thought she despised, or at any rate for some of the circumstances which such easy money could provide. So that, like a whole lot of other characters, what she did wasn't always or nearly so intelligible as what she believed that she thought; and though she scorned Mrs. Babbacombe for her wealth and the preposterous influence which anyone so plain and shapeless wielded in the world of dress, yet she had come along this evening full of vague ideas that she was going to enjoy herself, and had been terribly disappointed when she had started by not enjoying herself at all.

In fact, and as is now reasonably manifest, this girl, also, was a slight prig; though slight prigs, it sometimes occurs to one, aren't necessarily the less admirable for that. And now, as she looked at Ned Plunket and talked to him and listened to him and kept finding so much to smile at, she would have been glad enough to be rather less fastidious and rather more romantic. Because honestly he was most awfully nice — so nice that she had quite forgotten how tired she was; and honestly it did seem a shame that her principles still warned her against anyone who fell so clearly within the suspected category. And if Ned Plunket had thought to tell her that the great shadow which at present lay over his life was the fact that he couldn't put on a suit of overalls and clock in at a big engineering works at an hour when most citizens are still fast asleep, who knows how swiftly she might have been swept right away, or how differently he might have spent the following two weeks and a half?

But he didn't want to bore her, and he didn't want to complain to her, and somehow or other it was astonishing how easy it was to keep chattering away on all sorts of general subjects. Not that he had any clear idea of what he was actually saying, for seldom had so many different thoughts whirled round in his head at the same time. 'She's marvellous,' he thought. 'Whatever happens, I must keep her here as long as I possibly can.' And: 'Of course I ought to go at once,' he thought, 'but, after all, it isn't as if I were drinking the cocktails, or as if one more or less can make any odds in a crowd like this.' And: 'By Jove!' he thought; 'it's extraordinary how much better I feel this evening, and just when it seemed I was going to go on feeling rotten for ever.' And: 'Gosh, look at her nose!' he thought. And: 'I'll never say a word against the Watsons after this,' he thought. And: 'Oh, lord, if only I had the nerve to ask her what her name is.' And a little later: 'Oh, golly, if only I were one of those fellows who know how to get girls like this to come out to dinner.'

And when the crowd began to thin, he talked faster than ever; first so that he shouldn't notice it himself, and secondly so that the girl shouldn't notice it either. And of course the girl noticed it just as much as he did, only by this time the chemical action, or the sympathetic vibrations, or whatever you choose to call it, had gone so far as to be quite out of her control. 'It's ridiculous,' she could still tell herself, 'that I can really be so attracted by someone I don't know, and of course if he goes on like this with a stranger, it means that he goes on like this with everyone.' But at the same time

she knew that he didn't, and at the same time her
heart kept beating so loudly that she had to laugh
to drown the sound of it, and at the same time she
felt so terribly excited about something that she
hardly knew what she was saying. Only of course
it was all impossible and absurd, because he was the
kind that went round the world, and she was the
kind who went to and fro between rooms in Earl's
Court and a shop in Grosvenor Street.

And she was sensible, and she'd seen what other
girls had done, and how it always ended by their
losing their jobs — and that was sometimes the
least part of it — when they started by losing their
heads with the rich, idle ones. So that still this
excellent though slightly priggish young woman
clung to her principles and prejudices, and told
herself that of course she wouldn't go out with
him, even if he asked her. And then she thought:
'But he might ask me, anyhow.' And then she
thought, which happened to be true: 'But perhaps
I'm quite wrong, and he's *really* different.'

And then she looked at him again, and the
chemical action or the sympathetic vibrations were
suddenly so abnormally violent that both parties
became convinced that all the lights had gone out
and that the room was spinning round on a very
eccentric axis. And they put out their hands to
steady themselves, and their hands met, and
several million volts seemed to shoot through both
their systems, and they both realised that they
had gone completely crazy, and made a couple of
supreme efforts, and jumped to their feet.

'Oh!' cried the girl. 'What is it?'

'Eh?' said Ned Plunket, wildly. And then:
'My hat! Everybody's gone. Blast! I must
clear out at once. I say!'

'What?'

'Do I — do I see you again?'

'Oh, dear!'

'Can't I ring up? Or something?'

'No. I mean, all right. Yes.'

'I may? Gosh! How marvellous! I say — are you going anywhere? Now, I mean? Shall I take you?'

Was the girl hesitating? Had he really said what he thought he'd just said? What was she looking at? He span round. Help! It was Mrs. What's-her-name. The hostess.

'Oh,' she was saying; 'I hope I'm not interrupting you, my dear. But there's something I just wanted to show you. It'll save me telephoning in the morning, and ——'

She gave a vague smile at her unknown guest, but her unknown guest had already bowed, gasped and gone. There was another door that led straight out into the hall where his hat and coat lay alone on a big *cassone*. He fled through it, snatched them up, and started tearing along the richly-carpeted corridor. It seems unquestionable that if he had been capable at this moment of even the lowest form of reasoning, he must have detected the grave blunder which he was committing. Even instinct, you might have imagined, would have kept him hanging around in the main hall or on the stairs until the vision was vouchsafed to him again. Actually, however, his movements appear to have been guided by some kind of palsied automatism. A complete blank descended on him as he drifted across the fortunately deserted streets, tottered up his own steps, pulled out his latchkey, and came blinking past the umbrella-stand.

'Hullo!' he suddenly thought; 'there's a butler.' And 'Hullo!' he thought again; 'it's old Merryweather.' And 'Hullo!' he thought for the third time; 'what's he doing with those soup plates? Gosh, I must be late for dinner!'

Consciousness continued to return, and he hurried into the dining-room.

'Hullo, Mother,' he said. 'I'm frightfully sorry I'm so late. Only ——'

'It's all right, dear,' said Mrs. Plunket. 'I remembered where you were, and I knew it wasn't worth waiting. Never mind about dressing,' said Mrs. Plunket. 'Come and have your dinner while it's hot.'

'Oh,' said Ned, in a slightly stupefied manner. 'Right. Thanks.'

'And did you enjoy yourself?' asked Mrs. Plunket, breaking off a bit of toast. 'Did you have a nice time with your friends?'

'What?' said Ned. 'Oh, yes. Rather, I mean. At least ——'

His jaw dropped. Blackness swept over him. The family portraits rocked and shuddered in their sumptuous frames. Luckily Mrs. Plunket was now helping herself to a whiting, and had no eyes for anything else. But no one on earth could have realised the extremity of horror by which her hapless son had suddenly been stricken and overwhelmed. He hadn't the faintest notion how he was ever to find the only girl in the world again.

31

HE MIGHT, you say, have taken up his pen. 'Dear Mrs. Babbacombe,' he might have written; 'you don't know me and I don't know you, but I came to your party without being asked and stayed there for the best part of an hour and a half, during which time I found myself exceedingly attracted by a fair-haired girl in a brownish sort of frock with some kind of lace on it. I enclose a stamped and addressed envelope, and would you mind telling me ——'

But of course he couldn't write a letter like that. Don Juan himself couldn't have written a letter like that, and if he had, does it seem credible that

Mrs. Babbacombe would have answered it? Most
certainly she would have done nothing of the sort
— though she might possibly have handed it on to
the police — and then, again, can there ever have
been a more unpractised lover than Ned Plunket?
Admittedly he was acquiring experience about the
pains and torments of the profession at the most
startling rate; but except for that mad moment
when their hands had touched and he had so
astonished himself by offering to take the girl
home, he knew nothing whatever about the other
side of it all. The thing had come on him like a
thunderclap, it had knocked him silly — particularly silly, less serious-minded characters might say
— he'd said and done all the first things that had
come into his head, and now he was in the position
of one who beats wildly, and with ever-increasing
annoyance and discomfort, against the empty,
mocking air.

The girl had gone. He'd lost her. He didn't
know her name, he didn't know her address, he
didn't know anything about her except that she
had apparently been on her feet all day, that Mrs.
Babbacombe — curse the old hag! — had given her
a lot of trouble, and that he could no more get her
face or voice out of his system than he could grow
a new appendix. There was no one in whom he
could confide. There was nothing whatever that
he could do. The whole situation was so fantastic
that sometimes a high, agonised titter burst from
him as he lay awake in the darkness of the night,
or scowled over his textbooks, or went for long
walks all round the London parks. Sometimes
the remains of his reason took hold of him, and
he saw himself as he supposed that other people
would see him. As a fool, in other words; as a
blithering idiot who'd gone half off his nut or
onion over somebody who, of course, had never
thought of him again. In these moods he piled

it on, covering himself with opprobrium, calling himself every contemptuous name under the sun, doing everything in his power to shake off the enchantment which bound him.

'I've done it,' he thought, as he came sweating out of one of these paroxysms. 'I'm all right now. I've got over it. I see what an ass I've been.'

Phew! He drew in a deep breath, flung back his shoulders; and at once the same fair-haired vision returned, far, far more clearly than before. He cowered, staggered and groaned.

'You darling!' he muttered, and then coughed because Merryweather had come round the corner with a basket of logs and a couple of evening papers.

'Beg pardon, sir?'

'Nothing,' said Ned Plunket, kicking his own metaphorical hindquarters with his own astral boot. And 'Gosh!' he thought; 'it's getting worse instead of better. Gosh, if only I could forget!'

'And how's Ned?' asked B, Y and Z over the bridge-table up in the drawing-room.

'Getting on splendidly,' said Mrs. Plunket, 'and going for such lots of walks, I'm glad to say. Poor boy, I think he realises what a mistake he made in going off to those dreadful works, and getting so ill like that. My deal, is it? And of course he can really do anything that he wants to at home.'

If Ned had heard her, he wouldn't have said anything. It was now half-way through March, and at the end of the month he was going back into his overalls, whether his mother liked it or not. Last time he'd been sorry for her, and had taken the trouble to argue; but this time it was a question of his own lingering sanity even more than of his keenness or his career. He was still devoted to his rich, fat, middle-aged, unreasonable, easygoing mother, but he'd made his plans, and he'd squared the doctor, and he'd *got* to get out of this house and work, if need be, till he dropped. That was the way to get over it. Everybody said that was the way to get over it. And he was going to get over it. He glared, steadily; then less steadily; and then he reeled against the mantelpiece and buried his head in his hands.

Ten more days still, and always the aching and the hunger and the bouts of wild resentment against his own weakness, and the abject reaction, and the face and the voice to haunt him whatever he did. Then a week. Then less and less than a week. Now he was going tomorrow, and still he hadn't told his mother. Because, he said, she had really been told at the beginning. And because, he felt, one more scene on the top of everything else, and he'd go out of his mind. And because, he knew perfectly well, he had funked it.

And then suddenly — and now it was after lunch on the very last day — he thought: 'Well, here goes. I'd better get it over now. I mustn't be a brute.' And he flung down the technical journal whose pages were so strangely full of misty girls in brownish frocks, and ran downstairs to the morning-room (as it was called), and there was his mother with no end of a hat on, and struggling into a pair of very new gloves, and she said: 'Ah, there you are!' And then she seemed to look as if he weren't there at all, and said: 'Oh, it's you, is it, dear? How stupid. I thought it was Evelyn Rivington.'

'Why?' asked Ned. 'Is Mrs. Rivington here, then?'

'No,' said his mother. 'That's just it. She isn't. And it's past half-past three, and I can't think what's happened to her, and it's really very tiresome because I asked specially for the tickets, and you know how crowded it always is.'

'What is?' asked Ned. 'A concert?' Though it didn't sound like a concert, and his mother hardly ever went to concerts, only perhaps Mrs. Rivington was musical as well as amusing, and what else started so late in the afternoon?

'No, no,' said Mrs. Plunket. 'It's a dress show. At Marianne's. Do you suppose she thought I was going to meet her there? Because I said distinctly...' And she looked at the telephone, and looked at the clock, and looked flurried and put out. 'So unlike Evie,' she said, 'to make a muddle; but perhaps I'd better leave a message and start. Can I drop you anywhere?'

It seemed to Ned that if he declined this offer, he'd have no other chance of breaking his news, because his mother was obviously champing.

'Which way are you going?' he asked.

'Just off Bond Street,' said Mrs. Plunket; and then she shouted for Merryweather, and gave him her complicated message; and then she said: 'Come along, then,' though Ned still hadn't said whether he were coming or not. But apparently he *was* coming — because what did it matter what he did, and he'd still got to break his news. And they both went out into the hall, and Merryweather escorted them down the front steps, and Pope, the chauffeur, leapt forward and saluted them, and thus they were both packed into the back of the big car and under a thick fur rug, and then Pope slammed the door, and sprang on to his own seat, and the engine buzzed and whirred, and away they went.

'Now, then,' thought Ned, as he began removing his own end of the fur rug. 'Now I must tell her.'

But he didn't, because Mrs. Plunket had still, apparently, to tell him all over again how she couldn't make out what had happened to Evie Rivington, and how awkward it was when Madame

Marianne was specially keeping two seats for them, because if one didn't use one of the seats, it made it so much more difficult not to buy her models.

'But don't you want to?' asked Ned. 'Isn't that why you're going?'

'Never,' said Mrs. Plunket, very impressively, 'buy anything at a show. You'll only lose your head, and get something you don't want.'

Here, for the first time for very nearly three weeks, Ned actually started to laugh. And then he stopped, very abruptly.

'Oh, lord, no,' he said. 'What an idea, Mother! I couldn't. I'd feel the most awful ass.'

'Only, I mean, if Evie's not there.'

'Yes, but she's bound to be there. Besides, think of it! I'd be the only man.'

'Oh, no, you wouldn't,' said Mrs. Plunket. 'There are always several men.'

'Good lord, are there really?'

'Now, don't be tiresome, dear,' said Mrs. Plunket. And now Ned thought that perhaps on this last day, of all days, he oughtn't to be tiresome; and that he still hadn't told his mother that it *was* the last day; and above all that of course Mrs. Rivington was absolutely certain to be there.

'All right, Mother,' he said — though he still felt a bit of an ass. 'I won't come in with you, but I'll wait a moment with Pope; and then if Mrs. Rivington really isn't there ——'

'That's it, darling. Now, then, what's the fool looking round at me like that for? There! Over there! On the right!'

And Mrs. Plunket bounced up and down and signalled through the front window, and Pope touched his cap and drew over to the right, and got out, and ran round behind the car, and opened the door, and touched his cap again. And Mrs. Plunket alighted, and crossed the pavement and disappeared.

'I'll give her five minutes,' thought Ned, 'and then I'll go and have tea at the Club.' And he sighed, and sank back, and gazed at the passers-by, and thought how miserable he was, and how stupid he'd been to let his mother do all the talking, so that now he'd still have to tell her the news at dinner.

But in three minutes — because you know perfectly well where Mrs. Rivington was, and why — a page-boy came out, and said something to Pope, and then climbed on the running-board, and put his head in at the window, and startled Ned Plunket by chirruping in his right ear.

'The lady says, will you come in, please, sir.'

'Gosh!' said Ned Plunket. But he got out and went in. And there was an atmosphere, not to say an actual effluvium, which made him feel remarkably coarse, gross and out-sized, as he followed the page-boy up a flight of Georgian stairs. And at the top he felt even more shaggy, clumsy and asinine, for here in a large room were hundreds of women, all congregated on little gilt chairs, and a lot of them darting up and down and trying to look over each other's hats, and the page-boy was leading him on a tortuous trail right through them and right up to the front row of all. Lord, what a place in which to find oneself, and good gracious, how old and ugly and unattractive they all were, and, great snakes, how he felt their eyes all boring into him as he tiptoed after his guide!

'Hullo!' he said, as he slipped into the seat from which his mother obligingly removed half her person and a defensive hand. 'I say, Mother; I don't see any ——'

'Sh!' said Mrs. Plunket; so that now he was made to feel that he was in some pagan but intensely ritualistic church. And he blushed, and hunched up his shoulders, and wondered how the dickens he was to get out of his coat. And neither dared to look round, to see if there were possibly one other man after all, nor scarcely to raise his eyes from the parquet in front of him lest he be blasted for sacrilege against these appalling feminine mysteries.

And gosh, it was hot, and heavens, it was stuffy, and crikey, but it was an eye-opener on the way that money was wasted. 'Number Seventeen!' announced a priestess by a pillar, and there was a rustling of programmes and muttering of appraisement, and Ned Plunket looked cautiously up and saw a girl in evening dress and a fur wrap drifting and undulating across a black velvet platform. Quite expressionless, quite inhuman in every stilted pose and movement, not even blinking in the spotlights that blazed on her. 'I wonder,' thought Ned Plunket, 'what *she* thinks of it all.' But there seemed no more hope of guessing than if she had been a bird, or a fish, or even a tree. Artificiality *in excelsis*. She earned two pounds a week and commission, was engaged to a motor-salesman and had a passion for mixed grill; yet if one touched her — not that Ned Plunket would have dreamt of touching her — it was quite obvious that she would melt like the foam from which Venus was born.

She writhed and floated, she took off the fur wrap, turned round, put it on again, and passed from the scene. Another girl followed her, and a third, and a fourth, each distinguishable yet indistinguishable, each greeted and dismissed with the same urgent whispering. 'I wonder,' thought Ned Plunket — but he was staring now, and why shouldn't he stare? 'I wonder,' he thought, 'how long they keep it up?' And he tried to glance at his mother's programme, though the priestess's announcements seemed to follow no known arithmetical progression. Mrs. Plunket, forgetting for a moment who was beside her, jerked it away. He abandoned the effort; looked back at the platform. His heart suddenly made a complete circuit of his mortal frame, and returned to its original position with a thud. The girl who was standing up there, the girl who had seen him, recognised him, and given a quick start, was — figuratively speaking — once more the only girl in the world.

'Whee!' said Ned Plunket, as his eyes popped out of his head.

'Sh!' said Mrs. Plunket.

'Sit down!' said a voice from behind.

So Ned Plunket sat down. But his eyes continued to pop, his hands and feet continued to twitch, and his very soul continued to transmit the most emphatic wireless messages over those three and a half yards of parquet. 'Look at me again!' it cried. 'I'm here! I've found you! Where've you been? Do you remember me? How can I speak to you? Where can I meet you? When do you escape?'

And the girl turned, and postured, and bit her lip, and passed into what you might call the wings. 'Look sharp, Nancy!' said the assistant stage-manageress. 'Hurry up, dear. We're all late as it is.' And the girl hustled off to the communal tiring-room — to a place where even our thoughts should scarcely follow her — and started changing her frock like lightning, and all the time she was thinking: 'Oh, dear, oh, dear! It's him. I've seen him again, but of course it's just an accident. Of course it doesn't mean anything. Because, why did he run away that night, when he could so easily have waited? I wasn't more than two minutes, but he'd gone, and of course he was sorry he'd been kind to me, and of course that was why. And of course he's just what I was afraid he was, or he'd never be wasting his time at a place like this. I *loathe* the kind of men who come here and stare at one — horrible, rich, idle

brutes! Yes, I do. I loathe them, and I loathe
him. But — oh, dear! — that isn't true. And, oh,
dear, now it's all far worse than ever! I was
forgetting him — I *was* — I *was*; and I suppose I'm
absolutely raving mad, but now — but now ——'

'Step on it, Nancy,' said one of the other beauties.
'You're next, old dear.'

So Nancy stepped on it, and also into it, and
experts rushed at her and patted and pulled and
jerked and pinned, and so she went across the
fire-escape — to the great pleasure and entertainment of a number of occupants of neighbouring
buildings — and back into one of the workrooms,
and from there back again on to the temporary
stage.

'That's good,' said the voices in front. Or:
'I don't care for that one.' Or: 'It's all right
for *her* figure.' Or: 'Well, I saw something just
like that in Paris.' And Nancy went through all
her carefully-prepared movements, and again she
caught Ned Plunket's eye, and again he made the
most extraordinary faces, and again she bit her
lip and looked away, and again both their hearts
pounded like gas-engines.

Five more times and in five separate creations did
she appear from the left and vanish towards the
right, and on each occasion the invisible barrier
reared itself up and held these two luckless lovers
apart. 'Don't fidget,' said Mrs. Plunket. 'It's
nearly over now, and you can't possibly leave
till the end. Really, Ned, you must be more
patient.'

But Ned only took in one word, nor could he
tell whether that held hope or utter despair. If
only it *would* end, so that he could speak to her —
somehow and in spite of all the other and almost
insuperable barriers. He ground his teeth, clenched
his fists, scowled at the rival mannequins, and
leant forward in the most daring and unpopular

manner whenever his adored one reappeared. And
then suddenly there was a great shuffling of chairs,
and herding towards the staircase, and now he
didn't know what to do or where to go; but he
muttered something to his mother and started
bounding and clambering towards a side door.
And opened it, and found himself in a passage;
and turned to the left, and hesitated; and advanced, and darted back; and then — oh, gosh!
— there was a glimpse at the end, and he rushed
forward, stumbling and gaping and looking like a
madman.

'I say! Just a second. Please! May I say
something?'

'Oh, but you mustn't come in here.'

'I know; I know. But I'm not looking at
anything — except you. Listen — I *must* see you
again. I *must* talk to you. When do they let
you out? My gosh, you don't know what this
means to me. I want to explain. I want to tell
you something. When ——'

'Please! I'll get into awful trouble, if ——'

'I know. I'm going. But when ——'

'In ten minutes. Go round to the mews at the
back. There's a door there with the name on it.
Perhaps —— Oh, please!'

Ned Plunket ran back along the passage, pushed
and shoved his way down the main staircase, bolted
out into the street, shot round the first two right-
angles, began pacing the mews with a greater
appearance of insanity than ever. Suddenly he
stopped. What had she meant by 'Perhaps'?
Gosh, what if it meant perhaps she couldn't meet
him at all! Surely it was more than ten minutes
by now. He looked at his watch. He began pacing again. He frowned ferociously at a chauffeur
with a hose-pipe. He blew his nose, and wiped his
forehead. 'Perhaps.' Had there ever been such
a horrible, tormenting word? Ah! Thank God!

'I — I ——'

'Wait a second. I've got to go somewhere — with this note. That was how I managed to get off. But it's urgent.'

'All right. We'll go in a taxi.'

'Yes, but ——'

'And I'll explain everything. Come along. There's one at the end there. Hi!'

They both ran. They both leapt into the taxi. The girl gave an address out of the window, and the man tugged her in again by the arm.

'Listen!' he said. 'I want to tell you my name.' He told it her. 'And you? Quickly!'

'Oh, dear! I'm Nancy Ledbury. But ——'

'Good! That's all right. Listen! I lost my head, you know. I ran away that night because I lost my head. Gosh, what I've been through! I say, I've got to be sudden about this. I'm leaving London tomorrow, and I can't help it. I — don't be frightened — but I'm in love with you. It's been hell. For heaven's sake, will you marry me, or ——'

'Oh, dear!'

'Yes, I know. I know it's the most awful shock for you, but there's no time. We've wasted so much. You did hear me, didn't you? I'll tell you anything else in the world you ask. I — this sounds rotten — but I — I can afford it, you know.'

'Yes, I know.'

'What? How do you know? Do you mean, all this time ——'

'No, no. But look at you. Look what you do. Look at the difference ——'

'There isn't any difference. Gosh!' said Ned Plunket. 'Do you think I spend all my time at cocktail-parties and dress-shows? I'm an engineer, I tell you. I've been ill; that's all. I had my appendix out; but I'm going back to the works tomorrow, and I tell you there's absolutely no difference at all, except that you're ten million times too sweet for me, and I've never been in love with anybody before, and I know it sounds impossible, but I've never stopped thinking of you for one solitary second, and ——'

'Oh, dear! Oh, dear!'

'What?'

'If I hadn't seen you again! Oh, I've been so miserable! Oh, I think I'm clean off my head! Oh, let me think!'

'Well, gimme your hand.'

'Oh, dear!'

'Nancy! You did say it was "Nancy," didn't you? And you're not engaged to somebody else, are you? I mean, even if you are ——'

'No, no. Of course not. But you don't *know* anything.'

'I know,' said Ned Plunket, very firmly, 'that you're a darling. That's what I know,' said Ned Plunket. And: 'Gosh!' he thought. 'I'm in a taxi with her. I'm holding her hand. She hasn't taken it away. I could do anything now. What's more, I'm going to do something that's going to be the most marvellous thing I've ever done in my life. Yes, I am. Me, of all people! Just look at me, though. Here goes!'

He took a quick glance at the back of the driver's head, another quick glance at the deserted pavement of something that looked like a square; his other arm slid round the girl's waist, he pulled her towards him as masterfully as if he had been doing this kind of thing for years. Nor did she resist him. Nor did she stiffen, or turn her head. Their lips met, their eyes closed, the taxi rocked them gently to and fro.

'Oh, gosh!' thought Ned Plunket. 'Oh, dear!' thought Nancy Ledbury. They then became practically unconscious, and one can't help rather envying them at last.

32

CLINTON GARDENS could be nowhere but in London, and nothing but the seventies or eighties of last century could possibly have produced Clinton Gardens. The grey-brick houses were high and narrow, with slate roofs, with plate-glass windows flanking rectangular twin porticos, and, despite the six steps which led up to the last feature, with the deepest and most dismal areas. Inside, the rooms were ill-proportioned, afflicted with all that is most pretentious and ignoble in the way of doors, grates, dadoes and cornices, and again for the most part so high and narrow as to necessitate prodigious quantities of iron-banistered stairs. But the fabric was firm, heavy and solid, the walls were thick, the roofs and damp-courses were waterproof, and since the original leases had been for a period of ninety-nine years, there seemed but little chance at present of Clinton Gardens being replaced by anything more convenient or up-to-date.

That's the catch, of course, about civilised house property which conforms to civilised bye-laws. Few other fashions last for even ninety-nine weeks, but here all the money has been sunk, and all the tenants have come in, and it doesn't matter what happens to history or society or to habits, customs and tastes. The houses are there, their removal is impossible, they are, in a sense, perfectly habitable, and people have just got to go on living in them. Earlier and far more attractive rows of residences will come to the end of their terms, and will instantly be pulled down and turned into flats, shops, garages and cinemas. But one of the most terrible periods in British architecture stands secure in the protection of those musty engrossments in the lawyers' deed-boxes, and must remain as a monument to the very last syllable of recorded

time. If, it is true, the houses were planned on
so mammoth and monstrous a scale that no present-
day tenants can be found, then they may develop a
growth of extra door-bells and be transformed into
the most dreadful maisonettes. But the houses in
Clinton Gardens were merely monstrous, without
being mammoth at all; so people still lived in
them, and made the best of them, and even bought
and sold them occasionally, owing to the undoubted
convenience of the neighbourhood. And then,
again, once a thing belongs to you, it is extraordinary how uncritical you become. They were
rather a dull lot of people in Clinton Gardens, but
no one could say that they were particularly
unhappy.

That is the darker side of the picture. On the
brighter side one admits, quickly and agreeably,
that if the estate had been planned fifty years later,
it certainly wouldn't have contained even a quarter
of that open space at the back. And the open space
may be dirty (because it is in London), and the
trees may be sooty, and the paths may be slimy,
and the lawns may be poor in quality, and the
laurel-bushes may be positively Stygian in their
coating of metropolitan smuts; but at the same
time, and especially on a fine summer evening, it
is pretty good to be able to leavy your study or
dining-room by a flight of cast-iron steps — only
mind you remember to duck your head under the
plate-glass sash — and to find yourself at once in
a communal enclosure which is fully as spacious
as many a London square.

The seats may be a bit grimy and rickety, the
view of so many sculleries and pantries may be a
little urban, and complete seclusion may be a trifle
difficult to attain when so many of your neighbours
have had the same idea and both ends of the enclosure give on to public thoroughfares. But still
you *are* in the open air, and you *are* enjoying a

species of privacy, and you are at least getting
some kind of value for the very high rates with
which your property is encumbered. Decidedly, on
one of these summer evenings, there is a feeling
of peace and restfulness out here under the pale-
green skies. And as the twilight deepens and the
throb of traffic becomes less insistent and darkness
swallows up so much of the detail, there is even
a kind of mild grandeur about the long block of
grey brickwork; or, if you chance to be looking
the other way, a sort of sleepy simplicity about
the backs of the other and lower houses in Clinton
Place.

In autumn, winter and spring one may as well
confess that the grounds are little used by the
adult leaseholders — save in a few cases where age
or infirmity go pottering round, alone or on the
arms of long-suffering supporters. But — and on
this point Clinton Gardens is almost unanimous —
there's no doubt that they're a wonderful place
for the children. You just turn them out, and
they can run about and play together, and of
course it's far simpler than sending them up to
the park, and on the whole there's far less danger
of anything happening to them. Naturally, being
children, they will occasionally cut their knees and
faces open on the gravel, fall out of trees or down
areas, wedge their heads between the railings at
the ends, or suffer other injury from the broken
bottles which are embedded on the long brick wall
at the back. And no less naturally, for the same
reason, they will frequently strike each other,
scream, yell, howl and otherwise account for the
prejudice of the childless minority.

But take it all round, and considering how in
these days even nurses are perpetually expecting
afternoons off, there's no doubt that the gardens are
a tremendous practical convenience. 'Run along
and play in the gardens,' you say, in circumstances

in which it would be quite impossible to organise anything more elaborate, or to say: 'Run along and play in the street.'

'Oh, must I, Mummie?'

'Yes, of course. You can't stay indoors all the time, doing nothing. Now, go and put on your brown shoes.'

'Oh, need I, Mummie?'

Well, perhaps the gardens aren't quite so popular or quite so highly valued by the actual children themselves as by the authorities who send them there. Perhaps they don't seem quite so vast, luxurious and romantic as they appear to less fortunate children who gaze into them through the railings at the ends. Perhaps familiarity has bred, if not positive contempt, at any rate a pretty widespread sense of boredom. Nevertheless, convenience continues to triumph over whines, sulks and other symptoms of juvenile reluctance, and out they all go, and out they all remain until such time as they are summoned to return, and they play and talk together, and form cliques, gangs and juntas, and tell each other a lot of things which their parents have no idea that they know, and acquire a great deal of knowledge about the other families in Clinton Gardens which they keep carefully to themselves. Then they grow older, and the bonds are loosened by school, by fresh interests, by the development of self-consciousness or snobbery, by a general independence which releases them from the gardens altogether. But so far there have always been perambulators to supply a fresh crop of short socks and straight fringes, or Eton collars and round felt hats. At any given moment there always seem to be just as many children to run, chatter, laugh or quarrel as there were this time last year.

Thus, on the afternoon of this day that we're dealing with, towards the end of March, there were,

as usual, quite a number of sons and daughters
occupying themselves in their customary manner.
For it would be light until at least six, and the
temperature was no worse than seasonable — and
even seemed better, since the wind had dropped;
and although, after that particularly fine morning,
it had clouded over and rained sharply at lunch-
time, and hadn't exactly promised not to rain
again, this was precisely the kind of afternoon on
which the gardens were most valuable and useful.
Fresh air and exercise only a few yards from shelter
and nursery fires, and no risk whatever of being
caught and drenched while possibly as far afield as
the Round Pond.

'Must I?' the children had asked. 'Need we?'
But forth they had been driven, and perambulators had come bumping down the castiron steps,
and governesses and mademoiselles had withdrawn to their own bedrooms, or gone off to visit
their own friends, and once more any amount
of short citizens were wandering about over the
paths and lawns, gathering into intensely confidential knots, and exploring — though they knew
every inch of it — the dirty undergrowth by the
long brick wall.

Once more, also, two main factions were distinguishable in the wide enclosure; that which
followed the joint though frequently divided leader-
ship of Angela Potts and Marjorie Banting, and
that which congregated round the invisible standard
of a boy called Julian Sebright. Not that member-
ship of either party was fixed or constant, not that
these were rules, subscriptions, oaths of admission
or penalties for disobedience. It was just that
there were the children with the most vigour and
personality for their years; the naughtiest children,
very often, but never the dullest; and that thus,
at this period, their more ordinary colleagues
naturally gravitated in one direction or the other.

'There's Marjorie and Angela!' they would
say. 'Come on!' Or, if they happened to catch
sight of him first: 'There's Julian! Let's go
and see what he's doing.' And off they ran, and
perhaps Marjorie and Angela were feeling grown
up today, and told them to get out and not to
be little pests — only they were quite incapable of
obeying either instruction. Or perhaps Julian
would be feeling manly, and announced that he
didn't want any girls getting in the way — only
this never had any effect on his female adherents,
either. Or perhaps they were all three in an
inventive and encouraging mood, and welcomed
their admirers, and led them into some of those
delightful sports and escapades which yet so often
seemed to terminate in the tearing of garments and
the shedding of tears.

'Get out, you silly little fool,' they said. 'Yah!
Cry-baby! Boo-hoo-hoo!'

But the garments were repaired and the tears
were dried, and always the old fascination would
prove greater than shame or fear. In this miniature cosmos vigour and personality were just as
irresistible as in the greater world outside. Society
demanded leaders, and, as usual, society always
managed to find them. Looking back over the
past history of Clinton Gardens, a studious chron-
icler would find an endless succession of Angelas,
Marjories and Julians. Their reigns generally
started, with great suddenness, shortly after the
end of the summer holidays, and lasted until they,
like their predecessors, departed for boarding-
schools or abdicated because they were no longer
turned loose. The end was always quite as abrupt
as the beginning.

On the whole — and this seems quite right —
there were more boys in Julian's gang, and more
girls in the other. But oddly enough — or perhaps
not oddly at all — the only settled and inseparable

units in either collection were the very small males
who went trotting after Angela and Marjorie and
the very small females who were so openly devoted
to their rival.

'Get out!' said the two queens. 'You're much
too young, and you'll only spoil everything.'

'Get away!' said Julian. 'Why on earth can't
you go and play by yourselves?'

But nothing could shake off these extremely
junior members. They stood on the outskirts,
often on one leg, staring, worshipping, determined
to stick to the party of their choice. When the
running and screaming began, they nearly burst
their little lungs as they plunged about in aimless
imitation of the games which they couldn't understand. Nothing could be more ear-splitting than
the sounds which they emitted as they were caught
by their attendants, and taken in for meals or to
bed. But then, as they grew older, their original
loyalty faded. Their first hero or heroine had
vanished, and no successor could possibly exercise
the same magnetism. They drifted from camp to
camp, mercenaries who didn't exactly sell themselves to the highest bidder, but certainly attached
themselves wherever they felt that there would be
most entertainment. Since it is a fact, even in
later life, that anything from which you are temporarily excluded always seems more interesting
and amusing than whatever you have chosen to do
yourself, defections were constant and incessant;
but then so, for the same reason, were recruitments
from virtually the same source.

'All right,' said Marjorie or Angela. 'Go off
with those awful fools if you want to. *I* don't need
you. I can have much more fun without your
getting in the way.'

'Hullo,' said Julian. 'Come on, then. Yes,
lots of room as long as you behave yourself. We're
having a much better game than they are over
there.'

So it seemed at the moment. But then you heard your friends of yesterday laughing, or knew — though you couldn't quite see — that Angela was doing that extraordinarily witty trick with her dental plate. Had you made the wrong choice after all? You played defiantly and uproariously, which calmed your doubts, until perhaps Julian got rough and hurt you. You had forgotten how often Angela and Marjorie had been just as rough and given you just as much pain. In due course you ratted. So did a corresponding member whose place you had recently taken. The gangs were always shifting and changing like this; the one thing that they never seemed to do — at any rate, out here in the gardens — was to coalesce.

Perhaps one has conveyed the impression that there was some kind of system to govern it all. There wasn't. Chance and impulse ruled the whole business just as much as if these children had been twenty, thirty or sixty years older. None of them looked ahead, made plans for the future, profited from the past, or made the least attempt to alter the situation as they found it. A group of parliamentary voters couldn't have been vaguer, less settled in its convictions, or more liable to sudden changes of spirit. Only the great law of averages assured each party a guaranteed minimum of supporters, and each leader an inevitable counter-poise on the other side. Since there were no rules in existence, not even exceptions could prove them. Yet there's no doubt that there was something exceptional, if not unprecedented, in one of the leaders being at this period a boy.

Because boys, generally speaking, were stupider, slower, more backward and far less ready to thrust themselves forward. One isn't arguing about their comparative importance or intelligence in later life, and one would only be asking for the worst kind of trouble if one did; but it's a fact that between the ages of eight and twelve boys are often, if not always, as shy, prickly, diffident and indistinguishable as any hedgehog or porcupine. Civilisation, having noted this, has developed its own protection in the shape of preparatory and then public boarding-schools, which diminish the difficulty by at least two-thirds in point of time, and — apart from the expense — certainly don't add to it in any other direction. The boys vanish, are fully occupied, and are all the more welcome on their return. Suddenly they're grown-up, and then there's quite another problem to be dealt with.

But Julian Sebright had been a delicate baby and for six years an only child. Mrs. Sebright, his mother, had got into the habit of thinking and saying: 'Poor little Julian — one has to be so careful, you know; he's not like other children.' Then she gave birth to his sister Mercy, and, like her husband, was so much overwhelmed by this unexpected feat that it pretty well eclipsed everything else. Julian, not without a certain amount of reason, was violently jealous, sulked, raged and was automatically handed over to the doctor. The doctor, who had known Mrs. Sebright all her life and had become rather crystallised in some of his opinions, still stuck to it that Julian was delicate, prescribed queer foods and queer exercises, said that Mrs. Sebright couldn't be too careful, nodded, looked wise, and was really far more interested in the baby.

So Julian found himself established as an exception, and being no fool, took full advantage of it. If on the one hand he were cut off from certain attractive forms of provender, plagued about his scarf and his galoshes, and often forbidden to paddle when he wanted to, then on the other hand if there were anything that he didn't want to do, he only had to say that he felt sick and he got out of it at once. It was by this method that he succeeded in attending only seven dancing-classes in six terms, after which Mr. Sebright suddenly jibbed at the extravagance and the victory was complete. It was by this method that he was excused homework by the day-school to which he was sent, and — since he was no fool — learnt a great deal more by reading novels and newspapers instead. He was less fortunate over the gymnasium — which he detested even more than the dancing-class — because there the ancient doctor was definitely against him. Still, it's amazing how little exercise one quick-witted child can manage to take in these circumstances, when there are twenty-five or thirty contemporaries undergoing the same form of instruction. On several occasions, indeed, his entire contribution consisted of slouching along at the tail-end of the procession; yet when his grandmother gave him a little bicycle for his birthday, he thought nothing of doing three or four miles round the railed and walled enclosure.

In fact, long before he was ten, his delicacy had entirely left him and was nothing but a legend. But Mrs. Sebright never forgot that awful winter when he was two and a half, and Mr. Sebright was far too busy to see anything through his own eyes, and the ancient doctor, who had now lost almost all his other patients, still insisted that they couldn't be too careful. So his contemporaries went away, in tears or otherwise, to sleep in dormitories and to face their ferocious seniors; but Julian stayed on at his day-school in London, and had cream with his lunch, and took no part in the Tuesday and Friday afternoon games of football. They made him feel sick, he said, and he climbed trees in the railed and walled enclosure instead. Once he fell about eight feet and really did feel sick. But he never told anybody, and nobody ever knew.

Is one painting the portrait of a rather horrid little boy? Well, he was horrid enough at times,

but at times he wasn't in the least horrid. Just
as he was precocious in some ways, and ignorant
and inexperienced in others. Just as you thought
him polite sometimes, and on other occasions
thought absolutely nothing of the sort. He was
affectionate, heartless, truthful, inaccurate, sensitive, thick-skinned, honourable, deceitful, easily
influenced and astonishingly self-willed. In fact,
he was in every respect a normal and healthy
creature, except that somehow he had slipped out
of the ordinary kind of upbringing and it seemed
nobody's business to push him back. When he
was twelve, the ancient doctor died, and now
perhaps, if only he'd been more of a nuisance at
home, Mr. Sebright might have packed him off
to one of those dormitories. But you couldn't
really call him a nuisance. He lost his temper
sometimes, after which he sometimes apologised
and was really rather touching, and sometimes
didn't and everybody had forgotten about it in
the morning. So the moment passed, and nothing
happened. Mr. Sebright was busier than ever, Mrs.
Sebright was just as muddle-headed and silly, and
everything was just the same as before.

A little later the public school at which Mr.
Sebright had been educated, and where Julian's
name had been waiting, card-indexed and buried
away, since the week of his birth, suddenly sent a
printed form which might be summed up in the
short phrase: 'What about it?'

'What about it?' repeated Mr. Sebright, looking
over his spectacles and across the breakfast-table.

'Oh, no!' said Mrs. Sebright.   'Of course you
must explain.'

'Explain what, dear?'

'That we couldn't think of sending him.'

'Um,' said Mr. Sebright, for whom the present,
outside his office, was practically invisible, but for
whom the distant past was not without its glamour.

He thought, with rather exaggerated sentiment, of his own school-days. He also remembered the pride with which he had entered his first-born's name. He rubbed his nose, and looked a little disappointed.

'No,' he said. 'I suppose it's no use.'

Mrs. Sebright shuddered, and again her first-born was two and a half, and they were giving him oxygen.

'Of course it's no use,' she said. 'Of course it's quite out of the question. Surely you realise ——'

'Yes, yes,' said Mr. Sebright. 'Seems a pity. All right, dear.'

Nevertheless, he wrote to the school and said that although his son was too delicate at present (which he fully believed), he did hope that if a vacancy occurred later on — and so forth. If he had written this letter just after the war, it seems quite certain that the school wouldn't even have answered it. But times change, and, besides, the head master had actually been Mr. Sebright's fag. 'I'm so sorry,' he wrote, 'to hear about Julian' — he took the name from the card-index, but Mr. Sebright felt quite a flutter at this intimate touch — 'but I think, in your case, we could always manage to find room for him.' And so forth, again.

Mr. Sebright had an impulse. Sometimes, on the eve of a board meeting, he came home early with a bag full of papers, and made his final preparations in the little study. It was on one of these occasions that he found the head master's letter, and — a little later — Julian copying an essay out of his *Encyclopaedia Britannica*. Julian, naturally, leapt up and slipped towards the door.

'Just a moment,' said Mr. Sebright.

'Now,' thought Julian, 'he's going to ask me what I was doing, or tell me not to touch his books.' A choice of about six alternative misstatements sprang into his mind; his eye was firm; only his mouth wavered.

'Yes, Daddy?'

'Listen, old chap. I say, do you ever feel you'd like to go to a real school? You know what I mean. Well, the kind of school *I* was at. Eh?'

'A b-boarding-school, Daddy?'

'What's that? Well, of course. A real public school, I mean.'

Julian felt almost as sick as when he fell out of the tree. He'd loathe it, hate it, go mad at it. He was petrified.

'Oh, no, Daddy! Oh, please not! Oh, I couldn't! You — you don't mean ——'

'Eh?' Mr. Sebright was unbuckling his bag, and looking round for his favourite pipe. 'No, of course it was only an idea. I mean, if you were a bit stronger, it wouldn't be too late. But I suppose,' muttered Mr. Sebright, 'your mother's right, and anyhow she'd have a fit. Run along,' said Mr. Sebright. And: 'Door!' shouted Mr. Sebright, as his first-born bolted from his presence. The door closed, the impulse was buried and forgotten. Mr. Sebright started shuffling and poring over his papers.

But outside, with his fountain-pen and exercise-book, Julian suddenly found himself the prey of extremely conflicting emotions. Relief was certainly one of them. But there was a kind of shame, also; and an inexplicable kind of longing. And a disgraceful feeling of disloyalty towards his mother. A complicated dual vision presented itself in which he saw two paths, two lives, two sets of experiences running side by side. He was fascinated, tempted, appalled. Relief came surging back, accompanied by deep gratitude for so narrow an escape. And yet...

He dropped his fountain-pen, picked it up, wiped it on his knickerbockers, and went off to the dining-

room, where he brought the essay to an abrupt
and uninspired conclusion. 'Very good on the
whole,' wrote Mr. Keller, at the day-school. 'You
should try to sum up more clearly.'

So everything went on as before, and the dual
vision sank into the background, and Julian hardly
ever thought about it at all. He atoned for the
feeling of disloyalty by a marked outburst of
affection, and Mrs. Sebright took him to a matinée.
None of that, of course, if you were doing what the
other boys did. And, besides, he was delicate.
He didn't know how or why, but he was. A jolly
useful thing to be, too, when you saw what it had
let you out of. And yet again — just now and then
— if only he weren't...

33

THAT was in the early summer. Then there were
June and July, and examinations. Then the
Sebrights all went away, first to Mrs. Sebright's
mother, and then to lodgings at the seaside. And
then they came back again, and now Julian was
more than ever an exception, a *rara avis*, a case of
sui generis. All his masculine contemporaries had
vanished, and for the most part he was delighted
that this should be so. He'd grown, he felt extraordinary well, his work didn't trouble him, and
suddenly he realised that part of the endless succession had fallen into his grasp. Very small girls
followed him about in the enclosure, other children
of both sexes said: 'Here's Julian. Hullo, Julian!
Come on, Julian, what shall we play at?' He felt
lordly, important, a figurehead. Even his sister
Mercy seemed to respect him. He sent her on
errands, ordered her about, was aloof when it struck
him that such treatment would be for her good.

Then one day his sister Mercy was missing from
the circle, and he became aware that he wasn't

ruling alone. An unnatural but powerful coalition between Marjorie Banting and Angela Potts — who but for his equally unnatural presence would undoubtedly have been on separate thrones — disclosed itself as an established menace, and Mercy had joined them. Without exactly thinking it all out, he led a brilliant attack on an encampment which they had made in one of the shrubberies; a miniature wigwam — somebody's birthday present — was seriously injured, and notes were exchanged between parents. Somehow or other Julian's responsibility became obscured in the general confusion, nor did he see any reason for admitting it. Calm followed the storm, and again he decided that he'd had a narrow escape. Supposing he'd been packed off to that real school! A hollow feeling struggled with a sensation of unaccountable discontent. In any case, however, there should be no more organised *sabotage* so far as his party were concerned.

Angela and Marjorie plotted the most ingenious forms of retaliation for several weeks, but never succeeded in getting any scheme under way. Divided counsels, no less than the phantasmagoric character of their following, preserved the armistice. The enclosure settled down to another normal year — normal, that is to say, in every feature except Julian Sebright. But even Julian Sebright fitted into the accustomed pattern as the days grew shorter and colder, and playtime in the enclosure sank to its nadir.

At Christmas the male contemporaries came home, bluff and boastful, yet swiftly sensitive to the prevailing spirit of parties, presents and goodwill. Julian was a little subdued for a day or two, a little careful in his dealings with these initiates. Then one of them made a slighting observation, and Julian knocked him down. It was as easy as all that, apparently, and the effect was quite conclusive. Nobody else made slighting observations,

and the victor again found himself top dog.   His
popularity, indeed, went some way towards his head,
but though he became a bit rowdy at home, this
was expected at Christmas and he never got quite
out of hand.   Some secret sense of inferiority,
though quite invisible to any beholder, was always
restraining him and holding him back.   He couldn't
name it or define it; his personality disguised it
even from those who knew him best; yet he eyed
his father once or twice, as though he feared something, or expected something, or even hoped for
something.

Mr. Sebright didn't notice it.   After his own
holiday of three days he was again for the most part
an immanence more than a presence.   In due course
the male contemporaries set off for the London
termini, and Julian resumed his duties at the day-
school.   Sometimes he experienced an abounding
sensation of escape.   Sometimes he looked round
for it, and it seemed to be missing.

In February, when there's a half-quarter-day, Mr.
and Mrs. Palliser moved into Number Seventeen,
bringing with them the conventional quantity of
furniture and a very nasty little daughter called
Esther.   She was distinctly pretty, distinctly intelligent and distinctly polite.   Nevertheless, she
was a nasty little girl, even though her parents
adored her, and she was spoilt in a deceptive,
intangible manner, and she didn't go to any school
at all, but had governesses and mademoiselles and
fräuleins, all of whom left, without giving any clear
reason, after a maximum period of about two
months.

Her education, accordingly, was what you might
call scrappy, but her self-assurance was extreme.
At first all the other children were staggered by her,
tried to imitate her, and in most cases were instantly
punished for impertinence.   In fact, at this early
stage, and if she had chosen, she could probably

have made history by founding a third party at an absolutely unprecedented season. But she didn't. She sneered, ever so slightly, at all their unwritten laws, and suddenly there was a tremendous reaction and everybody detested her. 'That awful Esther,' they called her, and the voice of the people isn't always mistaken. 'She's a beast,' they said. 'She laughed when her dormouse died.'

Julian heard this, and couldn't believe it.

'She didn't!' he said.

'Yes, she did,' they told him. 'And it was her fault, too, because she knew it wasn't asleep properly, and she left the cage open, an' it fell into the slop-pail.'

It was beginning to sound rather circumstantial. Secretly, Julian was shocked and disgusted, but outwardly he was committed to scepticism.

'Rot,' he said. 'And anyway,' he said, 'you're little sneaks, and you needn't look so pleased about it.'

But somehow he wanted to get to the bottom of the story, even if it meant unbending to the extent of asking Miss Palliser herself. For some time he eyed her walking round the enclosure with her new mademoiselle; he approached her; he felt that she was eyeing him also, and drew back. Suddenly she left the mademoiselle, ran quickly across the lawn, stopped in front of him, and put out her tongue.

'Don't stare,' she added. 'Don't you know it's rude?'

'I wasn't,' said Julian. 'Is it true about your dormouse?'

'Yes,' said Miss Palliser. 'It's dead. It died in the slop-pail, and I don't mind in the least. But,' said Miss Palliser, 'I like you. I don't like the others at all. I say, shall we pretend we're married?'

'No,' said Julian — a little stiffly, but he was

staring more than ever. 'That's a potty sort of thing to pretend. I hate that sort of game.'

'You needn't be so stuck-up,' said the nasty little girl. And she looked at him out of the corners of her eyes. And she caught hold of the flap of one of his pockets. 'Come on,' she said. 'I like you awfully, Julian.'

And Julian laughed, and felt very uncomfortable indeed. But he was flattered. There was something strange and mysterious about Miss Palliser; something quite different from all the other children. It wasn't only that she was cleaner, and neater, and had longer eyelashes, and said such extraordinary things. The point was —— Well, what *was* the point? He couldn't place her, he couldn't understand her at all. She rather frightened him. But it was so silly to be frightened of a girl.

'Shut up,' he said. 'Look — there's your governess waving at you.'

'I don't care,' said Miss Palliser, tossing her nasty little head. 'I'm going to stay with you. Let's go and hide from her. Let's settle where we're going to live.'

And she began running away, and Julian ran after her, and she didn't say any more about their marriage, but talked — eighteen to the dozen, and again quite differently from all the other children — about the remarkable behaviour of her Uncle Alec, and how she wasn't supposed to know anything of it, but she'd hidden under the dining-room table, and that was how she knew *everything*, and ——

'Don't swank,' said Julian.

Miss Palliser stopped; glared at him; bit her pouting little lower lip; and stamped on the ground.

'You're a horrid little boy,' she said. 'Go away. I'm not going to speak to you again.'

The great Julian simply gasped. It was Miss Palliser, tossing her head and kicking up her heels,

who rushed back to her mademoiselle, and left him
in that extraordinary state of confusion, and resentment, and something else.

'Stupid!' he muttered. 'Going on like an idiot.
I don't want to hear about her rotten uncle. She
needn't think *I'm* interested.'

But he was. He'd heard just enough to provide
a perpetual irritant at the back of his mind, and
when he went indoors to do his homework — for, as
you have gathered, he hadn't managed to avoid this
for ever — he still kept wondering and imagining,
and thinking about the nasty little girl at Number
Seventeen. Next day, when it snowed, he was kept
back by Mr. Keller and made to do his arithmetic
all over again, and nobody went into the gardens
at all. But the day after that the sun came out,
and the gardens were full of children throwing rather
dirty snowballs at each other, and Esther joined
his party without a word, and put a stone in one
of her missiles and lobbed it through old Miss
Hackett's pantry window; and a man rushed out
in a white apron and a black rage, and for some
quite unaccountable reason Julian said that he'd
done it himself; and the man said he'd tell his Pa,
that he would, and Julian was filled with panic
only slightly mitigated by a deep sense of his own
nobility, and avoided his father for nearly a week,
after which he decided that the message must have
miscarried, for the window was mended and no
more was ever heard of it.

But meanwhile the nasty little girl had attached
herself quite inseparably to his party, and seemed
to be waiting for him whenever he came out, and
never left his side until he went in again. And
then, suddenly, she wasn't there, and he couldn't
think what had happened, because she wasn't with
Angela and Marjorie, either, and he didn't know
whether he were pleased or not — though the rest of
his followers were delighted. And then, just as

suddenly, she was waiting for him again, and she caught hold of his coat, and asked him: 'Did you miss me, Julian?   Do tell me — did you keep wondering where I was all the time?'

'Why?' asked Julian.   'Where were you?'

'Indoors,' said the nasty little girl.

'Do you mean you had a cold?'

'Oh, no,' said the nasty little girl.   'I just thought I wouldn't come out.   Nobody can make me do anything,' she said.   'I stayed indoors and wrote a letter to you.'

'Well, I never got it,' said Julian.

'I never sent it,' said the nasty little girl.   'Don't you wonder what I said?'

And of course Julian wondered like anything what she had said, with inevitable results on his homework.   But he wouldn't ask, and Esther never told him, and indeed it seems more than likely that she had never written any letter at all. They were inseparable again, and he was rather pleased, and often rather uncomfortable, and once extremely angry — which was when Marjorie and Angela pointed at the pair of them and sang something indistinguishable but quite clearly suggestive and offensive.   No doubt, in fact, that the precocious Miss Palliser was distinctly adding to the vulgarity of the whole enclosure.   No doubt, either, that Julian Sebright was getting dangerously near a scandal and a mess.

Sometimes he said to himself: 'Well, I'm going to stop all this.   I don't like being pawed, and it's blithering the way she keeps ragging one, and then talking all that rot about being married.   It makes me sick.'   And he felt fresher and better and more sure of himself, and strode down the iron steps determined to put his manly resolutions into practice.   And then — every time, it seemed — either Esther was there and all his determination faded away, or else she wasn't there and he did nothing

but wonder why on earth she wasn't.   He knew now
that he was going to get the most shocking report
from his day-school, and he was terribly worried
about it — quite genuinely and quite apart from his
fear of his father; but some kind of secret chivalry
always prevented him from laying the blame on the
nasty little girl.   Quite often he would have given
anything to be safely away among boys and nothing
but boys in a proper school in the distant country.
But then he thought how he'd hate that too, and
of all the strangeness and extra discipline and
fabled terrors.   No, he'd be mad to make a suggestion like that, and give up his freedom for nothing.
Because it *was* nothing, really.   It was silly to
pretend that it was.   Just one stupid little girl,
who thought herself so clever and couldn't even do
long division.

For a time he tried to use his sister Mercy as a
kind of bodyguard, only he couldn't explain to her,
because he didn't understand the situation himself.
For a day or two she was rather flattered by his
attentions; then she got bored, and went off to play
with Marjorie and Angela.   To tell the truth, he
was just as sick of the association as she was, and
made no attempt to win her back.   So that wasn't
much use.

But one thing the nasty little girl did do for him,
and that was to drive him into the bi-weekly games
of football.   He joined up without telling anyone
at home — swopping a collection of Christmas
presents for a fellow-student's discarded boots —
and on the first occasion he thought he had never
experienced anything so baffling and unspeakable
in his life.   But Mr. Rodgers, the games-master,
patted him on the shoulder, and said he'd soon pick
it all up.   And he felt a glow, and next time he did
start picking it up, and Mr. Keller noted and was
delighted with a faint reaction in his other work.
'Not,' he thought, 'that a boy like that was ever

really meant for a school like this; but still, when
you've seen the mother...' And he went on
with his arduous, monotonous and unhonoured
task.

Mrs. Sebright thought that her delicate child was
staying late on Tuesdays and Fridays to do carpen-
try — and if anyone wonders why she thought this,
then it looks as if the delicate child must have been
at least partly responsible. But Mr. Sebright came
home early again one afternoon — to pack, this
time, and go north on business — and met Julian
sneaking up the kitchen stairs with a muddy face
and a bloody knee.

'Hullo!' he said. 'What's the matter, old chap?
Been tumbling down?'

Tumble! What a word to use to an athlete!

'No,' said Julian. He deliberately glanced at
the famous boots, and even his father's eyes were
fain to observe them.

'Good lord!' said Mr. Sebright. 'Have you been
playing football?'

Julian nodded.

'Does — I mean, does your mother know?'

Julian hesitated. Smiled nervously. Shook his
head.

'Well, but — I mean, look here, old man — I
mean, seriously...'

Seriously, what? It seemed so ridiculous to tell
a clumping great fellow like this odd apparition —
and part of the oddness lay in the blurred outline
which showed him just as clearly at five, seven or
eleven as at his present age of over thirteen; it
seemed preposterous to tell a boy like that that he
oughtn't to run about and kick a ball. On the other
hand he'd been forbidden to do it, and there was a
reason, or had been a reason ——

Ting! went the half-hour from the grandfather
clock in the front hall.

'Lord!' said Mr. Sebright. 'I'm going to be

late. I've got to pack. I've got to get up to Euston. All right, old chap. Run along. Don't worry me now. I'm busy.'

And Mr. Sebright went bounding up the stairs, two and sometimes three steps at a time, and forgot all about the strange incident as he yanked his clothes out of the chest-of-drawers in his dressing-room, and shovelled them into his suit-case. Forgot, that is to say, as completely as one can ever forget anything. A microscopic record remained in a microscopic cell, and perhaps if his old fag had written again, the cell door would have opened and the record would have walked out. But big public schools don't, and there is no reason why they should, go in for what is commercially known as follow-up matter. Mr. Sebright caught his train with just one minute to spare, and the cell door remained closed.

And Julian crept very quietly past the drawing-room door, and washed his knee and face in the bath-room, and changed his famous but slightly irksome boots, and came down again and wandered automatically out into the gardens.

'Hullo!' cried several children. 'There's Julian!' They came running towards him. 'Hullo, Julian!' they shrieked. 'What shall we play at?'

Their leader nodded at them, considering their numbers, intelligence, and the problem of the very short time that was available before tea. He was frowning as he turned slowly round.

'Hullo, Julian,' said Miss Palliser, sidling up towards him.

Julian muttered a very objectionable word which he had learnt from his colleagues at the day-school. And yet, he thought, he had been waiting for this moment all day.

34

THUS it drew towards the end of March, and there came this other day when it was so fine in the early morning and so wet at lunch-time, and then so unsettled-looking as the afternoon span itself out. And because of these conditions, as you were told, the gardens were as full of children as they had been for weeks, and the governesses had taken themselves off, and the nurses were trundling perambulators, and the nursery-maids were indoors manufacturing innumerable slices of bread and butter. The alliance between Angela Potts and Marjorie Banting had just reached one of its climaxes of affection and intimacy; gifts had been exchanged; arms were almost perpetually twined round necks and waists; civility had come to verge on goofiness. In short, every sign and symptom pointed towards the earliest and most violent friction — 'Gimme back that necklace; I only lent it you.' 'You didn't! Well, gimme back my book!' — but at the moment all was peaceful activity in the one camp, while in the other Julian Sebright was absolutely at the top of his form.

'Come on!' he said. 'I've thought of something.' And he snapped out his orders, and everybody obeyed, and the children scurried to and fro, and screamed and jumped out on each other, and were rewarded or degraded entirely at the despot's will.

'Now,' said Julian, 'I've got another idea. Listen,' he said, thrusting one of his smallest adherents aside. 'This is a new kind of hide-and-seek, and anyone who doesn't understand has got to wait till we've finished. Now, listen.'

He explained, carefully and elaborately, while everybody bounced up and down. 'Do you see?' he asked. 'Well, I'm going to start, because it's my idea. And don't forget what I told you, because everything I said was important. Now, then; you all begin by going right over there.'

Away they trooped, not without raising slight fears in the breasts of the rival queens. But they passed the other gang, still chattering and laughing, without any clash, and Julian — having first shuffled loudly on the gravel, so as to throw them off the scent — moved quickly and stealthily into the undergrowth by the long brick wall, hurried along beside it, and so came to the spot which he had been keeping up his sleeve, as it were, from the outset. Here, by the railings which gave on to the quiet side-street, he could both conceal himself and, by an ingenious interpretation of his own rules, escape in either direction at a moment's notice. He turned round, panting and pleased.

There was a crackling just in front of him. Gosh, it was that girl again!

'Look here,' he began, indignantly. 'Didn't I tell you ——'

'Yes, Julian — I know. But I want to be on your side.'

'Well, you can't,' said Julian. 'Buck up! Clear out. You're spoiling everything.'

'I won't,' said Esther. 'I promise I won't. I'll do whatever you do.'

'Yes, but ——'

'*Please*, Julian!'

Well, if she left him now, she'd only show all the others where he was.

'Oh, all right. Only do keep quiet.'

'I will, Julian. Thank you awfully, Julian. Julian!'

'What's the matter now?'

The matter was that she was stroking his sleeve again. Sidling in that typical and tiresome manner.

'Julian.'

'Well, what is it?'

'Shall we pretend this is our house? When we're married, Julian, what sort of house ——?'

'Oh, stop it!'

'Please, Julian. Julian, I do think you're so awfully nice.'

Prickles running over the unfortunate hero's scalp. Feelings that he hated. Feelings that at the same time softened and unmanned him. He squirmed. He turned away again.

'Look,' he said, for no reason on earth. 'There's a taxi. One of those new ones.'

'Oh, yes!' said Esther, staring at it. So that for the moment they were both staring at it, and as it was indeed one of the newest taxis with the largest possible expanse of safety-glass, they both saw, quite distinctly, what the two passengers inside were doing. The man, who was Ned Plunket, an engineer-apprentice with considerable private means, was passionately embracing the woman, who was Nancy Ledbury, a mannequin-assistant at Madame Marianne's in Grosvenor Street. He was madly in love with her, he had just offered her his hand in marriage, the very second that he stopped kissing her she was going to accept it. Thankfully, gratefully, with sobs of choking happiness.

Honk! went the taxi-horn, and the vision vanished. The two figures inside the sooty railings remained motionless; but one of them — the boy — was almost literally paralysed with shock, horror and disgust. His face turned a pale, clammy green, his whole inside seemed to drop away, leaving a hollow, shuddering space in which the remains of a few jumbled organs heaved and crawled and wrestled hideously with each other. He'd always known that there were dreadful things in life, but never, never in his worst nightmare moments, had he dreamt that grown-up people

could be so shameless, so revolting, so absolutely
and utterly abhorrent. He knew things, of course;
he knew perfectly well that they were only kissing
each other; it never even occurred to him that he
had witnessed anything worse. But to see it all
like this, to see it when one wasn't expecting it,
to have beheld that abandonment, that nauseating
frenzy, that clutching, that terrible singleness of
purpose — only a few yards away, right in front of
him, just opposite where he was still gaping and
gasping — oh, it was horrible! All the purity of
which he was so ignorant, to which he was so
indifferent, all the purity which he would have
disclaimed so roughly and indignantly if anyone
had ever accused him of it, came surging up in wild,
sickening protest, and shook him, and clawed at
him, and battered and beat at him, and left him
wishing only for death, oblivion and extinction.

Grown-up people. Real grown-up people. This
was the kind of thing that they did — everywhere,
probably, all over the place when they thought no
one was looking; the loathsome, abominable beasts!
This was what all the sniggering was about; this
was what people meant, and talked and wrote
about, and even made jokes about, and all the time
— well, couldn't they realise? Couldn't they
understand? Couldn't they see how — no, not
filthy — but how *cruel* it was? How it tortured
one, how it made one hate everything and everybody, how it turned the whole world into a place of
unutterable degradation and slime?

Thus, foolishly, pathetically but inevitably — for
you had such a shock yourself once, though you
have probably forgotten it — did Julian Sebright
react to the harmless spectacle in the taxicab.
Thus did his soul descend into the pit, while blackness closed over it and the burden of his own
innocence weighed it down. It wasn't his fault
that no amount of novel-reading could prepare him

for the blow when it came; it wasn't his fault that
normal children don't glide into this kind of enlight-
ment, but are doomed to achieve it in painful and
individual jerks. Indeed, one might even say that
it was to his credit, in a sense, that he suffered as
acutely as he did.

But he did suffer. And in his suffering he now
turned abruptly from the spot at which he could
no longer bear to look, and his palsied gaze met
that of the nasty little girl whom he had quite
forgotten. At first he was merely conscious of a
fresh wave of shame that anyone else, whoever
he was, should have shared his unmentionable
experience. Then, suddenly, he saw the look on
her face; the look of cunning, the look of knowledge, the look of intimacy, the look of diabolical
invitation. With a choking, groaning sound, he
forced his limbs into action. He burst from her,
he thrust his way through the laurel-bushes, he
started running across the lawn.

'Julian!' she cried, as she tore after him. 'Wait!
Julian! Stop!'

'Go away!' shouted Julian Sebright, still
holding his lead. 'You don't understand. Go
away!'

But there were the other children, all bearing
down on him in triumph; all calling his name,
and spreading out to catch him. He swerved.
He hesitated. And again somebody touched his
arm.

'Julian——'

One regrets, for many reasons, to report so
entirely disgraceful an action, but it's no use
dodging the truth. Julian Sebright — there in the
middle of the open lawn — stopped, turned round,
pushed Miss Palliser violently on the right shoulder,
and knocked her flat. He then ran straight up his
own iron steps, sped in at the window, crossed the
dining-room, bolted into his father's study, slammed

the door, and was on the point of flinging himself
face downwards on the leather sofa, when he
suddenly stopped again, and gave a loud, gulping
cry.

'Good heavens, old chap!' said Mr. Sebright
— for, as it happened, there was to be another
board-meeting tomorrow. 'What the devil's the
matter?'

So Julian flung himself against his father's waist-
coat.

'Oh, Daddy!' he gasped. 'Oh, please — *please*
send me to your proper school instead! Oh, please,
Daddy — you *must*, Daddy — *please!*'

'All right, old chap,' said Mr. Sebright. 'Good
lord, yes. Rather!'

He sent just one glance at his study ceiling,
which in another sense was also the drawing-room
floor. But the men in the Sebright family were
together on this point; and the men were going to
win.

35

FOR years people had said to Graham Rutland:
'But of course it's different for you. You're not
tied down like ordinary people.' Usually they
added: '*You* can work wherever you like.' And
then if they were men, they looked a little envious,
while if they were women, they looked a little
condescending, and in either case there was also
a surreptitious suggestion that the work which
Graham Rutland did wasn't really work at all.

In his earlier days he had been accustomed to
rise to this unspoken taunt, to argue, to prove, at
any rate to his own satisfaction, that even novel-
writing required a certain amount of time and
labour; and to realise, when he had done so, that
he had produced just as much effect on a popular
illusion as if he had kept his mouth shut and spared
his breath. So now, when he was getting on to-

wards fifty, he merely smiled — and there's no doubt
that Graham Rutland had a charming smile — and
let them all, men and women alike, believe whatever they chose and think whatever suited them
best.   After all, it was the results that counted,
and the money that the results brought in.   And if
people preferred to picture him as flitting like a
butterfly from place to place, and occasionally — if
he happened to be in the mood — tossing off a couple of thousand words as he lolled back on a sofa,
perhaps it would only make them admire him less
if they discovered the actual truth.

And he liked their admiration.   Quite frankly
he revelled in it.   He went out, though not often,
to parties, and got the most genuine kind of kick
when people said: 'No!   Not *the* Mr. Rutland!
Oh, but I must tell you, I simple *adore* your books.'
At these moments his secret gratification was quite
as profound as his outward air of modesty.   He
smiled, charmingly; he was gracious, witty, and at
the same time delightfully humble.   The admirers
were enchanted with him, and he knew it.   Only
on the way back from the party did the inevitable
reaction set in.   'Showing off again,' he muttered.
'Coming the great man at 'em, and playing the
blasted hero.   Lord, if they knew what luck it all
is, and how little I've learnt in all these years!
Lord, if they knew what a bungler I really am!'

So then he hid himself away, and avoided parties,
and went on working like a beaver.   And of course,
judging by results, he wasn't a bungler at all, and
knew a great deal more than he thought he knew,
and certainly had no more luck than his talents
and application deserved.   Only there's this about
the profession of authorship; that when you're
young, you have all the ideas and can't write;
and when you're older, you've mastered the writing
part of it and haven't got any ideas.   If only, you
reflect, you hadn't put twelve plots into your first

novel, and if only you weren't too honourable to pick them out and use them all over again. But it's too late to take up another profession now, and as a matter of fact — and for all your present sufferings — you wouldn't take up another profession if you could. So you sit and sweat, and grumble and groan, and painfully evolve stories which, if you only knew it, all come out of your first novel anyhow. And there are moments, of course. Praise is still sweet. The double line that you draw at the end of the last chapter can yet transport you into a temporary elysium of relief and achievement. Not least, there are evenings of perfectly gorgeous literary shop with your contemporaries and rivals and friends.

But if there were one point on which Graham Rutland's acquaintances were utterly and perpetually mistaken, it lay in that original assumption that he could work wherever he liked. There existed, as he knew, friends, rivals and contemporaries who could take a typewriter on to an hotel balcony, or balance it on their knees while swaying in a lower berth, and still continue to turn out sentences with subjects and predicates which, added to similar sentences, grew into intelligible paragraphs and more. But he couldn't. He'd tried, and he knew he couldn't. More than once, when on his travels or staying in other people's houses, he had been visited with a genuine idea which experience told him was sound, and practice informed him should fall readily into the required shape. And he had shut himself up, and set to work with his fountain-pen and a writing-pad, and occasionally had succeeded, with the utmost agony, in covering perhaps a third of one sheet.

Then, however, it suddenly appeared that the table was the wrong height, or there was a mysterious draught, or the light was throwing disturbing shadows, or there were noises to interrupt him, or his hosts elected to have another of their incessant meals. He had struggled on, but always he had regretted it, made a mess of things, gone from bad to worse, and finally seen the so-called idea vanish into a chasm of corrections from which no amount of subsequent industry could ever retrieve it. The fact, indeed, was quite obvious that he would have been considerably better off if he had left that so-called idea alone. At least, then, he wouldn't have destroyed still more of his self-confidence, and with it all chance of ever employing the so-called idea again.

So he had learnt his lesson, and the lesson was that in that intangible world of touch and go where a writer wanders without guides or friends, he must have his own table, his own chair, his own surroundings and his own devices for keeping the more material world at bay. Perhaps, he often thought, this was weakness; but he'd fought it, he'd been beaten, and there was absolutely no point in returning to the attack. For years, now, the same ritual had accompanied his daily efforts to carry on his solitary profession. Always he began by locking the door. Always he proceeded to disconnect the telephone, to seat himself at the same angle, to provide himself with the same quality and size of writing-paper, the same pen, the same pipes, matches and tobacco. Invariably the first twenty minutes were occupied in staring at nothing and wondering why on earth he didn't retire; the next ten minutes were spent in copying out, but scarcely ever altering, the last sheet which he had written yesterday. And then, as abruptly but unconsciously as one passes from wakefulness into sleep, the pen took up its real labours, the mind, presumably, directed it, and another almost inevitably successful novel resumed its growth.

All this, for some reason, has been slightly subjective. Objectively, Graham Rutland was in complete control of his destiny — at any rate he'd never had a real failure yet — his public stuck to him, his publishers almost worshipped him, only the very youngest critics ever sneered at him, and a uniform edition might be expected at practically any moment. Naturally he didn't explain, and possibly it wasn't true, that the whole edifice depended on such details as an old leather chair and a special relationship to the fire-place and window; but this was what he believed, this was what he imagined that trial and error had proved, and when the lease of his old flat ran out, and it became necessary to seek fresh quarters elsewhere, he went through weeks of positive conviction that he'd never be able to write again.

The publishers didn't know this, of course; nor did the editors, nor the critics, nor the booksellers and librarians, nor the public which kept all these hard-working characters in their jobs. The general opinion, in fact — which turned out to be perfectly correct — was that someone called Graham Rutland would continue to produce novels of from eighty to a hundred and twenty thousand words as regularly and successfully as he had been doing ever since a great many people could remember. He was a novelist. It was his business. Why on earth should he ever stop?

But Mr. Rutland lay awake in his bed, and sweated with ridiculous and baseless terrors. 'I can't tell them,' he thought. 'No one would believe me if I tried to tell them, and anyhow what's the use? Lord knows what I'll do with myself when I run dry; but it's coming; it's getting nearer every second; I've never been more certain of anything in my life.'

Thus did Mr. Rutland's strange temperament plague him in the watches of the night. But a less sensitive side of him knew well enough that he'd got to live somewhere, whether he wrote or not, and he

appealed to Mrs. Lowthian — with whom he was
having one of his mild and extremely literary flirta-
tions at this period — and Mrs. Lowthian said that
of course they must go house-hunting together, and
he'd better lunch with her on Thursday.

'I'll get a list,' she said. 'I know just what
you want. Not a flat, this time, Graham — I can't
think how you stand it. But a dear little house
somewhere, with a garden, perhaps, and a lovely big
workroom.'

Mr. Rutland sighed and frowned, as he thought
how useless it was. But then he smiled, because
it was he who had taught Mrs. Lowthian not to
say 'study,' and undoubtedly there was something
pleasant in seeing one's influence at work.

'It's very kind of you,' he said; 'though as a
matter of fact ——'

'Kind?' interrupted Mrs. Lowthian — and, by
the way, it was her habit of interrupting which had
originally attracted him and eventually drove him
very quietly out of her circle. 'Kind?' she said.
'Not in the least. I know just how helpless all
you clever men are. You leave it to me.'

It was one of Mr. Rutland's by no means exceptional habits to become, for the time being, whatever
his friends thought he was. Although, therefore,
he didn't honestly consider himself either helpless or
clever, he looked both, and renewed his expressions
of gratitude, and said that lunch on Thursday would
be too charming for words.

And he turned up, what's more — looking a bit
dazed, as he always did after a hard morning — and
Mrs. Lowthian took him round in her car, and
after they had seen three houses which weren't
in the least like anything that she had so carefully
specified, they arrived, at about four o'clock in the
afternoon, at Number Fourteen, Clinton Place.

'This is more like it,' said Mrs. Lowthian. 'You
couldn't be quieter, Graham.' And: 'You could

make something of this,' she was saying a little
later. And then: 'Look! What a dear little garden.' And then, turning to the caretaker: 'Is that
another room at the end there?'

'Yes, mum,' said the caretaker. 'That's what
the last gen'leman 'ad built for 'is stoodio.'

'Of course!' said Mrs. Lowthian, hurriedly
consulting the house-agents' summary. 'I knew
there was one with a studio, and — Graham!
Where are you?'

'Here,' said Mr. Rutland, who was still standing
forlornly at the foot of the stairs. 'What is it?'

'A studio!' cried Mrs. Lowthian. 'That's just
what you want to make it perfect. Think of the
quiet, Graham. You can shut yourself in, and you
might be a thousand miles from anywhere. Come
along quickly and look at it.'

The studio was still full of the last gentleman's
canvases, and was at once cold, musty and gaunt.

'There!' said Mrs. Lowthian. 'You don't know
what a wonderful room we can make for you out of
this. Listen! You can't hear a sound.'

If the windows had been open, one would certainly have heard the voices of the children playing
in Clinton Gardens. But all that Graham Rutland
could think of at the moment was that he was tired,
that it didn't really matter tuppence where he lived,
and that if he went tramping over any more houses
he would probably collapse.

'I can't see ——' he began, despondently.

'Of course you can't!' interrupted Mrs. Lowthian. 'But you wait till we've cleaned it up,
and got you some nice furniture, and a carpet, and
bookcases, and a new grate. Why,' said Mrs.
Lowthian, 'I believe I could write myself in a room
like this!'

Somehow this notion jarred on the sensitive but
self-centred author. He did wish that women —
even charming women like Mrs. Lowthian — could

see that this kind of imitation was anything but
flattering.   Writing, thought Mr. Rutland, was,
after all, something more than a side-line or an occupation for a wet afternoon; and when a man had
given the best years of his life to it, and had suffered
so much for the sake of it, and now knew that he
was finished and yet couldn't bear the thought of
existence without it... Well, in short, Mr. Rutland
remained, as always, temperamental and a little
ungrateful; but he took the house because — although for some reason he wouldn't admit this even
to himself — it was just the house that he wanted.
And Mrs. Lowthian produced her clever friend
Mrs. Flowerdew, who did it up so that no house
can ever have more closely resembled the residence
of a literary bachelor, and made the studio look
almost like a novelist's study on the stage.   And
when she had done this, Mr. Rutland brought in
his old desk and his old leather chair and his old
pipes and papers and paraphernalia, and burnt
a few holes in the carpet, and disarranged all the
books, and left things lying about and refused
to allow anything ever to be cleaned, tidied or
moved.   And although this conduct was ulti-
mately responsible for his break with Mrs. Flowerdew — ('After all I've done for you,' she said. 'Are
you going to stop fussing me, or aren't you? he
asked) — yet in some mysterious and quite unexpected manner he was still writing just as many
thousand words a week as before the great upheaval.
Looking back, it seemed incredible; looking forward, he still saw nothing but doubts, difficulties
and despair.   But in the present — which of course
kept moving along with him all the time — he continued to write and write and write.   Presently he
had been in the new house nearly seven years, and
had finished nearly seven more novels.   An outsider would have said that it was inevitable; that
the creature couldn't help writing, and that this

result was scarcely distinguishable from the act of falling off a log. Yet not a month had passed without the creature groaning, moaning and chucking great sheaves of manuscript into his waste-paper basket.

'I'm done for,' he said. 'I'm written out. I'm probably going off my head. Lord, how happy I was when I used to live in that flat!'

A lie. A whole series of lies. He'd always used the waste-paper basket like this, his average output had hardly varied for the past twenty years, and reaction and fresh creation were as certain to follow this ridiculous whimpering as dawn succeeds to darkness. An outsider could have told him this, and some of them did, though he never believed them. A curious existence, if it weren't so common in the literary world. Is one sorry for him? No, not particularly.

And one of the reasons why one isn't particularly sorry for him is because during all these seven years — and for considerably longer, if you insist on knowing — Graham Rutland had sucked sympathy in the most cold-blooded manner imaginable from a long list of kind, foolish, generous and good-natured women. Look at the dedications in that shelf of his novels, and you'll find an almost complete catalogue. Mrs. Lowthian was by no means the first, nor was Mrs. Flowerdew by any means the last. One by one he used them, exhausted them, and flung them aside. None of them had any hold over him, for few gentlemen have been more steadfastly platonic, and from the moment that they bored him their doom was instantly sealed. At once they were neglected and forgotten, and at once the charming smile was directed elsewhere. If anyone had called him a philanderer, he would have been shocked, indignant and disgusted. Had he ever kissed them? Had he ever even held their hands? Of course he hadn't, but if a bachelor mayn't make friends, or if a bachelor must be compelled to keep all the friends whom he has made, surely that's going a good deal beyond the written or even unwritten law. Besides, he was never deliberate about it. Each change was always an accident, and quite unavoidable. He'd been gloomy, but he'd never been cynical in his life.

So after Mrs. Flowerdew there was Lady Pilcher. And then there was Augusta — he couldn't quite remember her surname. And then there were Mrs. Partridge, and Miss Harvey, and an American woman with a French title. And others. And if anyone had thought of tracing these bright companionships in the form of a graph, they might have noticed that while Mr. Rutland himself — as was only natural — grew steadily older, his friends became unsteadily but distinctly younger. Mrs. Lowthian, for instance, was actually his senior. So was Mrs. Partridge, though only just. But since then the line had never risen so high, once it had dropped as low as thirty-four, and now as it still wavered round forty, there seemed more than a hint that it was about to plunge deeper than it had ever been yet.

Masters, Mr. Rutland's manservant, who saw everything but said nothing, knew well enough that another change was imminent. Mrs. Selwood was still telephoning, her notes and letters still arrived three or four times a week. But twice Mr. Rutland had said: 'I'm busy. Ask her to leave a message,' and he hadn't written himself for over a fortnight. These were signs that there was no mistaking, and in Masters's case no thought of criticising, either. But whether the next item in the catalogue would prove to be Mrs. Playfair or that young lady who'd already given Mr. Rutland her photograph, well, here even Masters found himself unable to decide.

Nor, of course, could his employer, because in
this business his employer had never decided anything. He knew, certainly, that Mrs. Selwood had
become a thundering bore; in fact, he'd already
more than half forgotten her existence. But it's
just as certain that he wasn't looking about for her
successor. He'd met Mrs. Playfair, he'd liked her,
she'd come to dinner with him — though not alone
— he'd been to dinner with her, and already he was
using some of her phrases in his new novel. So far,
indeed, it seemed more than likely that this kind,
foolish, generous and good-natured woman would
occupy at least the next six months in Mrs. Selwood's discarded shoes. Mrs. Playfair herself was,
at this stage, prepared to make it even longer, and
this without a thought of passion or indiscretion or
any of the things with which Mr. Rutland had
always contrived to dispense. She was forty-five,
and no one, thought Masters, could possibly have
been more suitable.

But then Mr. Rutland had gone to a party,
and at the party he had met this girl called
Gwenda.

36

'HULLO!' she said. 'How do you do? I say,
this is a bit of a thrill.'

'I beg your pardon?' said Graham Rutland.

'Meeting you, I mean. I've read one of your
books, you know. I *adored* it.'

'That,' said Graham Rutland, with his charming
smile, 'was very kind of you. I wonder ——'

'What do you wonder?'

'Which book it would be.'

The girl threw back her head and laughed.

'Serves me right,' she said. 'I thought if I
said "one" like that, you might believe me. As a

matter of fact, I never read anything. But I'm
fascinated by success!'

'Are you?' said Mr. Rutland. And if she hadn't
been so young, and so cheerful, and so pretty, and
so amazingly refreshing at this distinctly dismal
party, one rather doubts if he would have said any
more. Not that he was conceited, but she'd at-
tacked his dignity and blown a definite hole in it.
In fact, though she was hardly out of the schoolroom, she'd laughed at him. But then she'd
flattered him. So that in two minutes she'd done
exactly what she meant, which was to be introduced
to the only lion in the room, attract his attention,
keep it, and see what happened next.

'And you think I'm successful?' asked Mr.
Rutland.

'Oh, yes. The Dewhursts are awfully proud of
having you here. I don't suppose they'll let me
talk to you for long.'

'Don't you?' said Mr. Rutland. 'Isn't that
rather my affair?'

'I say, that's rather sweet. I say —— '

'Yes?'

'I have *heard* of you, you know. And if I did
any reading at all —— But everything's such a
rush, isn't it?'

Mr. Rutland was amused.

'Is it?' he asked. 'Well, you're still young,
aren't you?'

'Am I? Guess.'

'I beg your pardon?'

'How young do you think I am?'

Mr. Rutland found himself a trifle embarrassed
by this question, but while he was still hesitating,
the girl supplied him with the answer.

'I'm nineteen,' she said.

'Good lord!' said the novelist and, as he liked
to think of himself, the student of life. Quite a
shock, for, of course, when he had used that un-

spoken phrase about the schoolroom, he hadn't meant it literally. About twenty-five, he'd have thought; but of course in these days ——

An alert, calculating light suddenly shone in his eyes, for there was a girl of exactly nineteen in his new novel, and it had just struck him that perhaps she needed a bit of altering. He'd been quite satisfied with her until a moment ago, but now she seemed colourless, inaccurate, altogether old-fashioned.

'Good lord!' he repeated, half to himself. 'Then you're only just out!'

'Out? What do you mean, Mr. Rutland? Nobody's ever in, nowadays. I say, aren't you funny!'

Sophistication, thought the student of life. Sophistication and, at the same time, ridiculous gaucherie. He could make something out of that, something quite new, and interesting, and rather appealing. Just look at the way this child had plucked her eyebrows and curled her hair and — yes, there was no doubt of it — made up her odd little face. And all the time, of course, she knew nothing at all. She couldn't know anything. What a character!

It must be admitted that during the rest of that first meeting quite three-quarters of Graham Rutland's mind were occupied in planning just how he could graft this new character on to the existing framework. How far, for instance, would he have to go back? How was it going to affect the rest of the story? How, particularly, was he going to get rid of her at the end? But the rest of his by no means blunt intelligence, and quite ninety per cent of his undoubted charm, just cut loose and enjoyed themselves. He sat back with his hands clasped over an elevated knee, and he talked and he listened, and he chattered and he laughed. Seldom if ever had he found things so easy at a party, and

what did it matter if he were being a little rude to his
hostess when all this was really part of his work?

Usually he left such entertainments feeling not
only aged and exhausted, but also sensible that he
had done worse than waste his time; that he had
in some manner lost a part of his precious individuality; had had it scraped and knocked about
and rubbed off. 'Lord!' he would mutter, as he
drove home in his taxi. 'Why do I do it? All
those faces. All those voices. All that deadly
sameness and falseness — and me making a dull ass
of myself again.' But this evening he smiled to
himself, as the lights flickered through the windows;
he felt young, clever and amusing. 'Nice child,
that,' he reflected. 'So busy trying to be grown-
up, and so appallingly innocent all the time. Such
a quick little brain. Such a cheerful, stupid little
fool. Honestly,' he thought, 'it was real luck
that I went out after all. Yes; I see just how I can
mix her up and work her in.'

It was so clear, as he went humming and whistling
to bed, that he never even troubled to set down any
of the little phrases and snatches of dialogue which
kept bubbling into his mind. There were a notebook and pencil by his bedside — there always had
been — which were intended for this precise purpose; but tonight he just glanced at them, chuckled,
and turned away. Why bother? Why worry,
when the thing was going to come out as easily as
winking? He read, he switched off the light, he
sighed, he fell asleep.

But in the morning the thing absolutely failed
to come out. He could destroy, he could erase, he
could alter the original girl's name, and of course
he hadn't forgotten the new twist which she was to
bring into the plot. But as for adding, as for re-
constructing, as for recalling any of those little
phrases or snatches of dialogue — why, it was hopeless. He groaned and moaned. He strode round

the workroom, glared blankly from his window at the perambulators in Clinton Gardens, sat down again and scratched his head until all his hair was standing on end. Supposing he abandoned the new idea, then; supposing he went on as before. He would. He tried. He couldn't.

At lunch-time, when he was feeling dizzier than ever, Mrs. Playfair rang him up.

'Hullo!' she said. 'How are you?'

'Ghastly,' said Mr. Rutland. 'Everything's gone wrong this morning. I've torn up about fifty pages' — this was an artistic exaggeration, but he *must* have sympathy — 'I can't go backwards, or forwards, or sideways. I'm just stuck!'

'Poor dear,' said Mrs. Playfair. 'But of course you've been overworking.'

'Do you think so?'

'I'm sure of it,' said Mrs. Playfair. 'You must knock off. You must try and put it right out of your mind, and then you'll find — quite suddenly — that everything's all right again.'

'Will I?' asked Graham Rutland, a little doubt-fully.

'Of course you will!' cried Mrs. Playfair. 'And to begin with, do you know what I'm going to do? I'm coming round in the car, and I'm going to take you for a nice drive — and perhaps we might get out and walk a bit — in Richmond Park. Fresh air, Graham; that's what you need. Now, promise me not to worry till I see you. I'll be along di-rectly after lunch.'

'That's very kind of you,' said Graham Rutland, and, indeed, companionship was exactly what he felt he needed. A good-hearted creature, Kitty Playfair; sensible, understanding, a real friend. He was just thinking, with a brief spasm of distaste, how boring Mrs. Selwood would have been in similar circumstances, when suddenly the telephone bell rang again.

'Hullo?' he said, off-handedly. 'Yes?'

'Can I speak to Mr. Rutland?' asked a voice.

'You are,' said Graham. 'Who is it?'

'It's me, Mr. Rutland. Gwenda Greig.'

'Oh! Hullo!'

'I say ——'

'Yes?'

'I say, you did mean what you said last night. Didn't you?'

'Eh?' said Graham. 'What did I say?'

'About my coming and seeing the place where you work. I'd simply love to, you know. In fact, I'm terribly keen. Shall I come this afternoon?'

Lord, thought Mr. Rutland, had he really said that? Well, as a matter of fact, he knew he had — or something just like it; only, of course, he'd never imagined —— Dash it, it would be rather fun, though. It might cheer him up. Only what would Masters think? Or Mrs. Masters? Or the girl's parents? Never mind, he was nearly old enough to be her grandfather, and —— Oh, lord! He'd forgotten. Mrs. Playfair.

'Do you know ——' he began, hastily. 'I mean, I'm most awfully sorry, but ——'

Here he suddenly remembered that it would be dark by half-past four, and that neither he nor Mrs. Playfair had said anything about what was to happen after the drive. Tea might have been presumed, but it hadn't been mentioned. An author could always say that he'd got to work.

'— well, look here, I'm busy just at the moment. But what about five o'clock?'

'Oh, lovely!' said the girl. 'That's just what I meant, really. You see, we're going to a cinema first. Thanks awfully. I'll be along.'

'"We"?' thought Graham Rutland. Was she bringing a friend with her, then? She hadn't said so, but perhaps it would be a good thing if she did. Or perhaps it wouldn't. He was a little fussed, a little nervous — a little prim, too — about the whole business.

'Oh, Masters,' he said, just as he was starting out. 'I've got a — a lady coming to tea.'

No, not a young lady. He wouldn't say that, and if Masters chose to think he meant Mrs. Playfair, well, what the dickens had it got to do with Masters?

'Very good, sir,' said Masters, who knew perfectly well that it wasn't Mrs. Playfair. And then Mr. Rutland climbed into the big, comfortable car, and a rug was placed over his and his companion's knees, and away they went to Richmond Park, and started trundling round it. For some reason he found himself in a conversational mood, and he wasn't in the least disappointed when his companion said that the grass really seemed too wet for a walk. They trundled and talked. What a pleasant, intelligent woman Kitty Playfair was! It grew colder and darker, and the car turned homewards.

'You'll come in for a cup of tea, won't you?'

Graham Rutland gave a twitch and a start.

'Do you know,' he said, very earnestly, 'I'm terribly afraid I can't. It's my work, you see. I had such a rotten morning, and if I don't try and catch up...'

Mrs. Playfair cooed and mooed and quite understood. The novelist felt rather a cad. A little later he felt rather a fool, because there were the tea-things in his little drawing-room, and the curtains were drawn, and the lights were all arranged, and he'd washed his hands and brushed his hair, but it was after half-past five and he was still quite alone.

'Dashed bad manners,' he said. And: 'I *ought* to work,' he said. And: 'Dash it!' he said; 'I'll give her just five more minutes.'

And: 'Ah!' he said. 'Here you are. Come along in and get warm!'

'Am I late?' asked the girl Gwenda.

'No, no. Not in the least. It doesn't matter, I mean.'

'We went to the most marvellous film,' said the girl Gwenda, 'and I just *had* to stay to the end. I *must* tell you about it.'

She did, and it sounded quite drivelling. But as she told him, and as they had tea, it again came over Mr. Rutland that of course he could make the most wonderful character out of his visitor, and that it was perfectly obvious where he'd gone wrong this morning, and perfectly simple now to get it right. 'Yes, yes,' he kept saying. 'I see. Yes, that sounds awfully good.' And then suddenly another problem was solved for him, though he wasn't sure that he was best pleased. 'We' had been Miss Greig and a young man called Neville. And they'd been alone together, quite clearly. And quite clearly his visitor thought nothing of this; but he did. He felt a little prim again, and critical, and anxious. Masters came in to fetch the tea-things, and he wondered what Masters was thinking. To hell with Masters!

'Come and see my room,' he said, abruptly.

'Oh, yes — of course!'

'This way. Mind all these steps.'

'How exciting! I'm thrilled!'

'Just a second, and I'll turn on some lights. There we are!'

'Oh, I say — what fun! And that's where you actually write?'

'Yes.'

'Well, sit down and show me how you do it.'

'You don't really ——'

'Yes, I do. Go on!'

Mr. Rutland felt rather a fool again as he obeyed her orders. But she hardly glanced at him. She was walking round, looking at all his books. He got up.

'Oh!' she said. 'Do you want me to go now?'

'No, no; of course not. Sit down.'

'Well, may I have a cigarette?'

'I beg your pardon. Of course! Here you are, Miss Greig.'

'Thanks. Do you mind calling me "Gwenda"? Everybody does, you know.'

'Do they? Very well, then. Here's a match — Gwenda.'

She eyed him steadily, and was it a little pityingly? He didn't care. He knew just what he was going to do with his novel.

He was charming. He drew her out, and she came out — like chewing-gum. He was hearing all about her family, and her friends, and her absolutely amazing existence. And it all fitted, it was all going to hang together and give just the characterisation that he wanted. Fine! The clock struck seven and he never heard it. But a few minutes later Masters suddenly reappeared.

'Hullo!' said Graham Rutland. 'Yes? What is it?'

'Beg pardon, sir. Mr. Buller has called for Miss Greig.'

'Mr. ——?'

'Heavens!' cried the visitor. 'It's Reggie! I told him to come at seven, and it can't possibly —— Yes it is, though. I must fly!'

And she flung her latest cigarette more at than into the fire, and leapt to her feet, and patted Mr. Rutland on the upper arm, and said that she'd had a marvellous time and that he'd been too sweet to her; and then she smiled radiantly at Masters, and dashed past him down the steps into the garden. 'Good night!' she called back. 'Thanks awfully. Thanks tremendously. See you soon!' And then, presumably, she met and connected with Mr. Buller somewhere in the hall, for by the time that Mr. Rutland reached the main premises himself there wasn't a sign of either of them.

'Lord!' he thought. 'What an extraordinary girl that is!'

But he did two hours' real writing after dinner that night, and he knew more than ever that his new nineteen-year-old character was absolutely running rings round the old one. Wiping her out, sending her to blazes, blowing the poor colourless creature to smithereens.

37

UPS and downs after this, as were only to be expected. Sometimes the novel moved, and sometimes it was bogged. Sometimes the author thought: 'I don't need her any more now. I can really do better without her' — and whenever this happened, you could be certain that he was seeing Mrs. Playfair instead; and sometimes he thought: 'Well, I *am* nearly old enough to be her grandfather, and if it really amuses her to come here ——' But there was no question of his being in love with her, for there was absolutely no question — and there never had been — of his being in love with anybody. All that part of him had always gone into his books, and perhaps this was a reason why he was so successful — though one admits that it isn't necessarily a part which invariably wins success. And, again, if anyone thinks that he was drawing a portrait of the girl Gwenda as he wrote and wrote, then all one can say is that he wasn't; or that it was quite unrecognisable, if he were. The girl in the novel, whether she were meant to be or not, was as different as chalk from cheese. Because novelists don't draw portraits, and if they did, they wouldn't be novelists.

Can one explain what it is that they do draw? One can't. No more can they. No more can

anyone else. If one tried to explain, it would only
sound as if the whole business were a kind of
spirit-writing, which it most certainly isn't. But
think of all the physical and spiritual stages which
separate the observed from the observer, and what
the observer writes from what the observer per-
ceives. Besides, one is assuming that Graham
Rutland was an artist, and artists don't even try
to tell the truth. They know so very well that it
isn't true.

So he cut and sliced, and added and altered.
And the axis of the whole novel shifted slightly,
but never had he written faster or been more convinced that he was writing well. He was happy,
and Mrs. Playfair felt it, and was flattered; and
flattered him in return, so that he became happier
still. Of course there were still hitches and hin-
drances — there always would be — but the book
grew; he saw the end no longer as an almost un-
attainable goal, but as a bright light drawing
nearer and nearer. He had lost that painful sensation of climbing and struggling. He was looking
down from the heights.

And all this time, also, the girl or child Gwenda
rang him up on the telephone and said should she
come and see him. And he said: 'Yes. Do.'
And, generally speaking, she did; and she prattled
away, and smoked his cigarettes, and continued to
relate her adventures while he continued to think
and to make mental notes. What was *her* game?
One can't explain that either. There she was,
free, unguarded, inquisitive and irresponsible, all
at an age at which no previous generation had been
out of leading-strings. What on earth would she
find to do with the rest of her life when she was
bolting the first mouthfuls so voraciously? She
neither knew nor cared, and no more did the rest
of her circle, as they dashed about together in
cars, and to cinemas, and to dance-restaurants and

to theatres. One mustn't be bored, one mustn't be out of things, one mustn't waste a moment of one's time.

Some critics might say that the whole lot of them did nothing else, but that didn't trouble Mr. Rutland. She was a type, and she amused him, and she'd helped him out of a literary hole. They both went on talking, and the surface of his brain became slightly pitted with the names of all her friends, though he knew none of them by sight, and with the details of their remarkable and tireless folly.

'How's Betty?' he would ask. 'What's *she* been doing lately?'

Gwenda laughed and began telling him, and he walked about and smoked his pipe and very often hardly even listened.

'Wasn't that priceless?' she finished.

'Priceless,' agreed Mr. Rutland. 'And Sam? What's old Sam been up to since he fought the taxi-driver? Eh?'

'You are absurd,' said Gwenda. 'That wasn't Sam at all. That was Bunny.'

'Well, never mind. Bunny, then. Go on.'

One applies oneself with the utmost assiduity to the riddle of this girl or child Gwenda, and one is driven to the conclusion that her game — if it were a game — was based solely on the fact that she'd done something that none of the others had thought of doing. She'd collected a celebrity, though she still hadn't read a word of his writings, and what one did next she really didn't know. Something, of course. One couldn't stand still. He was a kind, funny old thing, but one did sometimes want him to *notice* one a bit more. Suddenly, one day she arrived with that enormous photograph.

'I've brought something for you,' she said. 'Look! It's just been taken. Do you like it?'

'Eh?' said Graham Rutland. 'Good lord! Do you mean this is for me?'

'Yes, of course. Don't you want it?'

'Oh, rather. I call that awfully kind of you.
Most awfully kind. Makes you look a bit old,
doesn't it?'

'I'm not a baby,' said Gwenda.

'No, no. Of course not. Well, thank you very
much indeed.'

'Shall I put something on it?'

Before he quite understood this question, she
had seized the photograph and snatched up one
of his pens and scrawled 'With love from Gwenda'
across her own shoulder.

'There!' she said. 'No, don't blot it. Wait
till it dries.'

He hadn't been going to blot it. His impulse
had been to hide it quickly, before Masters or
Mrs. Masters came in and saw it. After the girl
had gone, he did hide it — in his boot-cupboard —
and of course Masters came across it within twenty-
four hours, and read the legend, and speculated
profoundly. But said nothing.

Was the next development a result or a coinci-
dence? Suddenly the other girl — the girl in the
book — got quite out of hand. She'd served her
purpose now, she'd more than justified his labours,
he hadn't a thought of returning to the original and
inferior young woman; but he couldn't get rid of
her. She was supposed to fade out; in the earlier
version nothing could have been simpler; but now
he'd gone and made her so vivid, or she had become
so vivid, that one couldn't just drop her like that.
She refused to be dropped. By every artistic
canon, by every requirement of his own conscience,
her disappearance had got to be explained. He
started trying to explain it, and she clung to the
fabric more firmly than ever. Not only was she
wasting his time now, but she was definitely up-
setting the balance of the story. She was shoulder-
ing aside the real principals, she was becoming

larger and more lifelike every moment. If he put her — or bits of her — in the waste-paper basket, she only emerged with far more vitality than before.

'Lord!' muttered Graham Rutland. 'This is getting past a joke. I'm just where I was a week ago, and every time I try and hurry things up I only get more long-winded than ever. You would think,' he growled, 'that after writing all these years I'd be able to go the way I want. But I can't. She's fine up to a point, and then —— Well, what *am* I to do with her?'

He complained to Mrs. Playfair, and Mrs. Playfair once more oozed with sympathy.

'You're overworking, you poor dear,' she said. 'Now, why don't you put it all on one side — put it right out of your mind and forget about it? I'm sure that's the only sensible thing to do. And then later on ——'

'No,' said Mr. Rutland, doggedly. 'You don't understand, Kitty. If I let this thing beat me now ——'

He made an awkward and even alarming gesture to indicate the depth of his determination, and when Mrs. Playfair asked him to come out for another drive with her, he refused so violently that the poor woman blinked. She forgave him, of course; they always did. He was a genius, she told herself, and geniuses must always have their own way. But for the time being it must be confessed that her sympathy rather failed in its main purpose, rather lost itself as it poured from her kind and foolish heart, rather trickled down the waste-pipe.

He didn't complain to Gwenda, for what did she know or care about his work? Nothing. In fact, he was perpetually on the point of telling Masters to say that he wasn't at home, or of failing to answer the little ill-spelt notes that she kept sending

him.   Not that he blamed her for his troubles,
but honestly — no, honestly he wasn't in the mood
for all her youth and froth and high spirits.   He'd
got to finish this novel, and then, perhaps ——

While he was still hesitating, still feeling dubious
and a little resentful, she blew in again to ask for
tea, or a mis-spelling suddenly pierced the joints
of his armour.   'What a brute I am,' he thought.
'What a selfish, superior swine!   I don't care
what anyone says; she amuses me, she takes me
out of myself, she stops me worrying about this
infernal mess that I'm in.'   So he was charming,
and wrote charming little acknowledgments, and
got into a worse mess than ever.   Even Gwenda
herself began to notice it.

'I say, Graham,' she said — for this was what
she was calling him now; 'you're looking awfully
bored about something.   Is it me?'

'No, no; of course not.'

But Gwenda decided that it was.   And to tell
the truth, she was getting just a little bit bored
herself.   Not exactly with her celebrity, for there
was still a thrill here, but with the way that the
situation seemed to be slipping into a rut.   She
hated ruts; she wanted change, excitement, uncertainty, perhaps danger.   Well, not danger for
herself, but danger in the air.   The kind of danger
where other people lost their heads, and she didn't.
One evening she asked Mr. Rutland to take her
out to dinner, and he laughed and said he was far
too busy.   As a matter of fact, he was a little
shocked, and as a matter of fact, she was more
than a little piqued.   Later he was a little annoyed
with himself for being such a prude, and she was
still more annoyed with herself for not doing it
more cleverly.   She retreated, and he followed a
few steps — though not nearly so far as she had
hoped.   She had another idea, and it seemed
virtually foolproof.

Because it was his idea, really, or sounded like
it almost at once.   He'd been ragging her about
all the films that she saw, and she'd been ragging
him on account of his ignorance.   'You just don't
know what you're talking about,' she said.   'Everybody except you goes to cinemas.'

'Do they?' said Graham Rutland.   Well, perhaps they did.   And perhaps ——

'And you *ought* to go,' said Gwenda.

'Ought I?   Why?'

'Well, think of the ideas you'd get.   Thousands.
Millions.'

'By Jove!' said Graham Rutland.

'Come on!' said Gwenda.   'I'll take you to
one.   I mean, you'd have to pay, of course,
but ——'

If she hadn't said that, he wouldn't have laughed.
But as soon as he laughed it was quite obvious
that she'd won.   And why not?   What harm
could there be in it — in the middle of a crowd, in
the middle of the afternoon?   None.   And then
all those millions of ideas.   Well, if he could only
find one...

'Tomorrow?' she was asking.

'All right.   You'd better come and have lunch.'

'Oh, Graham, I can't!   I'm lunching with
Jimmie.'

'Well, never mind,' said Mr. Rutland, suddenly
sounding almost relieved.   And perhaps he was.
'I ought to be working, really.'

The girl or child pouted obstinately.

'The afternoon's a rotten time,' she said,
'anyhow.   You come and call for me about a
quarter to five.   Then we'll go to a perfect film.
That's settled, isn't it, Graham?   Isn't it, Graham?
Yes?'

Apparently it was settled.   Ridiculous to question
one's own conscience when the girl herself clearly
thought nothing of it, and when one was nearly old

enough to be her grandfather. He couldn't guess
that no one ever took Miss Greig to a cinema at that
hour without subsequently offering her dinner, and
that she had already decided exactly where they
were going to dine. But undoubtedly there was a
little disturbance in the atmosphere, and he felt
it, and rather liked it, and she had gone before he
could possibly examine it more closely or realise
what it might conceivably mean.

'Rather fun,' he was still thinking at dinner.

'Potatoes, sir?' said Masters.

'Oh — thanks.' No, perhaps it wasn't rather
fun. Perhaps he was being a bit of an ass. No,
he wasn't, though. Or was he?

'Well, I won't do it again,' he thought. And
then he thought that perhaps he *would* do it again.
And then he was confused and perplexed. And
then he started worrying about his novel once
more. And then he knew that he wasn't really
worrying about his novel at all, but about something else. He felt very strange, and was a long
time falling asleep. When he woke up he knew
at once that something rather unusual was going
to happen today. He remembered what it was,
and felt pleased. At breakfast — a meal at which
Masters was never in evidence — he still felt
pleased, and rather excited. At lunch, though
dizzy after a maddening morning with the waste-
paper basket, he felt positively impatient.

'Could you speak to Mrs. Playfair on the telephone, sir?'

'What? Oh, certainly.... Hullo, Kitty — is that
you?'

'Oh, Graham, I do so want to hear about your
work.'

'Eh?'

'Is it going any better?'

'No; it's not. In fact, I think it's worse.'

'What a shame!' said Mrs. Playfair. 'Now

do, please, for my sake, leave it all and come out for a drive this afternoon. I'm sure this rain isn't going to last.'

'Can't,' said Mr. Rutland. 'I've *got* to go on.'

'Oh, Graham! Well, would you feel like dropping in for a little tea — later on, I mean?'

'Sorry,' said Mr. Rutland. 'I — I've got an appointment later on. I mean, it's awfully kind of you, Kitty, but —— What?'

'Nothing,' said Mrs. Playfair. 'It's all right. I quite understand. Only don't forget ——'

Mr. Rutland deliberately ceased to listen, and only just stopped himself from whistling as his devoted friend assured him of her devotion. He was ashamed of himself, however, when he said good-bye, and added something vague about to-morrow which made him still more ashamed when he heard how it was received. Nice woman, Mrs. Playfair. Good sort. Heart of gold. For a moment he found himself almost clinging to the echo of her voice.

'Masters!'

'Sir?'

'I'm going to work now. Don't bother about tea unless I ring for it. And, by the way, I'm going out afterwards and I might be a little late for dinner. Tell Mrs. Masters, will you?'

'Very good, sir.'

Mr. Rutland picked his way past the puddles in his garden, shut himself into his workroom, poked the fire, lit his pipe, and sat down in his old leather chair. 'Now then,' he thought. And got up again because his pen seemed to need filling. And filled it, and looked out of the window, and returned to the desk. 'Now then,' he thought again. And he scowled at his manuscript, and rubbed his head, and wrote three words and stared at his bookshelves. 'Odd creature,' he thought; but he didn't mean himself, or Mrs. Playfair.

'I suppose it's all right,' he thought. 'I suppose I'm not by any chance going a bit far. Well, of course I'm not. I'm nearly old enough to be her grandfather — curse it!' He stuck his tongue into one cheek, and became partially unconscious. 'Supposing——' he murmured; and shook his head. 'Absurd!' he muttered; and wriggled his shoulders. 'And yet——' he mumbled. He dropped his pen; he sighed. What was he feeling so queer about? What was it that he expected, wanted, and at the same time dreaded? What was this curious vision that lured him on, and at the same time scared him and warned him to go back?

'Rubbish!' he said suddenly. And the sound of his voice startled him, and he looked guilty, and snatched up his pen again. Now then. This wouldn't do. He'd got to concentrate.

He did concentrate, fitfully. He wrote a little. He read what he'd written. He snarled, and tore it up. Then for perhaps five minutes he did nothing at all, except gaze out of the window, and wonder, and ponder, and feel nervous. 'Perhaps,' he thought, 'I *have* been overworking.' But he knew that wasn't it. He knew that whatever it was had got something to do with — what? He'd lost it. And yet there was this sensation of something imminent and immanent. Dash it, and talking of words like that, there was also his work to be done.

Now then!

He grunted, he scribbled, he got his notes out of a drawer and read them for about the thousandth time. He found himself marching round the workroom, and sat down again. What *was* he to do with this confounded girl? What *could* he do with her? Coming bursting into his story like this, doing everything for it up to a point, and then entirely refusing to leave. Not that he cared what happened to her, but if she went any further she was going to ruin the climax, and if she did that, he'd jolly well ruin the book. Now, supposing...

The sun came out and began to dry the puddles. It began to sink, and the shadows became longer and fainter. It vanished behind a high wall of cloud.

'Blast those children!' growled Graham Rutland, as their infant laughter reached him from over the long brick wall. But he soon forgot about them, and they didn't really disturb him, as the complicated struggle went on. Now it was the girl of flesh-and-blood who teased him and puzzled him and made him screw up his eyes like that. Now it was the pen-and-ink counterpart that baffled him and annoyed him and yet wouldn't leave him alone.

The air grew heavier and heavier with tobacco-smoke, and the desk and the carpet all round it were strewn with sheets of paper. Tea? No, thanks. Not while he was still in this sort of mess; not while he was still losing the battle; not while he felt that the least interruption must destroy his last hope. Dead silence in the workroom. Or perhaps a gentle hissing from the fire. Or perhaps the unsteady scratching of a pen. And then dead silence again.

'Lord!' said Graham Rutland, at five minutes to five. And then, suddenly, his eyebrows shot up and his mouth opened, and he jerked forward in his old leather chair. He hadn't realised that he was staring out of the window at all, but he'd just seen the most extraordinary, the most unaccountable and incredible sight. A boy had come rushing out of the bushes on the left, and a little girl had come running after him; and the boy had stopped, and turned round, and swung his arm, and ——

Good lord! Flat on her back. And the boy — little devil! — had gone. And the other child was roaring and screaming — he could hear her all right; and a lot of other children were hurrying up and pointing and shouting, and —

Whew, what a little savage! What an abominable way to behave! What an unspeakable thing to do! What a —

Just one smack like that, and —

And, by Jove, that was exactly the way to deal with the girl in his story! It was the only way, it solved everything, it did the trick and made the climax absolutely terrific. Get everyone puzzling, just as he'd puzzled; get everyone wondering what one earth he meant to do with her, and then — Biff! Send her to blazes, and go right ahead like a fire-engine. Why the devil hadn't he seen it before? And what the devil had he been worrying about?

He seized his writing-pad, he sucked furiously at his empty pipe, he wrote and wrote and wrote. It was all coming out now. It was all falling into place. He saw everything as clearly as if he'd finished the book already, and at this rate he would have finished it — good lord, yes — in less than a week at the very outside. Nothing could stop him now that darned girl was out of the way. Nothing could hold him back. Nothing could ——

'Shut up!' he snapped, as the telephone-extension started to buzz. But his left hand had switched it off even while his right hand still raced over the page. Not another thought did he give it as he wallowed in the glory of this headlong progress. He was inspired, oblivious, lost to the entire world, and quite tremendously happy. Did he deserve it? Had he earned it? Why, what pointless questions to ask!

38

'SHUT up!' said Gwenda, also — but this was a few moments earlier. 'Don't make that filthy row, everybody. Oh, Tubby — do turn off that gramophone!'

Somebody, whether Tubby or not, made a long arm, and the alleged music ceased. The rest of the filthy row, however, continued quite as powerfully as before, and Gwenda clapped her free hand over her free ear. 'Hullo!' she repeated. 'Is that Mr. —— Oh, is that you, Masters? Masters, it's Miss Greig. Do you know where —— Oh, shut *up!* No, not you, Masters. What's that? I can't hear. Oh, he *is* in, is he? Well, look here, I want to speak to him. Put me through, will you? Yes, it's all right; he ought to be here really, you see. Thank you.'

Sound of humming — the same *leit-motif* that had just been cut short on the gramophone — more or less associated with the swinging of Gwenda's long legs as she sat perched on the table in the corner. Pretty continuous uproar from the six or seven visitors who were lounging and sprawling over by the fire.

'I say, Gwenda ——'

'Oh, do stop it, Val. Can't you see when a person's talking to somebody?'

'Yes, but you're not ——'

'Yes, I am! Hullo! Oh, Graham —— What's that?'

Masters's voice again.

'I'm sorry, miss. Mr. Rutland's busy.'

'Busy?'

'Yes, miss. He's working. He's in his room.'

'Well, can't you put me through?'

'I'm afraid not, miss. If he don't answer his bell, miss, it means he's switched it off. I'm sorry, miss, but that's Mr. Rutland's rule, miss.'

'Rule? Rule!'

'Yes, miss. Could I take any message?'

'No!' said Gwenda. 'Not if ——'

She dropped the receiver back on its rest. Pushed the whole instrument away from her. Sat there

with her eyes flashing, biting her lower lip, still
swinging her long legs; furious, raging, insulted.
She'd been snubbed, then.　He couldn't have
forgotten about her — that was impossible.　He'd
done it on purpose.　She'd gone out of her way to
play up to him, she'd wasted hours and hours in
being nice to him, and now he just hid there and said
he was busy.　For two pins she'd go round and find
out what he *was* doing.　Tell him what she thought
of him.　Tell him he needn't expect any more of
her visits.　Tell the old stick-in-the-mud ——

'I say — look at Gwenda!　Look at her!'

'What's up, Gwenda?　Who's been annoying you?'

'Nobody.　Shut up!'

'Help!　She's going to throw something.'

'Don't be a fool, Tubby.　Put on that record
again.'

'What?　Oh, all right.　I say — shall I change
the needle?'

'Do — if it amuses you.　Val!'

'Hullo?'

'I say — Val ——'

'Yes?'

'Come here.　Listen.'

The young man called Val stepped over a pair of
silk stockings and a pair of trousers, and joined his
hostess.　The musical accompaniment was now in
full swing again.

'Listen, Val — I'm bored with all these idiots.'

The young man called Val looked distinctly
interested.

'So am I,' he said; 'if it comes to that.
Only ——'

'Only what?'

'Well, you needn't have brought 'em all back.'

'Don't preach, Val!　I can't stand it.'

'Oh, all right.　Sorry.'

'And don't keep apologising.　I can't stand that,
either.'

'Well, what *am* I to do?'

The hostess looked at him. She was still sore
enough and raw enough inside. She was still angry,
and nothing would induce her to go near that in-
sufferable, swollen-headed old man again. But here
was somebody else who would do whatever she
asked him, and partly she wanted to prove this all
over again, and partly she wanted to punish somebody — anybody, in fact — for the tone of Masters's
voice. Only it must be quickly. And how?

'Val — where's your car?'

'Outside, Gwenda. Why?'

'Come on, then. Don't say anything. Oh,
don't *look* like that. Just go out in the hall. I'll
be there in a second.'

He started to shrug his shoulders, but she gave
him a push, and he went out of the room instead.

'Where's Val gone?' asked one of the girls.

Nobody answered her, and it didn't really
matter.

'Go on, Tubby. Give us another tune.'

'Which are the new ones, Gwenda?'

'On the floor there. Look out, clumsy! Don't
go and tread on them.'

'I'm not,' said Tubby. He dipped behind the
end of the sofa, and came up with a handful of
discs. 'Oh, good!' he exclaimed. 'This one's
a beauty!'

'What is it, Tubby?'

'Put it on, then. Don't talk so much.'

'Buck up. Don't keep us all waiting.'

'All right, all right, all right,' said Tubby.
'Don't speak to the man at the wheel.'

The music started again. Everyone was staring
at the gramophone. Then, as they all began talking at once, Gwenda slipped out of the door.

'Here I am,' she said, closing it behind her.
'Come on, Val.'

'Yes, but I say — what's the idea?'

'We're going for a drive.'

'But I thought you said ——'

'Well, I'm not. I've changed my mind. We're going for a drive instead.'

'Oh. All right, Gwenda.'

'Of course it's all right. What do you mean?'

'Well, isn't it getting a bit ——'

'You've got lights, haven't you?'

'Of course I've got lights,' said the young man, indignantly. Criticise his car, and you struck, beneath his apparently mild, not to say enervated surface, something in the nature of a tigress defending her young. 'What do you mean?' he asked. 'What are you talking about?'

'You're not arguing are you, by any chance?'

'What? No, of course I'm not arguing. Only you said ——'

'Well, never mind what I said, unless you want to go off by yourself. Do you?'

'No, listen, Gwenda — of course I don't. I don't mind where we go.'

'Nor do I,' said Gwenda.

And again she looked at him, and again she thought: 'Yes, you're the one that's going to pay for all this. You're the one I'm going to take it out on. You'll never guess why, and nobody'll ever guess why, but as long as I can make a fool of somebody — and it's going to be you this time, my dear — I shan't care who's made a fool of me.'

Not very creditable sentiments, but you took the risk, one supposes, if you joined a gang like Gwenda's gang. If you entered that luxurious jungle, then it was your own fault if you couldn't protect yourself. It seemed safe enough, with all its mockery and superficiality and utter absence of sentiment. So perhaps you assumed that there were rules and laws, even that the whole jungle was nothing but a painted representation of the real thing. If so, you'd find out, presently, that you were wrong.

'All right,' said the young man, just as if he hadn't seen the look, and just as if it hadn't excited him and given him that queer feeling behind his waistcoat. 'What you say, goes. Got a coat or something?'

'Yes, here it is. Be quick.'

She slipped into the coat before he could help her, and now he looked a little disappointed. 'Good!' she thought, for she knew all about being helped into coats. So the next thing, of course, was to catch hold of his arm.

'Come along, Val. Don't let's have them all asking where we're going.'

'Oh, rather not. But I say — where *are* we going?'

'Oh, don't be so dull. Anywhere.'

'Anywhere. I see. Are you in a hurry?'

'No. I told you I was dining with somebody, but I'm not sure I haven't changed my mind about that, too.'

'Well, here's an idea ——'

'No. Let's start first and talk afterwards. Let's go miles and miles.'

They got into the car, and the car moved off. As the driver felt its familiar touch and its familiar embrace, the old passion swept over him again and he almost forgot that he wasn't alone. Then as they lurched round the first corner, the passenger was tilted against his left arm; and as they straightened out, some of the pressure still remained.

'Cold?' asked Val.

'Not in the least. I'm boiling.'

'Well, open the window if you want to.'

'But what about you, Val?'

'Me? Oh, I'm all right.'

The car, you might almost understand, would temper the wind to its idolator. Gwenda decided to leave the subject of the car alone.

'Val!'

'Hullo, yes?'

'Tell me something.'

'Well, go on. Fire away.'

'Val — do you think I'm spoilt?'

'Just a second,' said the young man, as he stretched across to weaken the mixture. He listened for a moment. Accelerated, and was satisfied. Glanced at the oil-gauge, and looked thoughtful. 'What?' he said. 'Spoilt, Gwenda? Who says you're spoilt?'

'Never mind about that, Val. Am I?'

She wriggled a little closer against his sleeve.

'Not particularly,' he said.

'Val! You are disgusting! I know just what that means.'

'Eh? What does it mean?'

'That you think I *am* spoilt.'

'No, it doesn't,' said Val. 'It means I think you have a dashed good time. That's all it means.'

'Like now, I suppose?'

'What? No, don't start rotting me, Gwenda. And anyway ——'

'Yes?'

'Nothing.'

'I know what that means,' said Gwenda. 'You're a bit of a cad, Val, I must say. You know I *adore* motoring.'

And that was a good thing to say, wasn't it?

'With anybody?' asked Val.

Decidedly it had been a good thing to say.

'No, of course not. You know I don't go out with just anybody. Now, don't be tiresome, Val.'

'Sorry, Gwenda. Only sometimes you're so — so ——'

''M?'

'I dunno. Are you having dinner with me?'

'Are you inviting me?'

'That's the idea.   If you like it.'

'Well, am I spoilt?'

'No, of course you're not spoilt.   You're a bit odd sometimes, I mean.'

'Oh, am I?'

'Well, you know what I mean, Gwenda.   You generally get what you want, don't you?'

'Do I?' said Gwenda.   She hadn't got something that she'd wanted this evening, or she wouldn't be here now.   But what was it that she *had* wanted? Nothing, perhaps, and perhaps that was why ——

'Val!'

'Hullo, yes?'

'You do *like* me, though, don't you?'

'Well, of course.'

'If you could choose, Val, would you be taking *me* out now, or — well, or one of the others?'

'Which others?'

Good.

'Well, any of the others.   Come on, Val.   I'm not making you shy, am I?'

'Good lord, no.   I was just wondering how much petrol I'd got.'

'I must say, you're terribly romantic, darling.'

'Eh?'

'I must say, you're terribly romantic.'

'Oh.   Well, perhaps I am a bit.   I dare say you think I'm a fool ——'

'Oh, no, I don't, Val.   I can't stand fools.'

'You can't, eh?   Well, if it comes to that, I can't stand most girls.'

'What a hero!   Why, what's wrong with them?'

'I dunno.   They're hard.'

'Oh, give them a chance, Val.   Perhaps they're frightened of you.   You know, I was rather frightened of you — at first.'

What a lie!   But what an excellent idea!

'Were you, Gwenda?   I was scared stiff of you.'

'But *I'm* not frightening, Val, darling. Am I?'

'Well, not at the moment. Not when one gets you alone.'

'How ridiculous! You talk just as if you never did get me alone.'

'Well, I don't — very often.'

'You don't try,' said Gwenda. And then — for although everything was going splendidly, there were still hours in which to play this stimulating and soothing game — she suddenly began chattering about the party last night, and how terribly funny some of the people there had been. And then, still leaning so slightly but insistently against the driver's arm, she spoke of the streets through which they were passing, and of how awful they were, at the same time emitting lightning personalities about the various citizens who were at large in them. 'Did you see that policeman's face, Val? He was just like a badger. Wasn't he exactly like a badger, Val?'

'Ha, ha!' laughed the young gentleman. 'So he was. Jolly good. Yes, rather.'

But then he wanted to tell a really impossible story about another policeman with whom he had had a passage of arms on the subject of his silencer. So presently Gwenda stopped leaning against him, and that finished the story because he broke off, and said: 'I say, did I tell you all this before?'

'No, darling,' said Gwenda. 'Only a lot of other ones just like it. Do go on.'

Naturally he didn't go on. But Gwenda was so pleased with the defeat of her mechanical rival — exquisitely as it was sweeping her through space — that she leant sideways once more, and said something so companionable that the driver merely laughed again.

'You don't mean that,' he said.

'Yes, I do, Val. Val, darling, I *always* mean what I say. I say — isn't this all fun!'

'Think so?'

An emphatic, enthusiastic nod.

'Well, so do I, Gwenda.   Gwenda!'

''M?'

'Do you remember...'

And so on.   It was easy now.   It was all going
swimmingly.   Poor old Val, what a bore he was,
really; but rather sweet, too, the way one could do
anything one liked with him. ˙ And it was funny to
think of all the others wondering where she was;
and it would be funnier still if that blithering old
Graham could see her.   No rawness or soreness
now — at least, practically none — and presently,
after they'd had dinner, and when she became
really encouraging...

'Oh, Val — I am pining to smell the country
again!'

'So'm I, Gwenda.   Gosh, I've thought of just
the place, too.   Only that reminds me ——'

'What, darling?'

'Petrol.'

To the passenger's extreme annoyance, they
swung off the main roadway, straightened out again,
and stopped.   On their right stood a row of those
monstrous growths—draped in their own serpentine
tubing and topped with the familiar, hydrocephalous,
anæmic, featureless bald heads—which have spread
all over England so that man may spread himself still
faster.   On their left was a dingy mixture between a
shop, a chalet and a small railway-station.   Beneath
them was a strip of shiny, greasy concrete.   Beside
them was an interrogatory attendant wearing a
dirty cotton overcoat and, as it happened, one of the
finest quiffs or rampant fringes that can ever have
cheered the eye.

'Yerss?' he inquired, thrusting this adornment
through the offside window.

'Fill her right up,' said Val, jerking a gloved
hand towards the appropriate pump.

It then naturally followed, since the attendant spent all day and every day in performing this precise service, and since there are, roughly speaking, only two possible places where a petrol-tank can be situated, and since the whereabouts of any individual petrol-tank may be ascertained by one glance at any individual car, that — instead of looking, thinking or reasoning — the attendant started opening the catches of the bonnet, beneath which there was no petrol-tank at all.

'Whoa!' shouted Val. 'Not there! At the back!'

'Eh?' said the attendant, continuing on the false scent with considerable energy. There was a screech and a clank, and the driver came leaping out on to the concrete.

'Mind my paint!' he expostulated. 'What on earth are you doing? Can't you see the tank's at the back?'

'Aow!' said the attendant. 'That's right. So 'tis.'

There were two suggestions in his tone; one that tanks were always dodging about all over the place, and the other that it wouldn't really have made any difference if he had gone ahead and poured ten gallons directly on to the engine. Not what you might call a really sympathetic or intelligent character; not, perhaps, that you would radiate these qualities yourself if you were tackling the same monotonous job. But Val had driven too many thousand miles to think of disputing the points. His only object now was to close the bonnet himself, and to do it with additional tenderness so as to make up for what it had just suffered.

You know, however, what happens when such an owner once catches sight of all those rods, joints and other oily organs. He can't leave them alone. First he must admire them, and then there's always that little adjustment to make, or that spot where he suspects the looseness or leak, or the bit that needs wiping off, or the grease-cap or filter that might just as well be given another turn. So Val released the cover and leant forward and felt and touched and prodded; and frowned and considered, and prodded again.

'I say!' he called out, suddenly. 'Gwenda!'

'Yes? What's the matter?'

'Nothing. Just open the throttle a bit, will you?'

Gwenda pouted, and obliged.

'No, no. Not the hand thing. Do it with your foot!'

Gwenda shifted over into the driver's seat.

'Like that?' she asked.

'Yes. That's it. Now again. Not so fast this time. Go on doing it slowly.'

The rod went jerking to and fro, Val's fingers became covered with oil, and presently he came round and took a screwdriver out of the side-pocket.

'Is this going on all night?' inquired the passenger.

'What? No, I've nearly finished. It's the slow-running. That's all.'

'Well, it's slow enough,' said Gwenda.

'No, it isn't. That's just the point.'

She pouted again. Really, to sit here, in this horrible place, while Val fiddled and fiddled like that, honestly it was enough to try the patience of a saint. Honestly, he was perfectly drivelling about his footling old car; and which was he supposed to be taking out, her or it? She was just about sick of getting about a quarter of his attention, while he stood on his head and grovelled in all that mess. What did he think she was? Just a bit of luggage?

'Val!'

'Hullo, yes?'

'I say, do buck up. This is ghastly, you know.'

He stood up. He still looked longingly at his handiwork, but now the attendant had come round again with a paper ticket, and there was another vehicle tooting irritably just behind.

'Pay at the orfice, will you, sir? Wipe your 'ands on my rag?'

'Oh, all right. Thanks. I say, Gwenda!'

'Well?'

'Just move her forward a bit, will you? Back in a jiffy?'

So Gwenda trod on the starting-button, and drove a couple of car-lengths, and stopped, leaving the engine running. 'Sickening old car,' she muttered. And yet there was one way, wasn't there, in which she could put the rotten thing in its place? She could stay where she was. She could go on driving it; and if Val didn't like that, he could jolly well take her home. But if he did like it, or anyhow if she got her way, then at least he'd have to listen to her when she spoke to him. And she wasn't going to speak to him about motoring, either — because any fool could drive a thing like this — but on the contrary she was going to make up for lost time and get on with something that really amused her. And again she thought angrily of her first plan for the evening. And again she was quite determined that Val was going to be led the dance of his life. Throttle, indeed! She'd teach him to talk about throttles before he was very much older.

'Hullo, Val! Listen — I'm going to drive now.'

'Oh, I say ——'

'And don't be tiresome. I know just as much about it as you do.'

As the young man still hesitated, she smiled at him ravishingly, and once more pouted through her smile.

'Now, Val, darling — you're not going to be

selfish, are you? You do realise, don't you, that
I don't go out like this with just anybody?'

The young man's memory and reason seemed
temporarily to desert him. No question that his
companion knew all about smiling.

'Oh, all right,' he said, as he dived in and
slammed the door. 'Be careful, though, won't
you, Gwenda? Don't go and lose your head.'

She just looked at him. True that by doing so
she missed a sand-bucket by three-eighths of an
inch, but what the wing doesn't hit the heart rues
not. Besides, the heart was beginning to have
something else to attend to.

'There you are!' said Gwenda, as the car
picked up speed. 'Did you hear a sound from
your precious old gear-box? Of course you
didn't.'

She touched the horn, and a pedestrian skipped
hastily out of the way.

'I adore this, Val,' she said; 'and it *is* sweet
of you to let me do it. Straight on?'

'That's right. Just follow the tramlines, and
then ——'

'No, don't tell me till we get there. I shouldn't
remember; and, besides, I want it all to be a
surprise. Are we going somewhere awfully nice?'

'I hope so,' said the young man.

'What, Val, darling?'

'Steady! Mind that bicycle!'

'Don't worry. I saw it. I say, Val!'

'Hullo, yes?'

'This is better than going somewhere in London,
isn't it?'

'By Jove, yes. Rather.'

'Dear old Val. You are a funny old thing,
aren't you? Aren't you, Val?'

'Well, am I?'

And Gwenda laughed, and the young man's head
began to spin a bit faster, and the car went surging

along the dark roadway, and the dialogue became extremely staccato and obscure and allusive. And Gwenda, conversationally speaking, kept leaping forward and darting back, and the young man plunged and tripped, and was perpetually wondering if she meant what she might have meant, and was in consequence filled with curiosity and interest and still more confusing emotions. But it's a psychological or mechanical fact that — unless it's in charge of a real bungler — your own car always seems to go better when someone else is driving it. You don't feel those little extra vibrations through your feet and hands. You're not called upon to sympathise so frequently as the engine strains or the brakes react. And because you've been so sensitive to all these details before, you imagine now that there's never been such a car on the road.

You're soothed and delighted, and Val was soothed and delighted. So contented was he, in fact, and at the same time so constantly stimulated by the girl who still leant against him, that he became indeed the very instrument that her mood required. His laughter grew more foolish, his utterance thicker, his eyes rounder and his boldness, as he conceived it to be, more dashing. Once or twice he held her hand for a moment, and even when she took it away it was never as if she had minded. 'Gosh!' he was thinking. 'She's marvellous!' And: 'This is more like it,' thought Gwenda. 'He thinks he can do anything now, and he'll go on thinking it, and then, just the very second that I've had enough of it — oh, how surprised he's going to be, and, oh, what a fool he's going to look, and oh, what an amusing evening I shall have had!'

And she laughed again, and Val laughed, as he thought, with her. And still the tramlines stretched ahead, and still the car went bounding forward. And again her left hand dropped on to his right knee, and again he held it — only this time she gave a gasp, and snatched it back.

'Whoops!' she added, as she stamped on the brake-pedal, and if only that horse-van in front hadn't been exactly on the tramlines, or if only the driver hadn't just decided to get off them, she could have slowed, accelerated and forgotten the whole incident in a flash. But you've seen what happens sometimes when the wheels are narrow and the rails have once seized them. The front pair pulled over to the left, but the back pair grated, dithered and suddenly leapt to the right. Also there was a tram coming the other way. Also the horse-van had a projecting tail-board bearing part of its load of wooden boxes filled with flowers. The car's bonnet slipped under it, but that was all there was room for. There was a crash, and one of the chains snapped. There was another crash, and the bonnet was covered with earth and daffodils. There was a third crash, and the horse-van pitched slowly over on the starboard side, while one of its ancient wheels disappeared in splinters beneath it.

'Whoops!' said Gwenda again.

'Oh!' cried a number of fascinated spectators.

'Nah, then!' contributed the tram-conductor as his huge vehicle swept him regretfully from the scene. People began running out from the pavements. Other vehicles hooted, swerved, and avoided them by inches. The van-driver presented himself, uninjured, but in a condition of obvious frenzy. Bystanders, and among them an exceedingly active bystander with one leg, began gathering up the débris. Val got out and directed a trembling and agonised glance at his own paint. Idiot, he was thinking, to let any girl drive his poor, outraged car! Scratches, dents, a twisted bumper ——

The van-driver caught him by the arm, and he shook him angrily aside. Gwenda addressed him through the open door.

'It's all right, isn't it, darling?' she asked.
'You're insured and everything, aren't you?'

'Insured!' shrieked the young gentleman.
'What does that matter? Can't you see what
you've done to my paint!'

Gwenda merely pouted and slammed the door.

'Yerss!' added the van-driver. 'An' cancher
see wot you done to my wheel? You wait till
the copper —— Ar! There 'e is!'

Nobody saw the one-legged bystander shuffling
off with his armful of flowers. It was dusk, the
policeman was the new focus, the speeding traffic
soon hid him. Half a dozen long leaps with the
aid of his battered crutch, and there he was —
back by his lamp-post, silhouetted by the neon-
lights of the big suburban cinema; the daffodils
to which he had helped himself hidden by the old
box and the old bit of tarpaulin which staked out
his pitch; his eyes once more searching for possible
customers, his voice again whining the merits of his
original wares.

'Vi'lets!' it announced. 'Luvly vi'lets. All
fresh. All luvly. Tuppence a bunch. Luvly
vi'lets!'

But presently, when the copper had gone and
the van had been moved from the fairway and
the crowd had dissipated, the one-legged flower-
seller would stoop and feel behind the tarpaulin,
and up would come his treasure-trove and a new
cry would assail the passers-by. A bit of luck, in
fact, had come his way, and findings were keepings,
and nobody could identify five bobs' worth of
daffodils and his friend at the market would always
back him up if necessary.

'Luvly vi'lets! All fresh. Tuppence a bunch!'

The crowd was dispersing already. The horse
and driver had gone. The wreckage had been
shouldered and levered against the further pavement. The policeman had pocketed his notebook

and gone his way. The car suddenly snorted, shot round in a wide sweep which took it in and out of Edgerley station approach, and sped back under the archway in the direction from which it had come.

'Because if you think,' said Gwenda, 'that I'm going out with anybody who speaks to me like that, then that's just where you're wrong. It wasn't my fault anyhow, but even if it was, I should have thought I was more important than a few tiny little scratches that nobody can hardly see. Going for me like that in front of all those people! Losing your temper and behaving like an absolute cad. No, don't argue, Val; I don't want to talk about it any more, and I'm not going to. But there's just one thing that I never can stand from anybody, and that's rudeness. Now take me home, and don't worry me any more. I'm terribly, terribly disappointed. That's all.'

So Val drove in surly silence, and with bitter thoughts in his heart. The mechanical rival — his first and only true love — had triumphed after all. The test had come, and its sufferings were from that moment the only thing that mattered. Girls, indeed! Good lord, no! He was through with girls. He wouldn't have gone on to that inn to-night if he'd been paid. Calling them tiny little scratches like that. What next!

He scowled at the road in front of him, and Gwenda pouted at his profile. But there was still time, she was thinking, to ring up one of the others — even if they weren't still waiting around the gramophone — and to have a really amusing evening instead.

39

IMMEDIATELY after a quarter to six a subtle change takes place in the atmosphere of Hamhurst's vast establishment, and from then until closing-time it becomes more marked with every instant that goes by. The myriad swing doors still admit you, the lights are still glazing, the lifts are still running, the assistants and customers are still hard at it in every one of the seventy-two departments, tables are still occupied in the restaurants and the car-park outside is still as crowded as ever. But each moment, now, the air of welcome grows falser and more perfunctory, the urge to drive you forth more noticeable and irresistible. You feel it whether it be your first or your thousandth visit. You put on speed as you pass through the long aisles, you find yourself hurrying in your choice between the two qualities or the three sizes, and though the staff are as civil and apparently soulless as ever, they don't hesitate now to tap with their pencils, to address each other from counter to counter, or to show other signs not exactly of impatience but of foreknowledge of an approaching curfew.

A little later the thing becomes franker still. The door-keepers are more obviously in your way if you try to enter, the lifts somehow seem to go down far oftener than they go up, here and there folded dust-sheets have suddenly appeared, and big, wheeled baskets for the collection of the day's litter. It's quieter, too, and the rhythm of the whole scene becomes broken. The other customers have suddenly taken on a fantastic, unreal look, and before you know where you are, you're beginning to feel a bit unreal yourself. Your one wish is to escape before the dream vanishes and takes you with it, but though common sense may tell you that here you and Hamhurst's are entirely at one, you find yourself afflicted with a nightmare sensation of leaden soles to your shoes as you struggle towards the nearest exit.

'Other way out, sir, if you don't mind. Other way out, madam.'

It's almost with panic that you turn, retrace
your steps, dodge an enormous step-ladder which
has mysteriously manifested itself in your path,
and join the stragglers who are herding towards
freedom. Already the remaining assistants are talking in loud, careless voices, and you are appalled
by the bravado of a madman who is actually
arguing with the next janitor, and trying to force
his way in.

'Sorry, sir. Just closing. Too late tonight.'

Thank heaven, the madman collapses and retires.
You bolt after him, hustling against strangers like
the very worst kind of passenger in a sinking ship,
not daring to look back for fear of the monstrous
dissolution which you are convinced would meet
your eyes. Thank heaven, again, you're in the
fresh air of the street. Your breathing becomes
more regular, your heart stops pounding, you con-
nect with the comparative stability of your ordinary
existence, and, indeed, you have already forgotten
the terrific emotions which so nearly unseated your
reason. You don't believe, in fact, that you ever
went through anything of the sort. But you did.
And when the circumstances are repeated, you will
go through precisely the same shattering experience
again.

Thus, nightly, is Hamhurst's cleared of the clients
who have made it and built it and raised it from
one modest draper's and haberdasher's to an island
site with its own bank and post-office, its twenty-
eight lifts, its seventy-two departments, its two
hundred and forty delivery-vans, and its two
million pounds of share capital. But though the
doors are barred now, and the little blinds behind
them are drawn, though the car-park has melted
like snow and the watchmen and firemen have
already started on their rounds, Hamhurst's is still
far from being empty.

Typewriters are still rattling and clicking, cashiers

and accountants are still labouring at their ledgers,
heads of departments are talking to buyers, the
board-room is filling up for a conference, and at
this moment—while the humbler assistants are still
hurrying to the staff cloakrooms and a fresh army
of cleaners has come in from outside — the popula-
tion of Hamhurst's is still larger than that of many
a fair-sized village.   Yet the lights are gradually
going out in the seventy-two departments themselves, and more and more the humbler assistants
go crowding down the glazed stairway which no
client has ever seen, to slip their cards into the
relentless clock, to nod good night to its uniformed
guardian, to stand for a moment in the blinding
light which never seems to trouble his all-seeing
eyes, and so to vanish as shadows into the greyness
without.

    'Good night,' said the voices again.   'Good
night.'   'Good night, old man.'   'Well, it's
stopped raining again; that's something.'   'No,
I haven't seen her, but she was up there just now.'
'Well, good night.'   'Oh, hullo!   So you got
here after all, did you?'

    A burst of flighty, enfranchised laughter from a
knot of girls, and away they go too.   Matches are
being struck in the street outside, where the delivery-
vans are still backing and manœuvring, and
cigarettes are appearing in dozens from cardboard
containers.

    'Good night.'

    'Oo, sorry, I never saw you.   Good night, dear.'

    A stocky yet hollow-chested figure appears in
the blinding light, shuffles towards the clock, per-
forms certain automatic movements with the
automatic mechanism, and is transformed in turn
into a black silhouette.

    'Good night, Mr. Coffin.'

    'Eh?   Oh, good night, Mr. Hobbs.'

    It isn't really dark yet, save by contrast with

the blinding light. The sun has just set and the
sky has clouded right over, but even in this narrow
ravine it is still only dusk. Something less friendly
about it, thinks Mr. Coffin — second-in-command in
the turnery department — than about the blacker,
earlier nights. When one comes out like this,
exhausted and eternally conscious of one's boots,
it is pleasanter in a way to be swallowed up in
obscurity than to begin seeing all the familiar
surroundings again. Well, if it comes to that, there's
a lot to be said for the real summer, when one
can still potter about in the garden after supper;
but that's a long way off yet, and his fortnight's
holiday (thinks Mr. Coffin) is further ahead still.
This twilight business isn't really one thing or the
other. It annoys him. It makes him worry about
all sorts of things. Such as his health. Such as
his age. Such as life.

And tonight, of course, such as Em.

All day there'd been that undercurrent of per-
plexity and anxiety and baffled attempts to forget
them both. 'Got enough to do here,' Mr. Coffin
had thought, 'without bothering my head about
that.' Yet his head was still bothered. Missing
his train — well, it hadn't really mattered. Nobody
except the clock had noticed that he was late, and
so far as his work went, it had made absolutely no
difference at all. But if you started with that
feeling of hustle — well, of course it upset you.
He'd felt like losing his temper more than once,
with customers, with that traveller who'd come in,
with that clumsy girl in the canteen. He hadn't,
though. Every time he'd bottled it up, and kept
his mouth shut, and controlled himself. But that
didn't make it any easier next time. If anyone
cared to know the truth, it only made it worse.

Now, in fact, as Mr. Coffin joined a rush of
pedestrians through the traffic in the main road,
he felt a pang of regret that he hadn't lost his

temper. A vision presented itself of a glorious scene in which he stormed and raged, and all the other people blenched and apologised. A muttering escaped him, in which a few offensive adjectives might vaguely be distinguished. 'Silly idjit,' he growled. 'Wasting my time,' he mumbled. 'And 'oo do you think *you* are?' he demanded.

He felt better. One of his flat feet struck a slight irregularity in the pavement, and he nearly pitched on his face. He didn't feel in the least better now. Somebody, he imagined, had tittered, but even if he had been more certain who it was, the will to storm and rage had left him. The shock, fright and recovery had merely dislodged the pretence with which he had been trying to hide the truth. It was Em who was at the bottom of all this. It was the row with Em, the argument over Mrs. Bowker, the insult to his pride, the rank ingratitude; he couldn't get them out of his mind. They'd been gnawing at it all day — they and nothing else — and now, after nine hours of irritation, they came surging up again and nearly choked him.

'Look 'ere, my girl,' he began. 'Now, jus' you lissen-a-me. Wodjer suppose ——'

But words failed him. What was the use of words where a woman was concerned? They didn't care. They didn't understand. They let you work and slave for them, they took your money and all the comforts that it provided — took the whole thing for granted, too — and then, the first little difficulty that came along, the first little thing that didn't go absolutely smoothly, and what did they do next? Argued. Started going for you. Put their heads out of the window and shouted. And if the neighbours heard them, oh, dear, no, they didn't bother about that.

All right, then. He knew just exactly what he was going to do. If Em didn't appreciate having all that work done for her like that, then he'd tell

Mrs. Bowker she needn't come in again. He wouldn't tell Em; he was through with any more discussions on that subject; but perhaps when Mrs. Bowker didn't come in, and when he said nothing about it, but just started saving her wages again, well, then, perhaps ——

Mrs. Bowker, though. *Why* hadn't she come in this morning? Suddenly his rage switched over to the daily woman, and her quite unpardonable behaviour. A new scene suggested itself in which Mrs. Bowker came crawling to him for the half-week's money which he supposed he owed her, and he told her to sue him for it — with Em listening, of course, and realising the kind of man she'd married. That was what he'd do, though. And she *could* sue him if she liked; she could sue him until she was black in the face, but whatever it cost him she'd soon find out that it cost her a good deal more. He was in the witness-box now, giving them all the truth about her. He was telling some other applicant for her services exactly what he thought of her. He was hounding her down, ruining her, dragging her in the gutter. And if Em tried to say as much as a word in her defence — well, he'd show them both; that was all. He'd just show them!

Thus did Mr. Albert Coffin yield to his less creditable feelings and whet his own appetite for revenge, as he hurried and stumbled through the streets which he knew so well. And thus, though his mind never ceased for one instant to plough its ferocious furrow, custom halted him at the crossings and set him to the left or right as other bodies bore down on him, and even enabled him to glance at the big clock over the jewellers' and to make his nightly calculation from the position of its hands. It was all right. He needn't go quite so fast. He was a minute earlier than he'd been yesterday evening. No danger of missing the 6.35.

He instructed his fallen arches to take it easier, and they thanked him. But only for a moment. They'd received this order before, but somehow they could never obey it. Scores and hundreds of other feet were now all converging on the big terminus, and it was impossible not to be swept along with them. The urge was too insistent, the pace too unanimous to withstand. One might, perhaps, stop altogether—though nobody did—but no individual who moved at all could hope to resist the tide. There they all went, like grain pouring into a hopper, their eyes focussed on nothing, their limbs bearing them onward with ever-increasing inertia. At the actual entrance to the big terminus there was an illusion that the stream was running downhill or being sucked forward by powerful fans. Yet quite half the crowd were managing to buy evening papers, and even occasionally to receive change, without apparently checking the tremendous flow.

Almost night now. Full night, in fact, under the smoky glass-and-steel roof, where the steam locomotives hissed and panted and bellowed, and the electric trains came grinding in and went grinding out. The stream divided and swept towards its various wickets, passed through them, spread out along the platforms, dived into the lighted coaches, was jostled, shoved and compressed to the limits of endurance; set forth over the roughness of innumerable points, gathered speed, vanished, and was already renewed at the source.

How on earth did they all know who was who, and whither they were going, and did any of them pause even for an instant to consider why? No sign of this question in the pale faces that came swarming along under the greenish gas-lamps. Something had brought them here, something was driving them onward, and something forbade them to stop. That was all. And they did, in some

miraculous manner, retain their myriad identities
and force themselves into their appropriate carriages
and continue to be remoter from each other than
stars in space, as their ribs were crushed and their
feet were trod on and the whole swaying load went
roaring away in obedience to mortal and immortal
laws.

And whistles blew, and lanterns were flashed,
and the men in the signal-boxes strained and tugged
at their heavy levers, and still the empty trains
came in and the crowded trains went out, and
treasure and invention were lavished so that those
who worked might work again tomorrow, and
money might circulate, and human beings might
live until presently they died.

And Mr. Albert Coffin stood in a crowded smoking-
compartment and in a haze of Virginian tobacco
and on his flat and weary feet, and was held more
or less erect partly by the season ticket holder's
sense of balance, partly by pressure from other
passengers, and partly by bouncing with a shoulder
or levering adroitly with an elbow as the long
train tilted round corners and drew up with a
grating and a squeaking and set off again with a
hiccup and a jerk.   And somehow or other Mr.
Albert Coffin, also, had acquired a copy of the
final edition of his favourite evening newspaper;
and somehow or other, though the lights sometimes blazed straight into his eyes and at other
times heavy shadows fell between them and the
print, he managed to read and to assimilate and
to add to his fleeting knowledge of what was news
tonight even though it might never become anything more permanent.

Still at the back of his mind there was that
nagging sense of grievance, that muddled determination to refresh it and renew it as soon as he reached
his journey's end.   But yet, as he peered at the
headlines and sucked up the smaller type, he could

and did approve, criticise, philosophise, analyse or
reflect.   Good job, he thought, as he read that
someone had been arrested for the Paddington
murder at last.   About time, he thought, though
it was disappointing how, as usual, they never gave
one any of the most interesting details.   And,
hullo, he thought, another of those big City companies had gone smash, had it?   Well, obviously
that was what the newspaper believed itself—though
again it was rather aggravating in its vagueness
and reserve — because if this man Fink couldn't be
found anywhere, you could bet your boots he'd
bolted. Mr. Coffin drew in one or two sharp breaths
at the enormous sums of money which were mentioned, and found them distinctly stimulating.   An
inset photograph of Lord Midhurst's face and part
of his top-hat scarcely attracted his attention at all.
There was little or no thrill in a director whom
he'd never even heard about, but those figures....
He drew in his breath again, shook his head, shifted
one of his feet, and passed on.

Another photograph — this time of a bride and
bridegroom with a conventional background of
blurred attendants and blurred policemen and a
blurred crowd — was noted, but hardly demanded
even unspoken comment.   What did Mr. Coffin
know or care about titled women who were married
on a scale like this?   Nothing.   It was a different
world that the photographer and the block-maker
had once more offered for his inspection, but a
world so remote that it couldn't even arouse envy.
Em, of course, would read anything about anybody's wedding, and if she'd been anywhere near
that church ——

Em!   Mr. Coffin's mouth twitched, and he
turned impatiently from the woman writer's special
description of the ceremony.   He'd forgotten about
Em for the moment, but now that something had
reminded him, the grievance still lurked and gnawed

and smouldered.   All the trouble he'd taken, all he'd
done for her, and then ——

He read on, hurriedly, greedily, treating the
newspaper more than ever now in its capacity as a
companion of the same sex.   He dismissed its lapse
over that wedding, and plunged into a column
headed: 'Big First Night Postponed.'   Here one
of those knowing gentlemen with a knowing pseu-
donym—one of those characters who convince you
that they exist in the fullest of evening dress and
sup nightly in the society of the most radiant stars
— had communicated a red-hot narrative of the
disaster at Mr. Corbett's theatre; all very know-
ingly set forth, all packed with personalities, and
all — since, as a matter of fact, it had been written
almost entirely by Mr. Corbett's own B. J. Hanson—as compact of inaccuracy as it was full of
alluring references to the spectacle which would
most positively be presented next week.   'Certain
changes in the cast,' it ended, 'are also to be
made during this interval, as a result of which
Mr. Corbett tells me he is satisfied that the show
will be materially improved.   "This is my first
postponement," he said, "and naturally I am disappointed.   But if it enables me to retain my
previous high standard, then I am sure that eventually there will be nothing to regret."'

And Mr. Coffin lapped it all up, and nodded, and
though he had absolutely no thought of attending
any performance at the Empress Theatre, whether
Mr. Corbett's new production ran for two nights or
two years, yet he felt pleased at certain vague
thoughts of luxury and extravagance, and a little
uplifted by a fleeting vision of lights, laughter and
legs, and more than a trifle stirred by Mr. Corbett's
gallantry in facing such rough treatment at the
hands of Fate.

Then the train slowed down again, with more
creaking and dithering, and more wage-earners

started struggling towards the doors, and Mr. Coffin was compelled to lower his newspaper while defending himself from a good deal of jostling. And then the train stopped, and the appropriate wage-earners leapt out on to the platform and began herding towards the ticket-collector who should release them into their own suburb and their own section of the night. And then the train quivered and set off again, and Mr. Coffin gave a faint sigh and at last dropped into a vacant seat; still without any too much room for his elbows and still without any too much air for his lungs, but he was off his feet, and his feet were extraordinarily grateful. He sighed again, settled his eyeglasses, and went on reading.

More slowly, though, and with decreasing concentration. Subconsciously, also, it was now more necessary to follow the train's progress through the darkness, so that at the right moment he in his turn might disembark and make the last effort of the long day. The illuminated front of a big factory, the distinctive rumbles of a bridge, a cutting and a short tunnel, all sent familiar messages which were noted, checked off and put on some invisible file. And now the train had bumped over another set of points and was once more definitely on the loop. And the newspaper, like its morning contemporary, had suddenly become all small type about sport and finance, or pages of little advertisements at which one scarcely even glanced. 'Saturday's big match,' it said; but Mr. Coffin read no further. 'New Low Record for Associated Enterprises,' it said, but what did that matter to Mr. Coffin? He came to the last page of all. He turned it sideways for the stop-press column. Racing results; New York prices. Then some heavier but no blacker print. 'Officially announced that Sir Blundell Hascombe has tendered resignation.'

Mr. Coffin blinked; felt that he ought to remember who Sir Blundell Hascombe was; but felt incapable of making any more effort. Besides, another message had reached him through those subconscious channels. The train was slowing down for — so far as he was concerned — the last time. He folded the paper and stuffed it into his pocket. He edged forward on his seat. He waited for the exact moment at which the slackening of speed would assist in thrusting him back on to his feet. It came. He tottered, and caught at the door-handle. Other doors opened, other feet came hovering out over the gliding kerb of the platform. It ceased to glide, and already some of the feet were running. Bang, bang, bang, went the doors. A whistle. A throbbing, a drumming, and the train was off again. Squealing against the guard-rails of the curve. Smaller and smaller. Nothing but a red light now in the distance. And now nothing at all.

Mr. Coffin joined the stream that was making for the barrier, fished out his season ticket, exhibited it in silence, and passed through the booking-hall. 'Ugh!' he grunted, as the sharp descent towards the main road heightened the discomfort of his boots. Should he hurry so as to get it over, or move more slowly so as to feel it less? No decision came to him, though actually he was hurrying, because suddenly the grievance had seized hold of him again. Fatigue and the newspaper had lulled it, but he'd known there was something wrong in the booking-hall just now, and his mind had felt for it and hunted for it, and first he had remembered how he had missed that other train this morning, and then he had remembered why he had missed it, and now, more clearly than ever, he recalled each incident before, during and after the row.

He clenched his jaws, he glared into the dark-

ness, a welter of angry phrases came churning up
from his heart.   Yes, he was thinking, that was
what he'd say to Em.   And that.   And that, too.
He'd walk straight into the house, and it didn't
matter what she was doing or how she tried to
greet him; he'd start right away, he'd tell her
exactly what he thought of her, he'd let her know
exactly what she'd done, he'd go on till he'd finished,
and then ——

'Luvly vi'lets!' croaked a voice by his side.
'All fresh.   All luvly.   Luvly daffodils.   Come on,
sir.   Luvly daffs!'

Mr. Coffin stopped short, and there was a puzzled
expression under his bowler hat.   What was it?
What had happened?   Why did he feel that he
was still rushing towards Marefield Road, and yet
realise that he was suspended here outside the
Regency Cinema, blinking at a bunch of daffodils
flourished at him by a dirty fist?   What was the
meaning of this sudden softening, this sudden
bewilderment, this sudden and utter change in his
soul?

'Come on, sir.   Luvly daffs.   All fresh.   Come
on, sir.'

'Eh?' said Mr. Coffin.   And, 'Gor!' he
muttered, for he knew what it was now.   That day
that he and Em had got married.   That day they'd
come back to those first furnished rooms.   That
vase on the table.   Those flowers that he'd put
in it.   Em's face when she caught sight of them.
Em bending over and smelling them.   Em looking
up again, and turning towards him, and moving
towards him, and —— Oh, all the years they'd
been together since then, and all she'd done for
him and given to him and gone on giving to him!
And just because of a silly quarrel about an ugly
old woman who came snuffling round the house
and getting in the way ——

'Come on, sir!   All this lot for one an' a tanner!'

The last bunch, sir. Shan't be 'aving no more tomorrer. One an' a tanner, sir. Come on!'

And Mr. Albert Coffin came on. Still in a dream he unbuttoned his overcoat, dived into his pocket, and fetched out a handful of coins. Mostly coppers, and not such a large handful at that. But there was a shilling, and there was a sixpence. His thumb edged them forward, and they dropped into the one-legged ruffian's other fist.

'There you are, sir. That's a bargain, that is. 'Ave a bit of noosepaper to put 'em in?'

But Mr. Coffin didn't seem to hear this suggestion. Without refastening his overcoat, he had taken the bunch of flowers by their damp stalks, and had turned round and was moving quickly away among the loiterers in Edgerley High Street. The glare from the neon-lights changed to a glow from the terrace of shop windows. He stepped out past them, faster and faster, deaf to all the sounds from the traffic, blind to all the figures that bore down on him, and dodged him, and sometimes looked back and stared at him. Yet his feet didn't forget that gap between the confectioner's and the undertaker's, and led him without faltering into the darkness of Marefield Road. And diagonally across it, presently, towards the undersized pillar-box and the wide-spaced lamp-posts of Ardlers Road. And along its northern pavement, and so for the second time to the right. And now, as always at this point, his other hand went into another pocket and drew forth a little key-ring on the end of a chain; and felt for his latch-key, and found it, and shook the other keys out of the way — everything being timed, though tonight without the least conscious direction, so as to be ready for this tired little shop assistant just as his legs slowed down, and paused, and had landed him on his own miniature doorstep.

In went the latchkey, and up went one of Mr.

Coffin's knees.   The door opened, the key-ring went back into his pocket, and the door closed.   He took off his bowler hat, but his shabby overcoat remained where it was, for somehow those flowers mustn't be released, even for a moment, until they were handed to Em herself.

'Em!' he called out.   'I say, Em!   Where are you?'

Nobody answered him, but suddenly he was aware of voices at the end of the narrow little passage.   The kitchen door, as he now saw, was ajar, but what female visitor would be in there with his wife at this time of night?   Why weren't they in the sitting-room?   He frowned, opened his mouth to call again; changed his mind and advanced along the passage.

Good lor, it was — of all people — that old devil Mrs. Bowker!   Sitting there, if you please; and with her hat and coat on, and no sign of an overall. And Em was sitting on the edge of the kitchen table, and they were talking, talking, talking — absolutely as if — as if ——

'Ehrm!' said Mr. Coffin abruptly.

And the two women stopped talking, and Mrs. Bowker jumped up and Em swung round.   And Em looked at the figure in the doorway, at first almost as though he were a stranger or an eavesdropper, and even a moment later with no sign of welcome, but rather as if she resented his return, as if she had been meaning to resent it all day, as if she, also, had been nursing a grievance and was still the Em who had shouted after him and sent him running so angrily towards the station.

'Well?' she said.

An inexplicable look of excitement flashed across her face, and vanished.

'Well?' she repeated.

Mr. Coffin's right hand came shyly out from behind his overcoat.   He held up the bunch of daffodils. He blinked. His mouth gave a little quiver.

'What?' said Mrs. Coffin.

And then, suddenly, her face was full of every kind of inexplicable expression at once, and she slipped off the table, and she darted across the floor, and she caught hold of her husband's hand where it still gripped those damp stalks.

'For me?' she cried. 'Oh, Elbert! Oh, Elbert, and I thought —— Oh, Elbert, did you — did you remember?'

Mr. Coffin's mouth twitched again as he nodded solemnly.

'That day?' persisted Mrs. Coffin.

'Yes,' he said. 'And I — I'm sorry, Em ——'

'There, now,' interrupted Mrs. Coffin. 'We've forgotten about that, haven't we, Elbert? It was my fault, I dessay.'

'No, it wasn't, Em.'

If only, he was thinking, Mrs. Bowker wouldn't stand there all the time; grinning like that, too. He wriggled in his impatience and annoyance, and Mrs. Coffin felt the movement where her hand lay on his arm. She caught the look in his eyes, and suddenly her own excitement seemed to return.

'Now, Elbert,' she said, smiling at him; 'you're not to blame Mrs. Bowker, neither. Do you know she's come round specially to tell us the news, and it'll be all right again tomorrow morning — won't it, Mrs. Bowker. She couldn't help it, you know; really she couldn't. All night she was up, an' of *course* she couldn't let us know. Just fancy, Elbert! It's their first, an' he weighed nearly seven pounds, an' the Sister says ——'

'Here! Steady, old girl! What's the idea? Whose sister are you talking about? Eh?'

'Oh, you are funny, Elbert. The Sister at the 'orspital, of course. Now, don't gape like that. Haven't you never heard of people having babies

before? Go on, Elbert! Say something. Don't
you understand Mrs. Bowker's turned into a grandmother?'

Mr. Coffin looked stupefied. Despite a faint
feeling of masculine disgust, excitement was also
beating at his ribs. He glanced at the grandmother, he looked hastily away again. He shuffled,
he wriggled, he started scratching his cheek.

'Go on!' said his wife, waving the daffodils at
him. 'Go on, Elbert! Cancher say nothing?'

'Well, well,' said Mr. Coffin. 'Well, I mus' say.
A — a little boy, is it, Mrs. Bowker? Eh?'

'That's right, Mr. Coffin. You never seen such
a little beauty. I mean, of course I know it was a
hinconvenience, me not being able to let you know
but ——'

'Not at all,' said Mr. Coffin. 'Not at all,' he
repeated. 'That didn't make no difference, Mrs.
Bowker. I meantersay —— Well, really, now.
just fancy that! I'd no idea —— I meantersay,
what's 'e going to be called?'

Almost in the same instant he had congratulated
himself on escaping from a distinctly awkward
avenue and realised that somehow or other he had
landed himself in another one. Em was looking
at him kindly still, it was true, but also pityingly.
Perhaps, then, he shouldn't have asked a question
like that when the baby was still so young. Perhaps, for some reason which only women understood, one mustn't make this inquiry at quite so
early a stage. He was outnumbered, he was only
a man, and for a moment he almost thought of
backing hurriedly out of the kitchen.

Instead, as it happened, he shot a nervous glance
at the child's grandmother; and the child's grandmother beamed at him.

'There, now!' she said. 'Fancy you taking
such a hinterest, Mr. Coffin! Oh, yes, it's all fixed
up, Mrs. Coffin. Soon as she sees 'im, she says:

"I know what we'll call 'im, Ma." "Good 'eavens,"
I says, "wotever 'ave you suddenly thought of?"
An' there was my son-in-law — 'e's driving a lorry
at night now, so 'e come along almost as soon as 'e
'eard the news — all big an' clumsy; *you* know what
men are like. "Yes," 'e says, "wot's the idea,
Nellie? This is the fust I've 'eard of this," 'e says.
An' my girl's lying there, an' she says: "I'll tell
you both, then. 'E's goin' to be called David."
"David!" says my son-in-law. "'Ooever 'eard of
anyone in our family called that?" "That's just
it," she says. "I've always fancied the name
any'ow; an', besides," she says, "I'll tell you
another thing, only I don't suppose you know it.
David," she says; "that's what the royal fam'ly
calls the Prince of Wales!"'

And Mrs. Bowker began to laugh, and Mrs.
Coffin began to laugh, and in another second Mr.
Coffin began laughing, too. Perhaps he didn't
quite know why, but he knew — he had no doubt
of it now — that, just for another of those fleeting
instants, he had never been happier in his life.

40

So THE child David lay in a cot in the maternity
ward of the Edgerley Memorial Hospital, and he
weighed nearly seven pounds, and his face was
red and rather mottled, and his nose scarcely
existed and his mouth was loose and floppy, and his
tiny, little receding chin was the weakest feature
that ever you have seen, and his eyes were tightly
closed, because the child David was asleep. But
he'd had a hard day, even if it is possible that he
didn't exactly know it, and no character in the whole
length and breadth of the country was more honour-
ably or fully entitled to his evening's rest. He was
still barely twelve hours old, but in those twelve
hours his influence had reached out all over the

capital among high and low and rich and poor. He had comforted the unfortunate, he had strengthened those in peril, he had administered justice, he was responsible for wide and far-reaching decisions, he had brought lovers together, he had saved the Government, he had sent a murderer towards the gallows, and in one critical moment he had struck right round the globe and sharpened the knives which were to bring peace to a distant Possession. He had been bold, then, and when necessary he had been merciless, yet looking back on his crowded record one can scarcely ever accuse him of deserting the angels. This life to which he had just been introduced was no simple thing. Perhaps he realised how human beings still want to be happy, and some of the extraordinary means which they adopt towards this indescribable end, and some of the remarkable confusion which results from their perpetual and preposterous efforts. Perhaps in selecting the hour of his own birth, he also said to himself ——

But no. When one comes to think of it, that's rather preposterous, too. He was only a newborn baby. He couldn't say anything to himself, and we're absolutely convinced that he didn't. Besides, with a chin like that...

And yet again, on the other hand...

THE END

bW·M1013d

WITHDRAWN